London Borough of Tower Hamlets

91000008084546

KT-237-574

Library Learning Information

To renew this item
download the **Idea Store App**
on the Apple App Store
or Google Play Store

Or sign in to the library
catalogue at
www.ideastore.co.uk

TOWER HAMLETS

ISLANDS OF MERCY

BY THE SAME AUTHOR

Novels

Sadler's Birthday
Letter to Sister Benedicta
The Cupboard
The Swimming Pool Season
Restoration
Sacred Country
The Way I Found Her
Music and Silence
The Colour
The Road Home
Trespass
Merivel
The Gustav Sonata

Short Story Collections

The Colonel's Daughter
The Garden of the Villa Mollini
Evangelista's Fan
The Darkness of Wallis Simpson
The American Lover

Non-Fiction

Rosie: Scenes from a Vanished Life

For Children

Journey to the Volcano

Islands of Mercy

ROSE TREMAIN

Chatto & Windus

LONDON

1 3 5 7 9 10 8 6 4 2

Chatto & Windus, an imprint of Vintage,
20 Vauxhall Bridge Road,
London SW1V 2SA

Chatto & Windus is part of the Penguin Random House group of companies whose
addresses can be found at global.penguinrandomhouse.com.

Penguin
Random House
UK

Copyright © Rose Tremain 2020

Rose Tremain has asserted her right to be identified as the author of this Work in
accordance with the Copyright, Designs and Patents Act 1988

First published by Chatto & Windus in 2020

penguin.co.uk/vintage

A CIP catalogue record for this book is available from the British Library

HB ISBN 9781784743314
TPB ISBN 9781784743321

Typeset in 12/14 pt Garamond MT
by Integra Software Services Pvt. Ltd, Pondicherry

Printed and bound in Great Britain by Clays Ltd, Elcograf S.p.A.

Penguin Random House is committed to a sustainable future for
our business, our readers and our planet. This book is made
from Forest Stewardship Council® certified paper.

MIX
Paper from
responsible sources
FSC® C018179

To Richard, with love

'Many a green isle needs must be
    In the deep wide sea of Misery,
Or the mariner, worn and wan,
    Never thus could voyage on.'

~ *Lines written among the Euganean Hills, 1818*
Percy Bysshe Shelley

Part One

THE RUBY NECKLACE

She came from Dublin.

In that crowded city, she had worked for a haberdasher and presided over the slow death of her mother, after which she'd discovered in herself an unexpected yearning to leave Ireland and see the world. Her name was Clorinda Morrissey and she was thirty-eight years old when she arrived in the English city of Bath. The year was 1865. She was not beautiful, but she had a smile of great sweetness and a soft voice that could soothe and calm the soul.

Clorinda knew that Bath was not exactly 'the world'. But she had been told that it was built on seven hills, like Rome, and that it hosted 'galas and illuminations' in the spring and autumn seasons, and these things took on some splendour in her mind. It was also, she heard, a place where very many rich people assembled, to take the waters, or simply to take their leisure, and where the rich congregated, there was always money to be made.

Poorly lodged at first on Avon Street, at the lower end of the town, where the gutters were choked with refuse, among which dozens of pigs wandered in the daytime and at night lay down to sleep in their own comfortable filth, Clorinda Morrissey began her sojourn in Bath by working as a milliner's assistant in the cold basement of a shop on Milsom Street. This work was punishing to the hands. Though she kept reminding herself that it afforded her a 'living', she soon came to feel that this living resembled nothing so much as a kind of 'dying' and it made her furious to think that she'd left Dublin only to find herself suffering from feelings of collapse and decline. She vowed to alter her lot as quickly as possible, before her spirit failed her.

I

The only article of value she possessed was a ruby necklace. It was an object of some beauty: twenty blood-red stones strung upon a delicate gold thread, with a golden clasp. It had come to Clorinda recently from her dead mother, who, in turn, had had it from *her* dead mother, and she, in monotonous rotation, from hers. For long and featureless years, this necklace had been passed from one place of safekeeping to another. It had hardly been worn by any of its owners, but rather had taken on the petrified status of an heirloom, kept in a satin-lined box, dipped in methylated spirits once in a while, to clean it and show its brilliance to the air. For long periods of time, it was forgotten completely, as though it didn't exist at all.

Rumours that the great-grandmother had got it 'by dishonourable means' seeped down the generations, but these, if anything, only made each successive inheritor more keen to hang onto it. All of them believed that the ruby necklace would one day 'find its true purpose'. But what that purpose might be, even if it was speculated upon, was never decided. The necklace remained hidden away in peculiar places: under floorboards, inside a broken long-case clock, in the secret compartment of an empty wall cupboard where bowls of hyacinth bulbs were nurtured through the winter darkness.

Now, however, Clorinda Morrissey, toiling over stiff bonnets and the fabrication of cloth flowers to attach to them, in her cold base-ment, made a vertiginous decision regarding the ruby necklace. She was going to sell it.

To the voice inside her which protested that she was betraying the status of the necklace as an heirloom, to be passed on to future generations, she replied that she *had no children*, so there was no 'future generation' to pass it on to. To the idea that, by moral right, she should leave it to one of her brother's girls back in Dublin, she gave scarcely any consideration. These two nieces, Maire and Aisling, meant nothing at all to her. They struck her as dim, morose children, who probably did not even know of the existence of the necklace. And the rubies, she now saw uncommonly clearly, had no value whatsoever to anyone, until or unless that value could be realised. Surely, after all these silent generations had lived and died, it was time for someone to put them to use?

She took the necklace first to a pawnbroker. This elderly person applied a cup-shaped object to his eye and gazed at the rubies through it. Clorinda Morrissey, watching him with her sharp gaze, saw a tiny froth of saliva escape from his mouth and dribble down his chin. She deduced correctly from this that the man had at once understood that, among the dross of gilt, brass, glass, ivory and pewter habitually offered to him, here at last was a thing of uncommon beauty and value. He laid the cup aside, wiped his lips with a limp handkerchief, cleared his throat and made Clorinda an offer.

But it would not do. Mrs Morrissey was intent on changing her life. She knew that what was being proposed, although more than she could earn in six months at the milliner's, was miserly. A violent hatred towards the cynical pawnbroker surged up in her breast, a loathing as red and heartless as the jewels themselves. She didn't argue with the despicable man. She snatched up the necklace, replaced it in its box and prepared to walk out of the shop without another word. As she got to the door, she heard the pawnbroker call her back, raising his offer by a fraction, but she kept going.

The following day, she paid sixpence to borrow a fancy bonnet from the milliner, arranged her hair carefully beneath it, put on her best coat and clean shoes and marched into a high society jeweller's on Camden Street. Her entrance into this shop set ringing a little melodic bell above the door, and she took this for a sign of welcome.

The money Clorinda Morrissey obtained for the rubies, paid in gold sovereigns, signed for on an embossed Bill of Sale with as much flourish as she was able to muster, put her into a trance of what she called 'pure purpose'. She did not sleep. She sewed the sovereigns into the hem of a cambric petticoat. She chose to believe that her thirty-eight years of life had been lived in a kind of semi-darkness, but that now she would journey towards the light. And she knew exactly where she wanted that light to fall.

Further down Camden Street there was an empty shop premises. It had formerly been a funeral parlour which, Clorinda was told, had gone out of business 'due to insufficient deaths in the city'. It was explained to her that although Bath had a very high population of sick and suffering people, these were mainly 'imports to the town' who came hoping to be cured by the healing waters and who were indeed cured – or else went back to their homes to die. Bath's indigenous population was extremely long-lived. The steep hills around the city kept the people's hearts beating strongly. The air they breathed – at least in the upper part of the city – was very pure, compared to London and many other cities. Entertainments of all kinds kept them from despair. Reasons for dying were comparatively few.

The funeral parlour, however, was large: a handsome office at the front, where examples of coffin design were still on display, bolted to the wall. At the back, two rooms, kept as cool as possible by an arrangement of iron pipes ventilating into a sunless back alley and once furnished with expensive fresh-cut flowers, had served as 'viewing parlours' for those bereaved relatives who could stomach the sight and stench of an embalmed corpse.

Mrs Morrissey walked back and forth between these two areas, arranged to accommodate the conventions of English burial. And she saw immediately how her Irish spirit could adapt them very satisfactorily to her need for what she liked to think of as her *resurrection*. She stood at the window facing Camden Street and watched the scores of beautifully attired people strolling past. Her mind returned to the ruby necklace. She half expected to see it, adorning the crumpled neck of some wealthy dowager, but then she reasoned that it wasn't necessarily the kind of jewel to be worn in the daytime, but rather saved for one of these 'gala evenings' that had been allowed to acquire such splendour in her mind, but of which she had heard little since arriving in Bath. And anyway, the necklace was no longer itself. It was on the very precipice of becoming something else.

Once she'd signed her lease and engaged workmen to refit the premises, she wrote out a notice and attached it to the front door of the shop with milliner's glue. It read: *Opening soon in this place. Mrs Morrissey's high class Tea Rooms.*

What Clorinda Morrissey wanted from her enterprise was not only to make the kind of living that had nothing of the 'dying' about it, but also for *herself* to become known – a landmark, a magnet, a destination in her own right. Though she had had many friends in Dublin, it had always seemed to her that in the great life of the city she had had no importance whatsoever. She was invisible in her haberdasher's shop.

In the taverns, where she could match the men, mug for mug of ale, nobody paid her any special attention. She'd had a suitor once, a carrot-headed boy who had walked with his head in the clouds and been run over by the night mail coach. Later, she had had a proposal from a Norwegian sailor and wondered for a while whether she might enjoy lying in arms so strong and foreign, so inured against the cold. But in the end, she'd decided against him. The carrot-headed boy had died with his face turned to the sky; the Norwegian would probably fall into the sea and drown. And it came to her then that she didn't really want to live with a man – or at least not yet, not until she found someone whose gaze was steady and whose feet were planted firmly on the earth. She wanted to live *for herself*, to travel her own road. By the time she set sail for England, she'd reinvented herself as a widow, because widows survived far more cleverly in English society than spinsters – or so she'd been told.

And now she was going to have her name in gold script above the shop: *Mrs Morrissey's High Class Tea Rooms*. The future was going to be perfumed with raspberry jam and freshly baked scones and fragrant lemon cake. With a dairyman on Carter Street, she placed a substantial twice-weekly order of Devon clotted cream.

ONE AFTERNOON AT MRS MORRISSEY'S

Perhaps because of its excellent location on Camden Street and because Mrs Morrissey's builders had unearthed a pretty fireplace, with a serviceable chimney, from behind the coffin samples, where she was able to install a coal fire to warm her clientele on cold autumn afternoons, the Tea Rooms soon enough drew people to them in highly satisfactory numbers.

Word also went around Bath that Clorinda Morrissey could make a Victoria Sponge as light as a goosedown pillow, that the tea was always Best Assam, with no added dross, and that the atmosphere of the place was such as to make people feel that this particular teashop was a place *outside time*, an oasis or a fragrant island, a place where nothing bad could ever come upon them while they were there.

This was due not only to the brightly burning coals and to the excellent cakes, but to the personality of Clorinda Morrissey herself – to her quiet movement among her guests and to her sweet Irish voice, which was like a kind of soothing music permeating the air. She greeted all her clientele – whether duchess or daughter-of-trade, whether baronet or baritone in the local choral society – with a smile of exquisite courtesy and compassion, as though she had known these strangers through all the vicissitudes of their lives.

More than this, she was pleased, as time went by, to stumble upon the realisation that some people soon began to choose *Mrs Morrissey's Tea Rooms* as a favoured location for conversations of great intensity or confessions of the utmost importance. Watching from her service counter, from behind the bewitching array of jam tarts, crumpets, iced buns and fruit muffins, she could see them displace to one side the cake stand which she always set down in the middle of the table, in order to lean towards each other, so that their heads were almost touching. She saw gloves removed and hands grasped. She heard sighs and laughter and sometimes glimpsed tears sliding down an alabaster cheek and falling into the Assam. These things gave her great gladness of heart. She was someone at last. She was Mrs Morrissey of Camden Street and humanity came gathering to her sheltering bosom.

On this particular afternoon, the man arrived first.

Mrs Morrissey knew him as Dr Valentine Ross, one of the scores of medical men who made a good living from the cavalcade of invalids who came to Bath to take the waters and who liked to be encouraged in this and other cures for their ailments by reassuringly expensive doctors.

He was a strong-looking man in his thirties, of mid-height, with dark hair beginning to recede a little. Perhaps there was a suggestion of cruelty in his narrow blue eyes, but his manners towards Mrs Morrissey had always been impeccable. Often he'd come alone to the Tea Rooms, not to eat anything, but to sip tea and smoke a cheroot and seem to ponder some tangled or wayward question lurking beneath his conventional outward appearance. Sometimes, he'd engage Clorinda Morrissey in courteous conversation, asking her about the city of Dublin, its joys and woes, its prosperity and its poverty. He always listened carefully and once said to her that he was 'ashamed' to know so little of the world outside Bath.

His younger brother, he told her, was an explorer in the field of Natural Science, currently working on the island of Borneo in the Malay Archipelago. This extraordinary adventurousness of his made Valentine Ross feel 'parochial', or so he admitted, but he added that there was nothing to be done about it. He was not the kind of man who yearned to see raging cataracts and rainforests where no light fell. He couldn't completely understand, either – so he told Clorinda Morrissey – the white man's desire to discover 'lost tribes' in parts of the world nobody had yet mapped, being inclined to think that these people might be happy in their 'lostness' and living lives of quiet content.

'I'm perfectly sure you're right!' Mrs Morrissey had replied. 'Now me, I like all the clamour of the city. But when I was a girl, our Mam used to take us all to see our Grandpappy, who was a lobster fisherman off the West Coast of County Clare. And you could argue that he was a 'lost' man – living in a low cottage miles from anywhere and facing straight out into the heartless ocean. But he didn't want it any other way. He'd gather sea pinks for a jug on his old worm-eaten table and samphire for his supper. When we visited, we had bread and cockles for our dinner, and spent all our days running wild by the shore. He was kind to us, but what he liked most was to be left alone. When we left, he'd celebrate with a jug of stout! "Off you go!" he'd say. "Off, off!" So if you were a forest man and never on any map, might you, perhaps, be like him and the very happiest of people? But who can really say?'

Now, as Clorinda Morrissey approached Dr Ross's table, she noticed that his hand was shaking as he endeavoured to light his cheroot. His complexion, which usually suggested a calm demeanour and the obedient circulation of his blood, appeared pale and there was a faint beading of sweat on his brow.

'Doctor Ross,' said Clorinda. 'Are you well, Sir?'

'Quite well, Mrs Morrissey. And yourself?'

'Oh yes. Enjoying the autumn sunshine. Will I bring the usual Assam?'

To this question, Ross hesitated and cast an anguished glance at the door. 'No,' he said. 'Thank you. I will wait. I am expecting a guest.'

'Oh now, that's nice for a change,' said Mrs Morrissey. 'You may be wanting the cake and scones, then?'

'Yes,' said Ross. 'But I will wait to see ...'

At this moment, the door of the tea rooms opened and a young woman came in. One should say that she *strode in*, rather, and the eyes of those already enjoying their tea turned towards her, for the simple reason that she was excessively tall. Mrs Morrissey guessed that she must have been six foot two inches – or more. She wore no bonnet or hat, but her dark coat was fashionably waisted and trimmed with fur. She held her head so high that, at first, as she looked around her, her gaze fell upon the papered walls and not upon the clientele seated at the tables. This gaze of hers, Clorinda Morrissey at once perceived, was of a stern and penetrating kind.

At the sight of her, Valentine Ross laid down his still-unlit cheroot and stood up. A nervous smile creased his cheek and he raised his hand. The tall young woman did not return the smile, or else had not seen it. She hesitated a moment, as though she might be short-sighted and feared to stumble on the pathway through the tea tables to where he stood. So he began to move towards her. Mrs Morrissey watched him greet her with a formal little bow, then offer his arm and she took it and they returned together to where he had been sitting.

Clorinda Morrissey pulled out a chair for her, realising as she did so that she, who had sometimes been considered tall in Ireland, only came up to the lady's chin, her starched lace cap notwithstanding.

'Mrs Morrissey,' said Valentine Ross, 'may I present to you Miss Jane Adeane. Miss Adeane is the daughter of our renowned surgeon, Sir William Adeane, with whom I have the honour to work.'

Mrs Morrissey, though she was the *patronne* of her own enterprise and now known by name across most of the city of Bath, was nevertheless scrupulous about curtseying to those she served. This curtsey, however, was more a charming little bounce, as though her shoes contained invisible springs, and she noticed that it sometimes made people smile. She wished to tell them that she performed it in this way, not to amuse them, but simply to save time, that the proprietor of a tea room must be forever scuttling from one task to the next, from stove to kettle, from sink to linen cupboard, from jam jar to cream dish, from formal greeting to Bill of Sale – and all without seeming to be flustered or discommoded in any way. She really had no leisure for curtseys.

Clorinda Morrissey performed her bounce now and saw a smile break out on the stern features of Miss Jane Adeane. Miss Adeane held out her hand in greeting and Mrs Morrissey took it.

'I have heard,' said Miss Jane, 'about the lemon cake.'

The coal fire burned a volcanic red. Among the tea-drinkers, one small dog lay watchfully under a table, waiting for time to pass, waiting for his mistress to remember how much he longed to walk in the fresh air. At another table, an elderly man – or gentleman, as he would have preferred to be called – sitting alone, appeared to be a Person of the Cloth, but was, at that moment, in the very act of staining that cloth with clotted cream and sticky crumbs from his scones. Though he did not appear to notice his own clumsiness, others among Mrs Morrissey's clientele may have looked up and been amused by the mess he'd made.

If these same people had glanced at Valentine Ross, they would have taken him, at first sight, for the dependable, hard-working and prosperous man that he was. Those hard blue eyes, perhaps, suggested a certain ruthlessness in his character, or that he had moments of inappropriate yearning or imagining, yet it was of course impossible to guess what these might be.

But the person they kept staring at was Jane. Perhaps some of them whispered to each other that they'd never in their lives seen a woman so tall and a few of the women may have wondered how much extra material had to be ordered for her skirts and petticoats and what the cost of this might be.

Jane Adeane was used to the gaze of strangers falling on her and remaining there. She had grown impervious to this kind of intrusion. It had often been said to Jane that nobody knew where this exceptional stature 'came from'. Her mother, who had died giving birth to her, had been a small, neat woman. Her father – a thin man of ardent countenance and abundant grey hair, whom one might have mistaken for the conductor of an orchestra – was not particularly tall. Portraits of the Adeane grandparents and relations on her mother's side had often been taken out and examined afresh, in the expectation that some mighty ancestor would be spotted, trying to conceal his or her tallness by sitting in a low chair, but Jane had always known that none would be found. The six feet and two inches were hers and hers alone.

And the true fact was that she actually *doted on them*, these improbable extra centimetres of flesh and bone. They were at the heart of what made her exceptional in her own eyes. She sometimes imagined that the people around her – the very ones who stared at her so impolitely – were all struggling not to drown in the surging sea that is human life, but that she was quite safe from the dark deep. She was her own lifeboat, or her own small island. Her head and shoulders would always ride above the waves.

Clorinda Morrissey returned to Valentine Ross's table to take his order for tea. She saw Miss Adeane looking anxiously at him, quite as though she thought he was about to ask for the wrong things, and Mrs Morrissey was aware that when he requested his 'usual Assam', together with two rounds of hot-buttered toast and some slices of lemon cake, his voice was shaking.

Perhaps he was ill? It was known in Bath that the doctors, who had to spend so much time among the diseased and the dying, were prone to sudden sicknesses. Clorinda Morrissey had been told that arguments still raged between the Contagionists (who believed that disease spread via 'animalculae' brought into England with imported food produce) and the Anti-Contagionists (who thought that illness was generated spontaneously from filth and decay and then transmitted through the air as vapour or 'miasma') but little was truly understood about how infections spread from person to person, and so few precautions could be taken to prevent this. But why, Mrs Morrissey asked herself, if Dr Ross was ailing, had he invited Miss Jane to tea?

She hurried to make the toast and cut the cake. She then took everything to the table, setting the cake stand in the middle of it and retired with another of her little bouncy curtseys.

While at her serving counter, with her young helper, Mary, preparing food for her other customers, she couldn't stop herself from glancing, from time to time, at Dr Ross's table. She saw Miss Jane pour out the tea and then begin eating her toast rather hungrily. (Mrs Morrissey wondered whether that large frame of hers might need a lot of food to sustain it.) Ross took a piece but did not eat it. Jane seemed to be talking quite fast, but her companion only looked at her anxiously as he sipped his tea.

Then, when Jane had finished her toast, Dr Ross moved the cake stand aside, so that he might have a better view of his guest. He reached a hand across the table, as though he wanted to take hold of Jane's hand, but she moved hers away and helped herself to a slice of lemon cake. Now, Mrs Morrissey saw Ross begin to talk very earnestly, seeming to convey important news.

The little scene at the tea table, Clorinda Morrissey sensed, had all the makings of a drama, quite as gripping as any she had attended at the theatre in Dublin, but afraid to be seen observing it too closely, like some uncouth groundling gaping at the actors, Clorinda Morrissey turned back to her work and sailed forth into the room with an order of iced buns for the proprietor of Tilney's Department Store and her friend, Mrs Earle. She exchanged a little conversation with these two ladies on the subject of the new French fur muffs, sable and mink, which Tilney's was now acquiring 'before the winter comes upon us'.

'A wonderful Christmas gift,' boasted Mrs Tilney, 'or why don't you pop into the store and buy one for yourself?'

'Ah,' said Clorinda. 'Well, of course I would prefer to receive such a lovely thing as a gift, but alas, I do not have in mind an appropriate *giver.*'

This made the ladies laugh, but the laughter did not quite cover the noise of a chair being pushed back violently and when Mrs Morrissey turned, she saw that it was Miss Adeane's chair that had been moved and that Jane was now standing and tugging on her coat. Valentine Ross was looking up at her great height with an expression of profound dismay. On Miss Jane's plate lay the uneaten slice of cake. She turned to nod politely at Mrs Morrissey, then made her way to the door and shot out of it very fast, as though afraid she might be pursued up the street.

THE ANGEL OF THE BATHS

There was something mythic, something almost ghostly in the name by which Miss Jane Adeane had become known in Bath. She was described as 'The Angel', or sometimes as 'The Tall Angel' or 'The White Angel' or, more frequently, as 'The Angel of the Baths'. It began to be said that, if you could hire Jane as your personal nurse, then your search for a cure in the city would be successful. Men, in particular, were susceptible to this superstition. To be led to the waters by Jane's strong arm was to feel almost like boys once again, surrendering to a mother's care. Sometimes, the touch of her hand on their foreheads could make them weep.

It had been noticed, of course, by very many residents of Bath, that Miss Jane was a stubborn young woman, intent always on doing and saying exactly what she wished to do and say. Society was inclined to blame her father (if 'blame' was the right word) for doting too much upon his only surviving child. And it was true that Sir William Adeane was deeply attached to Jane, finding her presence in the house entirely comfortable and sometimes discovering himself to be uneasy if she wasn't there, quite as if he were a child and Jane his adored mother.

But Sir William should not be held to account for Jane's refusal to heed any but her own judgements upon what was the right path for her to follow in her life. The refusal was all hers, just as the startling height was all hers, and she was proud of them both. At the age of twenty-four, she had begun to suspect that one day, she and her magnificent inches would accomplish something the world might find extraordinary. That she didn't yet know what the thing was troubled her not at all. The thing was just 'The Thing', a gleam in her soul. She was content to wait patiently to find out what that gleam revealed.

She liked to wear white. Though her sleeves and the hem of her skirts often had to trail in the waters, or were tainted with specks of blood or phlegm, she kept these snowy garments as starched and impeccable as she was able. As well as wanting them to be clean, she wished them to impart a subtle reproach to her patients. For what she saw in the crowd of invalids shuffling their way to her father's practice in Henrietta Street was how very unclean they were. Sometimes, their teeth were black and loose and their gums filled with pus. Their beards were malodorous nests, nurturing tiny particles of rotting food. Their armpits stank of invisible pond life, their private parts of the sewer. And as for their feet … the prevalence of gout among them made the putting on and taking off of footwear such an agony that some poor sufferers slept in their boots and never washed their feet for days or weeks on end – with terrible corrosive consequence.

It was thus Jane's belief that immersion in the waters of the Hot Bath, by rinsing these bodies of some of their grime and allowing the skin to breathe, brought them relief in itself. And – beyond the reproach that the whiteness of her uniform implied – she also felt that, with its suggestion of purity and virginity, it gave unexpected solace to minds crammed with worldly distress. She did not wish to believe, though her father and Dr Ross were the true physicians in the premises on Henrietta Street, that she herself had no power to cure. She knew otherwise.

Her methods were varied. 'Strength through gentleness' was a motto she often repeated to herself. Her hands, her arms, her shoulders were powerful and their careful massaging of aching limbs often put her patients into an almost religious kind of sleep, from which they would wake praising God that they were suddenly free from pain. But they knew that the alteration in them wasn't due to any miracle, but to the inexpressible gift of the Angel of the Baths.

Jane had also learned from her father how to extract rotting teeth. She saw clearly that a contaminated mouth could poison and weaken a body, right down to the soles of its feet. Jane promised anxious patients that she could set them on a path to recovery without pain. They had only to inhale a little Nitrous Oxide to experience a feeling of exaltation, to start laughing at the very idea of suffering and the fear of suffering, at which moment, Jane's strong left hand would hold their mouths agape and with her right she would manipulate her shining Leopold Extractor, to twist and pull out the rotting tooth almost before the patient understood that his jaw had been touched.

The swabbing of putrefaction with a pad soaked in distilled carbolic acid left the site of the extraction as free of infection as could be expected. When the euphoria of the Nitrous Oxide wore away, Jane would gently take hold of the patient's first finger, dip it into a jar of Oil of Cloves and instruct him to 'become an infant for a while', sucking upon his own hand to take away the pain.

She never hurried a patient out of the quietly furnished room where she performed her dental work, but knelt by him and held his gaze, eye to human eye, until he could stand up and walk out into the bracing Bath air. This holding of a person's features in the balm of her brown eyes always seemed to bring upon them feelings of calm, and Jane came to believe, without ever having witnessed the work of Monsieur Mesmer, that her will could still the agitation of a frantic heart.

It was quite natural, then, that patients longed to return to her and even fancied themselves in love with her, so effective were her cures and so powerful were her presence and her touch. Some of these sufferers, over the years, had forgotten themselves so absolutely, when lying on her massage couch, as to whisper to her that their only cure lay in her willingness to massage other parts of their anatomies until they arrived at blissful relief. It was even put about one summer that the Angel of the Baths would do this, in exchange for a guinea, thus emboldening more patients to ask for it. But there was no truth in the assertion. None. Miss Jane derived considerable satisfaction from her ability to help the sick and the dying; the very idea of using her powers to commit acts which would defile her made her feel sick. The truth was that she respected men, sometimes for their bravery, sometimes for their skill and sometimes for their dauntless yearning to be heroes. She also pitied them for their child-like natures and their emotional cowardice, but she did not love them at all.

You might have believed, therefore, that Dr Valentine Ross, who had worked side by side with Jane for almost two years and come to know her as well as any man, apart from her father, would have comprehended this. He was not an unobservant man. But his hopes for a cure for his own troubled emotional state were misguided. They were vain hopes, absolutely vain, because they counted on a cure which – he had quite failed to see – was not there to be given.

Ross did indeed feel that he was 'ill' with love for Jane Adeane. His dreams were haunted by visions of her alabaster body. When he worked beside her, the soft perfume of her hair so beguiled his senses that he sometimes lost concentration and had to pause in the middle of a cupping or a cutting. He understood, too, what a clever nurse she was and allowed himself to rhapsodise over the brilliant practice he would be able to set up, outside the shadow cast by Sir William Adeane, with the Angel of the Baths at his side. He saw money flowing to him in a shining river.

But now he had made a fatal blunder.

All of his sexual and monetary ambition had led to a shockingly inappropriate proposal of marriage in Mrs Morrissey's tea rooms. After stammering out his feelings of adoration, Valentine Ross had said, 'Of course I will do everything as it should be done. I will go to your father and ask for your hand. But I need to know from you if my suit finds favour with you.'

Miss Jane had said nothing for a moment, but only looked him up and down with disapproval, as though he might have been a child who had buttoned his clothes all wrong.

'Oh, your *suit*,' said Miss Jane, at last. 'Well I like your frock coat well enough, but I am not certain that the waistcoat is not a little loud – for a doctor, you know ...'

Ross had been dismayed to realise that she was mocking him, as he knew she might – for her wit was keen and mockery was Miss Jane's instinctive choice in any conversation. But he wished she had not yielded to the temptation to use it here.

'Do not mock me,' he had pleaded. 'I love you, Jane. I think I have loved you for so long that it is beginning to hurt me, and so I'm seeking out this remedy.'

'*Remedy*,' she said, after a while. 'That is a peculiar word to use.'

'It is the right word,' said Ross. 'My love for you is a kind of malady, from which I know I will not recover. I will only be cured if you agree to marry me.'

'Ah,' said Jane. 'So now it is the humble nurse who must find a cure for the doctor?'

'Yes! Take pity on me, Jane. Do you remember when we attended a recital of Chopin preludes at the Assembly Rooms last autumn, and you—'

'Oh yes. I very much like the melancholy of Chopin. I know it isn't to some people's taste, but I feel, really, that this is their *loss*, and—'

'And you wore a scarlet gown and some tall contrivance in your hair …'

'Contrivance? It wasn't a "contrivance". It was a peacock's feather.'

'Was it? Well, my brother would have recognised it, I'm certain, but I did not. All I know is that I longed to touch the plume, to touch your hair. And then to feel your hand in mine. And ever since that moment, this malady of love has been with me and all I want is to make you mine.'

Jane Adeane had now drained the last dregs of tea left in her cup, as if she yearned to make some diversion from the subject of contrivances and hand-holding by drinking it. Then, she'd looked round the room and her gaze had taken in the dog now yapping fretfully at his mistress's feet. The dog wanted to escape and this was also now what Jane desired – to be far away from Valentine Ross. As for him, he must surely have understood that his proposal had been a mistake of the gravest consequence and that his life – and Jane's – in Bath would never be the same again.

Jane had adjusted her posture, raising her head as high as she could make it go, and looked down upon Ross.

'I am sorry,' she said. 'I am truly sorry that you should feel ill on my account, but there is nothing to be done about it. The cure you want is not within my power to give.'

She unfolded herself from the chair and stood up. Any short-sightedness she may have betrayed on entering the tea room, was no longer apparent. She glanced back at Mrs Morrissey waiting at the cake counter and nodded politely to her. Then she strode quickly to the door.

That night, Valentine Ross pondered his behaviour and Jane's prior to the tragedy (or perhaps it was merely a farce?) that had occurred in the tea rooms. For a long time, he'd believed that there was an absolute logic to this marriage and that no man had ever been more certain about where his future lay. He had even congratulated himself on holding back from asking for Jane's hand for several months after coming to the realisation of all that she meant to him. He had held back in order to look for signs that his affection for her might be returned – and he'd thought he'd found them. But he now saw that what, in fact, he'd found was not much more than Jane's polite respect for him as a doctor and a fondness for teasing him, which he'd fool-ishly mistaken for sublimated passionate regard.

He cursed himself for being blind and dumb. And yet there had been one or two occasions when Ross believed he'd caught a glimpse of romantic feelings in Jane.

One of these had been the night of the Chopin Recital at the Assembly Rooms – so ineffectually referred to across the cake stand. Before this, he had always remembered the evening with furious joy. Jane had appeared so magnificent in her blood-red dress and her bird's feather that the eyes of many other concert-goers had lighted on her, as they walked through to the concert *salle*, and, as if to shelter herself from these admiring looks, Jane had taken his arm and when he'd placed his hand upon hers, tucked into the crook of his elbow, she hadn't taken it away. Indeed she had smiled at him. *Smiled!* As if to say, 'yes, we are comfortable like this. You understand it and I understand it. So perhaps this is how we might remain?'

Then, when the music was nearing its end, Miss Jane had begun to cry – so moved was she by the sweet sadness of Chopin and by the talent of the pianist. Feeling her sobbing next to him, Valentine Ross had felt bold enough to take her hand and to lean in closer to her, so that his shoulder just touched hers – and she had not resisted him. When he'd passed her his clean silk handkerchief with which to dry her eyes, she had not returned it but tucked it intimately into the bodice of her dress.

'What in heaven's name,' Ross now asked himself, in this night of sleepless agony, 'was I meant to deduce from gestures like that? Are they not, precisely, the responses of a woman who feels herself to be loved and begins to bask in that affection? Would not other men have felt as I did, that this was proof of love? And – damn her to hell! – she never returned the silk handkerchief!'

This question of the handkerchief tormented him as much as any other. Was it simply an additional act of mockery on Jane's part, or might he ... dare he ... take it as a ruse to summon him back, as though she were saying to him, 'one stumbling offer of marriage might be sufficient for some women's taste, but not for mine. I am Tall Jane. I am the Angel of the Baths. My exceptionality demands that you reflect on your words and improve them and then come to me again ...'

But as the morning light began to show at his window, he was disposed to fear that were he to ask a hundred times for Jane's hand, she would still refuse him.

GOLEM

When Jane had arrived back at Henrietta Street, the moment she stepped through the familiar door, she knew that she now had to find some means to escape from Bath for a considerable while. The mere idea of working side by side with Valentine Ross, pretending that nothing had occurred between them, made her feel faint with dread.

She retired to her room and wrote a quick letter to her beloved Aunt Emmeline in London, asking to come and stay with her 'for a consoling stretch of time'. She then went to her father and, as calmly as she could, without betraying to him – by a single gesture or any alteration of tone of voice or articulation – that anything unusual had happened, told him she had been missing Emmeline and now desperately wanted to go to London to spend time with her aunt.

Given that he was faced with hiring a new nurse to replace his daughter and would now have to oversee the running of the house as well, Sir William was disposed to feel cross with Jane for putting him in a vexing predicament. But he could never really be cross with his daughter, and Jane knew this. Crossness was not a feeling he could tolerate in himself in regard to her. So all he did was to take her hand in his and say, 'you must do exactly as you please, dear lamb. You have worked very hard this season. Emmeline will be delighted to see you. And as for us, we will manage excellently, I'm sure. I will give you money for London fashions.'

Miss Emmeline Adeane lived alone in London with a solitary maid-servant, Nancy, in a tall house at number 2a Tite Street, Chelsea. A handsome woman in her fifties, of rarefied taste and with a fondness for outlandish clothes, including brightly coloured turbans, after the fashion of Madame de Staël, Emmeline Adeane had been able to make some headway into the male-dominated London art world, by exhibiting her paintings in small galleries and by her willingness to paint society portraits, in the manner of Sir Thomas Lawrence, which flattered their subjects – men and women both, and all their exquisitely dressed children, however fat or plain.

A known artist of the 1840s, Mr Jocelyn Hulton, had fallen in love with the beautiful young Miss Emmeline, encouraged in his feelings by the flattering ardour she expressed for his work. Emmeline Adeane and Jocelyn Hulton had struck a bargain in 1847. She would become his mistress, if he would look kindly upon her youthful talent and help her to become the great portraitist she knew herself to be.

This arrangement lasted some five years, during which Emmeline became pregnant no less than four times. To her sorrow and shame, she was unable to carry a child to full term. In exquisite pain and bloody mess, her half-formed babies, one by one, were expelled from her womb into a heavy porcelain dish and put by the Hulton servants into the night-soil bucket, eventually to join with all of London's fearful evacuations in the waters of the Thames. After the fourth miscarriage, Emmeline was ill for a long time and fell into a deep sadness.

Although Jocelyn Hulton was by then tired of her and what he termed her 'infernal head-gear', and had acquired a younger paramour, her predicament moved him. He was rich enough to buy her the house in Tite Street, where he furnished a fine studio for her. He told her that she had no more need of him. She was now a painter 'of admirable skill and originality'. He gave her, as a parting gift, a handsome pottery wheel and two hundred pounds of clay.

Before he left, he set up the wheel and gave Emmeline one lesson in pottery technique. This lesson was a strangely intimate and troubling thing. It required Jocelyn Hulton to stand behind his once-beloved mistress, would-be mother of no less than four children, press himself closely against her and put his arms round her, to guide her hands in the shaping of the turning clay. These gestures were so tender and the task in hand so sensual that, for a moment, Emmeline was aware of Hulton's returning desire and wondered whether, after all, he wouldn't make love to her once more and then change his mind about leaving her. But he moved away quickly, quite as though he were angry with himself for becoming aroused. He told Emmeline she had no need of further lessons; she could now teach herself to make anything she pleased.

One morning, some weeks after Hulton's departure, with a cold spring rain pelting the skylight of her studio, Emmeline cut a lump of clay and moistened it and kneaded it, before setting it on the wheel. The sound of the rain was like distant applause and Emmeline, who had spent much of the previous time in a state of collapse, dosing herself with laudanum to still the pain of her heart and mind, congratulated herself on standing upright at last, with her hands committed to a new endeavour.

She wondered what she should make. She decided on a simple bowl. She had in mind a ewer – which, later on, she might glaze and decorate. She was suddenly taken by a strange feeling of excitement.

She pressed the foot treadle to spin the wheel and used her thumbs – as she had been briefly instructed by Jocelyn Hulton – to begin to mould a hollow in the clay. She was at first surprised by how easy this seemed to be. Yet, soon, however hard she tried to make her bowl perfectly round, the thing persisted in an obstinate *lean* to the left. Again and again, Emmeline's careful hands encouraged it towards the shape she wanted it to take, but each time, it refused. It not only gravitated towards its leftward lean, but began to manifest a peculiar narrowing of its neck, as though it yearned – without any instruction from the potter herself – to become a drinking vessel.

Emmeline stopped the wheel, stood back and regarded it. She wondered whether experienced potters sometimes had to contend with this kind of mutiny of their material, or whether it had come about simply because of her lack of skill. She looked up as a growl of thunder made the house appear to tremble. The deluge upon Chelsea grew fiercer. It felt to Emmeline as if the driving rain might now crack the skylight above the studio and leave all her precious paints and canvases open to the sky. And indeed, after another few minutes had passed, Emmeline saw that the water had found a tiny fissure in the glass and was now falling, drip by drip, onto the half-formed object on the pottery wheel.

As she watched this happening, her heart began to beat very fast and she snatched at her blue laudanum jar and drank thirstily. It now seemed clear to her what was occurring: Nature itself did not look kindly on the vessel she'd made. It wished for something else.

Emmeline had told the story about the pottery wheel to very few people, but one of them – whom she had come to trust with many of the secrets of her life – had been her niece, Jane. Before she had revealed how the tale ended, Emmeline had said to Jane, 'People are disposed not to believe it. You, my dearest Jane, will trust in it, I know, because you and I do not lie to each other, but others suggest that my mind was deluded into seeing something in a state of alteration, because I was taking laudanum for my pain and my sadness. But I was not deluded. You could more truthfully say that I was witness to something phenomenal.'

'Ah,' Jane had replied, 'that is my favourite kind of thing! If only there was more of the phenomenal in Bath ...'

Jane had been reclining upon the couch in Aunt Emmeline's studio, settling her skirts comfortably around her, and had felt enthralled already by what she was about to be told. The world, Jane already knew, reeked horribly of old, exhausted things. Day could follow wearisome day without a single original or exciting moment stirring her pulse. But now Aunt Emmeline – by far the most exceptional and independent person in the Adeane family – was going to reveal something *new*. Jane felt ready to hug her aunt before the story had even begun.

Emmeline, whose habit of taking laudanum was growing more acute than she knew was wise, had snatched a sip from her jar and had then begun to pace about the room. Jane's intelligent brown eyes had watched her quietly and patiently. Emmeline passed a hand across her brow and, after describing her attempts to make a bowl while a thunderstorm raged over Chelsea, began to narrate the events which happened next.

'They all happened in the space of not much more than an hour,' she said. 'And yet they have lasted a lifetime in my mind. I think I will remember them, still, when I am very old.'

'Oh,' said Jane, 'I have done nothing yet which I will remember when I am very old, but I am determined to remedy that.'

'You will, Jane. Your life is going to be a rare thing. We all know it. Your father even *fears* for you.'

'Does he? Well, that cannot be helped. But let us not move from your story towards my future. I am dying of impatience to hear what happened ...'

'Well, this was the order of it. The storm raged on, and I stood back and let the rain fall. I watched as, drop by drop, the water leaking from the glass skylight began to pock the clay, so that, very slowly it began to be flattened by the persistence of the water. What had been round and full fell in upon itself, like a balloon emptied of air.'

'You let the rain transform it?'

'Yes. I *wished* for the rain to transform it. And what I saw, as the thing collapsed – or some would say, what I *chose to see*, was that what I had inadvertently made was a model of my own womb. It was not heavy with life any more. It was flat and empty. And the poor embryos of children who had yearned to be brought to human life within it ... where were they? They had seeped away through the womb's neck. They had vanished into the storm!'

'Oh,' said Jane. 'Oh.'

'But this idea engendered a kind of wildness in me. You could say that I was enthralled. I saw some other hand at work than mine. I waited until the "womb" lay flat and shapeless on the wheel, then I hurled myself on it and took up the soaking clay and began, on my work table, to squeeze some of the water from it and to dry it with a cloth.

'Then from this same lump of matter, I began to sculpt a figure. I wanted it to be beautiful, as I believed a living child of mine would be beautiful. I had many times done drawings and portraits of young children and babies. I knew how to arrange human features into a pleasing aspect. But I could not do it with the clay! The thing I made was a little stooped homunculus, a kind of miniature golem.'

'Could you not alter it? Knead it and pummel it and begin again?'

'I tried. I kept trying. But however urgently my hands moulded and remoulded it, it would not take any kind of admirable human form. It was deformed – hunched and bowed, with fat limbs, a too-large head and a sad face. I worked on and on and the rain stopped and I was weary beyond any imagining. I recalled Mary Shelley's terrifying evocation of the birth of Frankenstein's Monster. I was appalled by what I had made. I took up the golem and threw it into the hot ashes of the fire.'

Emmeline had paused here and come to sit at Jane's feet. She took another sip of laudanum and offered Jane the jar and she drank, too. They did not speak. Jane felt the laudanum's instantaneous consolation enter her blood. She took her aunt's hand and held it tenderly. She knew the story had not reached its end.

After some time had passed in silence, Emmeline continued: 'I went back to my room and lay down. I fell asleep and didn't wake till morning. And when the morning came I remembered what had happened and I got up and went and stared at the ashes of the fire. I expected to find that the golem had burned away, but of course it had not. It was merely *baked* as though it had been put in a potter's oven. It had refused to die.

'I fetched a clean cloth and wrapped it round the thing and brought it onto my lap. I rubbed it to get the ashes away. It was hard and brittle and cracked here and there, but I cradled it in my arms. I felt that I loved it.'

'You loved it? When you made it, it dismayed you, but now you felt love for it?'

'Yes. And in that feeling of love was great consolation. I had been so unhappy – to lose my babies and then to lose my lover. And some of that sadness ... I felt it leave me. I felt I could go on with my life and my work.'

Emmeline had got up and begun to walk about the room. Jane's eyes followed her passage from the couch to the window and back to the laudanum jar.

'That is the end of the story,' said Emmeline. 'I used to think there might have been something magical, something supernatural in it, but now I see that it was just a *sequence of events* which led abruptly to an ending. So I tell you it only to stress my belief that our minds can be consoled by the strangest things. And it told me also that we cannot shape the world according to the delights society decrees appropriate for us. We must be unconventional in our joys and find them wherever we can.'

'That is my reasoning, too,' said Jane. Then she asked, 'Do you still have the little golem, Aunt Emmeline?'

'Yes,' said Emmeline. 'I keep it in an old wooden shoe-box, shaped much like a coffin. When I look at it, I still feel tenderness towards it.'

This story had been told to Jane by Emmeline some years ago, but Jane had never forgotten it. Compassion for her aunt, coupled with an admiration for her talent had led Jane to feel that Emmeline might be the person who would guide her towards the exceptional future she dreamed of. And now, in the tiresome wake of Valentine Ross's proposal of marriage, she was on a steam train to London. As the fields of Wiltshire and Hampshire went by the window, Jane put all thoughts of Ross from her mind and let herself enjoy being carried so swiftly towards Emmeline.

CAPERCAILLIE

After Jane's departure, Valentine Ross took to rising from his bed very early in the mornings, tugging on such clothes as came to his hand, winding a scarf round his neck and walking out into the cold mornings, almost before the sun had risen. Sometimes, there was a dusting of snow on the pavement. Sometimes, the wind was so strong that fallen leaves on the street were blown upwards into his face. But these things Ross observed, merely, and did not acutely feel. Let winter come, was his thought. Let the snow fall and consume Bath in a shroud of silence. Let everything feel as stifled and as bandaged as my heart.

His favourite walk was up Beacon Hill and across some grassy fields to the village of Charlcombe. Going up Beacon, he felt his lungs complain, but forced himself to climb faster, as though trying to test his body, even willing it to fail that test and to fall.

But it did not fall. One of the gifts he'd believed he was offering Jane was his body's strength. In his surgery, he could, if the need arose, lift his patients onto his examination table. The power of his hands and his refined knowledge of the human skeleton enabled him to be swift and effective at bone setting. And as for his stamina as a lover, the girls working in the upstairs rooms of the Neck Tavern on Avon Street, where Ross was an occasional visitor, had nicknamed him Sir Diehard and he was vain enough to feel proud of this.

He had so often imagined this gift of his strength being offered to Jane that it was now almost impossible to accept that she would never experience it. He wanted to say to her, 'let me show you how adroitly I can love you. Then decide whether you wish to marry me or not. To cast me away before I've given you the gift of myself is not reasonable nor fair ...'

But of course no such words could be spoken. Jane had refused him and he now had to find it in himself to turn away from her and reimagine a different future. But where and how was that future to be found? It was this which Ross vainly hoped his cold morning walks would reveal to him. Yet he was aware, as he urged his body to its ever-faster pace, that his mind was a terrible blank. He supposed that thoughts must be flickering in some part of his brain, but he couldn't actually *think* them. He wondered if this blankness was a prelude to madness or bodily collapse.

When he reached the top of Beacon Hill, he usually stopped and looked down. The perspective before him still engendered in him a faint sense of wonder. He saw, laid before him, the *orderliness* of the city, which had grown with time, as new streets and squares were laid out. Noting how Bath had redefined itself as the years passed, and didn't remain petrified in the past, he began to wonder whether he, a citizen of this tranquil place, could also achieve some alteration in himself. But he feared that the emptiness of his mind, this void of non-thinking, would prevent it.

One morning in late November, Ross was walking from the Hill towards Charlcombe across the fields. There was a thin crusting of last night's frost on the grass. The sun, now risen in a blue sky, gave to the meadow a sudden jewelled splendour. Ross paused and stared at this, letting it dazzle his vision. Then, at the corner of his eye, he saw an extraordinary bird, shining black and green against the whitened field. It was, like him, standing quite still, seeming to regard the silent scene with close attention.

It was a capercaillie, the large wood grouse, *tetrao urogallus*, a bird of exceptional rarity, hardly ever glimpsed in England, but which, years before, on a visit to Scotland, had so beguiled Ross's younger brother Edmund by its colouring and its display that from that day, Edmund had been determined to dedicate his life to becoming a naturalist. At once, Ross was transported to other fields, lanes and hedgerows where he and Edmund, as growing boys in Wiltshire and, always under Edmund's instruction, had given all their hours to collecting plants and insects and to trapping small animals and birds.

What chiefly came to his mind, as he and the capercaillie remained motionless in the sunrise, was the sound of Edmund's laughter, his inevitable way of communicating pure joy when his eyes alighted on something – a rare orchid flower, an adder coiled into a circle on a warm stone, a golden eagle flying above the trees – which few people ever saw, but which, to him, seemed as magnificent as the December fireworks in Sydney Gardens, as moving as a phrase of music by Mozart.

Edmund had so longed to possess and preserve all that he and his brother found that soon their shared room was hung with great squares of cork, set with meticulously pinned samples of beetles, spiders, moths and butterflies and the pages of every book he owned were interleaved with pressed ferns, grasses and meadow flowers.

In his father's wine cellar, Edmund had set up a dissecting table, where he had studied the anatomy of the weasels, stoats, toads, lizards and birds he and Valentine had managed to trap or shoot with their father's rifle. He had made drawings of wings and tails, mouths, internal organs, feet and eyes and taught himself the difficult art of taxidermy, so that he could continue to study the anatomy of the animals long after they were dead.

Not far from where Ross was now standing was a fallen oak tree. He moved quietly towards this, not wanting to frighten away the capercaillie, and sat down. Though beautiful in itself, with its shining green breast and the flash of red above its eye – its beauty somehow made more intense because these birds had been extinct in England and had only been reintroduced there a few years before by land-owners who primarily wished to shoot them for sport – the capercaillie had immediately brought before Ross's eyes fond images of his younger brother. He saw Edmund's tall, gangly frame, running along a lane with his butterfly net. He saw his blond hair, ruffled by the wind. He saw his careful and steady hands pinning beetles to his cork boards. He heard his shouts of joy.

Edmund had been away for a year, on a mission – in the footsteps of his hero, Alfred Russel Wallace – to study the flora and fauna of the islands of the Malay Archipelago. The young man doubted that he could make a glorious name for himself as a mere collector – with no revolutionary theory about evolution with which to dazzle the scientific world – but he'd told Valentine that his heart nevertheless beat with longing at the thought of his adventure.

Edmund Ross believed he had a true calling towards botanical and zoological study, and he hoped to discover at least some new species on Borneo or Celebes that had never before been catalogued. He counted upon finding and dispatching 'viable specimens, showing the region's unimaginable variety' to Kew Gardens and to Mr Richard Owen, superintendent of the Natural History Department of the British Museum. He'd acquired an agent, Mr Stephen Chancellor, who instructed him in the preservation of animal skins and insects in spirit-filled casks and who would make sure that, once arrived in England, these reached their destinations. Though Chancellor announced that he would pay himself one third of the money offered by the London institutions 'on account of mighty work and trouble', he had also promised Edmund high prices, provided his specimens were 'first rank and by no means decayed'.

Edmund Ross had studied at exhaustive length William Wood's 1821 *Illustrations of the Linnaean Genera of Insects* and was himself a good draughtsman. His infrequent letters to Valentine, together with his casks of specimens, put aboard slow vessels from Sarawak to Singapore, where they waited for merchant ships bound for England, had included beautiful drawings of butterflies, scorpions, leeches, beetles, bats, moths, centipedes and caterpillars. One letter described with awe Edmund's ascension of Mount Ophir on Borneo. 'Here,' said this letter, 'with low cloud making the air so humid that breathing seemed difficult, I found true wonders, including a pitcher plant nourishing itself on its collection of drowned insects.'

But a recent letter, dated September, found him at Kuching, 'where', wrote Edmund, 'I have been balked in my intention of journeying on to the Aru Islands, where Wallace found the Birds of Paradise, by succumbing to Malaria. I lie in a hammock and sweat and groan. One night, I woke to find a rat licking the salt sweat from the soles of my feet.'

Though worried for Edmund, Valentine Ross had consoled himself with the idea that, by the time the letter was in his hands, Edmund would have recovered. Now, with a sudden shiver, he understood that this might not be the case. He conjured an image of his brother lying in darkness in some fearful hovel, roofed with mud and leaves, suffering agonies of fever, dysentery and thirst, untended by any human hand. And immediately, Ross's mind, so shrouded in blankness on his morning walks, was filled with resolution: he had to leave England without delay. By some means – though he had no idea, yet, how this was to be done – he had to travel halfway round the world to Borneo and save Edmund's life.

He'd saved it before.

At their cold and violent boarding school, fellow occupants of Edmund's dormitory, objecting very strongly to the boxes Edmund kept under his bed, filled with soil, leaves, worms and live insects, had one day seized the boxes, tipped their contents out of a high window and prepared to bundle Edmund himself into the void, held only by his feet in their faithless hands.

Hearing him scream, Valentine had rushed into the dormitory, assessed at once what was about to happen to his brother, approached the largest of Edmund's antagonists, picked him up bodily, without staggering or faltering, carried him to an adjacent open window and stuck the boy's head and shoulders out of it, announcing that he would tip him 'entirely out' unless Edmund was released. To his satisfaction, Valentine had seen the immediate slack-jawed panic on the faces of the dormitory inmates. He pushed his captive further out into the air and heard his screams now join with Edmund's.

Moments later, Edmund was once again standing by his bed, white with terror and disposed to weep at the loss of his insect collection, but unharmed. Valentine tugged his victim back into the room and threw him to the floor, where he saw to his astonishment that the boy was losing control of his bladder. The sudden recognition of his own strength, his own *power*, thrilled him more than anything he had known. His voice was choked with excitement as he said, 'If you touch my brother again, I'll put you all into the Sanatorium for the rest of term.'

The capercaillie was still wandering about the field. That his presence hadn't frightened away the bird, Ross took as a sign that the spirit of Edmund was looking calmly upon the improbable idea that his brother could suddenly appear by his side at Kuching.

Yet now Ross exhaled a long, exasperated sigh. He saw that the whole plan was preposterous. Edmund would know – as he himself knew – that such a journey towards unknown islands, towards the green darkness of swamp and rainforest, presented to him the worst fears that he could imagine. Valentine Ross was a man who was fond of order. His dedication to doctoring was born of his idea that the physician's primary task was to identify the nature of the patient's 'disorder' and to do whatever he could to restore body and mind to harmony. To travel to a region of the world where the climate alone seemed designed to make men ill, where trees crowded the sky, where ants could swarm from the forest floor into every space occupied by humankind, where leeches could burrow into the body's veins and arteries, was a task so completely beyond his capabilities that he now wondered how it could ever have entered his mind.

As the capercaillie wandered away into the pines, leaving Ross with the feeling of being absolutely alone, with nothing else stirring in the field, he was invaded by an intense dismay at his own shortcomings. Jane Adeane, his adored 'White Angel', had looked down at him from her great height and found him wanting. He had searched for but could not find the courage to travel vast oceans in the hope of saving his brother's life. What in the world was to become of such a flawed and cowardly man?

RAJAH

In Borneo, things were no longer quite as Valentine Ross believed them to be. Edmund Ross, recovering slowly from Malaria, was not lying in the kind of 'fearful hovel' so vividly imagined by his brother, but had been brought to the grand, high-portalled house of a self-styled Rajah of the South Sadong Territories, Sir Ralph Savage.

Here, the young man rested on clean linen sheets. On Sir Ralph's orders, Chinese servants brought Edmund sweet water from a garden well, bowls of sticky rice and a potion made of bitter Jesuit's Bark and molasses, upon which he himself swore as a preventative against death from Malaria.

Edmund slept a fevered sleep. From time to time, Sir Ralph would come into his room and look at him. Pale from his sickness, his long-fingered hands resting on his chest, his dirty hair matted, as though to resemble thorns, Edmund Ross reminded Sir Ralph of nobody so much as Jesus Christ himself, and this strange likeness brought into the rajah's heart complicated feelings of wonder and yearning. He longed for Edmund to wake up for long enough, not just to sip the bark potion, but to begin to talk to him.

There were many rajahs in Borneo at this time. All had their hearts set to the ticking of the European clock and acted as rulers over the native peoples: Malays, Arabs, Malanaus, Dyaks, Bugis and a small contingent of hard-working Chinese. One of them had even waged a deadly war in 1863 on behalf of one Malay tribe against another, seemingly only to assert his power to command bloodshed and sacrifice, as if that was the one thing he yearned for.

But the rajahs differed wildly in their treatment of those who laboured in their fiefdoms. Most were incompetent, demonstrated an unnecessary cruelty born of fear, and – often to their own surprise – could detect no improvements in the quality of human existence which surrounded them, not understanding that if they had treated their workers with greater consideration, they could have begun to make things better in this singular part of the world.

Sir Ralph Savage, however – despite the terror that seemed to be written in his name – was not quite of this lazy and unthinking kind. He saw that rajahs and sultans could, if they chose, bring happiness and prosperity to those they claimed to rule over, provided they refrained from levying harsh taxes on the Malays and had the imagination to see where that happiness might lie. Sir Ralph was a man who adored being alive, who found beauty in things which others did not necessarily see, and who, despite his overwhelming appetites, believed that Jesus Christ would watch over him and bring him, by some means, to everlasting salvation, if he could only do some good in the world.

Brought up in India, he had then been sent by his wealthy father to Oxford, where he read Divinity. He had liked his studies, but had stayed in Oxford for only one year before deciding that the darkness of England was killing him by slow degrees. He returned to the subcontinent and joined the Honourable East India Company's Army, from which he was dragooned out after seven months for 'repeated and unacceptable acts of gross indecency'.

Unrepentant, his heart still raging with unformed ambition, he fitted out a fine schooner and sailed south-eastwards across the Indian Ocean in search of adventure, power, sexual nirvana and the opportunity to practise philanthropy. With the death of his father, he was now in possession of a baronetcy and a colossal fortune which he believed could help obtain for him a kingdom in the wild romantic East.

To come by this kingdom, he approached the Sultan of Brunei, who claimed distant rule over the whole peninsula. It was known that the Sultan gave out gifts of territory in return for favours and Sir Ralph presented himself as a man who would do anything that was asked of him. This, however, was not entirely true. He believed in the Sixth Commandment. He did not like killing people. When the

Sultan ordered him to help put down a local insurrection by Land Dyaks, he felt himself falter. But his dreams of his own fiefdom were stubborn. He could not envisage any other way of being happy than by waking each morning to look out on his own portion of the world. And so he contrived to gather round himself a group of Malays addicted to cock-fighting and pay them to leave aside their cruel sport long enough to subdue the head-hunting insurrectionists and to lay before the Sultan a basket of Dyak heads.

Sir Ralph's financing of this bloodthirsty episode haunted him for a long while, but the Sultan was pleased to be rid of the Dyaks. He kept the basket of heads strung up in a grove of Mediterranean pines and was interested to record at what terrible pace the flesh became mushy and melted from the bone. This slaughter of his 'enemies', together with sexual favours tailored to his imaginative needs impressed the Sultan sufficiently for him to bequeath to Sir Ralph a substantial parcel of land in Sarawak, irrigated by the Sadong River.

Now, the rajah designed a palatial house not far from Kuching. Using both Malay and Chinese labourers, whom he paid with minute grains of silver, he saw it rise – astonishingly white, like an iceberg towering up from the ocean waves – against the impenetrable green of the tropical forest. He chose to see it as a thing of beauty, a temple of civilisation in a chaotic world. He planted the gardens with scarlet Canna lilies, orchids, banana trees, bamboo groves and coconut and date palms, set round with manicured English lawns. He built an aviary and sent the local Malays out into the forest to snare casso-waries, toucans, chestnut-hooded thrushes, and umbrella birds, whose exotic cries and jewelled plumage reassured him that life, here in Sarawak, was designed to capture all that was extraordinary under God's heaven.

In spite of his extravagant desires, Sir Ralph Savage had little of meanness in him and as soon as he had installed himself under his colossal roof, with his favourite Malay servant, Leon, as his primary bed companion, he set himself upon his path of philanthropy. In Leon, Sir Ralph had chosen a remarkable man, someone who knew far more about Borneo's yearnings and dreams than the English rajah would ever understand. In the hot nights, holding Leon in his arms, he kept asking him, 'What is to be done here, Leon? How am I to improve upon what the Creator has given us?' He told his lover that he wished to go down in history as one who had 'enabled happiness'.

Leon advised him to begin by building a road.

'A road to where?' Sir Ralph had asked.

'Sir Raff,' said Leon. 'There is no "*where*" in Sarawak. There is only Nature. Men begin; Nature finishes.'

'Then what is the point of the road?'

'The point for the road is to *try to be*.'

Sir Ralph stroked Leon's thick, oily hair. Because he liked this answer and didn't want to argue with his lover, and because he was infatuated with Leon and wished to deny him nothing within reason, he began to design plans for his road straight away.

He announced that it would be called the Savage Road. A cruel quantity of stones had to be found, broken and crushed to form its base core. This stone, hewn from the hilly ground by Chinese labourers, gave it impressive stability, and when Sir Ralph showed this proudly to Leon, Leon said, 'White and strong, Rajah Sir – just like you and the British Empire!' and exploded with irrepressible laughter.

Sir Ralph didn't mind being teased by Leon, but when the Chinese road crew informed him that nothing else could be found for its surface but tamped earth and ground sandstone, he understood straight away that when the heavy rains fell, the Savage Road would appear to send tributaries of itself slithering away into the forest. And this dismayed him. He wished to feel proud of his road. His appetite for the Great Tasks in life was boundless, but he suffered when what he had seen in his mind was blighted by some unexpected flaw. After each drenching rain, he would walk out along the road, past the new settlements that he was building on either side of it: past Malay children playing in the mud, past the little stockade where cock-fighting took place by firelight and moonlight, and note how much earth had been washed away.

He cut a strange figure, dressed in a crumpled linen robe, with his greying hair tied back in a silk ribbon and wearing leather boots purloined from East India Company Army Stores, standing in the middle of the Savage Road and cursing the sky. The little Malay children laughed at him. The Malay women hid their laughter behind soft shawls. But Sir Ralph didn't care if people found him funny or ridiculous; he only hoped they didn't find him cruel. He himself had endured enough of cruelty from his peers in the Army of the East India Company to wish for a world in which it didn't exist. Sometimes he'd kneel in the mud and pray, to his beloved Jesus, to send rain in more modest quantities, to help him return the lost earth to its rightful place on what he sometimes called his 'providential highway'. But the rain in Sarawak was relentless.

Another thing troubled him. Leon had warned him that the Savage Road would have no proper destination; it merely ran to the limit of the land over which Sir Ralph claimed to rule and then stopped, and this he had to accept. But where it stopped, the forest once again reared straight up in its terrible darkness, and this made him slightly breathless with dread. Sir Ralph could hear and observe the forest's intent: seeds cascading from the branches to embed themselves in the earth, lianas groping towards the ground, roots sending out tentacles into the crushed stones, the wind in the high canopy blowing everything towards the road's end, where the shadows of the trees already moved over it in a restless tide. When he lamented to Leon that the jungle was his enemy, he was surprised when Leon replied, 'No, Sir Raff, my friend. Don't be a nin-poop. This jungle is the cradle of all things.'

After many days of sipping the bitter tree bark medicine and forcing down a few spoonfuls of rice, Edmund Ross was strong enough to be led to a tin bath and bathed in warm water by two Malay boys. His nostrils filled with the scent of carbolic soap. His wild, spiky hair was washed and tenderly combed.

He began to take in his opulent surroundings: ebony furniture made in China, fresh muslin curtains at the window, Indian rugs, jade statues, overstuffed brocaded armchairs, gold candelabra which would not have looked out of place in Queen Victoria's dining room. Sensing that these things, or rather, the person who had gathered them around him, had saved his life, Edmund felt a sudden profound gratitude towards him and was overcome by a fit of weeping. His attendants withdrew silently, leaving Edmund alone in the bath, wracked with sobs.

Trying to master himself by examining his legs and noting their shrunken state, as though they might have been the trembling white shanks of an old man, he was then surprised by a voice very near him, which asked in aristocratic English tones, 'Shall I assume that you know how to read?'

A towel had been placed on the rim of the bath and Edmund now reached out for this and dried his eyes. Seated beside him on a lacquered stool sat Sir Ralph Savage.

Edmund at once recalled that he had seen this person once or twice before, standing by his sickbed and regarding him with tender concern. Now, the man reached out and laid a caressing hand on Edmund's damp hair. 'I ask,' he said, 'because this is the one thing lacking from my life: somebody who can read to me in faultless English, preferably from the New Testament. Is that something you would be prepared to do?'

'Yes,' said Edmund.

'Oh,' said Sir Ralph, 'well, that is very, very consoling to me. You cannot know how much I long to hear these verses again, spoken with feeling. There are missionaries in Sarawak, but their voices are too loud and their hearts too hard. They shun me and I shun them. I am a lover of young men and these people affect to despise me for this and inform me that I am damned in the eyes of Jesus. But they are wrong. I have many times spoken to Jesus and I know that he understands me, because of his own great love for Saint John. And I judge that you will not despise me. I've been told you are a butterfly catcher. Your mind must therefore be open and attentive to all that exists under the sun.'

Edmund now looked closely at Sir Ralph. He saw an ageless face, tanned and lined a little by the sun of the tropics, with thick hair falling to his shoulders and eyes of a startling blue, reminding him of his brother, Valentine. His lips were narrow, but sensual. From one ear dangled an exquisite piece of carved ivory, this ornamentation alone giving him the air of a pirate. The thought thus passed through Edmund Ross's mind that the man might be holding him captive in his eccentric mansion, but if this frightened him for a moment he also knew that he was too weak to put up any resistance to his captivity. And he was alive. He was alive, when, only a few weeks ago, he had been near to death in a fragile hut roofed with leaves. Whatever was going to happen to him here, he would have to surrender to it.

The evening of that day found Sir Ralph Savage and Edmund Ross, now dressed in clean clothes too large for his emaciated frame, sitting on the veranda eating catfish and sweet potatoes and sipping arak, while all around them hundreds of fireflies came out and glowed in the darkness.

In the shadows, not far from them, crouched Leon. Sir Ralph appeared to pay him no heed and the crouching figure was so still, so soundless that Edmund almost forgot that he was there at all. But after some time, Sir Ralph turned to him and asked him to bring an oil lamp to the table, and Leon got to his feet and went quietly into the house.

While he was gone, Sir Ralph said: 'I pay Leon with small pieces of silver. If he stays with me, he will be rich one day. The only condition is that he must be available to me day and night. He is very clever and lovable. And he has the silkiest arse in Borneo. I hope I do not shock you by saying this?'

'No,' said Edmund.

Sir Ralph tipped back his glass of arak and drank it down.

'Men must speak of these things,' he went on. 'We must speak of all that our souls long to confess. We must speak of *everything* in the world and speak of it truthfully. That is my philosophy. Perhaps you will tell me yours?'

Edmund smiled, but it was too dark on the veranda for Sir Ralph to see the smile.

'I was born in Wiltshire,' said Edmund. 'I was raised to be obedient and silent, and to keep my body in a like condition, with the expectation that I would some day become a Minister of the Church. But when I was quite a young boy I discovered the world of the insects and the flowers. And that always felt to me like a small patch of paradise.'

'If you discovered paradise in Wiltshire, why did you come here?'

'Because I wanted to test myself – to see whether I could survive in an unfamiliar world. And I have tried to follow in the footsteps of Mr Wallace. My quest is to send back rarities to England, to make men marvel.'

'Very good,' said Sir Ralph. 'I got the impression that the English are a little starved of marvels. And I believe that if there is nothing of the marvellous in our lives, we begin to die.'

A PORTRAIT

It was one of Emmeline Adeane's favourite pastimes to hire a strong horse and go riding on the sandy highway of Rotten Row in Hyde Park. Although this was a popular place, among London society, to see and be seen, and many people liked to ride in companionable groups, talking as they went, greeting other riders, showing off their equestrian skill no less than their *à la mode* riding habits, right down to their exquisite calfskin gloves, Emmeline preferred to ride alone. She wasn't particularly concerned to be seen. What she liked was the thrill of the ride.

Always urging her mount to a fast gallop, she crashed her way round the Row at chaotic speed, almost in the manner of a riderless horse who stubbornly keeps ahead of all the other contenders in the race. Just the sound of the horse's hooves pounding the earth excited her. And as for the speed, she had frequently declared to her friends that she knew nothing in the world more exhilarating than this. Impatient with slow groups of riders who might impede her path, Emmeline often appeared at the stables near dawn, to take her horse on its wild ride around an empty track. Then, what she loved was to see the sun coming up over the eastern edge of the city, to feel an answering rise of colour in her own cheeks and to feel that, despite her years of lost children, despite her abandonment by Jocelyn Hulton, her life was still delivering something of wonder, something of grace.

With Jane now installed at Tite Street, Emmeline soon enough announced to her niece that riding would be part of their lives and

Jane had agreed. She joked that only 'a very tall horse, at least sixteen hands' would have to be procured for her, 'otherwise my boots will trail in the sand', and Emmeline sent her maid, Nancy, round to the stables with this instruction. On a cold autumn morning, Emmeline and Jane set off for their first ride.

Jane's horse, named Nero, was large and frisky and inclined to pull too hard at the bit in its impatience to gallop, but Jane, like her aunt, was a courageous rider and enjoyed her mastery of the animal, encouraging it, at moments, to slow to a stately walk, so that she and Emmeline could admire the burning colours of the leaves flying in the wind, the icing of frost on the grass.

It was during one of these walking moments that two riders, a man and a young woman, mounted on chestnut horses, overtook Jane and Emmeline at an elegant trot. Once past them, the gentleman rider turned in the saddle and stared at Emmeline and Emmeline stared back and her mouth opened, as if to utter a sudden cry. It closed again as the gentleman turned away and, with a word to his female companion, urged his horse into a canter. Jane saw that her aunt kept staring until the couple were out of sight. Then Emmeline said quietly, 'that was Jocelyn Hulton. With his latest mistress. I should not care a fig for it, he's an old man now, but seeing him has made me feel very dizzy and hot. I'm terribly afraid, Jane, that I'm going to faint.'

Jane tugged Nero to a stop and quickly dismounted. She took hold of the reins of Emmeline's horse and helped her down. Leading the two horses with one hand and letting Emmeline lean against her as they walked towards the frosty grass, Jane led her aunt to an iron bench set out under an ash tree. Here, Emmeline sat down and leaned forward, putting her head close to her knees. Afraid to let go of the horses in case they bolted, Jane could only stand close to her aunt and will her to recover. Nero threw his head up, jangling his bit, unhappy with the sudden stillness of everything, but Jane held tight to the reins.

'I'm sorry …' Emmeline whispered. 'I'm sorry, Jane.'

'No need for sorrow,' said Jane. 'Only the sorrow you feel. And how could you know when this would come upon you, even though the years pass? In my work at the Baths, I observe this all the time: the shock, perhaps long delayed, which suddenly arrives in the mind and lays the body low.'

That evening, after Emmeline had rested and recovered and drunk tea by the fire, she said to Jane: 'I have always seen goodness in you, dearest Jane, but it is tempered by something else, something harsher and more determined. I don't know what that harsh thing is, precisely, but I know how to find out. I would like to paint your portrait.'

'Oh,' said Jane. 'You want to paint me in order to find out who I am?'

'I know who I think you are,' said Emmeline, 'but now I feel that I do not know you right to your core.'

'And supposing, in my core, I turn out to be somebody very wicked?'

'Well, that would be interesting. Then, you might have to be restrained by some means, I suppose, but not by me because I know that restraint is never to your liking and I love you far too much to hurt you. Might we begin the portrait tomorrow?'

Jane wished to be standing, for the painting. She said to her aunt: 'I don't think you will see me correctly unless you depict my height.'

Emmeline regarded Jane closely for a long time. As always, when she began a picture, some words of Jocelyn Hulton's echoed in her mind. 'For your female sitters, call upon myth,' he had said. 'Think of Greek goddesses. For women like to feel immortal. You must make them look as though they will be worshipped for all time.'

It came to Emmeline that there was already something of the 'immortal' in Jane and all she had to do now was to capture it. She asked Jane to put on a white gown, as similar as possible to those she wore at the Baths, and positioned her in front of one of the tall windows which gave onto the small neglected garden of the narrow house.

The visible portion of sky was blank and pale, and at once, Emmeline could see how the tones of this picture might help suggest the 'immortal essence' of Jane Adeane: a study of differing shades of white – white sky, a lace of white frost on a briar patch, white face and hands and neck, white cotton fabric – all suggesting an affinity with a condition of a previously unblemished whiteness.

43

But what would make it strong and real would be the discoloration upon that very whiteness, showing how time and texture and season cast shadows on all things and rendered them unique and grave, but yet suggesting here the stoicism of the sitter in the face of time and decay.

As Emmeline set up a tall canvas on her easel, she already felt excitement about the picture. She was impatient to sketch in the rough outlines with charcoal and begin working with her beloved oils. But one thing about the composition wasn't yet right: Jane's long-fingered hands hung loosely at her sides, inert and slack, and Emmeline knew that this detracted from her goddess-like status, making her look idle and somehow at a loss.

She broke off from her preparations, rummaged in the low cupboard where the failed artefacts she'd made on the pottery wheel were stowed away in a clutter, like a collection of damaged toys cast aside by a child. At the back of the cupboard was the wooden box in which she kept the golem. She lifted this out, opened it and took up the little manikin. She stared at it for a moment. Then she crossed the room and put it carefully into Jane's hands.

Jane looked down at what she'd been given. She felt moved that this was what Emmeline wanted: for Jane to be the custodian of a thing (or should she call it a 'creature'?) which had been important to her.

'I already feel tender towards it,' said Jane. 'And in your portrait, you will give it new life.'

Emmeline reached out and touched the soft skin of Jane's cheek. 'Let me remind you,' she said, 'that it's *you* I'm searching for.'

The portrait was begun in the flat grey light of a winter London morning. After a long while of standing obediently still, watching her aunt's gaze make small movements between her canvas and her subject, Jane's mind began to be preoccupied with something she had never before seen so clearly – that Emmeline Adeane had survived sorrow and tragedy only through the intensity of her commitment to her art, that her gifts as a painter singled her out from the common roll call of humanity and made her capable of the kind of higher endeavour which ordinary people never even bothered to imagine.

When Jane remembered the shuffling, anxious and groaning patients she nursed at the Baths, she suddenly saw them all as pathetic clay, as beings as imperfectly formed as the golem in her hands, even as *substances* in thrall to a never-altering state of inertia and incompleteness. In magnificent contrast, she perceived her aunt as somebody who understood that surrender to the paltry limitations of the human body and the unenquiring mind was not to be tolerated, that *striving* was asked of her.

These thoughts led Jane, in turn, to look at her own life and dare to ask herself whether her belief in her own singularity, in her innate *magnificence*, might not be delusional. She knew that she was a clever and patient nurse and that, once in a while, she could seem to bring about relief from pain which appeared almost miraculous. But was she not working at something thousands of other women could have done? Had her head not been turned by hearing that she was known as the Angel of the Baths?

And what, in her, had justified her disdainful refusal of a man like Valentine Ross? Jane knew that, as a doctor, he was accomplished and strong, that he had done no harm in the world, that he was offering her an honest life. Yet she had treated him like a foolish boy, teasing and belittling him. Was this fact alone not proof that where she thought she was marvellous, she was merely haughty and full of pride?

And yet ...

It persisted in her – she knew that it did – this feeling that her life would one day bring her proof that she was exceptional. But how was she to advance towards that proof?

Jane looked down at the small figure in her hands. And it came to her that it had been suffering which had refined Emmeline Adeane. She herself had been through flames and had found the means to heal herself. Without realising that she was speaking aloud, Jane whispered, 'when or how will any flame engulf *me?*'

'What did you say, Jane?' asked Emmeline.

'Oh. I was just giving words to what was in my head.'

'And what was in your head? It's your mind as well as your body which this portrait is going in search of.'

'Yes, I know, dear Aunt. And if you find it, do please tell me what I'm thinking.'

'Naturally I will. But now you must tell me what you just said aloud.'

Jane turned her head for a moment, regarding the low day-bed where, she had been told, to her emphatic distaste, Mr Hulton used to lie and practise onanism while watching the young Emmeline's unclothed right arm at work upon a painting.

'Well,' said Jane, 'I was remembering that before I came to London I refused an offer of marriage.'

'Ah,' said Emmeline, pausing for a moment with her stick of charcoal in her hand. 'Whom did you refuse?'

'He is no one. Or that is how I can't help but see him. He proposed to me in a tea room.'

A broad smile now lit Emmeline's face. 'A tea room, indeed,' she said. 'What kind of cake were you eating?'

'I believe it was a lemon cake. And at a table not far distant there was a small dog which began to howl.'

'Ah. So the dog's howling helped you to make up your mind to refuse the man?'

'No. I knew I would refuse him. The name of the person is Valentine Ross. And I could never marry a man called Valentine, could I, Aunt? There is far too much romantic flummery in the name, isn't there?'

'Romantic flummery? And that, of course, is not to your taste?'

'No. It certainly is not. I like things to be stark and plain.'

Emmeline was silent. She turned back to her work on the portrait. Then, she said to Jane, 'What was Valentine's station in life?'

'Oh,' said Jane, 'he is a doctor, who works with my father at Henrietta Street.'

'A good doctor?'

'Yes. I think he is very good.'

'So I wonder why you see him as *no one*.'

'I suppose I mean that he has no place in my heart.'

'Are you certain of this? You know that acceptable offers of marriage do not come along very frequently.'

'Yes, I know it. But this one is not acceptable. And, anyway, marriage is not on my mind.'

Emmeline was silent for a moment, then she said, 'you probably also know that, one day – inevitably – it will be.'

'THE DESTINY OF THE STOMACH'

Sitting in his dining room, one early morning, completing his breakfast of toasted teacakes and bacon, Sir William Adeane was reflecting upon Professor François Broussais's conclusions about the 'normal' and the 'pathological' in disease. In particular, Sir William had always been interested in the French physician's challenging idea that very many illnesses are caused uniquely by gastro-intestinal inflammations, and, as he chewed his bacon, he began to wonder whether, in his daily work, he paid this diagnosis enough attention.

Broussais had observed that 'the destiny of the stomach is always to be irritated' and it was true that very many of Sir William's patients came to Bath primarily to find relief from this discomfort by drinking the pure waters. He treated them also by raising blisters on the skin of the abdomen. When these were punctured, allowing the fluid to run out, it was thought that any infection within the stomach would also be drawn out, and although this treatment was so painful that some patients fainted when the blister was lanced, it was thought, on the whole, to be effective.

Seldom, however, had the doctor enquired about the quality or quantity of the food his clients habitually asked their bodies to ingest. He was inclined to think that they ate too much. Their waistlines bulged and strained against their clothes. Their breath was often foul, indicating a surfeit of fat-laden acids and too much tea. But a physician is not a nursemaid; he can't watch over a man's daily vict-ualling. He has to believe that his patients are not deliberately causing themselves bodily distress by gobbling too many oysters, by drinking claret until their heads begin to spin or by being unable to tolerate a jam tart unless it be heaped up with Jersey cream. And, reasoned Sir William, even if I knew this to be the case, what am I to do about it?

At this moment in his deliberations, as he was wondering whether he should make greater use of oatmeal poultices in his attempts to ease the perpetual 'irritation' Professor Broussais had identified, his cook Mrs Hughes came into the dining room and approached the doctor's chair, asking if she could have 'a word' before his working day began.

'Of course, Mrs Hughes,' said Sir William. 'Do please speak to me.'

The cook was wearing a dirty apron and she was scrunching this in her work-reddened hands, as if almost to wring it out, and Sir William deduced from this nervous gesture that some anxiety was playing upon her mind.

'Is anything the matter?' asked Sir William kindly.

'Yes,' said Mrs Hughes. 'I'm afraid, Sir, that everything is the matter. And this is what I came to tell you, Sir William: that I cannot go on.'

'Mercy, Mrs Hughes!' said Sir William. 'Whatever can you mean?'

'I mean that I cannot do my appointed job in this house any more, because I am given no proper orders. How am I to know what you and Dr Ross wish to take for your lunch if there is nobody to tell me? When Miss Jane was here, she wrote out the lists of meals and orders from the fishmongers and the butchers and the greengrocers every two days. But the fishmonger has just called and asked, "What is your order? Am I to give you haddock or Dover sole? Winkles for tea? Herring for breakfast?" and I have to say to him "be gone and take it all away, for I am not a mind-reader. And the gentlemen care so little, it seems, for my work, that they give me no orders at all." And I cannot continue under these conditions.'

Sir William Adeane was a man who invariably had an answer to every question asked, every theory put up for debate, but here, in the face of the angry Mrs Hughes, he found that he had no idea what to say. Meals, in his household, for as long as he could remember, had just *appeared* at the appropriate moments. He had no memory at all of ever ordering them, except at Christmas, when he liked to be particular about how much rum and brandy and what quantity of orange zest was put into the plum pudding. Otherwise, breakfast, lunch and supper were like the weather: they changed from day to day, but they were always just *there* by some magic he had never thought it necessary to learn.

'I am speechless ...' he stammered.

'Well,' said Mrs Hughes, 'I'm afraid speechlessness will not do, Sir. As well as fresh produce, we are wanting very many dry goods in the kitchen stores, upon which Miss Jane always kept a careful eye, but since she's gone I have been given no money with which to replace them. More than this, Sir William, I have not been paid my own wages for two weeks, despite leaving written reminders on your desk. So I am saying it again: I cannot go on. I have been offered a place at Bramerton Hall by Lady Manners and I have agreed to take it – from tomorrow.'

Sir William Adeane looked Mrs Hughes up and down. Though he had sometimes visited the basement kitchen, primarily to verify that it was clean and that no vermin were visible, he had to admit to himself that, if asked to give a detailed description of Mrs Hughes, he would have found this difficult. He excused himself from this dereliction by remembering that he'd usually seen Mrs Hughes through a miasma of kitchen vapour, given off by boiling puddings and stewing meat. It was surely just this steam which had made her insubstantial to him, and not his own lack of curiosity about her, wasn't it? And was a busy physician expected to know by heart the features of his own servants?

What he saw now was that Mrs Hughes was a very thin woman, with sinewy arms and grey hair escaping from a dirty cotton cap. That the sustenance of his body had long been in the hands of such a person now surprised him. He would have preferred his cook to be rounded of form, pink of cheek and spotlessly clean. He let escape from him a long, mortified sigh.

'If your mind is made up, Mrs Hughes,' he said. 'Then there is nothing I can do. Only apologise to you for any oversight on my part.'

But how on earth, he asked himself, when so many strangers were flocking to Bath for the winter Season, renting houses and arranging elaborate breakfast parties, match-making teatime feasts and evening soirées, was one to procure a new cook?

Because Sir William's dead wife and then his daughter had always taken these kinds of domestic question upon themselves and not bothered him with them, he felt like a child presented with some arithmetical sum it did not know how to solve. He sat over the remains of his teacake and bacon, with coffee going cold in a jug, until Valentine Ross arrived to hold his morning surgery and then shared the problem with him.

Ross suggested buying the *Bath Chronicle*, in the expectation that cooks might advertise their services there. They sent their housemaid, Becky, out for the paper and looked through it carefully, but this solution did not seem to be accessible within its pages. Many employers were advertising *for* cooks, but no chefs were offering their services. Sir William said to Ross, 'Had we wanted a hod-carrier, a coffin-maker or a chimney-sweep, we would have had no difficulty, but this does not help us at all. Can a hod-carrier roast a chicken? Can a sweep confect a caper sauce? I think not.'

The two men looked at each other. Visions of featureless days, devoid of any hot food, leading soon enough to unbearable hunger – only to be assuaged at exorbitant daily expense in one of the Bath chop-houses – instantly oppressed their minds, and after a moment Sir William ventured, 'I think I will write to Emmeline and ask that Jane returns straight away. And she will find some means to solve the problem for us.'

He glanced up to see a stricken look on Ross's face, which he was trying to fathom when their doorbell sounded, indicating the arrival of the first patient of the day. Valentine Ross at once left the room to take up his position in his surgery and no comment was made upon the idea of Jane's return from London. Sir William found himself alone again, his mind in a state of severe puzzlement.

Taking matters into his own hands, determined that he should not be subjected to Jane's return to Henrietta Street until he had found some means to cope with the strain and heartache of working at her side, Ross hurried through his roster of patients as quickly as he could that day and then walked down to Mrs Morrissey's tea rooms.

Here, he ordered a pot of tea and a cheese scone, and lingered over this – spreading and re-spreading smaller and smaller quantities of butter on the scone – until Mrs Morrissey went to put up her 'Closed' sign. He then invited her to sit down beside him. He hadn't been to the tea rooms since the day of his disastrous proposal, and it oppressed him slightly to find himself there, in a place where he had been made to feel so foolish and unhappy, but he had made himself stay and now he said, dramatically, to Clorinda Morrissey, 'I shall come at once to the point, Mrs Morrissey. Sir William and I find ourselves in a difficult position – very difficult indeed – and we feel that you are the only person in Bath who can help us!'

Mrs Morrissey was then told about the severe domestic problem at Henrietta Street and asked if she could see any way out of it.

At first she smiled and said modestly, 'I'm a relative newcomer to Bath, Doctor Ross, as you know, but of course I can ask around, to see whether, perhaps, one of my clients could *lend you* a cook.'

'Lend? I am not sure that a borrowed cook is the kind we were hoping for.'

'Ah well, now I do understand that. Perhaps, on second thoughts, that is not really a practical idea?'

Ross finished his tea and said: 'What I was secretly praying is that *you* could offer us your services for a while, at least as far as providing us with a hot lunch, before you open your tea room for the afternoon. I know that Sir William Adeane would be immensely grateful and would pay you whatever you demanded.'

'Pay me whatever I demanded? Well, that would be plain foolish, wouldn't it, Doctor? For you know that I am at heart a cake-maker. For the rest of everything, I have no skill. All that I could make for you would be meat pies and pasties, with perhaps a steak-and-kidney suet pudding, or, at best an Irish stew with lamb neck and pearl barley, as my mother made it. I really have no other ideas, when it comes to savouries.'

'But you might be willing to make those things – the pies and the stew and so forth – starting tomorrow?'

'Starting *tomorrow*?'

'Or at worst, the day after. Please say you will. You could come to Henrietta Street with me now, to agree terms with Sir William.'

Clorinda Morrissey gestured round her room, where the coal fire had now burned to embers. 'Why must you be in such a rush, Doctor Ross? Look at all that I have to clear up now, with only one girl to help me, and never mind that I must begin baking for tomorrow.'

'I do see that I am being impatient. But if you won't do it, I'm not sure what we are to do, other than to starve.'

Clorinda Morrissey now measured Ross's blue eyes with her own, which were grey and narrow and could sometimes close in weary refutation of the very many things in the world which inclined her to anger. In a quiet but firm voice, she said, 'You must not use the word "starve", Doctor Ross. Not to me. Remember that I come from Ireland. And when I was a young woman in Dublin, what did we endure but the terrible sight of people driven off their land by hunger, and dying in our streets? Did you never hear of the Irish potato famine?'

'I'm sure I did, but I was a child and I had no understanding of it.'

'Blight coming to our staple crop and spreading and spreading until all the counties of the west of Ireland were laid waste. And the British Government, you see, doing nothing, or almost nothing, only sending a few paltry ship-loads of American corn, at prices very few could afford. And then putting in a foolish Programme of Public Works to give employment to the poor. And what did these "works" do? They made the destitute people lift turf and sod to fill in empty hollows – to no purpose. They made them work on new roads that led to no destination. It's a wonder, it is, that Ireland has ever forgiven you.'

Ross looked down at his hands. If what he habitually saw in these hands was their strength and their skill, what he now felt was that no part of himself – mind or body – was truly equipped to undertake the complicated demands of a human life. There was just too much about the world that he didn't understand.

'I am sorry,' he said.

He knew that this apology was embarrassingly inadequate to the subject which had suddenly been broached, but these were the only words he was able to find.

Luckily for him, Clorinda Morrissey now found herself so contented with her life in Bath that she – no less than that Dr Ross – was disinclined to dwell for long on Ireland's passage through her four years of famine, her four circles of hell. She put a gentle hand on his arm and said, 'I apologise for being so harsh. I will come and talk to Sir William. The beef pies I make have been praised back home, for I do not skimp on the meat.'

ACROBAT

No more than half an hour after Mrs Morrissey returned from agreeing terms with Sir William at Henrietta Street, to chivvy her young helper, Mary into completing the tidying and cleaning of her tea room, and to begin on tomorrow's baking, a second caller rang her doorbell. The name of this person was Monsieur Florian Bellenger and he was a Belgian acrobat.

He had met Clorinda Morrissey at one of those autumn galas which had so beguiled her mind when choosing Bath as the destination for her new life. There had been rather fewer of these than she'd hoped, but this one, held in Sydney Gardens, had been splendid. There had been a five-piece orchestra and a wooden dance floor laid on the grass. Suckling pigs had been roasted on two enormous iron spits. On trestles, laid out in magnificent numbers, veal pies, pigeon patties, boiled ox-tongue and oysters had been offered, together with jellies, flans and blancmanges, sluiced down with punch, beer and lemonade – all for the price of the three-shilling entry ticket. There had been a maypole for the children, a muzzled dancing bear, led round by a Sikh in a jewelled turban, a coconut shy, a gypsy troupe dancing to violins and castanets and, most popular of all, a team of acrobats, who began by walking round on stilts and ended by flying through the air on a trapeze contraption fastened into the grass with iron hawsers.

It had been a cold night, but Clorinda Morrissey, wandering alone among the crowds, had looked up at the stars above the town, heard the yearning of the gypsy violins and decided that she was, at long last, a rejoicing *citizen of the world*, in all its variety. She congratulated herself on coming to Bath and having the tenacity to realise her small enterprise. She blessed the ruby necklace for giving her the chance to take her place in a cosmopolitan society. When she thought of Ireland on this particular night, it almost seemed to her as though her homeland had floated away, out into the Atlantic Ocean, where, in its habitual surrender to persecution and suffering, it was now a small, striving speck of green in the vast wash of the swelling and unending sea.

It had been while she was engaged in this reverie that Clorinda had turned to see one of the acrobats on stilts coming towards her through the crowds. He was made up in a clownish way, with a red nose and a black moustache, and wearing billowing striped trousers. He seemed to walk without difficulty on his tall stilts, and Clorinda couldn't help but stare at him, wondering what his life could possibly be like, if this was his occupation – to perambulate among crowds, six feet above them, then to risk his life on the flying trapeze. She asked herself how the human mind arrives at its unexpected decisions and whether they sometimes float up, unnamed and unbidden, from the long, shadowy road that is the past.

At this moment, the first of the promised fireworks exploded with a mighty boom in the sky and the acrobat fell over.

He fell sideways. He landed heavily on the grass, no more than a stilt's length from an organ grinder with a monkey on his shoulder. The monkey screeched and jumped onto the organ grinder's head. People around Clorinda gasped with shock and yet no one ran to the fallen man, quite as if they believed he was entirely made of wood and couldn't be hurt. But Clorinda Morrissey ran. She knelt by him and put her hand gently on his shoulder. He had just had time to reach out with his arms to prevent himself falling on his head, but he was winded and gasping for breath. Mrs Morrissey talked to him softly, telling him to lie still.

Other people now clustered around. The stilts were pulled from the ridiculous trousers. Children came to gape, then to start playing mock battles with the wooden poles. Clorinda told everybody to move back, 'to give the poor soul some air'. And after some minutes, the acrobat asked Clorinda if she might help him to his feet. She held his arm tightly. She saw that his false moustache had been torn off in the fall.

The following night, this man, Florian Bellenger, who was nearing fifty, but with the taut body of a youth and a smile of infinite charm, had come round to the tea room, dressed soberly in a black frock coat, bearing the gift of some autumn flowers. In his fractured English, he had told Clorinda Morrissey that he felt 'great shame'.

'Shame for what, Sir?'

'Shame to fall.'

'Oh,' said Clorinda, 'well, it was all the fault of the fireworks creating such a fright to you. If you ask me, you are one of the bravest people I've ever met. To walk on two bits of wood, like that. And to do that swinging and flying business through the air, with no net to catch you. Are you a Roman Catholic, Sir? Because I honestly think Our Lady herself would have been impressed by you and she would not have you talk of *shame*.'

Florian Bellenger had laughed joyfully and pressed the flowers into Clorinda's arms. They were Michaelmas Daisies and the purple and yellow of them reminded her of the scabious and ragwort which sprang up in the parks of Dublin, for want of a scythe. As she buried her face in them, Florian Bellenger had leaned forward and kissed her ear.

After that, he had called several times. Mrs Morrissey had made him tea and offered him muffins, for which she did not ask him to pay. If she was working, his eyes followed her about the room. It wasn't difficult to deduce that he had decided to fall in love with her.

When she thought about this, objectively, her own responses puzzled her. She could see that, by her own standards – in which people of great singularity, even downright oddness, were always favoured over those who were merely replicas of a thousand, directionless others – Florian Bellenger was a perfect man. Foreign, fearless, with an unknown, exotic past, the body of a dancer and a smile of such sweetness that other women became instantly flustered by it, he was surely an alluring prospect as a lover. And yet Clorinda Morrissey didn't want him. She liked his presence, his voice, his kindness, but she just didn't want him in her bed. After a while, she wondered whether she didn't want him *because he had fallen*, even as her young carrot-headed suitor in Ireland had fallen and succumbed to death. And she concluded that the only kind of man she might take willingly into her arms was one *who would not fall*, but on the contrary, be steady enough to lift her up, to a higher position in the world.

Now, on the day when she had agreed to help Sir William Adeane and Valentine Ross with their domestic troubles and was already making lists in her mind of the dishes she might make for them, here was Florian Bellenger at her door once again.

Damp and hot from her cleaning of the tea room and the arduous mixing and beating of flour, butter and sugar, with her brown hair in wild, escaping curls, she was tempted just to signal to him through the glass, telling him to go away. But he was pressing himself very close against the door and holding up a parcel, suggesting that he had come on an important errand. So Clorinda sent her helper, Mary, into the back kitchen, dried her hands on her apron and let him in.

She saw that his cheeks were pink, as though he'd been running and there was an agitation in him which she had never seen before. He held up the parcel.

'I bring you this,' he said. 'I bring it in hope.'

Clorinda took off her apron. The late afternoon, with its visit to Henrietta Street (a house in great need of a good cleaning, she thought) had already been peculiar enough and what she now longed to do was to lie down on her bed and go fast asleep. Instead, she fell back into one of the tea-room chairs and couldn't stop a long sigh escaping from her throat.

'Clorinda,' said Florian, 'Clorinda, Clorinda! I say your name in my dreams. But I want more than dreams. Here is my gift.'

He placed the parcel into Clorinda's hands. It was wrapped in a strip of gauzy fabric and tied neatly with string.

'Open. Open!' said Florian. 'It is for the one I love.'

This utterance brought to Clorinda's face a look of severity, seldom seen since the opening of the tea rooms had brought her so much gladness. She looked down at the package and knew that, no matter what it contained, she didn't want to unwrap it.

'I'm sorry,' she said. 'I never accept gifts from gentlemen.'

Florian Bellenger smiled his seductive smile and said, 'Do not say such a disappointing thing, Clorinda. I am not any gentleman. You know that. I am a spirit of the air! So open my gift. Allez! I am sure you will like—'

'No,' said Clorinda. 'Please take it back.'

'I know what you think – that I want something in return, n'est-ce pas? Something you may not wish to give – yet. But écoutez-moi bien, you and I, we are not ordinary. We are not bound in chains. We are not slaves to propriety, like those English snobs and prigs out there in the street. You ... from your green island; me ... from far away. We are quite free.'

'About freedom, I am inclined to agree. We are free, if we have the courage to be so. But this also means that I am free to say no to you.'

Florian Bellenger now looked as downcast as a trapeze artist, whose face has taught itself to smile at perpetual danger, ever allows himself to look.

'Clorinda,' he said. 'This is a gift of lace, *Point de Bruxelles*, from my home. I give to you something precious. For friendship. For the hope that you can love me. You sew the lace onto your bodice and I ... so softly, like the fingers of a flower ... I will unlace it, to reveal to me what I long to touch.'

Clorinda was tired enough on this day to wish to remain sitting in her chair, but she made herself stand up and hand the package back to Bellenger.

'You are my friend,' said Clorinda. 'But you cannot be my lover. Now, you must go, Monsieur. I have much work to do.'

Bellenger took the gift of the Brussels lace and put it sadly into the pocket of his coat.

'Tomorrow,' he said, 'I go to Bristol, with my trapeze troupe. Then to London. I shall be away some time. But I shall hope. I shall continue to hope that when I return—'

'Do not!' burst out Clorinda. 'I cannot be doing with it when men are foolish! And to hope that I will change my mind is just pure stupidity. You are a beautiful man, Monsieur Bellenger, but I cannot love you and that is that.'

Florian Bellenger then did a surprising thing. He opened his frock coat and ran a caressing hand down the slim silhouette of his body.

'I *am* beautiful,' he whispered. 'Many women have told me. One lady from Switzerland committed suicide when she could no longer have me as her lover.'

At this, Clorinda Morrissey strode to the tea room door and opened it and a cold winter wind blew in and ruffled the curtains. She said nothing. She told herself that some of the vanities of men are simply not worth commenting on. She stood tall by the door and waited for Florian Bellenger to re-button his coat and walk out into the darkness.

'… AND OF HIS KINGDOM THERE SHALL BE NO END.'

Only when he'd regained a little bodily strength and felt his head clear of the fever that had given him dreams of inescapable terror did Edmund Ross come to the realisation that all his collecting equipment was now missing. He counted himself lucky that he still had his wad of money, sewn into his hat brim, his hand-made boots, and one of his notebooks, but where was his compass? He'd searched every corner of the room he'd been given in Sir Ralph's house, but did not find it. Gone, too, were his gun and the boxes housing the corked boards to which he'd pinned his insects. Also missing were his butterfly nets, his dissecting tools and his killing jars.

He asked Leon, 'Do Malay people steal from white people?'

'No, Sir, Mr Ross,' said Leon, 'other way around. You come. Take our gold. Sail away.'

'Gold?' said Edmund. 'There is gold on Borneo?'

'There *was* gold.'

'And?'

'I told you. Taken by white people. Nothing left.'

After this exchange, Edmund felt that to mention the things he'd lost would make him appear pathetic and puerile. He knew that he would have to reconstruct his boxes, made with such neurotic care in England, search the market stalls of Kuching for a compass and a gun. He would have to purchase jars and chloroform and fabricate new nets. All of this would take time, and from the way Leon looked at him – with unmistakable, long-lashed disdain – he at first began to wonder how far he could trespass on Sir Ralph Savage's hospitality without upsetting the complicated laws of his household.

One early morning, Edmund was presented with a white robe, some raffia sandals and a pair of spectacles. He was led by Sir Ralph to a beautiful, secluded glade in the forest, shaded by palms, where two hammocks had been strung. From the nearby aviary came the cry of the cassowaries and from out in the forest the distant shout of the gibbon. The sky above the glade was the colour of opals, shading upwards to a more insistent blue.

'Now you see,' said Sir Ralph, 'in this very spot, right here, one of the commodities that money can buy. It can buy peace. For this to achieve perfection, all I need is the poetry of the King James Bible.'

Edmund was told to lie in one of the hammocks and put the spectacles on. 'You may think you don't need them,' said Sir Ralph, 'but the Word of God must be amplified before our eyes. You see? Or else we fail. We are so blind to what is true. Only when we see clearly, can we begin to understand.'

Sir Ralph had opened the bible at the Gospel According to St. Luke and told Edmund to start reading at Chapter One, Verse 26.

'I have chosen the Annunciation,' he said. 'For what gladdens our hearts more than a new beginning?'

Edmund was tempted to say that he'd experienced a troubling 'new beginning' to his life the day he'd arrived in Borneo. Once he'd entered the forest, tangled in its own impenetrable lore, his perceptions of who and what he was had begun to alter in a way that – in his great hunger for his adventure – he had never predicted. Indeed, there were aspects of himself which he now failed to recognise. He no longer saw a person who walked with a fearless stride, who was master – moment by moment – of his own intent, but felt that he'd become a child again, or else some species of a dream-self, who could only wander in this green immensity in a state of deep unknowing.

A hundred times, Edmund had reminded himself that his quest to find and capture rare species of birds and insects had lodged in his heart since he was a boy and that all he could do was to go forward, overcoming terror, and never think of giving up his mission, but yet he knew that something had changed in him: he was somehow *lesser* than he had been before. And when at last he had fallen ill, his sufferings appeared logical to him – inevitable. His illness was the place towards which he'd been travelling all the time.

But he told the rajah none of this. He opened the bible and turned the filigree pages very slowly until he found St. Luke's Gospel. Wearing the spectacles, Edmund discovered that the words seemed to jump about on the page – now large, now suddenly small – and the sun, falling in ever-changing striations through the palm leaves, decked the verses with a silvery, flickering light, so that the reader had the impression that he was trying to recite, not from a linen-bound book, but from something obstinately alive.

As he began to read, Edmund thought he saw a figure standing very still at the edge of the glade. The figure wasn't hiding. It had just seemed to understand how, among the darkness of the trees, it could be master of its own ambiguity. When Edmund next looked up, the figure was gone.

Had it been there at all? Or had something else – some configuration of shadow and light – confused the watcher? Edmund took off his spectacles and paused in his reading. His gaze interrogated the forest. Nothing moved there. He saw Sir Ralph turn in his hammock and stare at him. 'Why have you stopped?' he asked. 'My mind was just beginning to fill with wonder. You must understand, Mr Ross, that I have been yearning to hear a voice like yours reciting St. Luke's Gospel to me for more time than you could imagine. Please go on and don't stop until I tell you.'

Edmund replaced his spectacles and resumed:

'And the angel said unto her, Fear not, Mary: for thou hast found favour with God.

'And behold, thou shalt conceive in thy womb, and bring forth a son, and shalt call his name Jesus.

'He shall be great, and shall be called the Son of the Highest: and the Lord God shall give unto him the throne of his father, David.

'And he shall reign over the house of Jacob for ever; and of his kingdom there shall be no end ...'

Edmund kept reading until his throat began to be sore and the sun, rising higher in the empty sky, cleared the shade of the palms and began to burn down upon him and he felt the first symptoms of his fever returning. 'Malaria,' his brother Valentine had warned him, 'once begun on its first vile visitation, has a habit of returning, without discernible reasons. Watch for this and when you feel the first signs of fever, lay yourself down to rest.'

Edmund closed his eyes, shielding them with the bible. He wanted to get out of the hammock but he felt too weak to move. Then, he was aware of Sir Ralph at his side, lifting his shoulders gently and placing a kiss on his head.

'We shall go on tomorrow,' said Sir Ralph. 'Now you must sleep.'

He slept for many hours and woke in the darkness. His head ached, but the fever he'd thought was about to come back had subsided.

He knew that he'd dreamed about the Birds of Paradise, about their singular magnificence. The dream had been lit by a multicoloured radiance, quite as though sunlight itself was streaming out from the bodies of the birds, to fall upon everything around them. What now returned to Edmund Ross was the promise that he'd made to himself when he'd set out on his great adventure – that he would not go back to England without at least one living pair of these birds. He'd been told that the Queen herself yearned to see them and would build 'some suitable edifice to house them, that they may be seen as marvellous additions to our kingdom'.

He knew that he was not certain to find them in Borneo. He needed to persuade the owner of a ship to take him further eastwards, to the Aru Islands. But what was he now? A man in a strange captivity. A naturalist who had lost everything he needed to continue his quest. How could his plans ever be realised?

Edmund had no idea what time of night it might be. From his window, he could see no moon, only an icy clustering of stars above the palms. He yearned for a light less cold, a candle, and then pen and paper in his hand so that he could write to his brother. Indeed this was what he longed for, he realised, in a fierce moment which caught at his throat: he wanted Valentine to be by his side, to heal him, to reassure him that he could, by some means, embark upon the next bit of his life.

'EYES WITH WHICH TO SEE'

Finding that he missed his daughter, and that his patients complained quite blatantly and loudly about her absence, Sir William Adeane decided to write to Jane, asking her to come back to Bath.

We have been troubled here, he wrote. *The nurse who has replaced you has but a quarter of the medical knowledge which you possess. Furthermore, the household does not feel orderly, as it always did, when you ordered it. The most vexing occurrence is that our once-trusted Mrs Hughes has left us and Dr Ross and I have had no luck in engaging another cook. For the time being – and this was Valentine's idea – Mrs Morrissey from the Tea Rooms furnishes us with meat pies, kidney puddings and the like and places these before us at lunch time. Becky – who has not left us, but who seems to have adopted a mood of insubordinate indifference towards the household – puts together some kind of cold collation for my solitary suppers.*

Mrs Morrissey is exceedingly kind and your poor father has found himself quite charmed by her and by her tales of her life in Ireland, which come pouring into many conversations and seem to imbue them with an unfamiliar colour, (which I suppose must be an emerald-green kind of hue ...) I am particularly moved, I cannot say why, by the image of Mrs M as a barefoot girl, gathering samphire on what she calls 'the strand' at the sea shore, with her grandfather, who fashioned clothes out of rabbit skins, and feel I could listen to these stories forever, so strange and compelling does her world seem to me, but she has her business to run and she tells me that, alas, this arrangement for pies and so forth cannot go on beyond Christmas.

Then there is something else, Jane. It seems to me that Dr Ross is in an agitated state, as though he were nursing some great trouble, of which I am ignorant. He has taken to going on long, cold morning walks, sometimes arriving here with ice on his beard. On more than one occasion he has been late for his first patient and it does appear to me that his work has, in some way, become distressing to him. By late afternoon, he seems very tired and anxious and instead of staying to take a glass of porter with me, or to share my meagre supper, he leaves abruptly to go to his own lodgings.

I have the feeling that if you were here, you would intuit what is troubling Valentine and find some means to help him recover his equilibrium. So please, dear Jane, see if you can prise yourself away from London and its delights, and from the smell of oils in Emmeline's house and return to us. I would not ask this of you if I did not feel the time to be so out of joint since you left. We must *contrive to restore some order to the house.*

From your loving father,
Wm. Adeane

Compassion towards her father – for his loneliness, for his lack of real understanding of any world outside the world of his profession – had always dictated that Jane Adeane tried never to vex him or hurt him, but now she felt that, for once, she could not do as he asked.

It seemed to her, that in London, just as Aunt Emmeline was trying to see into her niece's heart by painting her portrait, so she herself had begun in earnest an interrogation of her own future. She had come to believe – perhaps fancifully – that Tite Street, Chelsea was a more helpful address than Henrietta Street, Bath in which to discover the road to be followed in the next bit of her life. She believed that this road should have about it some *inevitability*: that it should point in some kind of unerring line, from which she wouldn't be tempted to stray.

Jane knew that – for all her fame as the Angel of the Baths, for all her pride in the cures she seemed able to bring about – she didn't wish to spend her whole life as a nurse. She knew that she had to arrive, one day, at something which could be mastered and possessed. And it was as if, though still invisible to her, that *something* would be more likely to reveal itself to her in Aunt Emmeline's studio (in the ethereal, turpentine-scented air, under the high skylight which had once let the rain fall on a half-made creation on the pottery wheel) than anywhere else.

She also made good use of the library Emmeline had amassed, liking especially to lose herself in the myriad worlds conjured by Mr Dickens, admiring the reach of his imagination, but somewhat dismayed by the sickly sweetness of many of his heroines and wondering if she might write to Dickens suggesting that Lucie and Estella – to name but two – were somewhat marred by their own perfection.

She felt tempted to remind the great author that girls could be 'as wayward in their minds as any young gentleman and might sometimes have dreams that did not begin with the letter M for Marriage'. It amused her to imagine a crestfallen look on the bearded visage of the famous man upon receipt of her letter, yet she knew that she would probably never write it. Instead, she began keeping a diary of her life in London, not only noting what she did but what she *felt* about everything and commenting very frequently upon her own reluctance to return to Bath.

She knew that she had a good reason to stay on in Chelsea. Emmeline was pleased with the way the portrait of her niece was taking shape. She told Jane that she was particularly satisfied with her capture of her height and the way the white robes she wore had about them a realistic heaviness, a heaviness which Jane's body seemed to bear with an upright stoicism – even with a kind of nobility, entirely fitting to her character. But Emmeline admitted that she had not made the same kind of progress in her work on Jane's face. The features, still only sketched in, did not yet even look like Jane. And the artist was frustrated by this. She made her niece promise that she wouldn't leave until 'at least you have eyes with which to see'.

Jane wrote to her father, commiserating with him upon the departure of Mrs Hughes, upon Becky's insubordinate mood, and upon the inadequacies of the new nurse, but explaining to him that the portrait was of great importance to her aunt and that she really couldn't desert Emmeline until it had been completed.

On the subject of Valentine Ross, Jane wrote: '*I am sorry that Dr Ross appears agitated and distracted. I have no idea why this should be so. But*

I venture one reason: perhaps it might be that he has been too long working with
you in Bath? Should you not ask him if he would not prefer to set up his own
practice in Swindon, or in Swansea? Men cannot always keep finding contentment
with what they have. Sometimes, they must move on.'

After her letter was posted, she decided to think of all this no
more.

And then something happened which surprised her so completely
that she wondered whether she hadn't wandered into a state of mild
insanity.

It occurred at one of the select soirées Emmeline liked to give
from time to time, to reassure herself that London Society (or at
least some bohemian section of it) still admired her and her work.
These took the form of late suppers, served with champagne, at
which the guests could come and go and wander, eat and drink as
they chose and sit anywhere they liked, whether at Emmeline's table,
in the studio, on the stairs, on a Turkey rug in front of a fire, or
even, if they wished it, in Emmeline's bedroom.

Patient serving staff, dressed in velvet breeches and white wigs,
progressed up and down the house, carrying trays of glasses and
dishes of chicken breasts in aspic. Guests might cry out from odd
corners of any room for champagne reinforcements. It had been
known, once, for sexual congress to take place in a wardrobe, causing
some disruption to Emmeline's long, brightly coloured gowns. The
ambience was louche and the talk mostly amusing and highly decorated. It was often remarked that, in this house, the guests felt wickedly
free to do exactly as they chose. 'Chez Emmeline' was considered a
marvellous place to be.

For this particular soirée, Emmeline had invited some thirty people:
artists, sculptors, musicians, writers, professors of moral philosophy,
publishers, actors and singers.

Finding herself in this thrilling company, wearing her favourite
scarlet dress and an opal necklace, Jane felt a hectic excitement take
hold of her, as though she might have been a tall ship becalmed,
which had suddenly found the wind filling her sails. She let her glass
be refilled with champagne many times, was amused and delighted

to have her 'beautiful height' commented upon by a mighty tenor, who had put no less than six pieces of chicken-in-aspic on his plate, to listen to the intimate woes of a writer, who found himself 'in a featureless desert of non-creation', and to trade some amusing banter on the subject of the ever-changing landscape of the London Art Scene with a sculptor whose only aim, he said, was to make ugly things, to provoke the world into scoffing at his work, 'for what people at first scoff at, later on becomes the thing of greatest value. I exist to make money. Patience is the only commodity needed.'

Feeling her head swim a little and needing to sit down, Jane took her plate of chicken to the staircase – a place where she habitually liked to perch for long periods of solitary time and listen to the lively passing and re-passing of horse-drawn traffic in this leafy corner of London.

Here, exactly where she always chose to sit, she found a publisher by the name of Ashton Sims, a small, serious man of forty-five, sitting alone with his food, and she asked if she might join him.

Ashton Sims, co-proprietor of the highly successful and lucrative publishing house of Kirkwall & Sims, stood up and bowed to her. He was, he said, an ardent admirer and purchaser of Emmeline Adeane's work and was 'more than enchanted to meet her niece'.

'I hear,' he said to Jane, 'that Emmeline is wrestling with a portrait of you. I wonder why she used the word "wrestling".'

'Oh,' said Jane. 'This is what people always find themselves doing with me. They want to capture me and I am reluctant to let that happen.'

Ashton Sims smiled. 'I imagine that is very wise of you. You must talk to my wife, Julietta. Julietta is very vehement on the subject of men's "ownership" of women. She says Western Society is primitive in this regard, and I suspect you would agree?'

'Well,' said Jane, 'I have never been to anywhere considered actually "primitive", such as a forest in Borneo, where I am told human heads are sometimes used as decoration, but I think Julietta is right; men use women as chattels and adornments. They just don't cut their heads off first.'

Ashton Sims exploded with laughter. At this moment, a dark young woman appeared at the foot of the stairs and Sims called out to her, 'Julietta, come up! You must hear Miss Adeane's joke!'

Julietta Sims paused in the hall to have her glass refilled, then made her way towards the stairs on which her husband and Jane were sitting. She sat down just below them. When Ashton introduced her to Jane, Julietta set down her champagne glass and held out a slim, soft hand and placed it in Jane's with infinite tenderness, as though the two women had been friends in former times and were now meeting up again after a long absence.

Jane felt the sweetness of the hand-clasp and risked letting her gaze dwell on Julietta's face for a lingering moment. It had long been apparent to all in Emmeline Adeane's circle of friends that Julietta Sims – Italian by birth but made rather exquisitely pale by her long immersion in London's sunless weather – was a person of exceptional beauty, but perhaps no one had ever been as enthralled by it as Jane felt herself to be at that instant on the stairs. The light was soft and flattering, coming only from candles in two wall sconces, but even taking this into consideration, Jane knew that she was looking at a kind of human perfection, seldom seen.

Julietta's eyes were, of course, large and dark and her nose admirably straight, but it was Julietta's mouth, wide but not fleshy, with a Botticelli Venus curve to the upper lip, which gave to this face such extraordinary seductive power. Jane knew that she should look away, that Ashton Sims might reasonably be disconcerted by the length of time she was staring at his wife. But it felt to her that, by drinking in the beauty of Julietta's features she was bringing nourishment to her very soul. She wanted to weep or cry out in wonder. And she soon became aware that Julietta's hand was still held in hers and that the intensity of her immersion in Julietta's face was returned by the young woman's enraptured gaze.

At length, Jane turned aside and Julietta turned away. When Jane dared look at her again, it was to gaze upon the back of Julietta's neck, lit so sweetly by the candlelight, and at her dark hair piled into an elegant arrangement, ornamented with jewels and feathers.

It was at this moment that Jane remembered Valentine Ross telling her how, at the Chopin concert in the Bath Assembly Rooms, he had longed to reach out and touch her hair, and some pity for him now found its way into her heart, for she at last believed she understood what he had felt. Jane ached to do what he, too, had longed for – to reach out and stroke Julietta's hair and then her neck and then her bare shoulders beneath. This longing was so overwhelming that Jane feared her hand might stray towards Julietta of its own accord, but she controlled it by reaching for her champagne glass and calling to one of the manservants in the hall to come and refill it.

As the servant ascended the stairs, Jane was aware of Ashton Sims staring at her with an unfathomable expression on his face, and even as he stared she felt something touch her foot. She did not need to look down to realise that Julietta's left hand had crept under Jane's skirt and was now tenderly encircling her ankle.

MICROSCOPE

A cold winter had now tightened its grip upon Bath. In his morning walks, Valentine Ross had to fight against spiteful peltings of sleet, or found his path up Beacon Hill covered with snow. Sometimes a freezing fog joined with the smoke from a thousand coal fires to wrap the city in a poisonous mist, and this, Ross felt, was the most punishing of all conditions – the one most likely to lay him low. Yet he pressed on blindly, determined to reach the top of Beacon day after day, not caring if he fell ill, or perhaps wishing to surrender to some fearful bodily condition that might still the agitation of his mind.

By the end of each day's work, he began to experience the kind of deep tiredness that he imagined afflicted infantrymen on their terrible forced marches towards enemy lines. And this was how he now perceived his predicament: that he was enduring the difficult present in order to keep walking towards some defining conflagration and that only when he had come through this would his life resume any kind of normality.

That he had no idea what form this catastrophe would take didn't trouble him at present. He knew that a man may live in close proximity to things he does not yet *see correctly*. What he must try to do is to be vigilant and attentive to all that surrounds him, in order to find the path he should follow.

To deepen this enquiry, Ross cleaned and polished his Rayer Microscope. He set it up on a table near the fire in his lodgings and spent his evenings examining – almost at random – minute entities swept from his floor: coal dust, threads of wool from his hearthrug, flower petals, a fishbone, crumbs of bread, the leg from a dead spider.

In every case, he was disposed to marvel at what he saw through the lens. The fishbone, in particular, struck him as a thing of complex beauty, containing within its cells a peculiar pearly light. The spider's leg, too, was admirable, like a tiny piece of medieval armour. The flower petal, so fragile and weightless, so dead-seeming, yet revealed an intricate branching of veins, as though it had the means within it to come alive again. And these things consoled Valentine Ross by their beautiful and secret complexity. He took to plucking out lashes from his eyelids, vainly hoping that the mild pain he inflicted on himself would still his mind. He placed the eyelashes under the microscope lens, examining the white bulb-like growth at each root, suggesting to him that if a lash was planted in the earth, it might begin to grow and, in due time, unfurl minute black leaves.

He knew that his thoughts were muddled – almost as if he were dreaming his life, instead of living it. But he told himself that his existence had too little of the strange and miraculous about it now that Jane had gone and his heart had nothing marvellous to feast upon. He remembered Edmund saying to him, as he'd prepared to traverse half the world, that he couldn't be reconciled to living 'without wonder'. And it soothed Ross to think that he could find 'wonder' in the detritus swept from his hearth or from a sliver of matter tugged out from his eyelid.

'The microscope,' he announced to Sir William, one morning, 'reminds us that we're born blind to the intimate secrets of everything in the world. We should perhaps make more use of it in our work.'

Sir William Adeane, it seemed, was unwilling to address this subject at present. He had been distracted in recent times. An epidemic of chest ailments had arrived in Bath. He did what he could for the sufferers, prescribing balsams and inhalations. But he was dismayed to realise that his patients didn't have a great deal of faith in these. They kept clamouring for Jane, for the Angel of the Baths to lead them to the Hot Bath, to cure them with her touch.

'I have a new nurse now, Nurse Peggs,' Sir William patiently reminded them, but they were not happy. They were heard, in their distress, not to blame their adored Jane for being in London, but to blame Nurse Peggs *for not being Jane*, and for possessing an ugly name. 'Square Peg' was how they referred to her, stressing that Square Peg was not at all to their liking. And when word of this nickname reached Miss Peggs, she dismayed Sir William by stamping her foot so hard on his surgery floor that some of his surgical instruments bounced up and fell off their tray into the dust.

He told her coldly that nurses should not stamp their feet. He made her crouch down and retrieve the lancet and the probe that had fallen and clean them with her apron. Nurse Peggs did this obediently enough. But as she did so, she began to sob uncontrollably, stammering out that she would not stay in Bath 'to be insulted with a vile nickname' just because she couldn't fit 'into a blasted angel's shoes'.

It came to Sir William then, hearing his daughter mildly but jealously disparaged by Nurse Peggs, that he, no less than his patients, did not like this woman at all. Indeed he earnestly wished her to depart from Henrietta Street and never return. But he knew that – on that very afternoon – he was going to operate on a man whose life he hoped to save by opening up his chest and taking out a tumour from his lung, and he could not possibly hope to succeed in this operation without the constant vigilance of a trained nurse.

He thus made himself help Nurse Peggs to her feet, and offered her the silk handkerchief he kept in the pocket of his frock coat. He could find no words to console her; he decided the handkerchief would have to be enough. But it was not enough. Nurse Peggs dried her eyes and flung the thing away. She then told Sir William that she was going to pack her suitcase and leave Bath on the first available omnibus.

'Why do you not take the train?' Sir William could not prevent himself from asking.

'Train?' said Nurse Peggs. 'Terrible invention! Ruination of the world! I will not set foot on one of them.'

It was at this moment that a knock on Sir William's door heralded the arrival of Mrs Morrissey, to announce to him what she had been able to bring for his lunch.

Seeing Mrs Morrissey's face, smiling as it often was, and hearing her beginning to talk about a dish of rissoles, Sir William beckoned her frantically into the room, even as Nurse Peggs banged down the now-tainted surgical instruments onto their tray and strode towards the door. She pushed rudely past Clorinda Morrissey and her footsteps could be heard running down the hallway.

'Away and away …' said Sir William. 'She is gone. The "Square Peg". And good riddance! But dear Mrs Morrissey, please do come in and close the door and tell me what I am to do.'

Sir William sank down into a chair and passed his hands through his abundant hair. Mrs Morrissey stood regarding him for a moment, then ventured: 'You will have to tell me what has happened, Sir. Or else what can I advise?'

'What has happened,' said Sir William, 'is that my world has fallen apart.'

Sir William indicated that Mrs Morrissey should sit opposite him, in the chair where his patients habitually sat during a consultation. He noticed that she consulted the surgery clock before she agreed to do as he asked and he knew that she couldn't stay long; she had her baking to return to, her tables to lay. But he fervently hoped that she would remain with him for a moment. Ever since Valentine Ross had introduced her to him, he had liked her. He saw in her the kind of independent spirit possessed by Jane, yet she was of a more amenable and gracious disposition and her voice was soft and calm.

'All my trouble stems from Jane's departure,' said Sir William. 'Not only do my patients clamour for her – on and on, on and on – but I can by no means get her to agree to come back to Bath, not even for Christmas. She will not do it, telling me my sister "needs" her in London for a portrait she is painting. And then my cook leaves. A lot of mumbling about dry goods and non-payment of wages and out she walks from one day to the next. But for you, we would have no lunch of any kind.'

'Well Sir, it is only simple fare …'

'It may be simple, but it has saved us. I thought all might go on calmly here after you helped us out, but now my nurse is scuttling for the omnibus. Some foolish business about a nickname!'

'A nickname?'

'Yes. And tears – as you witnessed – all for that futile reason. But tell me how I am to open a man's chest this afternoon and endeavour to save his life, under circumstances like these?'

Mrs Morrisscy fanned her face with her hand, as though it might have been too warm in the room, when in fact it was cold, with a damp fog pressing at the windowpane.

'Open a man's chest?' she said. 'Lord in heaven! And I sometimes think that folding enough air into a Victoria Sponge to make it rise is difficult enough!'

Sir William now found himself smiling. Only moments before, he'd felt as if he would have nothing to smile at again in all this present time, and now Clorinda Morrissey had succeeded in spreading a small grin across his severe features.

'We all have our talents,' he said, 'and I think it's high time I told you properly how much Doctor Ross and I appreciate your pies and puddings. I do declare that you are keeping us alive!'

'Well,' said Mrs Morrissey, 'but not alive *enough*, Sir William. Isn't that so?'

'What d'you mean, Mrs Morrissey?'

'Well, now. I'm thinking of Doctor Ross. To my eyes, he seems anxious of late and he does not look well.'

'I know. You are quite right. You have lighted on another of my troubles. There is something the matter with him. I have asked him many times what it is, but he won't give me any answer. If I were to lose Doctor Ross ...'

'He used to come to Camden Street quite frequently, to take some Assam and smoke a cheroot. But after that day when he met your daughter there, I do not often see him. I only observe him here and I note—'

'He met Jane in your tea room?'

'Yes. Just before she went away. And perhaps I should not speak of this, but it did seem to me as though there was a little misunderstanding between them, during the tea.'

'What kind of "misunderstanding"?'

'I don't know, Sir William. Miss Jane left rather abruptly and Doctor Ross seemed downcast after she'd gone.'

Sir William now fell silent. He began staring at the fire, which had burned very low. Clorinda Morrissey watched him with some tenderness. It came into her mind that many of the men she'd met since coming to England, including the amiable Sir William, appeared confused about one thing or another. She didn't know precisely why this should be the case, unless … and she knew that only a woman could have dared give voice to this thought … society expected such vigilance, such leadership, such perpetual certainty from them – about everything from politics to manners, from monetary investments to questions of morality – that their vision of the world was as crowded and cluttered as a vast emporium of second-hand bric a brac and that much of what passed in front of their noses they did not veritably see.

TUMOUR

The solution to being able to perform the lung operation that afternoon lay, in the end, with Valentine Ross. He put a sign on the front door of Henrietta Street to say he was indisposed and regretted that he could see no patients that day. He then studied such notes as Sir William Adeane had made on the case of the man with the tumour, helped Sir William prepare the operating table and stood ready to help with this difficult and dangerous task.

The patient was a florid man of, perhaps fifty-five years, a Mr Latimer, the prosperous owner of a glue-rendering factory situated at the lower end of the city, about whose noxious emissions of foul-smelling steam there was much helpless complaint. It was also known that many beautiful living horses were slaughtered only to feed the glue vats with their bones, their sad flesh cut away and rotting in heaps in the open air, which attracted vermin to the area. Bath residents were vocal in their condemnation of Latimer's 'fearful enterprise' and its despoilation of an entire area of the city. But Latimer had made very satisfactory money from his glue and would not be moved to change his practices or re-site his factory.

When Latimer came in, both Ross and Sir William noted that he appeared quite calm. As he lay down on the table and his shirt was removed, he told the doctors that he had 'great faith'. He said, 'my faith is of two kinds: a belief in God, that He does not wish me to die yet, and a belief in Sir William's skill.'

Valentine Ross privately thought that a third kind of faith should have been added to his list: faith in his money – that it could buy him the best private care that was to be had in Bath, thus avoiding being placed in a hospital bed, where contagious diseases put so many at risk. But Ross said nothing on this subject and simply went about his preparations with quiet care.

He told Latimer that in a few moments he would be given a 'Letheon', a dose of gas confected from sulphuric acid and ethyl alcohol and named for the River Lethe, in which, in Classical Mythology, souls immersed themselves in the waters of forgetfulness. This administration would make him immune to the pain which was to follow.

'I have not, alas, had the time, in my extremely busy life as a man of commerce, to study Classical Mythology,' said Latimer, as if this were a boast he could be proud of, 'but I take your word for it.'

'We will work very carefully, but as fast as we can,' said Sir William. 'Ten minutes from now, the tumour will be visible to us and we will sever it cleanly, so that nothing remains. Your lung will be cauterised against excessive bleeding and infection and your chest cavity sewn up. When you wake, you may feel you have suffered some bruising – as though a hard-hoofed animal might have inadvertently kicked you in the chest.'

'A hard-hoofed animal?' said Latimer. 'Do you mean a horse?'

'Not necessarily. It will cause you some pain, but we will put you into a bed and watch over you. You may take a little laudanum and then you will sleep again, confident that your tumour is gone. I foresee for you a long and prosperous life.'

'I certainly hope so,' said Latimer. 'I have just bought a new house in North Parade, much larger than my former property, and I wish to enjoy some soirées there. For what is life without entertainment?'

'Indeed,' smiled Sir William. 'Are you ready, then, to be entertained by the Letheon?'

Now, the two doctors were swabbing blood from Latimer's opened chest and peering in at the expansion and contraction of the left lung. What they had expected to find was a bulbous mass, a distinct heaping up of tissue like a carbuncle, which Sir William's lancet stood ready to slice away. But there was no such growth visible to them.

They kept swabbing and the flow of blood into the cavity slowly diminished, giving them better sight of the base of the lung, which was where Latimer had experienced pain so serious it had sometimes caused him to choke and vomit, and where they expected the tumour to be found. That it was not there puzzled them into silence. They kept looking at each other and then back into Latimer's chest. The patient snored. The doctors swabbed and stared and swabbed and stared again.

Sir William administered more Letheon. That a patient should wake during an operation was a rare occurrence, but not unheard of. Severe pain could nullify the effects of the ether, and the screams of those who found themselves awake in the middle of a cutting were terrible to hear. Many died instantly of shock.

After a few more minutes had passed, Ross, remembering the alteration of minute things he had seen under the microscope, bent down and put his face very close to the breathing lung, willing himself to look unerringly at it, as though his eye could transform itself into the microscope's lens. Above the operating table, the gas mantle cast a white light on the moving flesh.

Wielding a small probe, Ross explored the lung tissue and what he then perceived was that this tissue was not exactly as he knew a healthy lung should look and feel. It was, instead, *infested*. The infestation consisted of microscopic nodules, some as minute as a grain of caviar, some the size of a frog's egg. They were whitish in colour, but a few were now seen as veined through with a livid purple. There were too many of them to count.

Ross drew Sir William's attention to them. 'Not one tumour,' Ross said. 'But what appears to be scores of embryo *tumorae*. I think they will spread and choke the lung. By opening them to the air, we may have inadvertently hastened that spread.'

Sir William stared. He could now see the tiny poisonous nodules clearly, but, confused by this cruel diagnosis, he felt himself for once to be at a loss.

'What can we do?' he asked.

'We could cut the largest of them out,' said Ross. 'But beyond that, nothing. We are looking at a death.'

Sewn up and bandaged with infinite care, Latimer now lay in the back room in Sir William's house where those who had undergone traumas of all kinds were put to rest and recover. Normally, it had been Jane who presided over this recovery, if necessary sleeping on a cot at the patient's side or keeping vigil all night long. But there was no Jane, nor indeed any Nurse Peggs, so Ross suggested that they might take it in turns to nurse poor Latimer through the night.

Finding himself awake in a different room, in a comfortable bed, and being dosed with laudanum, Latimer was brought to the great hope that his operation had gone successfully and that his tumour now resided in some enamel dish, later to be shown to him as proof of his imminent recovery.

He turned his head to see Sir William Adeane sitting by his side, holding the laudanum jar.

'Sir William,' said Latimer. 'Was all well? Will I soon be dancing a quadrille in my new house?'

'I sincerely hope you will,' said Sir William. 'But I must tell you that your recovery may be slower than you expected.'

'Why so?'

'What we found was ... more than one tumour. We have excised all that we could find, but do not be surprised if the pain in your lung lingers a little. There are many small wounds, you see, instead of one. But we will send you home to your wife with a good supply of laudanum and we would advise you to rest.'

'You mean,' said Latimer, 'that I am going to pay you for something which is incomplete?'

'That is the nature of surgery,' said Sir William calmly. 'It can only cut out what it can see.'

In the dark hours, while Latimer slept, Ross came to take over the vigil from Sir William. Ross expected Sir William to go gratefully to his own bed, but the surgeon didn't move from the patient's side.

'Sit down,' he said to Ross. 'For you and I have things to discuss. And this quiet night seems a good time to talk about them.'

Ross did as he was told, but not without foreboding. He prayed that Sir William was not going to mention Jane's name. He was not a man who liked lying. Indeed, he detested Bath society, sometimes, for its *habit of lying*, and had resolved, in his own dealings, to follow a path of truth, as far as he was able. But he knew that if Sir William was going to ask him what had happened between him and Jane, he would have to lie. What was clamped about his heart, what he struggled with on his cold morning walks, what he longed not to feel … this debilitating sorrow and disappointment … was only bearable if he could conceal it from the world. To have to admit it to Jane's father – to the one man who loved her, in his own way, no less than he did himself – would only bring him further suffering by adding humiliation to his woes. He felt that his situation would then become so unbearable that he would have to leave Bath and never return.

Sir William got up and put some coals on the small fire. A northerly wind keened in the chimney stack and blew smoke back into the room. Sir William turned and asked abruptly, 'Was it on your account that Jane went away?'

'On my account, Sir? Why would you suppose that?'

'I do not necessarily "suppose" it. I merely note that *something* happened to send Jane to London without any warning – something she never spoke of to me. I also cannot fail to notice that since her departure you have not been yourself. There seems to be a matter that is causing you grief and I have begun to wonder whether it is Jane's absence.'

'Of course I miss Jane,' said Ross, as brightly as he could. 'We couldn't fail to miss her in this household – both you and I. But I am glad for her that she is enjoying London Society. She works so hard when she is here, it is quite right that she should have a change of scene.'

Sir William looked closely at Ross. 'A very careful answer,' he said, 'but one that tells me nothing. Have you not something else to add?'

'I don't know what it might be,' said Ross. 'Only that I have been worried lately on account of my brother. As you know, he is travelling very far away and I haven't heard from him since the letter which told me he was ill. I am very sorry if this worry has made me careless in my work …'

'No. I'm not implying that. Your work is always very good. It was you who discovered the small, multiple tumours in Mr Latimer's lung, when at first I could not see them. But I ask myself whether there have been other things that I have been blind to. For I heard today from Mrs Morrissey that you took Jane to the tea room, that there appeared to be some quarrel between you and that Jane made one of the sudden departures for which she is well known.'

'Oh,' said Ross. 'No, you have quite misunderstood. I did invite Jane to tea at Mrs Morrissey's, but we had no sooner begun our very charming half hour, when she remembered that she had agreed to escort a patient to the Hot Bath at five o'clock. She was enjoying her cake, but alas, she had to leave most of it uneaten. Such, as you know well, is her dedication to her duty.'

'Ah,' said Sir William. 'So there is nothing between you?'

'What is between us is what has always been there: respect and admiration, nothing more.'

'But cannot these – respect and admiration – undergo some metamorphosis which transform them into love?'

'Quite possibly,' said Ross. 'But not in this case.'

VANISHING ANGEL

The day after Emmeline's soirée, with the January darkness closing in upon the long afternoon, a caller arrived at the door.

It was Julietta Sims.

She was shown by the maid into Emmeline's studio, where the artist was once again struggling to capture the features of her niece in the half-completed portrait.

When Jane saw Julietta, she was unable to stop a deep blush from suffusing the very cheeks which Emmeline was tentatively sketching in with dabs of pink and white. Emmeline put down her brush and looked at the two faces so intently held by the gaze of the other, and believed she understood what was occurring.

'Julietta, my dear,' said Emmeline. 'Will you take some tea with us?'

'Thank you, Emmeline,' said Julietta. 'But I will not stay long. I fear I'm interrupting important work. But it was only ...'

'That you had something to say to Jane?'

'Yes.'

'Then let me leave the two of you together, unless you would prefer to go to Jane's room and talk to her there.'

'Well yes, why don't we do that? Jane?'

'Yes,' said Jane. 'If you do not mind, Emmeline?'

'Of course not. I have much to tidy up here. You need not hurry in your conversation.'

The two women went quickly up the stairs and as they went, Julietta reached out for Jane's hand. Julietta Sims, great beauty that she was, had had many lovers since her marriage to Ashton Sims and most of these lovers had been women. It was thus that when she found herself alone with Jane Adeane in her room, sensing perhaps that Jane was a virgin in all respects, she took it upon herself to make plain her passion at once, without any modesty or fuss.

She laid Jane down on her bed and kissed her mouth. Though Jane had never before been kissed in this way, Julietta sensed at once that the embrace awoke in her feelings so powerful that whatever Julietta had in mind to do, Jane would surrender to it.

Julietta took out the tortoiseshell comb which held her elaborate coiffure in place and let her dark hair fall in a silky curtain round Jane's face.

'Now,' she whispered, 'nobody can see us!'

'I do not care,' said Jane. 'I do not care who sees us. I do not care about anything except this. Show me how to love you.'

Julietta next undid Jane's bodice, and pushed the clothes aside to reveal her breasts, caressing them first with her soft white hand, then fastening her lips on them. She liked to do this, when she made love to a woman, to give the breasts tender attention, first sucking on them, then removing her own garments to take the other into her arms. She knew that this soft prelude, drawn out gently in time, could engender such a yearning wildness of desire in that select band of women lovers she named her 'beauties' that when at last her fingers reached down to begin to caress the almost-hidden place where real pleasure kept its audacious secret, they could make a *jouissance* arrive almost immediately.

Such was Julietta's power that this ecstasy never brought to an end their surrender to passion, but only increased it, very soon making them crave her tongue where her hand had been. And Julietta's tongue was very skilled. Among the 'beauties', the words *J'ai envie de la langue de Juliette* became a teasing code between them, telling each other that it was a woman's knowing touch they craved, and that they craved it now. Whispered among themselves in polite drawing rooms, this little phrase could make them wild with desire and sometimes lead them out into the dark night, telling their menfolk that they simply wished to breathe the night air, but in fact to lean against the trees of ancient parks and give each other the rapid but gorgeous satisfaction they almost never got from their husbands' attempts at love-making.

New to all of this, knowing nothing of the 'beauties', when Julietta's tongue touched the place she knew men dreamed of discovering in her, and she felt a white, pulsing delirium go through her, Jane cried out so loudly in wonder that Emmeline heard the cry two floors down, stopped in her work of tidying her studio and said to herself, 'now I know something more of who Jane is'. But Jane no longer knew who she was, only that she had found Julietta and that she wished to make love to her for all eternity.

When Jane and Julietta at last descended to Emmeline's studio, Julietta's hair once more neatly put up by the tortoiseshell comb, Jane's hand pressing against her lips, to conceal the small wound on them made by Julietta's kisses, they found a note from Emmeline saying that she had gone out.

The two young women sat down by the fire and Julietta said, 'I must leave very soon. Ashton will be home from his office and he likes to find me there.'

Jane got up and knelt down by Julietta's chair and clung to her skirts and to her slim body beneath them.

'What am I to do?' she said.

'Jane,' said Julietta. 'We must live in the world. We must conduct ourselves as though there was nothing between us.'

'But how am I to do that?' Jane asked. 'I've never known love of this kind before. People will only have to glance at me to know what I feel.'

Julietta stroked Jane's hair. 'We are lucky,' she said. 'Your Aunt Emmeline has defied society in her life and she will understand, I think, how you might now wish to defy it – just a little. She may allow me to come here from time to time.'

'From "time to time"! And what am I to do in the days and hours in between?'

'You will live them. You will take walks along the river and go riding in the park. You will play bezique. You will read. You will sit quietly for your portrait.'

'But I will scream out for you day and night.'

'And I will sometimes scream for you. For your great height. For your strong arms. For your ankle which I first touched on the stairs. Then, I will come to Tite Street.'

'Come tomorrow. Or come back tonight, in the middle of the night.'

'You would ask me to leave Ashton's bed in the early hours.'

'Yes. You cannot love Ashton. You love women.'

'I love both.'

'You let Ashton make love to you?'

'Yes. He's my husband. And I would like to have another child.'

'You have a child already?'

'Yes. My son, Marco. He is four years old.'

Jane looked up at Julietta's perfectly arranged features. Her thought was, I would like to be this little Marco, held in his mother's arms, the object of her adoration, flesh of her flesh, the living manifestation of her future, her only boy, the one she will never leave until her death.

At supper with Emmeline, which Jane was almost unable to eat, she said, when the maid had retired to the kitchen, 'I am lost to Julietta Sims.'

'Yes,' said Emmeline calmly.

'Irretrievably lost.'

'Yes, I know this.'

'Am I now in a play? A tragedy of some kind?'

Emmeline sipped her glass of white wine, regarding Jane tenderly over the top of the glass. After a long moment, she said, 'we must finish the portrait. I think I know how to finish it now.'

'I asked you if I was in a tragedy, Aunt Emmeline.'

'And I said that I knew how to finish the portrait now – to put passion, not tragedy, into your features. But this may not take very long. Then, I think, you must return to Bath.'

'You're afraid I'll make a scandal in your house?'

'No. Not at all. I'm afraid that your heart will be broken. It's known in a certain group in London society that Julietta ...'

'Has lovers?'

'Women, in particular. I've heard them referred to as "Julietta's beauties". She never chooses ordinary-looking people. She chooses those whom she finds exceptional. I expect she was infatuated with you straight away, the moment she saw you.'

'And I with her.'

'But you must not stay to suffer, Jane. Now that you know a little more about your body and its pleasure, why do you not agree to marry your doctor in Bath? From what you say, he is an honourable man – and such creatures are rare in English society. Of course all men need to be taught about women's sexual needs, because they have no concept of what they are, but they can learn to be very good lovers, too. Your doctor would soon learn. And you would have him in your bed every night.'

'I don't want him in my bed at all. I could never love him in that way.'

'Of course you think that now. But I merely plant the idea in your mind.'

Jane was silent. She reflected that while she'd been making love with Julietta, she had experienced a kind of near-drowning in some dark element into which she had never before fallen. It was as though, during the two hours she and Julietta had spent in sexual abandon, the White Angel had vanished – vanished completely, with all her power and intelligence, to be replaced by someone else, someone who was no longer any kind of 'angel', whose mind was clouded, whose eyes were blind, whose hands had no skill, who yearned for nothing except her lover's touch and who would surrender everything to lie in that deep ocean of pleasure.

But she realised that she did not at all *admire* this new person. Miss Jane had always carried her great height around with a manifest degree of self-congratulation. Now, she felt as though this tallness had been taken from her and that she had become small, so small that people might pass right by her and not notice her at all.

LEON'S NEW IDEA

After the first few readings from the Gospel of St. Luke, Sir Ralph Savage had made clear to Edmund Ross that a portion of each day was to be spent in the forest glade telling and re-telling the life of Jesus Christ. But it was only in this tranquil place that the rajah wished to listen to this narration. He told Edmund that the fusion of his English voice with the words of his Saviour and the 'orchestra of the forest' created in him an exquisite tranquillity of mind.

Now, however, great storms began to fall upon Borneo. The sky above the forest seemed to gather itself into a perpetual night, and let wash upon the world so vast a curtain of water that it obliterated everything moving beneath it. The gibbons hid away, cradling their young. The grasshoppers and crickets crouched motionless in havens of moss and leaves. The bats hung silent in their caves. Even the herons along the river had stepped back from the water's edge to the darkness of the mangroves and stood hunched under puffed-up feathers, watching the water rise. The snakes roped themselves to leaf-sheltered branches and closed their eyelids, opening them only upon the sword-slashes of lightning. In the glimmers of white light, the snakes' eyes were like jewels, unyielding and shining.

Edmund lay in his bed, glad that he was inside Sir Ralph's great exaggeration of a house and not in some fragile hut or stilted long-house, swaying in the wind. He felt anguished not at his own state of idleness, but rather at his cowardly savouring of this pause in his endeavours. He listened to the insect and animal world gone silent, making way for all that the storms could do. He heard trees falling. He meditated upon the realisation that everything upon the earth is *at the mercy* of something else. He knew that his life had paused in this place only because his collecting equipment had been taken from him and because Sir Ralph's mind had placed him in thrall to the daily bible readings. But now, the rains had come and the rivers were swelling and he still had not found the means to replace his lost equipment. How would he ever be able to continue with his journey?

Meanwhile, the rajah's mind was turning upon a new enterprise.

As with the Savage Road, the idea had come to him from Leon, who had begun to berate him for letting too many people under his supposed governance languish in poverty and idleness. The building of the road had brought them some relief from this, but now, apart from the cultivation of rice and vegetables and the rearing of fighting cockerels, they were falling back into a state of inertia and sadness. 'Theirs is a great sorrow,' said Leon. 'They are very poor. Some will soon run amok. Maybe they kill you. Plenty rajahs killed in Borneo in past time. Because they do not think of their subjects any more.'

'It is not true that I do not think of them any more,' said the rajah.

'I am not seeing it, that thinking,' said Leon.

'You may not see it. But my mind is always turning on ways to improve their world.'

'You say your mind turns. But this mind is an empty cage, like a mouse wheel. It does not go anywhere.'

Sir Ralph knew that there was truth in what Leon had said. And he felt that it was the Savage Road, in all its uselessness, which was to blame. If only the road had had some destination, had led to some mighty portal opening upon an enterprise where trading could have taken place, then both he and the people would have prospered.

'What more can I do, Leon?' asked Sir Ralph.

'You listen to me, rajah.'

'I always listen to you.'

'That is very right. And my mind has turned. But my wheel is not empty. I have talked to the people along the river. We make a plan for you.'

'What plan?'

'You will build a cannery.'

'A cannery? For what?'

'For fish. A cannery with steam power. Cut trees to burn. Bring engineers from Singapore to design the canning sheds and show how to shape tin and seal with lead.'

'Where have you learned all this?'

'I am vigilant, rajah. While you lie in your hammock, I am travelling to the markets in Kuching. I see inferior tins for beef and sardines. Everything leaking and stinking. But I will discover how to make tins properly sealed.'

Hearing of this new idea, Sir Ralph felt a familiar excitement at the prospect of starting something radical and unexpected. Nobody but he, after all, had imagined his magnificent house, but there it stood, in all its bewildering grandeur. If that could appear in the middle of the forest, then why not other miracles? Why not – when the rivers teemed with fish – a canning factory to give everybody work and pay and purpose?

Sensing that he had got Sir Ralph's attention, Leon went on, 'after the rains, hundreds big soft shell turtles in the Sadong. Come to feed near the mangrove banks. Men spear and kill. Women chop turtle meat, boil in brine. Then to the cannery and send for sale. Catfish also. Subaru and frogs. Import–export.'

'Oh, very good,' said the rajah. 'Import–export! Where did you learn that? From traders in Kuching? But I like it. Import free from the river, export to Singapore for silver.'

'That is it, Sir Raff. We make plenty money.'

'Excellent. You see how helpful you are to me? I will form a company. The Savage Cannery Company. No more sadness.'

'Good,' said Leon. 'And now, Sir Raff, no more Jesus-reading.'

Sir Ralph looked at Leon, who was standing in the darkness of the evening near a window. A garish lightning flash arrived and, for a moment, lit up his slender body in magnificent silhouette, confirming in Sir Ralph's mind the godlike beauty of his paramour, the wisdom of his own erotic choice. But he had not expected Leon's last request. He knew it was useless to try to explain to Leon the peace and harmony which Edmund's bible readings brought to his mind and the way they led him to a spiritual excitement that was not totally separated from bodily arousal and yet seemed to confirm, day by day, the loving Christ's tender understanding of his yearnings. He was sometimes able to believe that a lasting state of absolution was coming near, a forgiveness for all his sins, past, present and future. If his thinking about this was not perfectly rational, it did not stop him from believing that if the ecstasy in his mind – as he lay listening to St. Luke on his hammock – could be brought to a furnace so strong that he might faint from its power, then this gift of absolution would arrive from his Saviour.

'Edmund Ross talks to me, as if from my God,' he told Leon. 'You must not be jealous of this.'

'So you will not send him away?'

'I do not need to. In time, he will leave. He has his own mission to accomplish.'

'I wish him to leave you now, Sir Raff.'

'So you say. But I cannot grant this – not yet.'

'When will you grant this?'

'I've told you, he will "grant" it of his own accord. He wants to find and capture the Birds of Paradise. When the rains are over, he will leave. He will sail to the Aru Islands and he will not come back.'

WHERE THE RED ANTS LED

As suddenly as they arrived, the storms moved away.

The sun returned and the forest exhaled its lungfuls of water as hot vapour into the sky. The relentless cry of the gibbon was heard again. The island showed itself as a thousand shades of flickering and shining green.

Sir Ralph went out into his garden, where he found several small snakes on his lawn, motionless in the hot sun, the wet grass steaming all around them. He let them be and called Leon and Edmund from the house. He told them to put on their boots. They were going to walk out along the Savage Road, inspect the storm damage, then make their way to the river, to mark out a possible site for the cannery.

As Sir Ralph had feared, the road was disturbed. Much of its surface dressing had leached away into the forest and even the white stones beneath had moved, here and there, kicked up by the violence of the rain, so that parts of the highway now stood in a state of potholed ruin. It was littered with fallen branches and leaves, nuts and berries torn off their stems in the wind. Rats were busy ingesting this scattered debris.

Sir Ralph stood still and stared. That nature had been so harsh towards a thing built to endure, a thing which bore his name and over which so many had laboured, he felt as a wound to his heart. He kneaded his chest. Then he squatted down and took up a few white stones, pressing them back into one of the potholes, as if he himself now planned to cure the road of its suffering single-handed.

Leon went to his side. 'Don't be a nin-poop, my rajah,' he said. 'More rain will come. But after all the rains, the people will work to make the road better. You don't do it now.'

Sir Ralph knew his lack of patience to be a fault in him – for which Leon was justified in mocking him. While his house was being built, he'd walked around with a drover's whip, never letting it fall upon the backs of his labourers, but nevertheless cracking it against the walls, announcing his dissatisfaction with the slow pace of the work. And during his brief time in England, he had found himself driven to fury by the willingness of even the cleverest of men to stand and wait when, very often, they should have acted. He asked himself how anything was done or made in a country where stoic detachment and the prolongation of decision-making were considered to be such unspoken virtues.

Now, he felt like weeping. He would perhaps have wept had Leon not reminded him that they were going to the river to determine where the cannery was to be sited. But the word 'cannery' sparked a tiny flame of optimism in his brain. He could almost immediately see and hear the marvellous workings of such a place, like an enormous threshing machine, running on steam-driven belts. He stood up and they walked on, soon veering away from the road and taking the path to the river.

This path was slippery with mud, flooded in parts, and long before the three men reached the river they could hear the risen water in a new turbulent conversation with itself, growling up against boulders, laughing down rapids. Leon stopped and turned to Sir Ralph.

'Sir Raff,' he said. 'Before we can build the cannery, you must bring the Savage Road here, to this place where we are.'

'You are right,' said Sir Ralph. 'For the lumber haulage. For steam machinery.'

'But I would suggest that we must make not just one, but many branches of the road, all arriving at the cannery site. As soon as the rains are over ...'

Then began a discussion about how near the river the new enterprise should stand. Sir Ralph envisaged it, rising on stilts, an enormous longhouse, almost at the water's edge. To bring the netted fish and the wounded soft-shell turtles as near as possible to some system of belts carrying them to the building where they would be adroitly decapitated, eviscerated, cleaned, filleted and boiled before being sealed into the cans would ensure, he felt, 'the efficiency and speed of the operation'.

But Leon reminded him that the river was 'like the sea'. Nothing about it was stable or predictable. In days, or even hours, it could rise 'two heights of a man'. If the cannery was sited too near the river, it would be at risk from flooding. The success of the whole undertaking – of what Sir Ralph now called in his mind 'The Cannery of Salvation' – would depend upon getting the positioning of the factory precisely right. This, in turn, would depend upon engaging an engineer to work out a plan for the enterprise.

While Sir Ralph and Leon walked on, talking as they went, Edmund was distracted by glimpsing two large Swallowtail butterflies, well known to him as *Papilionidae*, sucking fruit and moisture from a fig tree not far from the path. He stood very still, observing them, moved as he always was by the jewel-like colours, metallic blues and greens adorning their wings, with here and there patches of crimson which always reminded him of the flash of red above a capercaillie's eye, a wonder seldom seen but one that had once moved him to tears.

Had he had his butterfly net with him, he might have captured both insects with one skilful flick of his arm. But without any equipment he was helpless. Edmund stepped quietly from the path towards the Swallowtails. He saw that they were so concentrated on the rain-washed figs that they didn't move at his approach. He longed to touch them, but even as he reached out his hand, they spread their huge wings and rose silently into the tree canopy.

Edmund stood where he was, watching the butterflies' graceful flight and listening to the forest alive once more with bird and animal cries. Looking down at his feet, he saw a column of red ants flowing across his boots and smiled at their insouciance. He didn't move, but let the column surge on. It was then that he noticed that he was standing in a small clearing and that nailed to a palm was a cracked and faded wooden sign which read: *Claims Office 500 yards*. An arrow pointed in the direction the ants were travelling and it amused Edmund to wonder if, where once a gold mine had been worked, these courageous tiny creatures had found ideal terrain in which to nurture the queen and establish the epicentre of their vast and complex society.

He shook the ants from his boots, but began to follow alongside the column. Although saplings and trailing lianas stood in his way, he saw that he was walking on what had once been a well-trodden path and while knowing that he should have turned back and rejoined Leon and Sir Ralph, he felt insatiably curious to discover whatever traces remained of what had once been a gold mine. Inherent in this curiosity, he knew with some shame, was the notion that man's search for precious metals, over the whole circumference of the earth, is a quest without end, yet also subject to his impatience, fatigue and disappointment, thus leading to the idea that wherever treasure has once existed, small vestiges of it can often remain, long after it has been abandoned.

After a few moments of walking, the ant column veered leftwards into the dense forest. But so certain was Edmund that the ants had selected the old mine terrain as their home that he decided to follow them. Feeling at once the absence of his kris, with which to hack away the vegetation impeding his progress, he nevertheless stumbled on, bending everything aside with his hands.

A cloud of moths shook itself from a fallen tree and rose into the air, passing directly over Edmund's head, some of them touching his hair with their wings, and snagging on it. Edmund brushed the moths away. He stopped for a moment, wondering whether, after all, he shouldn't rejoin Leon and Sir Ralph, but realised he had come quite far now. The ants still travelled at his side, in a smooth flow over roots and mossy stones. A large Monitor lizard darted suddenly from a camouflage of leaves, snapped up a mouthful of the insects and disappeared. A few of the ants began to run round in circles of distress, but the main column surged on, closing the gap on itself left by its dead comrades. And Edmund found that he now felt a sentimental affinity with the red ants. He wanted to follow where they led. He also told himself that if they were indeed leading him to the abandoned mine, he would enjoy apologising to the rajah for his sudden disappearance from the walk to the cannery site if he could put into his hands a tiny powdering of gold.

Most importantly, however, this feeling of being deep in the forest, alone, alert to everything that he might be about to witness – horror and wonder, both – brought back into Edmund's heart that familiar excitement which had fed his dreams of discovery and which, since his illness and his sojourn in Sir Ralph's house, he feared he might have lost for ever. He no longer minded that he didn't have his knife. His face was scratched as he moved forwards, his hands pricked by thorns and chafed by bark, but he was happier than he had felt for a long time. When he saw a king cobra coiled among the roots of a banana tree, he walked nonchalantly past it.

He didn't know how much time had passed when he became aware of a change in the light above the canopy. He stopped and looked up and saw that storm clouds were once again gathering. Thunder was just audible, far off as yet, but no doubt coming nearer. Edmund sighed. He had often before been in the forest in drenching rain, but he also knew that a chill always followed if shelter was not quite quickly found. Now, perhaps, he could have wished himself back on the path to the river with Leon and Sir Ralph, but when he turned and looked behind him he was no longer certain in which direction the river lay. He cursed his lack of a compass. Of all the things that had been stolen from him, the loss of the compass troubled him the most.

'Follow the ants,' he muttered. 'Have faith in their purpose.'

And he told himself that when the mine was reached – and it surely couldn't be very far off now – there would he come upon some remnant of a gold miner's hut or cabin, decayed with time but quickly made serviceable as a temporary refuge. In this place, he would wait until nature changed her mind again and the sun returned. And he fell to imagining what he might find there in the gold miner's hovel: some ancient cans of bully beef, a shovel with a broken haft, a sluice box, once rattled back and forth, back and forth, almost to its destruction, but yet still intact, still powdery with the dirt through which some wretched digger had hoped to glimpse the shining substance that would alter his life.

VALENTINE REVISITED

The year had turned and the first signs of spring were visible in Chelsea.

Emmeline Adeane, with Jane at her side, was now wiping her hands on a turpentine-soaked rag and looking with satisfaction at Jane's finished portrait.

The aspect which Emmeline had found for her niece's face was one of severity, suggesting both a clever mind and perhaps even a stubborn one. But for a long while there had been something missing from the features, something the painting had not caught.

Emmeline had seen at last what this was. She had then reshaped Jane's mouth very slightly, giving it an almost imperceptible upward curl on one side. The tiny alteration now suggested the humour and the fondness for irony which were so much a part of Jane's nature, but which had been absent from the portrait until Emmeline had made this final adjustment.

She now asked Jane if she liked the portrait and Jane said, 'I think I am going to like it as I like myself: on certain days not at all and at other times I am going to adore it immodestly.'

'Good!' said Emmeline. 'As long as those days of adoration occur quite frequently, I am happy! And now, Jane, we must talk about the future. I believe it is time for you to go back to Bath.'

Jane walked away from Emmeline and went to the window, looking out at the sunshine falling upon Tite Street. She thought, I have begun to adore everything here. I adore the grey pavement.

'Are you tired of me, Aunt?' she asked after a moment.

'No. You're not a person of whom I could ever tire. I am happy and amused in your company. And I love you very much, as I hope you know. But I have given much thought to the shape of your life, Jane. You are twenty-five. If it's in your nature to love women—'

'I don't know if it's "in my nature" to love women. I have never thought about it before. I only know that I'm enslaved to Julietta.'

'I understand that. Most people are "enslaved" at some point in their lives. But do you want to repeat *my* life? I have lived so much of it alone because the man I was enslaved to wouldn't marry me. There was a kind of bargain between us and then it ended. I was left with very little except this house. And it has been wearisomely hard and lonely. If Julietta is all you live for – a woman you can never be husband nor wife to – then your life will be hard, too.'

Jane said nothing. In these moments, she recalled the feelings that she'd had about her own loss of *being* in her surrender to the extreme pleasure she'd felt with Julietta, as though she no longer existed outside her lover's embrace. Did erotic love of a certain kind rob the self of part of the self?

'Listen to me, Jane,' said Emmeline. 'I know your mind isn't tending this way. But you have found somebody – the doctor whose name you mock, this poor Valentine – who seems to love you distractedly, from what you've told me. Your father writes to you that this would-be suitor is ill and I'll wager it is your rejection of him that has made him so.'

'I very earnestly doubt that is the case, Emmeline.'

'Well, I do not doubt it for one second! So please hear me out. If you are clever and make the right accommodations with this person, you will have a full and pleasant life. You would resume the nursing work you are so good at. You would stay near to William. You would have children of your own.'

'But Aunt …'

'I don't underestimate your passion for Julietta one bit. Do not think that. Did I not see it in both your faces? But you and she are resourceful people. Remember, she is married to Ashton Sims. She has borne him a child. But he seems unaware of – or else is blithe about – her trysts with women. I'm sure, if she can do this, then it is certain some meetings between you and her could be arranged, either here at Tite Street or in Bath.'

'But you are still asking me to marry someone I do not love …'

'No. In all truth, I am not. I am not. Because you *will* love him. I feel certain of it. You will love him no more and no less than Julietta loves Ashton. And he will give you a good life.'

'I don't want him in my bed.'

'You might decide you did, if you taught him how to love you. Ask Julietta to remind you how this may be affectionately and tactfully done.'

Jane found this conversation painful. She didn't like talking about Valentine Ross, most particularly because she felt sorry for him, but that night, alone in her room in Tite Street, she decided to examine the truth of what she felt about him.

What she discovered surprised her a little. She remembered Ross arriving to begin his doctoring with her father two years ago, a serious person showing immediate dedication to his work. She remembered saying to Sir William that she thought his new assistant 'very promising'. She had added that she was astonished to note that a man with such 'outlandish blue eyes' could look so steadily upon the maimed and the sick. In other words, her first reactions to Valentine Ross had been favourable. She had found nothing negative to say about him. It had also been true that he had settled into the Henrietta Street practice with graceful ease, neither presuming to loosen the bond that existed between Jane and her father, nor treating her as an inferior because she was a nurse and not a doctor.

In the two years that separated his arrival from the day in Mrs Morrissey's tea room when he'd proposed marriage Jane could recall nothing that had alienated her in Ross's behaviour. If she had been asked what she felt about him during this time, her answer might have been teasing. She might have said that 'for a *man*, he is quite passable' or 'considering that I only admire one man and that is my father, Mr Ross is working quite well on his aspiration to join this company of one.'

She might also have added that there *had* been moments when she'd felt something for him which was fractionally more than mere approbation. One of these had indeed been the night of the Chopin concert at the Assembly Rooms. She had liked strolling through the crowd on the arm of a serious and handsome gentleman and she had very much liked the feel of his closeness to her at the music's end, when tears overwhelmed her. He had made her feel cared for and he had made her feel beautiful.

It was only the proposal that had ended it all.

Jane simply could not see how Ross had arrived at something for which she was so unprepared. The chasm between liking him and wanting to be his wife and live with him for ever was extremely great. She had never thought of him in this way. How could he not have seen that? How could he not have known that Miss Jane Adeane had much more to achieve in the world before she committed to any such binding alliance? Even if she hadn't precisely known *what* she might achieve, the aspiration to excel at something had never left her. It was with her night and day. She was 'The Angel of the Baths' already, the one woman whose touch everybody yearned for. Yet she would do more. She was certain of that. She would go on and discover The Thing which would make her exceptional in the eyes of the world. But she would not discover it as the wife of Valentine Ross.

Yet now she wondered whether she had been wrong about this. Did not the wives of other men find the means to discover their gifts and their talents? Was not the mathematical genius, Ada Lovelace, a fine example of this? Might not the steady support of a man take from her sufficient material worries to allow her the space to commune more deeply with herself, so that The Thing would reveal itself to her more quickly and more completely?

And what of companionship? Like Emmeline, Jane had often had moments of feeling lonely. She pitied her aunt for all the years she had spent in a solitary life. True, that life had been an admirable one, but it had also been difficult, freighted with sadness and mourning. Emmeline had discovered a fine gift in herself and yet, for all that, she had not had the life she wanted.

Jane now tried to remember any moments when Valentine Ross had caused her irritation. He had stared at her sometimes, with a stare which lasted too long, but this had perplexed her more than it had annoyed her. In general, she had been perfectly comfortable and content in his company and it was only the terrible moment at Mrs Morrissey's which had brought about her fury.

After all this analysis of her memories and feelings, Jane realised that she now felt tired, but not at all sleepy. Her head ached. She had one of those strange moments of wishing that she were not alive at all to face the dilemmas which surrounded her.

She reached for her diary and wrote: '*Though the image of Julietta's beautiful face is never absent from my mind for long, tonight I am thinking again about my poor Valentine. But why do I describe him so, as though he might be a little wounded animal I had first rescued and then abandoned? So now I ask myself, are marriage vows sometimes brought to their fatal exchange because one party feels sorry for the other?*'

BELLE ÉPOQUE

The next day, Julietta arrived at Tite Street in a state of hectic excitement. She recounted how Ashton Sims was visiting Paris to talk to a well-known French author, a certain Guy Mollinet, in the hope of acquiring the translation rights to his new novel for Kirkwall & Sims, and had suggested that Julietta come with him 'to buy herself a new Paris wardrobe for the coming spring'.

'I told him,' panted Julietta, 'that it was a grand idea but that I would be very sad going shopping on my own and he straight away suggested that *you* come with us, Jane! It was his idea, that you should accompany me. He said he admires your wit and that you might make him smile at dinnertime and help to entertain Monsieur Mollinet. He loves to laugh, apparently, and speaks good English. Ashton will arrange everything. We leave on Thursday for Dover.'

Jane had agreed at once and then sat down and written the following note to her father:

Dearest Papa,

I know you must be despairing that I will ever return to Bath, but this is to reassure you that I will be coming back soon. The portrait is finished.

First, however, I have been invited to travel to Paris on Thursday with my new friends, Ashton and Julietta Sims, and I hope you will not begrudge me this great adventure. Ashton Sims is one of the owner-directors of the publishing house, Kirkwall & Sims and his Italian wife is a great beauty.

I promise to send you a Carte Postale of the Cathedral of Notre-Dame, or possibly of some poor beggarmaid prostrate at its portals. For I am told there are many dispossessed in Paris, on account of the city's redesign by Baron

Haussmann, but I believe I will have to endeavour to harden my heart towards
them, in order to go SHOPPING with Julietta! Emmeline is lending me
money for a few Paris fashions, but I have told her you will repay her.
   From your contrite, loving and heartless daughter, Jane

Now, after being brought a breakfast of coffee and French patisserie
in her room at the Hôtel Meurice in the rue de Rivoli, Jane was lying
naked on her bed making such wild love with Julietta that she felt
herself blush at her own abandon. Under Julietta's instruction, Jane
was now capable of exciting her lover to ecstasies – so she said – she
had never before experienced.

'Because you are so tall and strong,' whispered Julietta, 'it is as
though you are a man and a woman, both together. My mind flickers
in and out of seeing you as two people. And I cannot tell you how
impossibly erotic this is. But we can take it even further, Jane, if you
want to …'

'I want to.'

'Then I have a wonderful plan. It will be something about which
I've often fantasised, but I have never dared to do it. Only with you,
now, we are going to do it.'

'Tell me the plan,' said Jane.

'No,' said Julietta. 'Now we are going to dress very smartly in our
best day dresses and coats, and go out and you will soon see what I
have in mind. And I know that we are both going to go wild with
excitement. I feel almost faint thinking about it.'

Julietta's 'plan' took them in a *carrosse* across the Seine, which, like the
Thames, was awash with human sewage and all the detritus of city
life and yet was lit with such a beautiful spring light that the tides of
filth seemed only like intricate copper-coloured marbling on its sparkling surface. And in the variety of commerce on the river Jane felt
she could discern a place whose clamour was all for wild indulgence
and excess. She saw one barge piled up with nothing but bales of
mink skins, another with a mountain of pineapples, another with a
hundred cages filled with larks.

When they descended from the cab, in the rue du Bac, Jane noticed
how warm the air was and as she savoured this, she felt that she had

never been as enthralled by life as she was at this moment. Julietta had explained to her that Haussmann was tearing down the ancient, cluttered streets and wooden houses to lay out wide boulevards and apartment houses built in stone and embellished with ironwork and classical decoration. And the thought came now to Jane that she was Haussmann's perfect acolyte, not only casting an admiring eye on his beautiful new vistas but herself undergoing a radical transformation, becoming a new person in a new époque. Her past was demolishing itself as surely as the old, narrow streets of Paris were disappearing. With Julietta, Jane Adeane was being reinvented.

The cab had deposited Jane and Julietta opposite the doors to a large draper's shop named Boucicaut. Jane presumed they were going in there – to buy new gloves, perhaps, or new ribbons or petticoats – but Julietta gently took Jane's arm and led her a little way down the street and in through a narrow door to an ancient-looking emporium named *Tirard, Costumiers*.

As soon as they entered Tirard, Jane felt her mood veer unexpectedly from happiness to obscure dread. So crammed was this airless place with racks of theatrical costumes that the garments themselves seemed to exhale a strong human odour, as if ancient living bodies still inhabited them. It was the smell of perfume and the passing years, the scent of splendour and decay.

Then, when Jane tilted her head upwards, to try to take a gasp of purer air, she saw that another row of dresses – these ones embellished with pearls, sequins and feathers – hung suspended from pulleys roped to the ceiling. Jane knew that only an imagination as febrile as hers would see these as encasing the emaciated forms of actresses, down on their luck and close to death, but still sporting their ragged finery, yet this was how the clothes appeared to her and she was overcome with sudden sorrow and wished they had not come in here.

She was almost on the point of asking Julietta if they could leave when a frock-coated monsieur, sporting elegantly twirled moustaches, and a waistcoat of gold brocade, appeared out of the darkness at the back of the premises and greeted Julietta like a long-lost friend.

'Signóra Sims!' said this finely self-exaggerated person. 'Quelle bonheur de vous revoir! Toujours aussi belle, ma fois. Vous cherchez une costume pour une soirée musicale? Qu'est-ce qui va vous plaire aujourd'hui?'

'Monsieur Tirard,' said Julietta. 'Vous allez bien?'

'Oui, oui, très bien. Quelle ange vous êtes! Comment puis-je vous server ce matin?'

Jane had not understood every word of this, only that it was a gracious greeting. But Julietta now took Jane's arm, introduced her to Monsieur Tirard and then whispered something in his ear, which Jane couldn't catch. She saw a knowing smile pass over Tirard's features. He turned towards her and looked her up and down, noting, of course, her great height and seemingly delighted enough by this to begin to caress his moustaches, as if in anticipation of something pleasurable.

'Je vois, je vois,' he said. 'Je vois tout de suite! Venez avec moi.'

Julietta took Jane's hand and they followed Tirard into the great gloomy darkness of the rear of the premises. Here, Tirard made elaborate show of lighting a gas lamp, and by this strange white light Jane saw that they were surrounded now by rows and rows of men's costumes and shelves of assorted hats, boots and shoes and racks of canes.

'Voilà!' said Tirard. 'Vous avez beaucoup de choix. Qu'est-ce qui va vous plaire, Mademoiselle? Capitaine des Dragons? Magicien? Matelot? Ou simple séducteur?'

Jane looked at the clothes, more sober in their colours than the dresses of the first room, but nevertheless indicating the kind of flamboyance to be seen perhaps in London, but very seldom in Bath. Tirard pulled one ensemble from the racks, a dark red frock coat, narrow check trousers, red and black, and a silver waistcoat.

'Séducteur?' he said, with a raise of his manicured eyebrows.

He moved towards Jane with the costume, then held it close to her body, inviting Julietta to admire the way the vivid reds set off her colouring, and now Jane understood; she was here to complete the transformation she had already felt in herself. She was going to become a man.

More and more outfits were selected by Tirard and held against Jane's body. Each one provoked such excitement in Julietta that her pale cheeks were soon cherry-coloured and sweat began to glimmer on her beautiful brow.

'Jane, Jane!' she cried out. 'I love them all. Which do you like? Which shall we try on?'

Now Jane felt torn between the peculiar horror the place had provoked in her and Julietta's excitement at the idea of dressing her in men's clothes. 'In most conflicts between desire and other sentiments,' Emmeline had once said to her, 'desire always wins.' And Jane suspected that it would win now.

She and Julietta were led behind a silk curtain. Julietta reached up and gave her a long ardent kiss. 'Like this,' she whispered, 'I am going to love you more than I have ever loved anyone.' Both the kiss and Julietta's words stirred Jane to follow Julietta's breathless instructions. She obediently disrobed, her clothes being almost torn from her by Julietta's nimble hands, and put on a white shirt, green and black striped trousers, a green waistcoat and a black frock coat.

Julietta dashed out from behind the curtain to ask Monsieur Tirard for a tie and a top hat. She returned to arrange the tie very tenderly in a perfect bow, just as she might have done for her husband. Then she produced a tortoiseshell comb from her purse, brushed Jane's hair back from her face and secured it in a tight chignon. She handed Jane the top hat and Jane put it on. When this was done, she turned Jane round towards a long, tarnished mirror, draped with a feather boa.

'Look,' she said. 'Now we are the perfect couple. We can do anything we want. We only need one more thing.'

Julietta went out again and Jane heard her whispering to Monsieur Tirard and Tirard say to her, 'Signóra, vous êtes sublime! Mais vous savez ces choses-là coûtent chers. Ils sont defendus ...'

'Je le sais,' said Julietta. 'But I *adore risk*. You know me by now, Monsieur Tirard. I am in love this time. Please give me what I need.'

Jane heard them walk away into another part of the shop. She turned her gaze on her own reflection. The change in her was impressive and she would have been entertained, even mildly excited by it had she not been besieged by the sudden and devastating realisation that Julietta, greeted as an old friend by Monsieur Tirard, had surely been through this very same erotic game with other lovers.

She'd told Jane that she had 'fantasised' about doing it, but had never done it. But it was clear that this was a lie. She had often spoken of travelling to Paris, and Jane now believed that she had probably played this identical charade scores of times. First, she would have driven her lovers wild in her bed, then she would have flattered them with talk of their exceptionality and asked them if they wanted to 'go further' in their debauch – and they would have assented, just as she had assented, because nobody could refuse Julietta Sims. After that, she would have brought them here, and then …

Jane's mind turned back to the racks of costumes, still perfumed with the stink of sorrow and decay, even with the stale effusions of desire. In the shadowy little cubicle behind the silk curtain, she began to feel faint and sick. She was burning hot, then icy cold as sweat began to pour down her back. She flung away the top hat and dragged her arms free of the coat.

She was tearing at the bow tie when Julietta returned with a triumphant smile on her face, babbling that Monsieur Tirard had given her 'the very perfect thing we are going to need'.

'It's very expensive,' she whispered breathlessly, 'but we will enjoy it so much, we might die of pleasure …'

It was only then that Julietta noticed that Jane was taking off the green-and-black outfit.

'Stop!' she said. 'We're going to buy the costume, Jane, and I am going to take us to be photographed together, with you wearing it … "Monsieur and Madame".'

But Jane was now stepping out of the trousers and reaching for her own clothes.

'I'm sorry, Julietta,' she said. 'But I don't want to do this.'

Julietta immediately went to Jane and held her close against her breast, boldly sliding her hand between her legs, beginning to chafe her there and saying gently, 'You're shocked, my dearest. I understand. I thought you might be. I know I'm very, very wicked, but you will see—'

'You are only "wicked" because you lied to me.'

'Lied to you?'

'You said you'd never done this before, but it's clear from the way you're friendly with Monsieur Tirard—'

'Hush, Jane. Don't be so bourgeois, or I will have to send you straight back to Bath. Of course I've done it before. I've travelled every road to ecstasy with women that you can imagine, and probably some that you can't, because this is what I choose to do. But it is also to say nothing important at all, only to remind you that now I can be a very good lover to you. Isn't this what you want? Does anything in the past matter one jot? Now, steady yourself and press harder against my hand. Like that, yes. You see how quickly you surrender to me?'

MORGUE

Dinner that evening was at the Café Anglais on the Boulevard des Italiens.

Ashton Sims had arranged everything with quiet care, ordering champagne for his French author, and treating him with the utmost courtesy. Guy Mollinet demonstrated at once that he spoke quite passable English, but Ashton chose to lace the conversation with French, to show Mollinet his fluency in the language, and Julietta's as well.

Jane watched Julietta, dressed in a lilac satin dress with a low décolleté, flirt with Guy Mollinet and she observed how easily he seemed to let her reel him in. Most of what she said to him Jane was unable to understand, but Julietta appeared quite unconcerned about this and hardly looked in her direction. The goal of Signóra Sims seemed to be to seduce the author, at least to the point where he would agree to sell his work to Kirkwall & Sims, and to forget about everything and everyone else.

Although this was troubling, Jane resolved not to feel any jealousy. Mollinet, aged about fifty, was not in the least handsome. His mouth was sensual and his hands very fine, but Jane couldn't imagine that Julietta was attracted to him. What she was doing was play-acting. It was play-acting of a very convincing kind, but Jane knew that it was not real and she suspected that Ashton knew it, too.

Ashton explained to Jane that Mollinet's novel had for its principal setting the Paris Morgue. 'The novel reminds us,' said Ashton, 'that this is the place to which we all come in time. In Paris, it is a public place and the dead are laid out for inspection behind a glass partition for the living to gawp at. So what a profoundly enabling and original setting this makes for a book! I wouldn't be at all surprised if other French writers don't try to steal it and make it their own, and I think it will be read by thousands in an English translation.'

'What story does it tell?' asked Jane. 'I do think Miss Austen understood the importance of *story* so very well, didn't she, Ashton? For what is the impact of any setting, even one as macabre and original as a morgue, compared to it? All we beg to know is will Elizabeth Bennet marry Mr Darcy or not? Will Marianne Dashwood be betrayed by Mr Willoughby? Compared to these questions, everything else pales, doesn't it?'

'You are right, of course,' said Ashton. 'And we publishers are ever beseeching our authors to hook their readers with mysteries and unknowings, and remarkably few understand how to do this. But Monsieur Mollinet tells a marvellous story: to escape a murderous lover, a young woman feigns death and is put on show at the morgue – a place the vile man is in the habit of visiting every Wednesday afternoon, to gloat over his victims.

'Cold water is sprayed upon the bodies, to keep them from decaying too fast. The heroine of the story has to endure this without moving for several hours. And of course she has to starve herself, to appear emaciated and dead. All this is made possible by her connivance with the Keeper of the Morgue, who places an iron cage over her chest, so that her breathing is concealed. He falls in love with her, of course, and helps her to take up her life again. Then she's persuaded by the Keeper to take a job at the morgue and both of them slowly become aware that the dead are playing tricks of their own!'

'Oh,' said Jane, 'so the mood of the book is very heartening and uplifting?'

Ashton laughed. 'It's a work which asks a lot of the reader, not least a strong stomach. There is nothing like it in England. The French and the Russians are the only writers who follow a dark road like this one. Because they have no fear of scandal, no fear of fear. They show human life in all its difficulty. And they know that readers are wolves.'

'Wolves? I have never thought of them like that. Do you think Miss Austen's readers are wolfish?'

'Yes. Even they. They tear at the flesh of her stories. They love to see the wicked punished or humiliated. Do we not gloat when Fanny Price rejects Henry Crawford in *Mansfield Park*?'

'Yes we do. How wonderful it must be to have the power to move people to adoration or wolfishness with inventions that have sprung out of one's mind like birds from a conjuror's hat. Has Monsieur Mollinet mastered this power?'

'Yes indeed: his characters live and breathe upon the page.'

Hearing his name mentioned, Guy Mollinet interrupted the conversation between Jane and Ashton, to say that Julietta, on hearing that he'd written about the Paris Morgue, asked whether he could take them there the next day. Ashton turned again to Jane. 'What plans do you and Julietta have for tomorrow?'

Jane put down her knife and fork on her delicious plate of *Saumon Napolitain* and couldn't help but recall Julietta saying to her, 'Ashton has meetings with French publishers all morning. I will come to you after breakfast and we will lock and barricade your door and play at man–woman love. Tirard gave me the wicked *appendage* we will need. I swoon at the thought of it, don't you? But it involves much physical exertion, so after it we will be ravenous. We will go to lunch at Tortoni and eat oysters and *filet mignon* and ice cream.'

To Ashton, she said, 'I think Julietta wants to go shopping in the morning, but we would be free in the afternoon.'

Jane had imagined that the morgue – this house of the departed – would be very quiet, but as they passed beyond the foyer to the viewing chamber, the sound of living voices was loud and they found themselves in a great crowd of people pressed up against a wall of glass.

Beyond the glass, the bodies lay upon slabs of black marble, tilted at thirty degrees towards the spectators. All were naked, their private parts being covered with little strips of white linen no bigger than a woman's handkerchief. And, as Ashton Sims had described to Jane the evening before, fountains of water played constantly upon the dead, running in rivulets from their heads to their feet, in order to cool them.

Jane saw that one body was much smaller than the others and her heart ached to realise that it must be the body of a child. Not only this, but the child's body was in a state of more advanced decay than the others, suggesting that none among the daily crowds had come to claim it. The hair was almost gone from the head and the little neck seemed to have shrunk down, so that head and body were joined at the shoulders.

Jane stared at the child's body for a long time. With the water trickling over it, making the whiter flesh appear soft and malleable, it suggested to her an image by which she had long been haunted, the image of Emmeline's poor golem, damp from its rotation on the pottery wheel, forming itself into an ugly creature in Emmeline's hands. She longed to take up the child and bring it back to life.

She reached out to take Julietta's arm, and glancing sideways at her lover, saw that she was very pale. She, too, had seen the child's body and said in a querulous voice to Jane, 'I can't see that without imagining what I would feel if this were Marco, laid on the slab. Why does the mother not come to claim it?'

'Because she is heartless, or because she herself is dead.'

'There should be no death,' sighed Julietta. 'There should be only pleasure and delight.'

The crowd barely moved along the glass wall, though now new visitors to the morgue were pressing in behind.

'Vous voyez,' said Guy Mollinet, as the press of the living began to be stifling and uncomfortable, 'we have not simplement cousins et cousines des morts, but you have also the tourists, like we are.'

'Should we be ashamed of being here?' asked Julietta.

'*Non, non,*' said Monsieur Mollinet, 'we must look. We must understand. Ces morts, ce sont nous.'

Jane turned to Mollinet to say that she already had long experience, in her work as a nurse, of seeing the dead and that she agreed with him – that the living should not turn away. But her words were suddenly lost as an elderly man with a hectic look in his eyes pushed past her and began screaming that he had recognised his own corpse and was here to take it back.

In her room that night, Jane found that her whole body ached and she lay down on the bed in the serene comfort of her white nightgown, glad at last to be alone.

She knew that no day in her twenty-five years of life had been as strange as this one and she felt that she would remember it always: the visit to the morgue, the child's body, the memory of Emmeline's sorrow, and – superimposed on these sad images – a vision of herself that morning, with Tirard's obscene rubber 'appendage' strapped to her loins, making love to Julietta exactly as if she had been a male lover. The sexual power of this had been such as to make both Jane and Julietta cry out and they had been momentarily disconcerted to hear the occupants of the adjoining room banging upon the wall. But they hadn't been able to stop. The rest of the world had ceased to exist for them.

THE RIVER TURNED UPSIDE-DOWN

When Leon had heard the storm approaching, he and Sir Ralph Savage had not yet reached the Sadong, but they had come a long way – too far to make it back to the rajah's mansion before the rain fell – and under the darkening sky Leon led the rajah to the small longhouse inhabited by his mother, Taminah.

This woman had always moved Sir Ralph. She suffered from a skin disease, for which no cure had been found, and which blotched Taminah's face with patches of pure white pigment, as though a map-maker, beginning to sketch in the colours and contours of a world, had found himself at a loss and had had to leave portions of his work completely blank.

Taminah had lost all her sons except Leon, to drowning, sickness and the trade wars between the English and the Dutch. She, who had once been the matriarch of a large family, now lived alone and in semi-darkness. The two daughters she might have counted on to help her in her old age had married and gone to live in Singapore. Her husband, head-hunted by Dyaks for trespass on their tribal land, had died so long ago that Taminah had difficulty remembering his features. She still had dreams of the beloved head the Dyaks had cut off and strung up in the roof of their hut in rattan nets; she just couldn't recall what it actually looked like. To Leon, she said: 'It is better like that. If a head is separate from a body, then it must stay in the shadow of the mind.'

Now, Taminah, sitting by a small fire, received her son and the rajah. She stood up and bowed, pressing her palms together. Sir Ralph bowed to her in his turn while Leon went to his mother and embraced her, and the fire, stirred into new life by the current of air blown into the room by the opening of the door, flared bright coral for a brief moment. By this sudden light, Sir Ralph noticed that Taminah was sitting on an embroidered mat which had been a gift from him to Leon, but he was not disconcerted. His presents to Leon had been so numerous that his lover's small room in the rajah's mansion now appeared a little like a stall in a bazaar.

More than once, Leon had mocked Sir Ralph for his endless cascade of expensive offerings, but this had not prevented him from adding to it. His natural inclination, in his adoration of Leon, was to lay before him an unending quantity of material things. It was as if he imagined these objects would form a kind of protecting wall around his lover, ensuring that he would never leave and never come to any harm. His worst fear was that some quarrel with Leon would dismantle this fragile edifice and that he would be left alone, to pine for the rest of his life.

Always courteous to Taminah, Sir Ralph now sat cross-legged opposite her, while the smoke from the fire made ghostly patterns in its search of an escape through the roof aperture and the thunder began to roll overhead. The rajah apologised for disturbing Taminah, but explained that they had been journeying to the river when the storm began to threaten. They begged shelter from her until it had passed.

She began to talk very fast to Leon, lamenting that she had no food, only a pot of sticky rice and a little jar of tuak. Leon consoled her, saying they had no need of food, but Taminah, now anxious at her lack of hospitality, asked him if she should kill and pluck one of the tethered cockerels which strutted around her veranda. Leon told her to let the cockerels live and that if they got hungry, they would eat the rice and be content with that.

It was then that the rain began to fall on the palm-leaf thatching of the longhouse, battering it fiercely, as if with an avalanche of small stones. Whenever a deluge like this one threatened her house, Taminah imagined it as what she called 'the river turned upside-down'. Sometimes she feared that the rain would bring boulders and crocodiles and broken canoes tumbling down on her head.

Leon had warned his mother that this was 'muddled thinking' and that she should try to keep better control of her mind and not let it stray into the madness from which so many of the elderly seemed to suffer. But Taminah had not been moved by this warning. She had said to Leon: 'Madness is the end to which we all come. Suffering and loss take us there. You will see. In time, you will come to it, too. You will see the river falling from the sky.'

It was only now, seated in Taminah's house, breathing in the loneliness and poverty in which this woman lived, that Sir Ralph suddenly remembered Edmund. He'd thought that Edmund had been walking just behind him and Leon and had followed them into the longhouse, but now there was no sign of him. The rajah stood up and looked around, as if hoping to find Edmund standing in a corner of the room.

'Where is Mr Ross?' he said to Leon.

Leon didn't hesitate before saying, 'Oh you very blind, my rajah. Your Jesus boy, he turn back to your house. He say to me, on the path, I am turning back, Leon.'

'When did he say this?'

'When we hear the storm. He is cowardly.'

'But he was interested to see the cannery site.'

'Except he is weak. And you know he is quite mad. Collectors of butterflies and beetles; such men are very foolish.'

'No,' said Sir Ralph. 'They are not. They are trying to educate people in England about the things they have never seen and never even imagined.'

'Englung people want to see scorpions and snakes?'

'Yes. And birds and flowers. Why not? They want to learn about these islands.'

Leon shook his head crossly. 'Not learn,' he said. 'Only steal.'

'Well, never mind,' said Sir Ralph. 'What else did Edmund say to you?'

'Nothing. Only he is turning back.'

The rajah now went to the door of the house, which opened onto the veranda where the cockerels were tethered. He saw the scrawny birds touchingly huddled together against the storm, their eyes closed, their bright feathers ruffled and beaded by the rain and their tethers lying in a tangle around them. He began calling Edmund's name.

Taminah looked worriedly at him. She said to Leon, 'He must not go out. The river will fall on his head.'

Leon asked his mother to fetch what tuak remained to her and they would drink this and eat some rice and sleep a little until the worst of the rain was past. Then he called out to Sir Ralph, 'My rajah, giver of all gifts, don't be a nin-poop. Stop your calling and close the door.'

Taminah put a pot of sticky rice to heat above the fire and served Leon and Sir Ralph all that remained of her tuak. The rajah felt cold and worried and the strong drink soothed him a little. He disliked having arguments with Leon. Worse, he hated it when he suspected that Leon was lying to him, and he thought now that Leon had lied about Edmund. Surely, if Edmund had decided to turn back, he would have made this plain? Edmund perfectly understood that Sir Ralph was now both excited and troubled by Leon's idea of the cannery and he would have been interested to see where this great 'consolation' might stand one day.

But the rajah reasoned that there was nothing to be done until the deluge had ceased. He drank the rest of the tuak and ate a little of Taminah's rice. Leon sat close to his mother, on the far side of the fire and would not look at him.

When they'd eaten all she had, Taminah laid out mats for them and they lay down and slept, while the thunder rolled on and the waters of the Sadong rose still higher.

Sir Ralph had a dream of Edmund's voice reading softly from St. Luke, Chapter Five:

'*. . . now when he had left off speaking, he said unto Simon, launch out into the deep, and let down your nets for a draught.*

And Simon answering said unto him, Master, we have toiled all the night, and have taken nothing: nevertheless at thy word I will let down the net.

And when they had this done, they inclosed a great multitude of fishes: and their net brake.'

The rajah, in his dream, saw the fish thrashing in the heavy net, but the fish that he saw were not in the Lake of Gennesaret, but in the Sadong. There were so many of them that the banks were silvered and alive with their leaping, as though, in their multitude, they were one dancing and shuddering body.

The rajah's hands reached out, and other hands reached out and the fish were taken up and thrown onto a wide moving belt which conveyed the fish to the portals of the brand new cannery. The cannery workers scooped them onto slabs of stone and knives began to slice away their heads and slit their bodies to get out all that was unclean or sharp – anything in them that might hurt a man.

While the rajah slept, Edmund had walked deeper into the forest. He was still following the red ants, trusting in them as some kind of fortuitous guide, but he had strayed far from the original path to the abandoned gold mine and he had no idea, now that there was no sun in the sky, which direction he was travelling in. He berated himself for not staying with Leon and Sir Ralph. It came to him how many times in his life he had been distracted from the road he was on by the sight of some wonder of nature, a single orchid growing by a brook, a white owl in the dusk, gibbons at play in the high trees. He would lose himself in contemplation of these things and forget where he was meant to be going. Often, he had been saved by his compass, but now that vital piece of equipment had gone missing from his life.

The thunder was coming nearer, but no rain had yet fallen. Ahead of him, he saw that a heavy tree had crashed down across his path and the exertion of clambering over it now presented itself to him as a fearful ordeal, as though the fallen tree had grown in size to become a hillside of impossible steepness.

He looked down at the ants. How would they approach the obstacle? He had seen red ants make a bridge across water with their tiny, armoured bodies, sacrificing some of their number in the process for the survival of the group, and he was interested to see what solution they would find now.

He walked on. When the ants reached the fallen tree, they didn't pause, but quickly made a ladder of themselves, clambering one upon another until they had purchase on the tree trunk and the column could flow upwards and over it and resume its march on the other side. When the column reached its end, some of those who had formed the ladder had fallen onto their backs and lay stranded and dying. Edmund squatted down, picked up a small stick and righted the fallen ants, one by one. When one of them stung his hand, he didn't flinch. He watched as they moved this way and that below the log, trying to find purchase that would take them over it. Finding none, they hurried away, in search of a new route to their destination.

Edmund sat down on the fallen tree. He heard a shrill cry and looked up to see the wide wings of a Brahminy kite spread against the darkening sky. To certain tribes in Borneo, these were birds of ill-omen and seeing them always made Edmund shiver.

Part Two

'SOMEWHERE QUIET AND SOLITARY'

On a Sunday afternoon at the end of April Jane Adeane returned to Bath.

When Sir William, keeping watch at the surgery window, saw his daughter descend from her carriage and mount the steps to 28 Henrietta Street, he was so overcome with relief and delight that he thought he might dissolve into tears. He ran into the hall and took Jane in his arms. What he wanted to say to her was 'never go away again', but he knew better than to burden Jane with commands of such a peremptory and emotional kind. He well understood that, as his nurse and assistant, she would obey his every instruction; as his daughter, she was disinclined to obey any of them.

But Jane was moved to see her father. After she'd kissed his cheek, she stood back and looked at him and was amused to note that, in the many weeks that she'd been away, Sir William's stomach had increased in girth considerably more than appeared possible in the time that had elapsed.

'Oh Papa,' she said, laughing, 'where has my lean father gone? Who is this new father who is unable to fasten the bottom button of his waistcoat?'

Sir William smiled and patted his tummy, almost with pride, it seemed to Jane.

'There is but one person to blame,' he said, 'and that is Mrs Morrissey.'

'Mrs Morrissey? Oh, I am astonished! Have you been gluttoning on scones and cream?'

'No, no. I told you in one of my letters, dear Mrs Morrissey confects the most marvellous pies and kidney puddings for our lunches. Doctor Ross and I have become quite addicted to suet and gravy.'

'Well, so I see,' said Jane.

'And pastry,' added Sir William.

'Yes, I declare I can see the pastry, too! But never mind. It only means there is more of you to cherish.'

Sir William led Jane up the stairs, while the maidservant, Becky followed with her suitcases, now freighted with acquisitions made in Paris, several of which Jane knew would have to be placed securely out of sight.

When Jane reached her bedroom and looked in, noting at once that a little vase of primroses had been put on her dressing table, her first thought was how small the room seemed, compared to the one she'd occupied in Tite Street. The bed, too, appeared very narrow, almost like the bed of a child, and her heart, which had been lightened by her reunion with her father, now faltered at the idea of the constraints that would be placed upon her life as soon as she resumed her role as a nurse in Bath.

She knew better, however, than to let Sir William pick up any hint of this sudden dismay. She ran to the primroses and lifted up the vase and breathed in their soft perfume.

'How beautiful!' she said. 'I haven't seen a single flower since I left. There are none in London.'

'Oh,' said Sir William, 'I surely remember that Emmeline's house has a garden ...'

'Yes. A garden. But it's full of brambles. It is how she likes things to be: wild and unruly. She admires Nature's thorns.'

If Jane had immediately noticed a change in Sir William, he in turn was now struck by some differences in Jane. He was unable to describe these with any precision. It just seemed to him that Jane had become *more than ever Jane*, as though she had stepped out of a shadowed place into a blinding light. Her colour was high, her eyes very large and bright, and her hair shiny and coiled into a bold coiffure, kept in place by a comb of mother-of-pearl. She held herself with even more grace and *panache* than he remembered.

'You look well,' he said, ashamed at the inadequacy of his comment, but finding no other at present.

Jane had chosen Sunday as the day of her return in the expectation that Valentine Ross would not be at Henrietta Street. She wanted to spend the time quietly with her father, hoping that his dear presence would reconcile her to finding herself back in Bath.

At first, she had not been reconciled. As the coach had brought her from the station and she'd seen the familiar, well-ordered streets of the town rise up around her, she'd had a strong inclination to get out of the carriage, remove her luggage and take the next available train back to London. But she had resisted. She felt that her father's need of her had to be honoured – at least for a time. She told herself that she would 'try on' her old life and see what happened to her.

She would keep her love for Julietta secret, like a precious ruby held in her pocket. And if her yearning became unbearable, she would find some means to meet her. In her mind's eye, she imagined a wayside inn where, dressed in her man's clothes, she would meet her 'wife' and they would spend the night together. Already, she could see the mullion windows of the room, the candle burning at the bedside, her lover's soft white body, her hair spread out on the pillow …

But now, she had to try to accept once more the contours of her old home: the narrowness of her bed, the medicinal smell which hung in the air, the invisible presence of Dr Ross. When she thought about him, it surprised her to realise that, notwithstanding the two years they had worked together side by side in perfect harmony, she always pictured him in Mrs Morrissey's tea room, making his ridiculous proposal of marriage. It was as if that fateful day now obscured everything that had gone before it. Jane knew that this was a contrary way to think about him, but it seemed that her mind could find no other.

To distract herself from contemplating him at all, Jane opened her trunks and began to take out the new clothes she'd acquired in Paris. She caressed them as she hung them up in the narrow wardrobe where her nurse's uniforms hung like accusing ghosts. Making sure that her door was closed, Jane now unpacked the frock coat bought at Tirard. She held it against her body and pressed her face into the fabric of the shoulders, where a trace of Julietta's perfume lingered. Prior to their love-making, Julietta had liked to indulge in a little play-acting, pretending that they were husband and wife out for a walk in the Luxembourg Gardens. She had tucked her arm inside Jane's and they'd perambulated about the spacious hotel room, with Jane wearing her male outfit, and Julietta had remarked on the lilacs coming into bud in the park and the dogs yapping in the spring sunshine and the children at play with their hoops and skipping ropes.

A knock on Jane's door brought her out of this reverie. She threw the frock coat back into her trunk and closed the lid. Becky came in and announced that Sir William had ordered tea.

'He asks that you come down to the parlour,' she said. 'He told me to be sure to tell you that there are cakes from Mrs Morrissey's.'

Jane and her father sat at the tea table and both remembered how comfortable they felt in each other's presence. After a while, Sir William said: 'I know you have much to tell me, but I expect I will hear about it all over time, and you will show me all your Paris fashions?'

'I will, Father.'

'And talk to me about your new friends, the Sims. I know that Kirkwall & Sims have a fine reputation.'

'Indeed. And now they are adding a new French author to their list, Guy Mollinet. He was so charmed by Julietta over dinner at the Café Anglais that he signed a contract with Ashton Sims the very next morning.'

'Yes. I had heard that Mrs Sims is incomparably beautiful.'

Jane felt herself blushing and quickly bent her head and pretended to wipe her mouth with her table napkin. She realised that the very saying of Julietta's name could make her tremble and she told herself henceforward never to speak of her lover, lest her feelings revealed themselves in all their nakedness through the agitation of her body.

She poured more tea for her father, who was eagerly biting into a cream-filled brandy snap, and said: 'Monsieur Mollinet's novel is set in the Paris Morgue. And he was kind enough to show us round the place, where you know the dead are laid out for public inspection. Is that not a macabre idea?'

'Quite macabre. But it surely has a purpose: that the dead who are missing are found by their relatives.'

'Yet many people gathered there to gawp at them did not seem to be relatives. They appeared to think of the experience as an entertainment, as though they had been at a puppet show or a zoo.'

'It is normal. The dead fill us with gladness because we are not yet among them. But speaking of the dead, I am going to put into your hands tomorrow a certain Mr Latimer, on whom Doctor Ross and I operated a little while back. As we feared, he is dying. He has been told that his one last hope of life is to return to the Baths and be put into your care.'

'What is he dying of?'

'His lungs are congested with very small tumours. Doctor Ross saw them, when I could not recognise them for what they are. There is no doubt that he will die, but you will do your best for him, to ease his pain.'

'Can you not operate a second time, to take the tumours away?'

'He is not strong enough to bear it. And I certainly could not contemplate performing such an operation on my own.'

'Would not Doctor Ross assist you?'

'He would. But he left Bath yesterday. He will be gone a little while.'

'Oh, to where is he travelling?'

'I didn't enquire. He told me he is very tired and he has not looked well for some while. I think he will go somewhere quiet and solitary.'

Jane was silent. For reasons which she couldn't quite fathom in herself, she felt disappointed by this news. One of Emmeline's last instructions to her had been to 'look with a new eye upon your poor Valentine' and now she was to be denied so much as a glimpse of him. She wondered what 'solitary' place he would choose and what he would do there. Furthermore, she couldn't stop herself from wondering whether, in his new loneliness, Valentine Ross would think of her.

EBB TIDE

Ross travelled south across the Mendip Hills and into Somerset. He journeyed by small stages, putting up at quiet inns, not knowing what his ultimate destination would be. He talked to no one.

The May weather was fine and clear. In the ditches beside the quiet roads he was gladdened to notice an abundance of daisies, oxlips and violets. Like his brother, he'd always been moved by the modesty of small flowers.

Taken by a desire to see and smell the sea, he made his way to Watchet and looked out at the deep harbour, where, he had been told, the tides would ebb by thirty feet in every twenty-four hours, leaving all the vessels beached on the red-toned mud.

When Ross arrived there, the wind was blowing from the south and it felt to him as if this was hastening the ebb, as the water slapped around the hulls of the colliers and ketches and then, inch by inch, crept away from them, as though some mistake had been made and the sea was repenting of its earlier rush towards a man-made haven.

He watched the sea for a long time, waiting for the moment when it would be quite gone from the harbour and the boats would lie stranded, showing an ugly infestation of barnacles on their hulls and a tangle of seaweed on their rudders. When at last this came about, very much as he'd imagined it, he found it strangely troubling.

Valentine Ross was not a man much given to self-love or self-pity, but he now yielded to the idea that his own life was in the same state as the ships abandoned by the sea. He was beached and useless. The person who would have turned the tide and brought him back to a meaningful life felt nothing for him.

In due time, the incoming flow of the water would rescue even the great iron-hulled windjammer stuck fast in the mud at the outer corner of the harbour wall. She would be loaded with iron ore from the Brendon Hills and bound for Newport and the Welsh steelworks, under mighty sail. The luggers and ketches would make their way into the Atlantic fishing grounds and return with basket-loads of mackerel and herring, and the fishwives of Watchet would sing as they carried them ashore. All would regain their appointed reason for being, but he would not.

Ross sat down on a stone bench and watched the gulls circling and landing in the mud, swooping on tiny crabs and cockles. He looked all around him and found the scene desolate, despite the pale sunshine falling upon it. Scrawny cats were fighting over a few fish-heads strewn among the stones. A horse stood silent and still, in the traces of a collapsing cart. A fire smouldered, untended, in a rusty brazier.

At his back, Ross now began to hear the sound of tuneless singing and he turned to see a posse of men approaching the harbour, carrying jars of stout, far adrift on a companionable drunken tide. They walked in zigzags, bumping against each other, interrupting their song with happy laughter. They came and stood near to the bench on which Ross was sitting and one of them raised his fisherman's cap to him and belched and said, 'Don't mind us now, Sir. It's just our sea legs making us stumble.'

Ross raised his own hat and nodded to the men, one of whom was now pissing over the harbour wall, in blithe unconcern, singing all the while. Smelling the sudden medicinal mix of stout and urine, the thought now came to Ross that perhaps he should emulate these tipplers of Watchet and turn to drinking to soothe his mind. He wanted to ask how long it had taken them to set aside their troubles and reach a mood of such kindly merriment. But he was afraid to talk to them, fearing he might be mocked for his expensive clothes and for his melancholy. He stood up and walked away, glancing one last time at the stranded ships.

*

Now, he was in the Saloon Bar of an inn named The Plough and the Stars, drinking ale in great thirsty gulps until he felt some balm fall upon his anguish.

It was getting towards evening and men began to come in to the bar to find respite from the day's labours, and Ross envied them just as he'd envied the gulls and the drunken men at Watchet harbour, because they appeared content in the here-and-now. And he had a great longing to talk to one of these strangers about his life and how he had come from Bath to escape the proximity of the one person he cherished in the world.

Standing next to him at the counter was an elderly man, wearing a dog collar and a long priest's gown under a frayed coat. He was drinking cider and chewing on an old blackened pipe and Ross took him for a man who was much alone in his life.

Finishing his own flagon of beer he gestured to the landlord to refill it and then turned to the gentleman and said, 'May I buy you another one, Reverend? To celebrate the May weather.'

'Ah,' said the churchman, 'May weather, now. Trouble be, I'm not in the May-time of my life.'

'Nor I,' said Ross.

The man snatched the pipe from his mouth and looked at Ross. 'Nearer it than I,' he said. 'I got married round about your age and thought I would be happy.'

'But you were not happy?'

'Not a day was I happy. I married the wrong woman, but I was glued to her like a barnacle to a ship's bottom. There's no parting from a wife if you're a man of the Church.'

'And you're with her still?'

'No. Thank the Lord. She went silly in the head and died eating ragwort in Davy's Field out yonder.'

'She knew it was poison?'

'Or she didn't. Happen she thought it were a feast of snow peas. But it killed her. And I was free.'

'So you're a happy man now?'

'No, Sir, I am not. For my life was blighted. And now that I'm near the end of it and I see the great wasteland that it was. These days, there's only cider and prayer.'

Ross ordered more cider for the Reverend, then he said, 'life is savage. This much I've understood.'

'Are you married to the wrong woman, then? That will bring a man to bloody ruin, sure as anything can.'

'No. I'm not married. I'm quite alone.'

'That's not a good state, either. But there are remedies. This is a ships' town. Wait till the lamps are lit, and then go down to Harbour Cottages – them little hovels set back behind a stone wall at the eastern edge of the quay. The accommodation isn't the best, but the drabs aren't fussy there and some of them are bonny. Even I – all skin-and-bone that I am and wearing a bleedin' cassock – I had them all. The only thing you have to do is pay.'

Ross drank more beer. The shadowy room, lit by a smoky paraffin lamp, now began to take on an altered aspect, as if everything were moving slowly away from him, and he felt sickened suddenly, whether from the drink or from his proximity to the vicar with his filthy pipe and his tales of ragwort poison and prostitutes.

He asked himself whether this was what he wanted to do: find a woman and pour all his darkness into her. He tried to imagine some Watchet girl, fat in the rump, with a high colour in her cheeks and a slurred Somerset voice, trying to coax him towards desire with well-learned obscenities. But he knew that if he found himself with such a person, she would never satisfy his longings; he would simply want to kill her.

'I don't want a woman,' he said to the Reverend, 'I only want *my woman.*'

'Well then. What's your trouble? Drink up your ale and go to her.'

'My trouble is,' said Ross, 'she's not mine.'

Ross left The Plough and the Stars soon after this. He walked unsteadily away from Watchet and out onto the deserted road that climbed towards Kilve between hedgerows and fields of young green wheat. He'd drunk enough to feel sick, but not enough to reach that state of euphoria he'd seen in the fishermen at the harbour. He didn't ask himself where he was headed, or where he would sleep. These things didn't seem to hold any urgency for him.

It was dark now, but the moon that had risen above the coombs was almost full and lighted Ross's way. He stopped by an oak tree and vomited up the beer and was glad to get it out of him, and felt light-headed as he walked on, as though he'd been purged of some unknown weight that had held him to the earth.

He threw back his head and looked at the stars, feeling as if he might almost take wing and fly towards them. Then he was lost in a reverie of the sky, imagining the different constellations moving above the far side of the world, where Edmund resided. A longing to see his brother and hold him close to him now invaded him so fiercely it brought pain into his head. But the pain was followed by a slow seepage of something like happiness into his heart as he told himself that there *was* a way to move his life forward, to catch a flowing tide, if he could only find the courage to leave Bath, to leave everything and everyone behind and travel in search of Edmund. It felt to him as though Edmund was calling to him – as he had often called to him when they were boys – and that now he would answer. In his arduous, easterly journey to save his brother, he would forget Jane.

SUDDEN MERRIMENT

It was with some anxiety that Jane dressed herself the following morning. Rising early to tug on her nurse's clothes and arrange her hair under the white cap, she had the thought that all her skill in helping people to cure their ailments had probably left her. It had left her because she no longer truly cared to do it. She was in love with female beauty now; she was afraid that ageing and sick bodies, especially those of men, were going to disgust her, as they had never done before. The great store of tenderness and compassion which had earned her the name of Angel was diminished – or so she felt.

When Sir William saw her at their seven o'clock breakfast, clothed in the white garments which had always suited her so well, he couldn't but look admiringly at her and said, in a voice not devoid of profound emotion, 'Ah, Jane. Now everything is right once more with the world!'

But for her, it was not right. She let Becky pour her some tea, but when the maid set three rashers of bacon in front of her, fatty at their edges and on a chipped plate, she sent this away. She felt sweat on her upper lip and a sickness in her stomach. She wondered if she was going to faint. She nibbled a heel of white bread, as a squirrel might nibble it, taking tiny little mouthfuls, to try to soothe her discomfort. Meanwhile, her father read the *Bath Chronicle* and attacked his bacon with relish. Jane waited silently on her chair. She steadied herself by holding on to the rim of the breakfast table.

Latimer was brought to the house in a chaise at eight o'clock. What Jane saw was a pale, thin man, whose mouth hung agape in his tortuous search for breath. She, who had never seen the manufacturer of glue in his pomp and optimism nor heard him boasting about his new house in North Parade, was at once moved by simple pity for a poor soul whose lungs and heart were in such distress.

She helped him to Sir William's surgery and laid him on the couch and stood by while her father took Latimer's pulse and listened to the laboured breathing with an expression of dismay on his face, like a man listening to a favourite piece of music being played badly. While this was going on, Latimer looked pleadingly up at Jane, his eyes never leaving her features. And she intuited what he wanted to say — that he had heard about her, that she was the Angel of the Baths and that she was now all that stood between him and death.

She took up his hand, which was as cold as any marble, and held it tenderly. She said, 'I'm impatient to get you to the Hot Bath. The vapour and warmth will have an excellent effect on the congestion afflicting you. By the end of the morning, you will feel some relief, and then you will rest.'

It was difficult for Latimer to talk, but at length he said, 'I am told I should not hope. But perhaps *you* will give me hope?'

'Certainly I will,' said Jane. 'The waters have saved many lives, as I'm sure you know.'

'You see,' said Latimer in a choked whisper, 'I have not yet overseen all the decorations to my upper floors. My workers are so slow and my wife is very vexed that nothing is complete ...'

'Well then,' said Jane, 'should we immerse your painters and plasterers in the Baths also, to try to hurry them up?'

A wan smile now creased Latimer's wasted features. 'Or drown them?' he said.

'Ah yes,' said Jane, 'although as a rule, we try not to drown people, don't we, Father?'

'As a rule,' said Sir William. 'Now, Mr Latimer, Jane will come with you in the chaise and oversee your immersion, and you will soon be feeling the great benefit of sulphur and steam. I will visit you at your house this evening.'

'Yes,' said Latimer. 'Very good. But I remind you it is the old house you must come to, for the new is not yet ready for us. My men are such laggards ...'

*

Now, Jane was helping Latimer to climb into the Hot Bath. In its jade-coloured depths, the trembling legs of the other patients could be seen, their modesty-gowns folding and unfolding around them, like the drapery on a frieze of Roman statues.

Latimer clung to Jane's hand until he was immersed in the water up to his shoulders, but when he was in, he looked bewildered, as though something else was expected of him which he had not yet comprehended.

'Shall I move about?' he asked Jane.

'You have no need to move,' replied Jane. 'Just feel yourself at rest in the water. But you may walk, or swim, if you feel strong enough. Try to breathe as deeply as you can.'

Jane was now looking down at Latimer's head, where a few first stains of old age stippled his balding pate. What she – rightly – understood about this man was his overwhelming desire to remain in the world, to see his grand house completed, to marvel at decorated ceilings, at reeded skirtings and papered boudoirs. He was a person held to life by material splendour. Now he was forced to contemplate the loss of it all and Jane was able to imagine how hugely this filled him with despair – and this moved her.

Emmeline had reminded her that the human mind is capricious and does not always feel 'appropriately'; it can mourn for the loss of those who have done little that is deemed admirable in the world. Told by her father that Latimer was a 'wretched manufacturer of glue, who has made his fortune out of animal bones', Jane neverthe-less wished to make up her own mind about him and decided that she felt true compassion for his plight.

She watched Latimer wade out very slowly towards the centre of the Hot Bath and as he did so, a young woman, holding up a child in the water, approached her. Jane saw that the infant was a boy of about four years old. He clung to his mother like a baby clings, the centre of his being pressed to hers, his arms fastened round her neck. When they got to the place where Jane was standing, the young woman reached up and laid her wet hand on Jane's white shoe.

'I know you,' she said. 'You're the one they call the Angel of the Baths. Aren't you?'

Jane regarded them closely. She saw that the boy was very thin, his little legs almost wasted away.

'I used to be called the Angel, or so I heard. But I have been away for some time. I do not know who I am now.'

'Then none of us should put our faith in you?'

'I don't know. I've come back to Bath, to do everything I can, but if I ever had any power to heal, I fear it is quite gone.'

'Or perhaps it is not? Will you touch my son's head and bless him? He is dying of consumption.'

The woman gently prised the boy's arms from round her neck and lifted him up towards Jane. Jane saw the large brown eyes of the child afflicted with fear and pain. As she reached out her hands towards his damp head, she thought about a child she had never seen, Julietta's little son, Marco. She closed her eyes, to summon an image of him in her mind, so that it was to him, the son of her beloved, that she directed a simple, silent prayer, 'Let the child live and recover his strength and take his place in the world.' But, straight away, the boy began screaming and his mouth filled with blood. His mother snatched him back, to calm him.

'What did you do to him?' she cried out.

'I'm sorry,' Jane said. 'I'm truly sorry. I said a prayer in my mind. That was all.'

Jane took out one of the rags she always carried in the pocket of her apron and gently wiped the boy's lips. He spat blood into the water and then was silent.

'Are you the Angel or are you not?' said the young woman crossly.

'Perhaps it's wiser not to believe in angels at all,' said Jane. 'We should rather put our trust in human kindness.'

The young woman walked away, lowering her boy gently into the water and hearing him laugh now, soothed once more by the warmth of it. Further off, Latimer had discovered that, despite his weakness, he was able to swim, but what escaped from his afflicted body was not blood, but a little chuckle of sudden merriment.

Jane watched them both: the child who'd had such a short life, but who was loved so dearly by his mother; the middle-aged businessman whose empty heart was snagged on the contemplation of architectural mouldings and who was, perhaps, loved by no one. They would soon be equal in death, the cold clay of England sealing them in darkness, while far above the great medical cavalcade which drew people to Bath in such numbers would whirl on, untroubled by its failures and its derelictions.

At lunchtime, when Jane returned to Henrietta Street, the smell of stewing meat drew her down to the kitchen, where she found Clorinda Morrissey taking a great golden pie from the oven.

'The Lord be praised,' said Mrs Morrissey, when she saw Jane. 'You're here at last! I can't tell you how much your father has longed for this day.'

'Well, Mrs Morrissey,' said Jane, 'I cannot tell *you* how many words he wrote to me while I was away about your pies and puddings. I had no news of anything but these!'

'Oh get along now, this is simple food ...'

'Which is what Sir William likes. And I couldn't help but notice how one side of his waistcoat now has some difficulty reaching the other side.'

At this, Mrs Morrissey let forth a delighted peal of laughter and Jane thought the sound rather marvellous in this house – a strong woman's laugh, where there had been only men and their work and their silences, and sullen little Becky chivvied like a mouse from floor to floor.

'I do hope,' said Jane, 'that my father's demands haven't made the running of your tea rooms too difficult for you.'

'No, no. Not at all.'

'Now that I'm back, I can start looking for a permanent cook, if you wish ...'

Clorinda Morrissey snatched up a dish cloth and began wiping her hands on this. After a moment she said, 'the truth is, Miss Jane, Sir William has asked me if I would consider a ... permanent arrangement. And, well, he is so kind and thoughtful ... it was not very difficult for me to agree. I am saving up to buy him a new waistcoat!'

Again came the laughter, this time accompanied by a blush which Mrs Morrissey was unable to conceal and which, Jane decided, might have been the most interesting blush she had ever witnessed.

AFTER THE RAINS

Sir Ralph and Leon had spent three days and nights in Taminah's house, while the sky above them, deep purple in its darkness, had let fall a deluge into the Sadong and the surrounding forest that seemed to have no end.

Braving the rains, Leon had crept through the trees to the river which had risen by more than the height of a man, drowning the trunks of the mangroves, covering boulders, behaving like an inland sea, where waves formed in wind-whipped crests. He carried a sharpened stave and wanted to spear fish, to silence the hunger they were suffering, but even he, who knew the Sadong in all its moods, could see that the current of the river was running so fast that it might easily sweep him away.

And Leon didn't want to die. He planned to make himself the manager of the cannery, overseeing all its construction work and then putting himself first in line to make money from it once it began exporting its tinned fish. He had dreams of these tins being shipped, not just to China, but carried north-westwards into Russia. He'd heard that people were poor there. He imagined them seated in the snow, eating turtle meat from Borneo and praising its quality and its freshness in a strange language.

Instead of fishing, Leon gathered wild figs and bamboo shoots on a platter of banana leaves and took these back to Taminah, who roasted them over her fire and the rajah remarked that this 'gibbon diet' was much to his liking and that he would plant more bamboos in his garden.

Every time Sir Ralph mentioned the disappearance of Edmund Ross, Leon reassured him that he would now be safely in the rajah's house. But the rajah also remembered him saying, when Edmund had arrived in his sickly state, that 'butterfly catchers', whose gaze was distracted by every bird or insect they saw, got lost in the forest very frequently. He'd suggested mockingly that this, in fact, was the state they deserved – being lost. For only in a condition of lostness did they see clearly what actually surrounded them. They became alert and vigilant. They were compelled to put aside the 'wrong Englung maps' of the country they carried in their heads and start to assemble new ones which did not lie to them.

Sir Ralph now pondered this bit of undoubted wisdom, but he also prayed that Edmund had not strayed too far from the path on the way to the cannery site and that when they eventually returned to the house, he would find him there. But he doubted it. He feared for Edmund's safety. Without a compass and with the huge rains falling, he might succumb quickly to cold and hunger, or he might trespass – a white man alone and in distress – into Dyak territory and risk being killed. He judged that all these possibilities had now entered Leon's mind and perhaps enthralled it. Leon had decided to feel jealous of the 'Jesus Boy'. He not only wanted him gone; he might be made cheerful by the prospect that Edmund Ross had suffered and died.

In the dim dawn light of Taminah's dwelling, Sir Ralph watched his lover sleeping. There was no part of his body which the rajah did not worship. He would have liked to sculpt him in marble, make some marvellous 'David' out of him. Yet he also knew that the workings of Leon's mind were almost entirely hidden from him, that a hatred of white men lurked somewhere deep inside him and that the Malay stayed with him, not out of any deep love or devotion, but because the sexual power he exerted over him could buy him a rich and fabulous life.

To distract himself from the desire he suddenly felt for Leon, whom he couldn't touch in front of Taminah, Sir Ralph rose up from his mat and crept to the door of the longhouse. He opened it quietly and went out onto the veranda and smelled the pungent perfume exhaled by the forest, rinsed and irrigated by the rain. A dawn mist shrouded the vegetation and he found the scene before him a thing of great beauty. The deluge had ceased. Little by little, the cries of birds began to be heard again.

The rajah sat down on an old wooden chair where Taminah spent long hours wondering what her life had signified and how, if she so wished, she might be rid of it. The mist moved in ghostly eddies as a breeze crept through the trees and a pale sun began to rise. At Sir Ralph's feet, Taminah's cockerels, huddled together in a bedraggled little group, woke up and shook their blue-black tail feathers in the sunlight, to dry them and restore to them the lustre of which the birds always appeared so proud.

The smallest of their number had been killed, plucked and roasted by Taminah the day before and, in their hunger, she, Leon and the rajah had torn and eaten every morsel of flesh from its bones. But now the rest of them came, one by one, to where the rajah sat and looked up at him, hoping for millet or a husk of maize, and he talked to them softly, telling them that he had nothing for them. And he thought how the entreaty of the birds mirrored all the thousand other requests which those he called *his people* made of him, and how, though he sincerely wished to give them what their hearts cried out for, he very frequently failed.

When they left Taminah's house, Leon suggested that they continue their journey to the proposed site of the cannery, but the rajah refused. He wanted to hurry home as quickly as the swampy ground would permit, to see if Edmund was there.

'He may not be there,' said Leon.

'You told me that he had decided to turn back. Where else would he go?'

'I cannot know rightly, my rajah. Perhaps he is there, perhaps he is not. I have seen foolish butterfly men turning in circles. They do not understand the forest. And Jesus cannot help him.'

They walked slowly, their feet often pulled down into the flooded earth, and when they reached the Savage Road they stopped. The long rains had now borne away almost all the tamped earth of its surface and it appeared to Sir Ralph a lamentable ruin, as though it had been laid down long ago by someone else and forgotten, a road which nobody travelled, a gathering of white stones testifying to the labour of a multitude of souls, but now devoid of any purpose or function.

In contemplation of his blighted road, the rajah felt a great weariness overcome him, a weariness that was not habitual in his life. He thought of himself as a man of unbounded energy, whose brain boiled with schemes and endeavours, whose blood never cooled, and who would soon begin to undertake the great adventure of the cannery, which would bring work and prosperity to his people. Now, he felt that merely overseeing the repair of his road was not only beyond him; it was pointless. Whatever works he put in place, they would always be at the mercy of the rains and the encroachment of the forest. These things were its enemy. Only his great iceberg of a house rose high enough and displayed an audacity sufficient to withstand the climate. He was in a frame of mind to wall himself up inside his outrageous palace and never move again.

The sun was shining on the house when Sir Ralph and Leon arrived there. Servants came running out, crying out a greeting to the master they had feared drowned in the storms. The rajah was moved by this and stood still on his steps and held out his arms and took them all into a wide embrace, while Leon stood back and watched the scene with a face devoid of expression. He had often instructed the Chinese houseboys who worked for the rajah not to kowtow to him; he was just an ordinary white man who had been given a dishonourable discharge from the Army of the East India Company, not a king or a god. But he recognised an uncomfortable truth: those who cleaned and cooked in the Savage House felt some deep affection for Sir Ralph, for which he could not really see any explanation.

With the greetings over and the cook running indoors to prepare food for the rajah's return, Sir Ralph began to enquire about Edmund. But he was told exactly what he feared, that Mr Ross had not returned.

After they had eaten and Sir Ralph had retired to his great curtained bed to sleep, Leon made his way to the room that had been occupied by Edmund. He folded back the raffia screen at the window and let sunlight fall upon the Turkey carpet – one of many the rajah had shipped from Constantinople, whose beautiful intricacies always troubled Leon for the arduous labour that had gone into them, as if he imagined that into the exquisite madders and carmines of the weave the blood of Asian children had been wantonly mixed.

Leon walked slowly round the room. As he moved, a lizard on the wall sped upwards and began clinging to the ceiling. The place was tidy, with Edmund's few possessions laid out on a mahogany writing desk. Leon went to the desk and saw that a half-finished letter lay there, held down by a jade paperweight.

Leon's ability to read English was not as good as he would have liked, but Sir Ralph was a patient teacher and Leon a willing pupil. He understood that English was the language of the rajah's secrets and the existence of these secrets made him feel small, so he worked hard on mastering reading and writing.

He sat down at the desk and stared at the letter. There were some words which he couldn't understand, but he could read the recipient's address at the top of the page:

Dr Valentine Ross,
31 Edgars Buildings,
Bath, England

The letter began '*My dear brother*', and went on to describe the rajah's house near Kuching and how it was a place unlike any Edmund had ever seen elsewhere in the Malay Archipelago. It then began to set out Edmund's frustrations at the loss of his collecting equipment and his anxiety at his diminishing supply of money. It broke off suddenly with the words *I hope to …*

What Leon kept returning to was the name 'Valentine Ross' and the address in Bath. In the revelation of these details, he glimpsed immediately how his own future might achieve the kind of magnificent alteration he frequently dreamed of. He took up the letter and went to his room and placed it out of sight under his sleeping mat.

THE GREAT MISTAKE

Edmund had stayed still for too long, watching the red ants, whose courageous convoy seemed to have no end. When he'd woken from his 'absence' with the ants to remember where he was, the rain was already drenching him and he looked around urgently for shelter. The thick canopy itself could afford some protection from the deluge, so he made his way to a patch of forest where no light seemed to fall and stood under the broad leaves of a tall banana tree. It always astonished him, the silence that descended upon the forest when the rains came. It sometimes felt to Edmund as though everything had died in the storm, except himself, kept sentient only by the workings of his stubborn English soul. But surviving such acute loneliness had always tested his inner strength to its limits. When he'd first arrived in Borneo, he'd felt so confused and alone that he had adopted an orphaned orang-utan and was consoled by its presence, and man and beast had clung together, like parent and terrified infant, when the rains fell and the voices of the jungle faded to silence. When the creature died – of some disease which Edmund had no power to cure – he buried it in a deep grave and laid on it a worn pair of gloves, as a symbol of human friendship.

After a while, as the deluge gathered force, and the sky darkened to a night-time blackness, he felt stupid standing under the tree, like a child punished by being told to stand in a cold corner of the room. He remembered a day when, as a boy of seven or eight, walking home from school to his parents' Wiltshire farm, he'd been caught in a thunderstorm and had crossed half a field of plough to stand under a broad-leaved oak. It was autumn and the leaves of the oak were yellowing and falling all around him.

He'd thought the storm might quickly pass, but it didn't pass. And it began to feel to the boy as though it would *never pass*, but slowly turn the field to flood and his skin to slimy pink liquid – and yet he didn't dare move. He remembered wishing that Valentine had been with him, to tell him what to do, but Valentine was away at his boarding school.

He'd thought of his mother, waiting at the door, casting terrified eyes on the sky and on the empty road beneath, and knew that he should run home along the narrow lanes turning to gullies, and that if he didn't move, he might die. But he was afraid to leave the shelter of the protecting oak. And then the darkness of evening had come on and he could see nothing except the faint glimmer of the rain, and he had begun to cry.

After a long time, he'd seen the light of a torch flickering in the lane and heard his father calling his name and he knew that he was saved. Yet still he clung to the rough bark of the tree, and his father, in his heavy farm boots, had had to make his way across the ploughed field and pick him up and carry him home in his arms.

Now, remembering this, as though it might have happened only a year ago, instead of two decades, Edmund asked himself how long he was going to stand where he was, with the rain now sliding off the banana leaves and splashing onto his shoulders. And something in him told him he would probably stand there, unmoving, until the rain ceased. But he also knew that it might not cease, that the day was slowly passing and the night would soon come, and he asked himself what he would do then.

He made some decisions about this, and yet he knew that these were fragile – the kind of decisions other men would have made and acted upon, but which he, Edmund Ross, would probably be unable to carry out. Some other man – his great hero, Alfred Russel Wallace, for instance – would perhaps have gone back to the fallen log and, by the wild illumination of the lightning flashes, been able to work out the right direction towards the path, from which he'd strayed to look at the *Papilionidae*. If he'd found this, then possibly the distant sound of the river, towards which he'd been walking with the rajah and Leon, might be heard above the storm and following this might guide him to wherever they were sheltering.

Alternatively, if he found the correct path, this other courageous person, this true explorer, might have been able to follow it all the way back to the Savage Road and thence to Sir Ralph's house, and then his life would quickly resume its purpose.

But Edmund, understanding that this person was not him, knew why he didn't move from under the banana tree: the pain of being lashed by the storm was no more terrible to him than that which he now endured perpetually, in mind and body. He could remember a time, not so far distant, when this agony had not been there, but since his illness, it had been almost constant in him – the knowledge of the slow collapse of his whole enterprise. He could not go on. He felt more dead than alive. And he saw, trailing behind him, the great mistake that had been his belief in himself as a true explorer, as a man who could endure loneliness and deprivation, who could understand how to exist in other people's worlds, how to suffer willingly for the sake of the discoveries he would make.

But he was not this man. He was too frail, too cowardly ever to become this man. What he longed for was to be on the Wiltshire Downs, searching for fritillaries and orchids among the springy grass. He wanted to lie down on a bed of chalky earth. When he tried to utter the word 'England' it invariably choked him with weeping.

He moved just a little – from a standing position to sitting down on the damp ground under the tree. He reached out with his hands and touched moss and sodden leaves and the tatters of dead banana fronds and small pellets of matter which might have been the droppings of flying squirrels or rats. He dreaded to light upon the body of a snake. He knew that snakes would slither out as soon as the rains ceased.

He ceased his exploration of the forest floor. He closed his eyes. He felt that he had travelled a road so long and so hard that all he could do now was to stay perfectly still, while admitting that its end had been reached. He was shivering violently and knew that perhaps his Malaria was returning, and again he thought of his brother, so safe in his world of medicine and frock-coated order, and wished that he, more than any other living soul, was by his side and would hold out his hand in mercy.

HEIRLOOM

A few days after Jane's return to Henrietta Street, as she came home for one of Mrs Morrissey's sustaining lunches, she found Clorinda in tears.

A feeling that, in a short time, the Irishwoman had become her friend led Jane to go to her and put a consoling arm round her shoulders. Clorinda dried her eyes on her apron and told Jane that it was nothing, 'just some awkward news from Ireland' and that she must hurry away now, back to the tea room.

Jane let her go, for it seemed to her that this was what Clorinda wanted, but she decided nevertheless to mention Mrs Morrissey's upset to her father, as the two of them delved into the mutton stew left for them on the dining room sideboard. And Jane saw that this news claimed Sir William's complete attention and that after hearing it he fell very silent and had difficulty finishing his meal. As he rose for his afternoon surgery, he said to Jane, 'I do not like it that Mrs Morrissey is unhappy. I will go down to Camden Street to see her after my last patient has left.'

'Shall I come with you?' asked Jane.

'No, no,' said Sir William. 'A kind offer, Jane. But I think it is best if I go alone.'

Jane looked searchingly at her father, but he would not hold her gaze, so she turned away and said nothing more.

Clorinda Morrissey went about her preparations for her afternoon service of tea in her usual efficient way, even remembering to give instructions for some damask table napkins, newly bought from

Tilney's, to be put out and to congratulate Mary on the lightness of her latest batch of scones. But this show of normality concealed, in Mrs Morrissey's heart, a fearful little worm of terror.

She had received a letter from her brother Michael in Dublin. Michael had related to her how his eldest daughter, Maire, now aged fourteen, had been suffering for some time from 'a malfunction of the thyroid gland, giving rise to terrible symptoms – a foul goitre on her neck and a strange diminution of her faculties of comprehension'. He told her in the letter that 'the only hope for Maire' was an operation to remove all or part of the thyroid, but that this operation would cost far more money than he, who worked as a clerk in the back offices of the Anchor Brewery, could afford.

He now came to the request which caused so much dismay to Clorinda Morrissey. He phrased it politely, but there was no mistaking the firmness of his resolve.

I truly hope you will agree to what I suggest, he wrote, *which is that the ruby necklace – which fell into your possession after our mother passed away, but which is an heirloom and therefore the property of all the family and not yours alone – now be sold and the profits divided up between us. I believe this will enable me to pay for Maire's operation and probably to save her life. Do not refuse me, Clorinda. Your letters, I am glad to note, relate a new prosperity you have found in Bath and so I assume that you – unlike myself, who have seen no rise in my wages for so long a time – have no pressing need of money. In the necklace, I think, resides the one and only hope for my suffering daughter and I am sure you would not betray me by keeping for yourself something precious which belongs to us all.*

At the time when she'd sold the necklace and, at a stroke, changed her life, Mrs Morrissey had given scant thought to its status as an heirloom. The word had been mentioned in her mother's will, yet it was also clear – and had been acknowledged by Michael – that the ruby necklace would fall into Clorinda's possession, in the expectation that the thing would reside where it had always resided, in some place of permanent concealment.

Had she, perhaps, felt more affection for Maire and her sister, she might have paused more thoughtfully before extracting it from its dark hiding place (an ancient tea caddy) and bringing it sparkling into the light. But the truth was that while Aisling struck her as being a sorrowful, unhappy child, for whom she felt some occasional pity, she found Maire very irritating: a dull and stupid-seeming girl, with all her thinking so constrained by Roman Catholic dogma that Clorinda had sometimes commented adversely to herself on Maire's 'faculties of comprehension' and was now disposed to tell her brother tartly that his eldest daughter's condition was 'not at all new'.

The knowledge that, as their aunt, she ought to have loved these children, but could not seem to manage it, did nothing to ameliorate the moral dilemma Clorinda now found herself in. She recognised that she had acted selfishly by taking all the profits from the sale of the rubies for herself, but she had then worked as hard as she had ever worked in her life to establish her tea room, now patronised by so many in Bath that tables had to be reserved in advance. More than this, Clorinda had been able to give work to two more helpers, Agatha and Bessie, thus bringing alteration to lives which were badly in need of it.

Surely, all this militated in favour of her high-handed decision to exchange a family heirloom for hard currency? In her mind, Clorinda still told herself that she had done nothing wrong – or at least not completely wrong; she had simply chosen a better life than the one she would have had. Who was in a position to say that she was not entitled to choose this? No one. And it had not really occurred to her that one day, within her lifetime, Michael might ask what had become of the rubies. Yet she saw now that she could not possibly let her niece die. Telling Michael that she had sold the necklace was going to be difficult enough and might bring forth from him a storm of rage and a sermon upon selfishness and materialism. This she could endure. What she felt was unendurable was that she should become the author of a tragedy in the Morrissey family.

She began to look around for solutions. She knew that she could offer to send money for Maire's operation, but would the savings she had been able to put away be enough to pay for this? She could, perhaps, admit to having sold the heirloom but lie about the sum she had received for it, setting down, as an example, the amount which the old pawnbroker had first offered her. But she was not very comfortable with this blatant untruth. And might her brother be so furious with her in any case, no matter what she had got for the necklace, that he would engage a lawyer to hound her? What – in Heaven's name – would be her financial position if he brought a legal case against her for appropriation of family property? What would become of her beloved tea room and all her marvellous endeavours? She *loved* her tea room. She was insanely proud of it. She thought it the most comfortable and consoling place in the world, and she could not bear the thought of losing it.

Sir William Adeane came hurrying down to Camden Street just after six o'clock.

He found a 'closed' sign on the tea room door, but knocked urgently upon it and, eventually, Clorinda appeared and opened it. When she saw Sir William, the tears which she had been holding back all afternoon in front of her clientele came forth in sudden abundance. She just could not help them. And Sir William could not help what he did next, which was to take Clorinda Morrissey in his arms.

While Mary and the other girls peered at them over the service counter, Sir William held Clorinda close to his chest and laid a kiss on her disordered hair. And the truth was, he felt like crying himself because this proximity to the adorable Mrs Morrissey was something which he had dreamed about for weeks and weeks and yet he had never attempted any approach to her, dreading to trespass upon the integrity of her person and upon unrequited feelings.

Now, of course, he wanted to kiss her mouth and when she threw back her head and looked at him, with her pink cheeks all asparkle with her Irish tears, she seemed to be challenging him to do just this. It was so long since Sir William had kissed anybody that he wondered if he remembered correctly how it was done, but he was not left to wonder for long, for Clorinda brought her lips to his and pressed herself more tightly to him. That they were half in and half out of the tea room doorway as they gave way to their sudden passion only caused Sir William divine amusement. It confirmed in his mind the belief that life, so often so cruel in the way it thrust the human soul into prisons from which there seemed to be no escape, could some-times place it athwart an open door.

That evening, at supper, Sir William told Jane that his life was 'just a little changed' and that he had it in mind, when the summer came, to make Clorinda Morrissey his wife.

Jane got up from the table and went to her father and kissed his cheek. She told him she could imagine 'no greater happiness' for him than this and that she and Clorinda would be 'the best of friends'.

'There is just one more thing,' he said. 'I must go to Dublin with Mrs Morrissey without delay. Clorinda's niece is in need of a difficult operation and I have agreed to perform it, without charge. It seems it may be a matter of life and death.'

'In that case,' said Jane, 'of course you must go.'

'I will not be away very long. You will keep the house while I am gone?'

'I will,' said Jane.

'You may be a little lonely,' said Sir William. 'I had thought Doctor Ross would have returned by now. But I have a letter from him, postmarked in Devon, in which he says he is making his way to Plymouth, in search of a ship to take him half across the world to join his brother in Borneo.'

'Is he really going there?' asked Jane blankly.

'Yes. I believe he is. He says he will endeavour to use his doctoring skills among the native people. It is a noble aspiration, but of course we will miss him here, will we not? He will be very hard to replace.'

'Yes,' said Jane, then returned silently to her chair.

MAGIC FROM UNDERGROUND

The moment Jane had taken in the news of her father's trip to Dublin with Mrs Morrissey, she sent an urgent letter to Julietta, telling her that she would be alone in the house for at least one week and that she would introduce Julietta 'to the wonder of the Baths and to all that might follow from your exquisite immersion'.

As she wrote, she asked herself in what state her feelings towards Julietta now stood. Though she had initially been dismayed to find herself back in Bath and had often been choked by desire for her lover, she realised that she had, in fact, slipped back into her old life with quiet ease. She had succeeded in ameliorating the pain suffered by Latimer to such a degree that he had declared himself capable of 'cracking the whip upon my painters and plasterers once more', and had fallen to his knees with gratitude towards Jane, clutching the hem of her white robe and pressing it to his lips. This little performance, though embarrassing at the time, together with her tender care of other patients, had brought back to Jane the idea that she did, in truth, possess healing powers beyond those the waters could give. And these feelings of mastery of the nursing art, of becoming once more the Angel of the Baths, calmed her longing to be elsewhere.

Now, however, turning her imagination to all that she might do with Julietta in Bath, she felt a veritable desperation to see her come upon her. When Julietta did not immediately respond to her letter, she sent a second one, begging her to appear 'on Tuesday evening and no later' – by which time Sir William and Clorinda Morrissey, now officially designated his fiancée, would be safely in Dublin, or if not quite there, then at least well embarked upon the Irish Sea.

Oh, Jane, came Julietta's reply, *you cannot imagine the difficulty I am in! No sooner had I told Ashton that I wished to take the waters in Bath and to spend some time with you than he immediately dubbed this a capital idea and insisted that he would accompany me. As you know, he has a great admiration for you and simply will not hear of my coming to Bath alone. More than this, he says he is very tired and in need of just such a rest-cure. So I could not possibly entreat him to stay at home.*

We will arrive on Wednesday and put up at an inn called The Bear (known, Ashton says, to Miss Austen, as she places Catherine Morland there in Northanger Abbey *– and I am now struck by the many, many bits and pieces of arcane knowledge with which publishers cram their minds …)*

Will you dine with us at the inn on Wednesday evening and then perhaps you will come for us on Thursday morning and escort us to the Baths?

From your dearest friend, Julietta Sims

Jane's vexation and disappointment was profound. She had been imagining the elixir of entire nights spent with Julietta, but now her frustration was going to be unbearable. She would be with her lover. She would gaze on her beautiful body immersed in the green waters of the Baths, but not be able to touch her or be touched by her. Her mind turned and turned upon ways in which she could lure Julietta to her bed, but she could not see how, with Ashton by her side, it could be done.

Confiding her frustrations to her diary, she then sat down and scribbled out a desperate note: 'I long for your l. O Julietta, I want to be your h again and put on my Paris "attire" and kiss you while I enter your c …'

But she did not send it. She did not admire the coarse-grained, needy person who had written it. She tore it into small pieces and distracted herself by selecting which dress she would put on for dinner with Ashton and Julietta.

When she made her way into the dining room of The Bear, much admired by repute in Bath, and saw Julietta seated at a candlelit table, with her dark hair piled in curls on her head and an opal choker encircling her neck, her first thought was that her lover appeared even more beautiful than she remembered. Jane's progress to the table, following the raised arm of the maître d'hôtel, stalled for a moment as her eyes took in the sight of her beloved and when she reached her side she knew that she appeared flushed.

Ashton stood up and kissed Jane's hand and said, 'We're honoured to be in Bath, dear Jane, and much looking forward to our drenching tomorrow.'

'Oh, my poor Ashton,' said Jane, 'you make it sound as though I was inviting you to stand out in the cold and rain!'

Ashton laughed and led Jane to her chair. Julietta's eyes, made large and soft by the candlelight, now rested on Jane's face and the two women nodded politely to each other, quite as if they had been strangers, their minds unencumbered by any secret knowledge.

Jane sat down and wine was poured for her and Ashton began talking about Guy Mollinet's novel, the translation of which he had undertaken himself.

'I am regretting it,' he said. 'Not because the novel is not very fine, but precisely because it *is*. It is my own work that I am finding poor.'

'Well,' said Jane, 'I have always supposed that translation is a difficult art. Anything which is near to perfection has great trouble in becoming something else. Does the way forward not consist of breaking up the language into shards and reassembling them in a different but poetical way?'

'There you are, Ashton!' said Julietta. 'Jane has solved it for you at one stroke. Perhaps you are too afraid of breakage?'

'Yes,' said Ashton. 'Jane is right. I think I am. I'm following too slavishly a word-for-word journey with it, and this is not working.'

'Is it not possible,' asked Jane, 'that Julietta, with her knowledge of Italian construction as well as French, might help you?'

'Oh no,' said Julietta, 'I have not the time nor the patience. I am honour-bound to spend a portion of each day on completely trivial things, such as the purchasing of table napkin rings, and the rest of it playing with Marco. Is that not so, Ashton?'

'I don't know,' said Ashton. 'What you do with your day has always been your own affair. Do you not think that is the secret of a happy marriage, Jane, not prying too much into each other's day-to-day business?'

'I cannot say, dear Ashton,' said Jane. 'I am not any kind of authority on marriage, for I have no experience of it.'

'Ah yes,' said Julietta, 'but perhaps you will have in the near future. This is partly why we are here, Jane, so that we can be introduced to the young doctor you talked to me about and see if he may be worthy of you. I have taken the liberty of telling Ashton all about him.'

'So she did,' said Ashton. 'But she told me that you didn't wish to consider his suit. Will you remind us what his name is?'

Jane now turned her gaze away from Julietta and looked down at the menu which had been placed in front of her. Some dishes listed there were written in French and Jane's heart was whipped by a longing to be in Paris, eating at the Café Anglais and savouring the exquisite idea of the following morning spent in bed with her lover.

'His name is Valentine,' said Jane quietly. 'I find it a foolish name. But it no longer signifies. He has gone away.'

'Where has he gone?' said Julietta.

'To join his brother, who is a botanist and travels the world and who lives by procuring rare species of plants and insects for Kew Gardens.'

'Plants and insects?' said Julietta. 'What a peculiar idea. Where is he intending to find them?'

'I believe he is headed for the Malay Archipelago.'

'Oh good gracious!' said Julietta. 'Where on earth is that?'

'The Far East: the other side of the world.'

'How vexing. You mean we shall not see him?'

'None of us will see him,' said Jane.

When, the following morning, Julietta and Ashton arrived at the Baths, to be met by Jane, they were accompanied by their five-year-old son, Marco and his Nanny, Miss Paley.

Struck by the beauty of Marco, who much resembled his mother, Jane knelt down and asked him whether he was looking forward to his immersion.

'No,' said Marco, 'because I am a bit afraid of water, aren't I, Mama?'

'Just a little,' said Julietta, 'but I will hold you up, and Jane, who is known as the Angel of the Baths, will watch over you.'

'Oh, and more than this!' said Jane, taking Marco's little hand in hers, 'for I will tell you a secret, Marco. Come closer and let me whisper it. The water here is not ordinary water; it is *magic* water. The moment you get into it, you will start to feel very warm and happy.'

'Will I? Why is it magic?'

'It's very hard to tell, because it comes from deep under the ground. We can't *see* its magic; we can only feel it.'

'How will I feel it?'

'Well, I think you may feel it in your toes, like a lovely tingling feeling, and then in your legs and then it will creep upwards and upwards until you feel it everywhere in you – even on the tip of your nose.'

Marco laughed. He touched his nose, which Jane saw was a small and very perfectly formed little nose. She realised that she felt an instant and profound tenderness towards this boy and when he asked her if *she* would be the one to hold him up in the 'magic water' she felt that she couldn't refuse him.

So it was that, instead of standing on the edge of the Hot Bath, Jane found herself wearing a cotton shift, side by side with Julietta in the translucent warm bath, holding Marco in her arms. At first the boy clung to her very hard, but then he told her that he was starting to feel some 'magic' in his feet and began to reach out with his arms, so that he could feel it 'everywhere'. Jane let him lie just under the surface, holding his head up and keeping him aloft but letting him splash out as he wished, and he began laughing with joy.

Julietta moved alongside them now. Her hair, piled up on her head with a slippery comb, began to fall free and streamed about her shoulders, and these floating tresses, together with the way her soft shift clung to her body under the trembling light and shadow on the water gave her the appearance of a mermaid, and Jane thought that she would carry in her mind this vision of her lover all the way through her life. A violent yearning to be with her absolutely, to kiss her and hold her risked taking hold of Jane and make her weak with longing, but she fought it off because of the boy, because the moment belonged to him, because the boy was a wonderful being who was now invaded by the 'magic' Jane had evoked and was finding the courage to embrace the element that had once made him afraid.

THE *RAINSFORD*

He had got this far.

Now, the tumult of the Plymouth wharves surrounded Ross and he was jostled for'ard and jostled aft, not knowing which way he was heading, but driven along by the great tide of commerce, incoming and outgoing, which was both the pride of a maritime nation and a living manifestation of her mercantile heart.

On every face – whether fishmonger or costermonger, carpenter or sail-maker, quayside drab or Jack Tar – he saw the animation of *purpose.* Everybody, it seemed to him, appeared convinced of the importance of the expeditious moment, their hearts bursting with anxious fervour for whatever small errand or mundane task drove them on. In Bath, by contrast, Ross mused, people walked about the city at a slow pace, with, on their faces, an expression of mild vacancy, as though they thought of themselves primarily as models for their clothes, or as if they were slightly surprised to find themselves there at all.

He stopped at a stall selling oranges, bought a single fruit and asked to be directed to the Harbourmaster's office. The orange-seller was a plump and kindly-seeming woman of fifty. Of the Harbourmaster she said: 'You be wary of his temper, Sir. He's much prone to apoplexy!'

'Thank you for telling me,' said Ross, 'but why should this be so?'

'Lord above knows! They say he suffers from colic. And he's too much pestered – by the likes of you, asking questions and more questions. I suppose you're looking to get aboard a ship, are you?'

'I'm trying to join my brother,' he said, 'beyond Singapore.'

'Beyond Singapore? The antipodes, you mean?'

'The islands of Malaya.'

'Oh. Well you won't find a ship in Plymouth going *there*. His Excellency the Apoplex will laugh you out of the room!'

'I know. I will have to disembark at Singapore and find some other, native craft to take me to Borneo.'

'Heavens alive, Sir! Know you how that is to be done?'

'By asking about, I presume.'

'Not at all. *Asking about* will bring derision upon you, if that is all you propose to do. Take silver in your purse and be prepared to spend it.'

Ross thanked the orange-seller for her 'excellent advice' and made his way to the Harbourmaster's office, a grand building which fronted the quays and from which the Apoplex could survey the tide of commerce beneath him and the waves which broke so dangerously near its feet.

The man was standing, his shoulders hunched over a heavy ledger on a tall desk. He didn't turn round when Ross was brought in by the clerk, but continued with his work, as though the interruption hadn't happened. Only when Ross announced himself again as 'Doctor Ross' did the Harbourmaster put down his pen and say, 'Medical doctor, or academic pretender?'

'Medical, Sir,' said Ross.

'Right then, state your business. Then you can examine my piles. See how I must work – standing up? My knees ache and my ankles swell, but I can't sit down on my bottom on account of the cursed haemorrhoids.'

'Are there no doctors in Plymouth who can help you?' asked Ross.

'Ships' doctors. All charlatans. They know how to prevent scurvy, but they are no use to me.'

'But you have consulted them?'

'All they try to give me is a vicious salve. It burns the skin but does not cure. Now tell me what you want of me and be succinct. The morning flurries on.'

Ross explained his desire to get aboard a ship bound for Singapore. When the name of the port was mentioned, the Harbourmaster said, 'I was there once. Beautiful women, by God. You can trade a tin tea kettle for a satisfying debauch in Singapore. Is that why you wish to go there?'

Ross quietly explained that he was going in search of his brother, for whose life he feared. This less colourful reason for his journey seemed to bore the Harbourmaster, who returned for a moment to his ledger before announcing that a brig, the *Rainsford*, carrying cargo, but accepting 'passengers of good standing', would leave for Australia in two weeks' time and make port in Singapore 'before the end of summer'. He added that the *Rainsford* was even now being refitted for her voyage and that Dr Ross was welcome to 'inspect the conditions prevailing aboard' if he so wished. He pointed to the furthest end of the harbour wall, where Ross was able to see the two masts of the brig and notice tiny figures aloft in her tangle of rigging.

'That's the *Rainsford*,' he said. 'Not a bad ship. Built for war – a fighting vessel. Now she's tamed down. Carries a cargo of rum and fancy goods for the antipodean taste. And the owners never overload her, they don't want Sheffield plate and Stoke pottery at the bottom of the ocean, so she sits right on her Plimsoll. You'll be safe on her.'

'I believe you, Sir.'

'Right. I will book a cabin for you, Doctor Ross, subject to your ability to make the requisite down-payment. She sails in fifteen days, tides and weather permitting. But forgive me, before we come to money, I must without delay get the breeks down and show you my Great Suffering.'

With the sight of the Apoplex's anus still raw in his mind, Ross was now being helped to clamber up a rickety gangway to the lower deck of the *Rainsford* by one of the ship's carpenters, a pleasant-faced man with pads on his knees and a smell of linseed oil on his clothes. Ross was advised to tread carefully about the ship 'on account of holes and traps all over the place where our repairs are unfinished'.

He was shown to the berthing deck, where the passengers would be housed in sleeping quarters designed mainly for the ship's officers. He opened the door of a tiny cabin and noted the narrowness of the bunk in which he would spend an endless number of nights. He took in, too, the darkness of the space and tried to anticipate his future acceptance of these conditions, telling himself that his life, in its disappointments, had made him small, and that a lightless hutch on an old ship of the line was probably an appropriate place for him.

But what troubled him more than the low, cramped cabin was the smell that pervaded the berthing deck. It was a sickly stench which Ross likened to the stink of rotting flesh and he wondered whether the crannies of the vessel were blighted by dead vermin which had lain there since its last voyage. He turned to the carpenter, who, perhaps noting that some of the colour had drained from Ross's face, gestured to the floor of the cabin and said, 'what you can smell, Sir, is the ballast. Sand and gravel. Innocent enough, sand and gravel, but whatever is lowest in a ship, where the ballast lies, down into that place seeps all the filth and spills, all the vomit and foul water left unmopped from the decks above. We call it the "graveyard whiff" or more properly "the mephitic".'

'I see,' said Ross.

'I thought I wouldn't get used to it. I thought it would make me ill, but it didn't – no more than the roll of the vessel. Two or three days out into the open sea and you don't notice it any more.'

'I'm glad of that.'

'But, if you don't mind my asking, Sir, why does a man like you – a doctor, you told me – want to leave the safety of our own sweet land?'

Ross asked the carpenter if they might walk up to the quarterdeck, where the mephitic might be less troubling, and when they got there, Ross sat down on a wooden chest which looked as though it might contain guns or ammunition, and took some gulps of the salty Plymouth air. Finding the orange still in his hand, he put this to his nose and comforted himself with its bittersweet scent.

The carpenter wiped his brow with an oily rag and stood at Ross's side, looking back over the ship's rail at the fervent life coming and going along the quayside.

'In answer to your question,' Ross began, 'you ask me why I want to leave what you called "our own sweet land" but let us consider, here in Plymouth, whether it is really so sweet. What I observe in everybody I see here is that they are driven and distressed by commerce, reaching after this thing or that thing and never resting or at peace.'

The carpenter smiled. 'If you don't mind my saying, Sir, how are you in a position to know that your "observations" are correct? Might a man not find what you term "peace" in humble trades, such as selling oysters – the smell and beauty of them, the money he will get? And take me. I may be an ordinary man, a low man, but I love my work. A perfectly crafted tongue-and-groove alignment can bring me wondrous happiness.'

Valentine Ross spent another two nights in Plymouth before returning to Bath. He walked about the town, not with any destination in mind, but going in wider and wider circles away from and then back towards the *Rainsford*, trying to reconcile himself to the moment, two weeks hence, when he would set foot upon this ship and be carried away towards an unknown life.

Visions of himself walking the decks of the great brig, travelling south into warm latitudes, becoming accustomed to the infinite horizon, to new stars in the sky, to the miles of lightless water beneath him alternated with moments of physical paralysis, when he would find himself stopped in his tracks by a different imagining, a vision of Jane Adeane in her white dress – tall Jane, *his* Jane, the only woman he would ever love. Always, she was walking towards him and on her face was a serene smile and she held out her arms, as if to beckon him to her, and then when he reached her, she was no longer there.

MIDNIGHT

Towards the end of his journey back to Bath, Ross found himself disconcerted by the smell of his own body. It was as if the mephitic stink of the *Rainsford* still clung to him, or else had insinuated itself into his nose so completely that with every breath he took he was forced to inhale it again.

Arriving late in the town, he went to his lodgings, found fresh clothes and took up the keys to the Baths, which, as a doctor, he had the right to visit after they'd closed for the night. The thought of the soothing waters of the Hot Room was so consoling to him that he found himself pacing fast through the streets in his impatience to get there.

Now, he stood naked at the edge of the bath and paused for a moment. In the midnight dark, with one candle lit in a sconce, its fragile light making tiny loops of brightness on the water, the place appeared magically beautiful to him and he entered into the warm depths with feelings of relief and gratitude. He immersed himself completely, not minding if the water stung his eyes. He stayed very still for a long moment, then slowly surfaced.

He rubbed his face and looked down the length of the bath. He'd assumed that he was quite alone there, but now he saw that, at the far end, just visible through the steam which rose from the heated water, there was a shadowy figure standing silently, watching him.

At once, his own nakedness embarrassed him. He'd spurned the conventional white shift which bathers were commanded to put on because he'd assumed that no one would be at the Baths at this late hour and because he wished every cranny of his face and body to be cleansed of the stench of the *Rainsford*. But he decided not to worry about this. He counted on the darkness and the steam to conceal his body and began, gently, to rub his skin clean. No doubt, he thought, the other man is a doctor – and what did nakedness signify to doctors, who habitually saw not just the whole exterior of a man, but something of his *interior*, too?

Then, by the disturbance of the bath, he realised that the stranger had begun to swim towards him. He rubbed his eyes. The candle flickered and almost went out, but flared up again more brightly. And in this instant of brightness Ross saw that the person coming nearer and nearer to him was Jane. She swam strongly. Her hair, plaited into a simple braid, caressed the sleeve of her shift. Ross blinked in awe and disbelief. That he should meet her here, in the deep midnight, in his nakedness, was so unlooked for, so wonderfully strange, that he almost felt like breaking into laughter. He called out her name.

She stopped swimming and stood still, some distance from him, regarding him with what he thought was a smile.

'Doctor Ross,' she said. 'You are returned.'

'Yes.'

'I am glad,' she said.

He was made flustered by the word she'd chosen. Glad? Was she resorting to teasing him straight away, before they had even had the chance to see each other clearly, or had she discovered, in their long absence, some genuine vestige of her former regard for him – before the disaster of the tea room proposal? Whichever it was, Ross didn't know what more to say to her. It was as if, having held her for so long in his mind, a beautiful ghost, the object of his fantasies and his sorrow, he was unable to communicate with the real Jane.

'I won't come any closer,' Jane said, 'for I think you have left all your clothes in a distant rainforest, and you would not want me to take advantage of that.'

He made no reply. It was as if Jane had emptied his mind of words.

She spoke again. 'By this light,' she said, 'the place is full of wonder, is it not? Does it not feel to you as though we were swimming in a dream?'

'It does.'

'And in dreams, everything may defy normal expectation. Is that not right?'

'Yes.'

'So if I were to come closer, if I were to ... but no, I can read your face in the dark. You would not want that. I will take my leave.'

Jane turned about and began swimming away from Ross. He watched her go. He felt too stunned by the encounter to call her back. Part of him was still refusing to believe that she was actually there at all. If he had not been naked, perhaps he would have swum after her, but he couldn't do this. He stayed very still, staring at her slow passage through the water. When she reached the end of the bath, Jane mounted the steps and went away.

Though he was tired – not just from the journey, but by all his lonely wanderings in the West Country, by the sight of empty hillsides and tides in turmoil and the terror of ships – Ross didn't go to bed, but sat by a yellow lamp in his rooms at Edgars Buildings, smoking a cheroot and wondering what – if anything at all – had just happened to him.

What he knew he would not be able to withstand would be a *pretence* by Jane Adeane to feel some regard for him, only for her to reveal within a short time that this was not the case. Even if he wasn't reconciled to the fact of her indifference, he had at least grown used to it, as if to a bruise on his chest, and he'd formed the hope that the bruise would eventually fade. He'd half believed that once he'd set foot on the island of Borneo and was reunited with Edmund he would – almost – cease to think of her.

Now, she'd swum towards him in the candlelit dark of the Baths, her words and gestures seeming to reach out to him in a seductive fashion. Or had he misread these? Was she simply choosing to welcome him back in an intimate way that merely took account of their old friendship? When the morning dawned, would she once again be cold and distant?

He thought this the most likely probability. But supposing she was not? Supposing her feelings towards him *had* changed, then what would become of his resolution, so arduously arrived at, to quit one life for another in a distant world?

To try to stop thinking about Jane, Ross summoned images of his brother. He imagined him sitting by an open fire, examining the butterflies he'd captured, then pinning them, in all their gorgeous colours, to his cork boards and rejoicing in their beauty. Above Edmund, a different constellation of stars moved slowly across the sky towards a cloudless morning.

Oh, my dearest one, Jane wrote to Julietta by a midnight candle, *it was the strangest thing you could imagine. I am just returned from the Baths. I took myself there in the darkness, hoping this would still the torment of longing for you and help me to sleep, and who should I find there, naked as a savage, but poor Valentine!*

Because I can't conceal anything from you (and because even now I am still thinking of all the places where I want to kiss you and be kissed by you) I will admit that I was indecently pleased to see him. I'd thought that he was quite lost to me, on some foolish expedition to find his brother in the Far East, but when I saw him, all your words and all Emmeline's words about trying to make a life with him came back to me. And I saw their logic. So I think that this is what I must decide to do now: bring Valentine Ross back to me, stir up his passion, and have him once more within my grasp.

And then, who knows?

Since I met your beautiful Marco, I have thought how much I would like to have a child of my own. Ross is handsome enough and an excellent physician and I believe he would be a kindly father . . .

Well, you see how my mind is tending?

But, oh my dearest, because I love YOU, there are limits, I know, to what I will ever be able to feel for him, or for any man. Whereas for my poor Valentine, I believe there are no limits. So by calling him back to me, am I not acting dishonourably?

Tell me, Julietta . . . tell me if I am behaving like a selfish witch, or only as we women must behave to stay afloat and not sink into invisibility and wretchedness in a world where men wish to make all the rules.

From your adoring friend, Jane

COMPLICITY

Early in the morning, Jane was woken by the urgent ringing of the doorbell.

She pulled on a silken robe and rushed to answer. The sight which greeted her was troubling. A carriage was driving off, but its former occupant, Mr Latimer lay prostrate on the steps of 28 Henrietta Street. The glue merchant's wife was bending over him, unable to stifle her sobbing but yet endeavouring to rally her husband, addressing him as 'Mr Latimer', quite as though this odd formality might be the very thing to stiffen his weakened sinews.

'Mr Latimer,' she wailed, 'for pity's sake, try to rise up, for I cannot lift you, all lean and thin as you have become ...'

Jane asked Mrs Latimer what had happened and the woman reached up to her and pleaded, 'Help us, Miss Jane! Mr Latimer was in the hospital, but this morning I was summoned there because he was crawling round on the floor, among all the unmentionable mess, asking for a chaise to bring him here. And when the nurses tried to restrain him, he attempted to strike them. He was crying out that only you could save him.'

Jane knelt down and used all her considerable strength to hoist Mr Latimer's inert form into her arms. His head, which seemed to her shrunken in size, lolled on her shoulder. Jane carried him into the house and laid him on the couch in Sir William's surgery. His body was very cold. His eyes rolled in their sockets. Instructing Mrs Latimer to fetch a blanket from an oaken chest, Jane put a steadying hand on Mr Latimer's cheek and leaned towards him until her face was close to his. His breath was sour and all colour had drained from his cheeks.

For a moment, Jane wondered if he had died in those brief moments when she was carrying him between the front door and the surgery, but no, his eyes still moved and when they focused on Jane, his mouth moved, trying to form words. But he could not form them. The attempt seemed to choke him and he coughed up some phlegm, dyed pink with blood.

'Mr Latimer,' said Jane, gently wiping the blood from Latimer's chin, 'you are at Henrietta Street. You are safe with me. I am going to make up a balsam for your lung and then you will breathe more easily.'

'No use,' whispered Latimer, 'too late.'

'No,' said Jane firmly. 'It is not too late. Now here is your dear wife, who will hold your hand while I prepare the balsam. Then you will see what excellent properties it contains …'

'Properties?' said Latimer.

The faint suggestion of a smile moved the corners of Latimer's mouth, and she felt the pathos in the fact that the word 'properties' had snagged at his heart. He gaped beseechingly at Jane, as if to say 'let me live! Let me inhabit my new property and rejoice in its perfectly crafted sash windows, its floral ceiling roses!' She knew that it was said in Bath that if you could hold the gaze of the Angel of the Baths for long enough to feel its power, then you might be cured by this alone. Yet Jane now realised that, since meeting Julietta, she herself was easily distracted, and could feel her own impatience to turn away from the stare of strangers.

She left Latimer's side, while his wife dried her tears and came to take hold of his pale hand. She went to the table where Sir William attended to what he called his 'chemical magic' and took down a vial of almond oil. For the balsam, she would need boiling water. Becky was not yet awake, so Jane descended quickly to the kitchen to put a kettle on the range. While she waited for the water to boil, she heard the front door open above. When she returned to the surgery with the bowl of hot water, Jane saw Valentine Ross standing at Mr Latimer's bedside.

Jane nodded a 'good day' to Ross and he inclined his head. In the kitchen, Jane had tied one of Becky's aprons round her silken dressing gown and she was glad of this now, to help maintain her modesty in the morning light, but she was aware that her legs and feet were bare and she saw that Ross couldn't help glancing at these, as she mixed her balsam.

'What do you think, Doctor Ross?' she asked. 'It is my own opinion that a tincture of bitter almonds will relieve much congestion in Mr Latimer's lung and then he will be more at ease.'

Ross did not reply directly to her, but only nodded and then bent down towards Latimer and raised him up, placing cushions at his back, so that he could bend over to breathe in the steam from the almond infusion.

To put the bowl on Latimer's lap, Jane had to move very close to Valentine Ross. The scent of his body (or perhaps it was just the scent of his clothes?) she recognised as if from long, long ago, as though it had been part of her childhood and she had always known it and liked it. She asked Ross to hold the bowl steady while she placed a towel over Latimer's head, put a gentle hand on his neck and told him to breathe deeply of the pungent steam. But he could not breathe deeply. He could only gasp. The vapour whirled about his face and his open mouth tried to capture it, like a child might try to capture falling snowflakes, but he could inhale very little.

This sight of her husband moving his gaunt visage this way and that, under the towel, attempting to take the balsam into him, brought his wife to another spasm of weeping and she began to babble that she had been brought out of a 'poor family' by Latimer and given a good life.

Jane supposed that she thought Latimer couldn't hear what she was saying because of the towel, for she ran on into a great storm of explanation of Latimer's wealth, saying that he had been unfairly derided for his glue factory, but that glue 'holds things together and how would society fare, indeed, if those things that needed to be attached to each other came apart?'

Neither Jane nor Ross said anything to this, but Mrs Latimer continued: 'All our lives, we had to suffer the taunting that we got our money from making stews of animal bones, but everything is made of something. What is a leather bag but cow hide? What is in a pillow but down plucked from geese? It was never fair to us.'

Ross said, 'It was surely never fair, Mrs Latimer. But most of what mankind attempts suffers derision from one quarter or another. There are those – very many, indeed – who deride doctors. They want us to be all-knowing, but we are not. The diseases of the body and mind are infinite and we lag far behind.'

'But what about you, Miss Jane?' asked Mrs Latimer. 'I was told you could work miracles, but you have not saved Mr Latimer.'

'He will live a while yet ...' said Jane.

'But not long enough! Our new house is almost ready, but he will never see it, never stand at an upper window and look down ...'

She wept again. Meanwhile, Latimer seemed to be in acute distress, struggling to breathe and giving voice to a howl of pain.

'Let him lie back,' said Ross to Jane. 'I will take the balsam away and bring laudanum.'

Ross removed the bowl and went out of the room, to his own surgery, which he had not occupied for a long while. Jane wondered briefly what his feelings would be upon finding himself there – whether the familiar room and all that it contained of his life would call to him and beg him to stay in Bath. But she had to give all her attention to Latimer now. The poor man was shivering and crying out, struggling for air, and a tiny rope of blood progressed steadily from the corner of his mouth down his chin. Jane kept wiping this away. She arranged the blanket more snugly round Latimer and his wife took off her own shawl and laid it on him. She sought to hold his gaze as she bent over him, but his eyes wandered and could not come to rest on anything.

'He is going,' said Mrs Latimer. 'He is going, Miss Jane ...'

Jane put her hand on Latimer's neck and could still feel a pulse, but she thought that his wife was right: he was dying. She heard the hall clock strike seven and was visited by the thought that it was strange to die at a moment when a new day was just beginning, when the people of Bath were travelling to work, when the errand boys were setting off on their deliveries, when the rich sat in their parlours and perused the *Bath Chronicle*, searching for news of their investments, when, in London, the Queen would be busy gobbling down a third helping of her favourite breakfast dish, Kedgeree ...

She also wished that Ross would return with the laudanum. When he did, she decided that she would signal to him to let Latimer drink it all. That way, the terrible last moments of his life would be passed, not in the agony he was suffering now, but in a soft darkness, or even in a dream of what that life had been, lived mainly among splendour and warmth and the sound and stink of a great factory alchemising bones into money.

When Ross came back, Jane left Latimer's side for a moment, to whisper her thoughts about the laudanum to him and he replied that he had already arrived at the same decision.

It was with some difficulty and slowness that Latimer swallowed the brandy and opium, but he managed it at last and its properties appeared to work very quickly in his afflicted system and his body ceased its struggles and his breathing became quieter. His eyes closed. Mrs Latimer laid her head next to his on the pillow and Jane and Ross could hear her tunelessly singing the words of a little Music Hall song:

> '*My sweetheart's name is the sound of the sea*
> *And his arms are my ship of rest*
> *His voice is the breeze which sings to me*
> *And tells me I'll ne'er be lost.*'

Jane and Ross moved away from the bed and sat down, either side of Sir William's desk, like patient and consultant, with Jane in the consultant's chair. They didn't speak, but only looked at each other with an enquiring kind of look, knowing they had been complicit in hastening Latimer's approaching end and silently asking each other whether any mortal sin was being committed.

STRANGER

To find herself once again in Dublin troubled Clorinda Morrissey far more than she had anticipated. She told her fiancé that 'it is as if everything which had once been familiar and dear to me has decided that I am *no longer dear to it*.'

'What can you really mean?' asked Sir William.

'Well,' said Mrs Morrissey, 'I turned my back on Dublin. Now, it rewards me by making me feel like a stranger from Canada.'

'Canada, my dear?'

'Yes. I mean like one who comes from very far away and recognises nothing and does not know the correct meaning of anything.'

She couldn't explain it more clearly than this. She knew, however, that her feeling of being shunned, or even disliked by her native city might have been brought about, not just by her desertion of it, but by the guilt she had begun to feel on the subject of the Morrissey heirloom.

Her brother Michael and his family lived in a tenement flat on Bishop Street, a road of once-handsome brick houses with Dutch-gabled roofs, now fallen into disrepair and having about it a feeling of peculiar emptiness, as though the wind which blew in off the river was intent upon turning everything that existed there to dust.

Clorinda knew this street quite well. In daylight, a few children played in the road, chalking out Hopscotch games or giving each other rides in an old baby carriage, their little legs hanging over the edge and their stout boots kicking the dented wickerwork. The bell of the Rag-and-Bone Man could sometimes be heard in the early evenings and shadowy figures might come out from the doorways, to see what they could sell to him for a few ha'pennies. But mainly the street felt like a place which a catastrophe had once visited, leaving behind it a feeling of anxious vacancy.

The Morrissey flat was small and cluttered with all the cheap household furniture which Michael and his wife Kathleen had bought for it over the years, now collapsing slowly where it stood, the table propped on wood blocks, a blanket chest gnawed by worm, a larder cupboard nailed up with broken chicken wire. Soot from the coal range blackened the ceiling and tainted the air. Toys Michael had made for his girls from bits and pieces of pine and plywood lay about the floors and got under everybody's feet. Mice fretted behind the skirting boards.

There were two bedrooms and in one of these Maire and her sister Aisling slept. Since Maire's illness, Aisling, too, had been in torment, kept awake night after night by her sister's snores and by her crying. One evening, she had crept down to the street and climbed into the baby carriage abandoned near the tenement door and tried to sleep in that, with her feet splayed out against the handle.

When Michael found her like this, he understood that things couldn't go on as they were. By some means, he had to find the money for an operation for Maire. He had to give them all hope in a better future. He stood in the empty street, looking down at Aisling's eleven-year-old limbs contorted in the attitudes of an exhausted sleep and it was at that moment that he remembered the ruby necklace.

Told that his sister would bring her 'fiancé', a renowned surgeon, to Dublin to operate on Maire free of charge, Michael felt confused. He knew, without needing to be told, that Clorinda felt little for her nieces, that her successful business in Bath had taken her very far away from Ireland and from the family, and the feeling that she had to pay some price for this – for a kind of betrayal of her Irish roots and her blood relations – was disinclined to leave him. But what kind of price? To press her about the heirloom – which he now reasoned, *must* have been sold to establish her tea room – seemed a good way to begin her punishment. Perhaps it would end with that, or perhaps it would not?

Now, he wasn't sure what to do. He could see that the offer she was making was generous. If Sir William Adeane were able to save Maire, then Clorinda would have to be forgiven and the moment, then, might seem inappropriate to a discussion of the ruby necklace. In Michael Morrissey's dreams, however, these things were strangely conjoined: the wound that would have to be made in Maire's neck; the circlet of blood-coloured jewels. To exchange one for the other had a symmetry about it which obstinately appealed to him.

But it soon transpired that Clorinda's plan would not work. For this life-or-death operation, Maire would need to be taken into hospital. It wasn't something which could be performed on a kitchen table. Michael Morrissey had hurried to the hospital to tell them that a great English surgeon, Sir William Adeane was offering to perform the procedure. But, the Dublin doctors, informed peremptorily that Sir William was proposing to colonise hospital staff and precious resources for his own use (and his own aggrandisement) chose the path of rebellion.

'How thoughtless,' they said, 'how very *English* of Sir William Adeane to believe that we would permit this!' But of course they would not permit it. If Sir William showed his face at the hospital door, he would be turned away.

Despite his anxiety for his daughter, Michael was not ashamed to admit to himself that he enjoyed giving this news to Sir William and seeing the disbelief on his face. The surgeon and Clorinda were seated in Michael and Kathleen's parlour at the time, where Kathleen had put a clean white cloth on the tea table, but the two girls just sat staring vacantly at their aunt and her ageing paramour. Maire plucked with nervous little hands at her goitre and Aisling, whose face wore an expression of deep sadness, played with a toy pig.

Kathleen stood at the doorway, as if ready to show the couple out before any tea had been taken. When the news descended into the sooty air, a silence fell over the room which was agonisingly complete.

But then, quicker than anybody could have predicted, Clorinda Morrissey stood up and said: 'this is of no significance. None at all. Sir William is one of the few surgeons who can perform this operation without endangering Maire's life, but *where* he performs it does not matter. We will take Maire with us to Bath. She can live with me until everything is made ready for the surgery, and when she has recovered enough to make the sea journey, I will bring her back.'

Michael looked over at Kathleen. Neither of them spoke. Sir William now rose up and put a protecting arm round Clorinda.

'There you are!' he said. 'There is the solution. What do you say, Maire? Would you like to go on a steamer to England? You would, wouldn't you?'

Maire did not answer. It was as if she had not understood what was being asked of her. Michael stared at his suffering daughter for a moment, then he said, 'perhaps it is a kind offer, but I really don't think this would be the thing at all. I can't have my daughter going to England. Since the famine—'

'Jesus, Mary and Joseph!' exploded Clorinda. 'Why be dragging the famine into this, when it's long past?'

'It may be long past, but nobody here has forgotten how England starved our people.'

'And now you would starve your own daughter of life rather than let it be saved in England?'

'I'm a man of principle – in case you have forgotten that, Clorinda. You may not remember the suffering in the forties ...'

'Of course I remember it. Didn't we go hungry ourselves? And sure, the English should have died of shame, but how would that have helped us? And now you're willing to sacrifice Maire to history, and I for one do not see the sense in that.'

Silence fell once more in the room. Kathleen moved a fraction further out of it. Sir William looked all around him at the drab parlour and noted one small item of value standing in a corner: a glass-fronted bookcase displaying a bone china tea service. This tea service tugged at his heart. He saw now – if he had not seen before – that Clorinda's life had been filled with deprivations and sacrifices of a kind he could not have imagined until this moment.

'I suggest,' he said, now chilled by the atmosphere in the room, 'that we leave you to think about this – about our taking Maire to

England – and that we return tomorrow and you can tell us what you have decided.'

'I made potato scones …' said Kathleen from the doorway.

'They will keep,' snapped Michael. 'You leave now, sister, but tomorrow we will discuss the matter I raised in my letter to you, but which you have not mentioned. We will discuss the necklace.'

FORGOTTEN STREETS

Clorinda woke early in her hotel room and, leaving a note under Sir William's door, went out into the city.

She walked to the river and saw the sun rise in a grey-green sky above the Liffey. As a child, she had liked to come and watch how the fishing trawlers and the merchant ships at anchor there moved all the time in the wind and how they pressed and bumped so closely against each other, as if they craved intimate companionship after their long, lonely voyages at sea.

In the scent of the river and in the sway of the ships – so it seemed to Clorinda – lay all the fabric of her distant past, and she breathed deeply of the salty air and let her eyes dwell on the leaning masts as the sun began to touch them. And it felt to her that here, in this bit of Dublin poised between returning and leaving, she was once again accepted as belonging to the great city and not shunned as one who had betrayed it.

She was grateful for the feeling of happiness and calm which this gave her. She remained a while longer, listening to the cry of gulls, watching life resume on the decks of the boats, as men were chivvied from their cramped sleeping places to swab decks, to sew shrouds, to mend fishing nets or to stow cargo: barrels of beer from the Anchor Brewery, where Michael was employed, bales of sheep's wool, livestock in crates and cages. She found herself glad of the way the commercial heart of Ireland – a place where suffering seemed, like rank weeds, to take root in every piece of cleared ground – kept stubbornly beating, of the witness it bore to *the continuation of life*, no matter what might arise to cast it down and make it cease.

And she resolved there and then that, blessed as she now was to be able to ask for Sir William's help, she *would* find a solution to the great matter of the necklace. And no, she would not give up her beloved tea rooms! Even in prosperous Bath, the human mind could find itself oppressed by care and sadness. Life was short and cruel. People needed places of sanctuary, islands of warmth and calm. She had opened a door on such a place and she would not close it now.

Later that morning, when they were back in the Bishop Street tenement, confronted now by Michael and Kathleen, but not by the children, who were in school, Clorinda and her fiancé listened quietly while Michael accused his sister of 'purloining the only thing of value this benighted family has ever possessed'.

'What do you say to that, sister?' Michael pressed on. 'And bear in mind that I will know by your face if you are lying to me.'

'I will not lie to you, Michael,' said Clorinda calmly. 'You were aware that I took the necklace, when our Mam died. I kept it safe for a long while, as I knew I must, but the only means by which I could start my business in Bath was to sell it. Here is the Bill of Sale.'

From a little beaded purse which Sir William had given her, Clorinda produced the document from the jewellers and handed it to her brother. He reached into a worn pocket for his spectacles and put them on. His hands shook as they held the paper.

'It was a simple exchange,' Clorinda went on, 'a transaction which transformed something which had been hidden in the dark for generations into a place of shelter and light.'

She saw Kathleen peer over Michael's shoulder. His shaking hand showed her the large sum, written in both figures and letters, which had been paid to his sister and then they looked up and stared at her and she thought it was the kind of stare a judge might give to some felon on whom he had just passed sentence.

'A place of shelter and light?' Michael burst out. 'What, in God's name, is *that* pretentious rubbish? You've committed daylight robbery and we will employ a man of the law who will hound you until you pay us our share.'

'That's right,' said Kathleen. 'Michael knows a law fella who works for the Brewery, don't you, Michael?'

'Indeed I do. And he will be willing to serve notice on you.'

'As I expected,' said Clorinda, 'except there will really be no need of your "man of the law", Michael. We will agree to divide the sum shown on the Bill of Sale and I will pay what I owe you.'

'How in the world are you to do that?'

At this moment, Sir William stood up. In his black frock coat, with his white hair, he might almost have been Michael Morrissey's 'man of the law', suddenly arrived like an apparition in the mournful room.

'Let me explain,' he said, 'that Clorinda has been very prudent with the money she's made from her tea rooms. She has a sum put by. But because it does not reach the amount owing to you, I have told her that I will make this up from money earned at my practice, and she will repay me as and when she can. I trust this is satisfactory to you. It will mean that Maire can have her operation performed here in Dublin, by your own surgeons.'

Michael and Kathleen fell silent. They looked from the Bill of Sale to Clorinda, then to Sir William, then back to the Bill of Sale. And Clorinda felt that she knew what was in their minds: that the relief they felt about Maire was tempered with something else – by a feeling that the world was a pitiless place, in which some people prospered unfairly and others were left to suffer in a forgotten, silent street, where the wind was always strong. She and they were on opposite sides of that divide now and Clorinda knew that, whatever happened to Maire, she would never be forgiven.

When they left Bishop Street, the beauty of the early morning had vanished and rain was falling. Sir William looked around for a Hansom Cab but Clorinda doubted they would find one in this part of the city and said that she didn't mind an Irish rain; it was always a gentle thing.

So they walked on, arm in arm, at the slow pace Sir William favoured, their fine clothes beaded by the drizzle, their faces growing shiny and pink and Clorinda thought, as they went on, that she'd never enjoyed any walk more than this one. She felt, at last, reunited with her city, at one with the quiet streets and the rain. And towards Sir William she felt the greatest tenderness she had ever felt for any man.

When the sun came out again and they reached a small park where the berries on the rowan trees glowed a marigold orange, and where an organ grinder was playing an old song Clorinda remembered from her time working for a haberdasher, she knew that this was where she wanted to go before they left Dublin, to show Sir William the tiny shop with its drawers of ribbons and bindings, which had been her last lowly billet in the city of her birth before her momentous decision to leave.

But on the way to the haberdasher's, they found a Coffee Room offering 'Fine, true coffee from the Americas, No Added Ingredients' and they went in and sat down. Clorinda looked about her, measuring the Coffee Room in her mind against her tea room. She ran her hand across the wooden tabletop and said: 'What do you think, William? Are people comforted here in the way I like them to be in Bath?'

'Not at all,' said Sir William. 'There is no fire.'

'That is because it is summer.'

'No. It is because there is no *fireplace*. And, worse than this, no visible means of ordering a brandy snap! But I am comforted because I am with you and can hold your hand if I wish.'

Clorinda laughed and Sir William thought once more what a sweet sound that laughter was and he grew grave, suddenly, with the thought that he would surely die long before his new wife and the gift of her laughter would one day go to somebody else.

'I hope,' he said, with a choke in his voice, 'that we will be married for a very long time. Though everything about us may disappear or undergo some infernal alteration which nobody predicts, I want you and me to be just as we are now: happy and at peace. And you laughing.'

DARK AND SHINING COLOURS

In ten days' time, the *Rainsford* would sail for Singapore.

Valentine Ross lay in his narrow bed and tried to weigh in his mind whether he would be aboard the ship, suffering in his hutch of a cabin, cold and seasick, yet embarked at last on his mission to find Edmund, or would he dare to postpone his sailing in one final attempt to woo Jane?

He'd returned from his travels in the West Country with the conviction that Jane Adeane would be cold towards him, that there would be nothing but awkwardness between them. But it had not been the case. First, there had been their dreamlike midnight meeting in the Hot Bath, his nakedness seeming to amuse Jane and goad her to a flirtatious exchange. Then, together, they had presided over the death of Mr Latimer, conspirators in the matter of the opium, bound together by what they had decided to do. And when that was over and Mr Latimer's body had been taken away, there had been a long moment when they had stood alone together in Sir William's surgery and Jane had taken his hand and said: 'I am glad. I am glad.'

What had she meant by this?

Had she been referring only to what they had done for Latimer, or did she mean she was 'glad' to see the person whose proposal of marriage had once been so evidently displeasing to her? She had left him then, to sleep for a while after the long vigil of the night and he had not pressed her to say more. But now his old yearning to be loved by Jane Adeane returned so strongly to him that he let himself hope that she felt something more than friendship for him. All his visions of a shared life, of sexual bliss with the woman whose magical touch everybody longed for, invaded him completely and drove almost everything else from his mind. Yet he knew that if he were to risk one last manifestation of his feelings and was rejected a second time, then his future was sealed: he would board the *Rainsford*; he would never see Jane again.

Noting that the weather was fair, and having no patients except those who might hope to consult him informally at the Baths, Ross set out on one of his walks to Charlcombe. On his way, he came to a decision that he knew was not logical, but rather the kind of hapless, childlike decision a gambler makes. The decision was this: he would walk in the field where he had once seen the capercaillie. He would linger there a little while and if he set eyes on one of these birds, why then he would take this as a 'message' from Edmund. And he would read that message as a summons to the Far East. He would consider himself bound by it. And if no capercaillie appeared ... he would take his chances and announce his love a second time to Jane, hoping that all memory of the tea room proposal had somehow been obliterated from her mind. The mere thought that he might be obliged to repeat some of the words once spoken at Mrs Morrissey's laid on his heart a feeling of suffocation.

When Ross got to the field, last observed with its covering of frost, he now saw that it had been planted with turnips. He'd learned from Edmund that capercaillies were not only rarely seen in England but that they were moorland-loving birds, feasting on insects which crawled among grass and heather. Crows might come and peck on turnip tops, but capercaillies would not.

Was his childish bet won, then? Was he saved from having to travel to Borneo? Ross stood at the edge of the turnip field and watched the wind moving the trees in the wood beyond it. The notion that the direction of every human life may often be determined by such infinitely small moments, by such superstitious arithmetic was a terrifying one and he berated himself for ever thinking up this ridiculous wager.

He turned away from the field and was about to walk on when his eye was caught by a fluttering of wings, as a large bird settled on a fallen log at the edge of the wood. He looked over to it and was relieved to see that it was a rook. But his gaze was held a while longer by what could almost have been a still life set before him: a bird standing silent and still on a dead, moss-covered tree trunk. It seemed to him almost as though the scene had arranged itself before him, to tell him something, but he was unable to say what it was.

He invited Jane to take supper in his rooms. He knew that this was a provocative invitation and he expected her to refuse, but she did not refuse. He sent out to a cook shop for smoked trout with a cucumber mousse and to the wine merchants for a bottle of Rhenish hock.

She arrived wearing a dress of dark brown silk with an amber necklace at her throat, as if dressed for a much grander evening than the one he was offering. She had woven brown satin ribbons into her hair. Against these dark and shining colours, her skin looked very white.

He poured her a little glass of hock and as she sipped it she said, 'So Doctor Ross, I suppose this is a little farewell supper, is it? You see I have chosen to wear an expensive dress, purchased in Paris, in your honour. When do you sail for Borneo?'

He was unable to speak. He had not imagined that he would be confronted by his moment of truth so very early in the evening. He'd presumed they might spend time talking about Latimer's death, or about the marriage of Sir William and Mrs Morrissey, but no, of course this was Jane, and Jane always liked to rush headlong towards the heart of any matter. She had little patience for small talk or conversational evasion of any kind.

'I believe,' Jane continued, 'my father told me you would sail in two weeks – or perhaps less? Is this right?'

'No,' said Ross.

'No? He was mistaken, then?'

'No …'

'Oh alas, Doctor Ross, I am confused now. Is there a difference in meaning between one "no" and another?'

It had to come out then. She'd begun to tease him, as she always did, and he couldn't let this happen at such a time. He believed he would kill her – he would put his hands round her beautiful white neck and *strangle* her – rather than let her belittle him and make him suffer as he'd suffered before.

Yet he found himself on his knees. He grasped Jane's hand. Part of him knew that he looked ridiculous, but it all had to be done and said now, all his pent-up love and passion had to be laid before her.

'Jane!' he cried out. 'I have tried and tried to cast you out of my mind. I've done everything a man could do. But I've failed. You haunt me every moment of my life.'

'Doctor Ross …'

'Don't speak! Please! Let me say what I have to say. I want to marry you. If you won't have me, then I will leave England and never come back, but I have to ask you one last time, will you be my wife?'

He was looking up at Jane, but could not read her thoughts. It seemed to him that there was a flicker of a smile on her mouth and he couldn't bear the sight of this mocking smile, so he lowered his head and buried his face in her lap. He knew this was beyond all modesty, but he didn't care. He understood that his whole future rested upon this moment.

To his shame, he realised that he was on the verge of weeping, that he wanted to claw at Jane's body, as a sorrowing child sometimes claws at his mother. And he couldn't suppress the sob that now came straight from his heart, the cry of an animal in pain, but the next thing that he felt was the touch of Jane's hand on his neck and she began stroking his hair. Then, she raised him up and held him close to her, face to face, looking into his hard blue eyes.

'Perhaps, after all, it is very simple,' she said. 'I will marry you and we will do what everybody does; we will strive to be happy.'

What followed next was not what would have followed with any other well-brought-up young woman except – at that moment in time – with Jane Adeane.

She kissed Ross and he found that her kiss was searching and brazen and deep. She kissed him again and told him that she thought it strange in society how men and women bound themselves in lifelong marriage without first finding out if they were compatible in bed. And he took this for the invitation it appeared to be. The supper and wine were forgotten. They went hand in hand to his bedroom.

Jane took off all her finery, loosened her hair from its satin ribbons and lay down naked on his narrow bed, caressing her own body as provocatively as any whore while she waited for him to join her, as if to display to him that, for all her extravagant height and strength, she was ready to surrender to him.

The sight of this, so long imagined, was as extraordinary, as full of wonder to Ross as the sight of a sunrise to one who has been held captive in darkness for long and frozen years.

Part Three

WOMAN IN WHITE

Emmeline Adeane was making final preparations for a midsummer exhibition at the Barlow Gallery in Mayfair. She would show twenty pictures. Mr Sheridan Barlow himself, visiting Tite Street several times, had professed himself to be 'encaptured' with Emmeline's work – most particularly by her portraits – and Emmeline had decided to be content with that and to refrain from asking Mr Barlow whether 'encaptured' was an actual word, which she might be able to find in Mr Ogilvie's *Imperial Dictionary of the English Language*.

For it did seem to be the case, she reflected, that the owners of art galleries were very frequently men who were unable to use ordinary language with any precision and who walked about in a horrible blizzard of peculiar superlatives and meaningless coinages, from which they tried to shelter themselves by a wild flailing of their hands. That it was these people to whose commercial souls she had to entrust her work troubled Emmeline, particularly when they liked to grab such a large slice of her sales receipts, but they were the custodians of her life. She could not, after all, sell her work in the street.

The picture by which Sheridan Barlow was most 'encaptured' proved to be Emmeline's portrait of Jane. She had titled it *Woman in White* (suspecting that Mr Wilkie Collins would not greatly care if she had borrowed the title of his wretchedly famous novel) and she was disinclined to sell it. But Barlow had hurled upon it such a confetti of praise, coupled with the promise of such a rich price to be got from it that Emmeline had given way and agreed to hand it over to him. Unframed, it had remained in her studio ever since Jane had returned to Bath and Emmeline had liked its presence there. Now, she had to load it into a Hansom Cab and cart it round to her framers, Messrs Hartley and Foulkes, skilled artisans of whom she had become very fond over the years.

It was while standing with Mr Hartley at one of his work benches that Emmeline was invaded by a sudden pain in her chest. It was a pain like no other, the feeling of a terrible iron nail being driven into her heart with repeated hammer blows.

She clung to Mr Hartley's counter with one hand and massaged her sternum with the other, hoping that this might cause the hammer to cease its terrible work. But it did not cease. Emmeline had a brief remembrance of Mr Hartley's kindly face staring at her with grave concern before she descended into darkness.

She fell sideways onto the dusty wooden floor. Mr Hartley rushed to her side and gathered up her hand, feeling for a pulse. At the same time, he shouted for Mr Foulkes, who was working in an ante-room, and Foulkes, who was getting on in years, immediately came limping in.

'What is it, Mr Hartley?' he asked.

'Behold!' cried out Mr Hartley, with all the dramatic intonation he considered suitable to the situation, 'Miss Adeane in a collapse!'

'Oh, woe!' said Foulkes, catching his colleague's tone. 'What are we to do?'

Mr Hartley was now attempting to revive Emmeline, by patting her cheek and urging her to wake up, but she lay still and pale before him, showing no sign of movement. Only the turban she was wearing that day had moved when her head hit the floor and was now lodged unceremoniously over one eye, like the hat of a jester. And all among Mr Hartley's dismay there lurked a fearful worry at this occurrence, taking, as it did, so much dignity from Emmeline's person.

'You must run to the doctor, Foulkes,' said Mr Hartley. 'You must urge him to come immediately.'

'Run?' said Mr Foulkes. 'You know I cannot run …'

'Hobble, then. Hobble as fast as you can. It is but two streets away.'

'No,' said Mr Foulkes. 'I have a better idea. Lay her on a stretcher and we will carry her there, between the two of us. That way, there is no toing and froing.'

'Admirable,' said Hartley. 'Except that we have no stretcher.'

'What are paintings but strong canvases stretched between four points, Mr Hartley? Put her on the unframed painting of the White Woman and we will convey her to the doctor on that. The unframed object will be lighter for us to carry.'

Mr Hartley stared at his colleague. In their long association, Mr Foulkes had often shown an odd originality of mind which Hartley knew he himself did not possess. His choice of mounting boards for watercolours had sometimes been too modern and daring for Hartley's taste, but had helped to give the firm its reputation for up-to-the-minute craftsmanship. Thus, when Foulkes made seemingly audacious decisions, Hartley was disposed to go along with them.

'We might damage the painting …' he ventured.

'No,' said Mr Foulkes. 'I will fetch a rug and lay it over the canvas. Then, all should go well. If she was fat, why then there might be a bending sort of calamity with the canvas, but she is so light, she will not even dent it.'

So it was done as Mr Foulkes suggested. The portrait of Jane was laid on the floor and covered with a tartan blanket and the two men gently lifted Emmeline onto it. Her turban fell off altogether and Hartley gently laid it on her chest – perhaps in the very place where she had felt the hammer blows. Then they set off, easing their strange conveyance gently through the narrow shop door and into the street, where a ragged urchin crossing sweeper stared at them with huge eyes and asked, 'is she dead, then, mister?'

'Get away, lad,' barked Mr Foulkes, 'she's a fine lady and we will not let her die.'

Emmeline woke up on the doctor's couch. She saw a face coming out of the darkness and positioning itself very close to hers. She wanted to scream with fright, the more so when a probing finger pushed up one of her eyelids so that the face could peer under it into the depths of her eye. But she found that she had no voice.

Then she felt something touching her chin and she realised it was a man's whiskers, and the tickling feeling was horrible and she tried to raise a hand to push the man away, but found that she could not raise it. She thought that perhaps she had been turned into some farm animal, penned into a crate and that the man was about to eat her.

Then she heard a voice and recognised it from somewhere, and the voice said, 'Is she awake, doctor? Is she living and breathing?'

The face disappeared. Emmeline was able to turn her head a fraction and tried to find words in her mind for what she could see. On a table not far from her, there was a collection of … what were they called? Shiny things, sharp things which looked as if they could wound …

The friendly, familiar voice said: 'It's Mr Hartley, Miss Adeane. Mr Foulkes and I thought it best to bring you here, to the doctor. You were taken with a bad turn on our premises. How are you feeling?'

She was able to nod her head, but not speak any words. She could see Mr Hartley's kind face and this was then joined by the lined visage of Mr Foulkes, who said, 'you gave us a bitter fright, dear lady. But you are safe at last, with a medical man.'

Now, she lay in a hospital bed. The ceiling above the bed appeared very far away and strangely clothed with dark, moving shadows. She stared at these and tried to give them form, but their form eluded her.

Down the length of the ward, echoes travelled. They were the echoes of footfalls and voices, but Emmeline's mind was unable to say whether they were in past or present time. And these confusions – the formless shadows moving without ceasing, the noises which came and went in a peculiar surging tide – led her to believe that some catastrophe had overtaken her. Its origins remained a mystery. The last thing she could remember was climbing into a Hansom Cab, holding something in her arms.

Some time passed, during which Emmeline fell into a light sleep and when she woke, she saw a figure in white standing beside her bed. The figure remained very still, looking down at Emmeline, who, seeing the white gown, knew that she should be comforted by this person in some way, but she was not comforted. She searched the features, thinking to recognise there something familiar, something tender, but she was looking at a dark brow, at close-together eyes and understood that the stranger would not help her.

She went away and Emmeline resumed her contemplation of the formless shadows playing across the high ceiling. She knew that she was searching for a name and that when she found it, she would have to try to say it aloud, for in this name resided her only hope of understanding what had happened to her.

She searched all night, or at least through what she believed to be night, and when the dawn appeared to break somewhere in the high room, she found the lost one-syllable sound that had been buried somewhere inside her, held down by her sick heart, and she summoned all her strength and began calling out, 'Jane! Jane!'

'ONLY SUBMIT'

When Sir William and Clorinda Morrissey arrived back from Dublin, in the early evening, they were surprised to be greeted at the front door of 28 Henrietta Street by Valentine Ross and Jane, who drew them into the parlour where a bottle of ruby port and four glasses had been laid out.

The tired travellers were touched by this. Port wine was just the thing to revive their spirits and they began to sip it gratefully, but it wasn't long before they understood that the wine had not been opened just to sustain them; it had been opened to celebrate something much more momentous.

Watched very intently by Jane, Ross stood up, took a fortifying draught from his glass and said, 'we have some news which we hope you will celebrate with us. I have decided not to make my planned journey to Borneo. Indeed, nothing would induce me to make it now. For my circumstances have changed for the glorious better! Two weeks ago, while you were away, I took my courage into my hands and asked Jane if she would consent to become my wife – and Jane has agreed.'

Mrs Morrissey – once witness to the failed proposal in her tea room – let out a gasp. Sir William put down his glass of port and opened his arms, as if to embrace the gallant finishers in a long and arduous race.

'My word!' he said. 'You could not have told me anything I would rather hear. Come and kiss your father, Jane, and my dear Ross, come and shake my hand.'

They did this, and in the next moment decided upon the kind of collective embrace not often to be seen in any Victorian parlour, and during which, finding himself the object of so much affection and rejoicing, Valentine Ross had a sudden fear that he was going to embarrass himself by breaking into tears.

As the little group separated once more, Clorinda Morrissey said, 'There were we, under grey skies in Dublin, not knowing one single thing about the sunshine falling here. It would have cheered us so much, would it not, William?'

'Indeed it would. But it is also a wonderful homecoming.'

'I'm aware, Sir William,' said Ross, 'that strictly speaking, I have not done things in the right order. I should have asked your permission for Jane's hand first, before approaching her. But what can I say? The moment arrived and had to be seized, did it not, Jane?'

'Yes,' said Jane calmly. 'The moment arrived.'

'Of course it did,' said Sir William, 'of course it did! Just like my reckless embrace of Clorinda, somewhere between the street and the threshold of her tea room, and this is how life is: we are overtaken by flashes of lightning and brilliant storms, and we can only submit.'

Jane took in this statement of her father's and, alone in her narrow bed in Henrietta Street that night, felt that it described quite accurately her relationship with Valentine Ross. Except that he alone – and not she – was the one who had been invaded by a great and turbulent passion.

With all her great curiosity about the world, it had been fascinating to Jane Adeane to experience a man's desire in its wildness and desperation and she had had no choice, once she had agreed to marry Ross, but to submit. It had even excited her a little, at first, to be the object of such adoration and animal striving, but as the attempts at love-making went on night after night, she had soon enough felt slightly suffocated by it and did not entirely enjoy being held beneath the body of a man, crushed even, as he cried and shouted his way to his own delirium.

Jane told herself that marriage would calm him and that they would settle into some kind of tranquillity in bed, yet this was not quite what she wanted either. She wanted to feel with Ross the same kind of yearning and the same kind of excitement and satisfaction as she had felt with Julietta, but she knew she was a long way from that. The 'flashes of lightning' were all experienced by him.

What was she to do?

Julietta had suggested to her that men needed to be *taught* how to arouse women and she had been bold enough to press Ross's head down between her legs, but once there, with his beard feeling rough against her thighs, he had not known what to do, except to kiss her a little, so the attempt was abandoned and never tried again. The *jouissance* Jane had arrived at so easily and so frequently with Julietta never happened with Valentine Ross.

It thus came slowly into Jane's mind that she would have to let marriage return her – paradoxically – to the state of virginity she had inhabited prior to her meeting with Julietta. Before she'd been touched by Julietta, her sexual self had been dormant, in a condition of quietude. All her passion had gone into her powers of healing. She was the Angel of the Baths and that had been enough.

Now, she would have to go back to that – to finding joy in touching people only to cure them and take away their pain. And she saw how she had to include her future husband in this, for what was his terrible passion for her except pain – unless it could be satisfied? And only she could satisfy it. She would submit herself to what seemed to be a very pressing and overbearing need and his sufferings would be assuaged.

Was she capable of doing this?

She didn't know.

She tried to let her mind embrace the other changes to her life that marriage to Valentine Ross would bring: a house of her own, the establishment of a successful medical practice, in which she would be given the status of an almost equal partner, the possibility of a child. She saw that, in the eyes of many, she was destined for a fulfilled and happy life. But she knew that if she was to find this happiness, then there was one task which she had to accomplish: she had to renounce Julietta.

And it seemed to her that this renunciation had to begin straight away. Always congratulated by her father for her 'great strength of purpose', Jane Adeane now knew that she had to call upon this and try to strike from her memory the rapture she had experienced with Julietta in Paris, even learning to describe what they had done together as 'wickedness' and letting it become something of which she needed to feel slightly embarrassed and ashamed.

Before she faltered in this resolve, Jane sat down at her writing desk and began a letter to Julietta.

My dear love, she wrote. *Because you and I were always so very honest with each other, I will not fuss you with a long and rambling letter, but get straight to my point.*

I have done as you and Emmeline suggested I should do and agreed to become the wife of Dr Valentine Ross. We will marry in the autumn. I am in no doubt that he loves me very much, for he tells me repeatedly that he has never loved anyone else and when I let him make love to me, which I have done many times, his desire has always appeared ... well, how can I describe it ...? I cannot, really. I will leave you to imagine its desperation. In me, there was no answering rapture, but let me say I believe my Valentine is an honourable man and that we stand a good chance of being contented together.

But I fear that this contentment rests upon one condition. It is the harshest condition, Julietta, yet I know that without it, I will be unable to submit to my future life.

You and I must never be lovers again.

I am in no doubt that you will often and often enter my dreams and a memory of what we were to each other in Paris will rise up and fill me with longing, but I must do my utmost to put you out of my mind altogether ...

Jane had reached this point in her letter when there was a knock at her door. It was Sir William, and Jane could tell by his pallor and by the taut set of his mouth that he had bad news to impart.

'Jane,' he said, 'I have word from London, from Emmeline's maid, Nancy. Emmeline has suffered a paroxysm of the heart. She calls for you. Not for me, but for you. I fear that you may be all that stands between her and death. I know that you would not wish this at such a time, now that you want to be at Ross's side and prepare for your marriage, but I must ask you if you would be willing to go to her.'

Jane turned from her letter, which she placed face-down on the desk and stared at her father.

'Is it too much to ask of you?' said Sir William.

'No,' said Jane calmly. 'Of course not. Poor dear Emmeline! I will go to London.'

She began to make her preparations straight away. Halfway through her packing, she returned to the letter and read through what she had written. She imagined Julietta looking at the terrible words, then setting the document aside, folding it into smaller and smaller configurations until it resembled some failed attempt at an origami figure. And she would hold this in her soft hand and feel that her life, too, had suddenly got smaller, that some vengeful spirit was intent on folding away her joy.

Jane took up her letter and crumpled it and threw it into the fire. To the obedient flames, which snatched at the paper and let it curl and char and fall to ashes, she whispered, 'I refuse to do it.'

THE HAND OF THE ENGINEER

He arrived in a prau from Singapore. He carried on the boat a cargo of gunpowder, for which the rajah had paid 'too much silver'.

Sir Ralph had not wanted to hire this man, but progress on the riverside cannery had been so disappointingly slow that Leon – whose dreams of the enterprise seemed to overturn all the other content of his mind – had insisted that the whole thing was doomed unless it were put into the hands of an engineer.

'We do not need such a man,' argued Sir Ralph. 'I oversaw the building of my house by Chinese labour. I can oversee the setting up of your cannery.'

'Not true, my rajah,' said Leon. 'All is desperation at the river. Logs jamming there. Men wounded. And mangroves still with feet in the water. A bloody chaos! We need gunpowder to blast – boom! Then we can begin properly. And for powder we need an engineer. I will go to Singapore and find him.'

His name was Septimus Scaife. He had learned his skills in the cold and grime of the factories of Northern England. A wound to his right hand, which left it with an unassuageable tremble, had caused his dismissal from his job as a builder of iron towers and railway bridges. Nobody in England wanted to employ an engineer with a shaking limb.

But Scaife had suspected that on the other side of the world, where methods of construction lagged behind those being tried in Manchester and Sheffield, he would be hired for good money – for his knowledge, far more than for his physical skill. And he was not wrong. He was taken on at Singapore by a Muslim rajah trying to build an aviary out of steel and wire, to satisfy his favourite wife's love of captive birds, and it was here, as he was finishing this beautiful construction, that Leon had found him and lured him to Sir Ralph's domain with promises of silver.

Until he had seen the river and the disposition of the forest on either side of it, Septimus Scaife had told Leon that he could not know whether the cannery scheme was workable or not. What he could say was that 'a good sufficiency of covered buildings' would be needed to house it and that it would be difficult to site these securely without first blasting the mangroves from the water.

The idea of clearing the land for the cannery 'at one boom' was thrilling to Leon. He'd borne painful witness to the slow progress of an arm of the Savage Road towards the cannery site and to the arduous attempts to cut down the mangroves, resulting in a river choked with trunks and branches and the Sadong obstinately flowing round them, to colonise yet more ground. Leon had a vision of all this miraculously gone and tracts of land made level and stable, ready for the canning sheds and the steam-powered rolling belts that would lift the fish from the water.

Scaife, a man in his fifties, had a bluntness of speech and manner which was inimical to the rajah. Sir Ralph noticed that Scaife was especially curt and rude to Leon, treating him as a person of no account, and this caused the rajah intense agony, knowing that he was unable to explain to a disagreeable engineer from the English North what Leon's true status was in his household without risking the man's immediate departure.

Scaife had presumed that he would be lodged in Sir Ralph's great palace, and he spent his first night there, but when he returned from a day's survey at the Sadong, he found all his possessions gone from the room where he'd slept the previous night. At a loss, and with his trembling hand suffering uncontrollable agitation, the engineer walked round and round the big house – both awed and disgusted by its opulence – in search of the man who had promised him a quantity of silver, but who had appeared displeased with him on sight. But he could not find him. Eventually, he was shown by one of the

Chinese houseboys to a 'cottage' in the grounds, a place built of wood and palm thatch by the rajah with the foreknowledge that only certain guests would fit in with his aesthetic choices up at the great house, and that the others would have to be banished to this simple dwelling.

Scaife found a pile of mats for sleeping on, a table furnished with paper and ink, a commode, a jug and ewer, and a quantity of rush-lights. A bevy of green parakeets snickered in the banana trees outside the cottage window. He thought all of this woeful. At the Muslim rajah's palace, he had slept in a tented goosefeather bed, in a large, quiet room, in which the oldest of the rajah's concubines had been 'on loan' to him during his visit. He had been treated with respect. His nights had been scented and rude.

Now, he saw that his status had fallen. Septimus Scaife was a man who, since his unfortunate accident, which had imbued him with a great store of self-pity, was quick to make enemies, and when he took in the amenities offered by the cottage, a violent loathing of Sir Ralph and of his 'henchman' Leon took possession of him. Sitting glumly on the pile of mats, he began to wonder how, while fulfilling his duties sufficiently well to earn him the promised silver, he might sabotage the project and bring ruin to men he deemed venal and lazy, living a rich life they had not deserved.

Did the rajah sense that this man would try to do him harm?

Perhaps not. He only sensed something about him that he mistrusted and disliked, the more so because Leon, apparently bearing the man's disdainful behaviour towards him without flinching, was behaving like a child in his excitement about the explosions Scaife would bring about.

Sir Ralph warned his lover that the 'black powder' was a fiendish substance which often surprised people by doing more damage than was intended, but Leon brushed this 'feeble talk' aside and spent his time showing Scaife 'the mangrove problem' at the river and putting in front of him designs for cans that the engineer immediately dismissed as useless, telling him that there was no capacity to manufacture cans on the rajah's estate and that these would have to be shipped to Kuching from China. The Chinese, he said, were the only people in this part of the world who knew how to make airtight containers. But if he expected Leon to be dismayed by this, he was wrong.

'China! China, Sir Raff!' said Leon, in a voice choked with excitement. 'I will cross the South China Sea. I will become Emperor of the Tin Can dynasty!'

'Hush, Leon,' said the rajah. 'I'm tired.'

'No,' said Leon. 'You don't be. Tired is very bad. I work. You see how hard I work with this engineer? Soon, I will be rich from this cannery – and then I will leave you.'

Sir Ralph made no answer to this. For as long as he could remember, Leon had tortured him with threats of leaving. It was an emotional trick played too often to be convincing. But on this occasion, perhaps because, for some days now, the rajah had indeed been feeling sad and listless, the idea that Leon might one day actually abandon him was suddenly so unbearable that it choked him and he was quite unable to speak. He felt his heart pound in his great barrel chest. Tears started under his closed eyelids and began running down his cheeks.

Instead of gently wiping away the tears, Leon began pinching Sir Ralph's face, as if to gather the tears up, like tiny fallen leaves, or spilt crumbs in his hand. This pinching felt cruel, and the cruelty excited Leon, but instead of moving, as he usually did, towards some sexual expression of his anger, he left the rajah's bed and began upon a terrible diatribe of how, whenever white men came to the rajah's house, they scorned him and belittled him – he, Leon, the man upon whom everything depended. He said he heard the word 'savage', unspoken but directed by thought alone against him and all his race. And the rajah – 'you whose very name is Savage!' – had never defended him. With the 'Jesus boy' he had communed 'in secret hammocks' and as for Septimus Scaife, why had this uncouth man not been told that Leon was to be treated with courtesy and respect? Was all this surely not proof that Sir Ralph did not truly love him, did not truly see him as an equal, but only used him as a slave to satisfy his carnal appetites? Let the rajah think upon this. For the time was coming when Leon would have made his own fortune, when he would lie down in his bed, not with any white rajah, but on a mattress stuffed with silver dalers. And then he would buy a prau and sail away.

He would become a prince in his own right. Malays could be princes and rajahs. He would go to Celebes or to the Aru Islands and fight primitive tribes and soon enough come to rule over others. He would cease his perversions with men – except when he felt a violent need for them. He would marry a beautiful woman and make her his Ranee and father children. He would carry a jewelled dagger at his waist and wear rings on his fingers and a golden anklet on his leg. He would found a dynasty in his own name, while Sir Ralph would die without an heir, die all alone, unconsoled by his treasures, as the forest bore down on his ridiculously named Savage Road and infested it with tangled vines and the roots of vigorous trees and the nests of snakes – with the true essence of Borneo, in fact, against which the rajah had waged constant war, but never understood …

This outburst of Leon's was so wounding that Sir Ralph felt himself descend into a feeling of helpless shock. He opened his eyes and through tears which now stung like nettles on his lashes, regarded his lover, who was pacing back and forth in front of the rajah's bedroom window, where a coral sunset provided a blazing background to the scene.

He couldn't speak, but his long and terrible thought was, 'all my happiness is going to be lost to a dream. And the dream will fail.'

CAT'S CRADLE

The next day, the rajah walked to the river and saw Scaife making preparations for what he called 'an explosion experiment', placing his paper tubes of gunpowder just shy of the water's edge, in the strange architecture of the mangrove roots. Wire fuses to set in train the explosion made tangled journeys in and out of the tubes.

'I will start with a little powder,' said Scaife, 'to gauge the resistance of the trees. Then, if I have calculated rightly, I will put all in train for a very mighty blast. Once the debris is cleared away, you will have clean land, on which you can begin to build your canning sheds.'

Sir Ralph watched the shaking hand of the engineer placing the pods of powder and inserting the fuses. Beyond him, he saw what Leon had described as the 'bloody chaos' of the river, choked by felled trees, which the current was not strong enough to carry away, and it felt to him that this place was a terrible landscape of what was in his heart.

He wanted to tell Scaife to cease his work, to go back to Singapore, but now, after Leon's diatribe against him, he feared to bring about more rage. He'd spent the night trying to work out exactly why Leon had said such hurtful things, trying to understand what it was like to *be* Leon. And he had seen, perhaps for the first time, that although he lived in comfort and luxury, Leon longed for something else: he longed to rule.

By advising the rajah to build his road, he had supposedly been showing the Englishman how to establish mastery over his lands, yet that mastery was fragile; nature kept on and on reclaiming the road – as Leon had surely known that it would. Perhaps he laughed a bitter laugh whenever the rains began? He had probably come to understand that no foreigner, whether Dutch or English, could hold sway for long in Borneo, because there was too much about the island that they didn't understand – and never would understand. They relied on clever Malays, like Leon, to tell them what to do. So why should he, Leon, remain in a position of servitude, when he was the one who possessed the knowledge needed by the ruler? All that kept him there was his lack of money.

Here, then, lay the reason for his enthusiasm for the cannery. He knew that Sir Ralph would wish to have little to do with such a complicated, messy enterprise, but that there might be hard currency to be made from it. And he, Leon, would put himself in charge of the accounting. If all went to plan and cans of filleted subaru and well-prepared soft shell turtle could be exported to China and beyond, then Leon's dreams of riches might be realised. And then he would leave. He would go in search of his own small empire to rule.

Dismay at the logic of these thoughts gripped the rajah's heart once again as he stood watching the engineer fumbling with his fuses. He saw how easy it would be for Scaife to be blown apart, and sudden compassion for the man overcame him. He thought, we all risk being defeated by some small weakness in us that we can't control. And then that is the end of us.

He didn't want to remain at the river. He had the notion that to lose himself in the forest for a while, to remind himself that nature could be sublime as well as unkind, would bring him some respite from sadness and worry. To return to his house, he would have walked due north, but leaving the Sadong behind until he could no longer hear its running over the rapids, he turned east and proceeded at a slow and careful pace.

He soon came upon a family of gibbons and stopped to wonder at their furtive little faces looking down upon the white man. They scattered as he moved forwards and this disappointed him, as if he'd hoped to have some kind of conversation with the animals and was hurt by their fear of him. And this foolish wish revealed to him how alone he felt himself to be.

Not far from where he was walking he knew there was a small Dyak settlement and he wondered if he might come across it and stop to rest there and drink a cup of arak and admire the pumpkins the Dyaks grew in strange abundance. The chief delight of this tribe had been to play a complicated form of Cat's Cradle – or what they termed 'Scratch Cradle' – with the rajah. And it always made him marvel at the different patterns they could make with the string, far superior to any he had ever learned in his fifty years of life.

The rajah began listening out for the sounds of human habitation, but all he could hear was the great orchestra of the forest and he held up his arms in a gesture of surrender to its music, which, when his own death came, would continue without pause.

Then he walked on, managing to find pathways through the trees into small glades, where the bush had been cut and where burning sunlight fell. In one of these glades, he noticed that the air was tainted by a foul scent and he expected to find a carnivorous pitcher plant growing there. Though these insect-eating plants always spoke to his curiosity, he also knew that they could emit a horrible stench, their bulbous stems being full of half-digested flies.

The rajah looked around and around. What his eye eventually lighted upon was not a pitcher plant but a shallow mound, covered with a few stones and branches of foliage. Sir Ralph knew that dead animals were seldom buried in the forest; they were eaten – by men or wild hogs, or vultures. Approaching the mound, he fought off the sickness that rose in his throat from the vitiated air and gave all his attention to measuring the grave in his mind. It didn't take him long to conclude that this was the fragile tomb of a man.

By the time the rajah reached the Dyak settlement, he felt weak from heat and thirst and from a new and terrible thought which had entered his mind: that he had stumbled, quite by chance, upon the last resting place of Edmund Ross.

He was relieved to have found the Dyaks. Though he had once fought them, as enemies of the Sultan of Brunei, this was not widely known along the Sadong. Indeed, some on the lands he now owned chose to regard him as a Deity-come-among-them, and this both moved and amused him. They did not merely bow to him, but liked to touch him, trying to ascertain if his skin, his hair, his fingernails and his eyes were made of flesh and blood or rather of some other immortal substance they would never be able to name. This touching of him sometimes felt like childish tickling and would make the rajah giggle and this pleased the Dyaks greatly and they would set up an answering clamour of laughter all around the white man, loud enough to silence the tree frogs and the bad-tempered toucans.

Once, he had been told by a Dyak woman that when he died, he would certainly be reborn 'just as before' wearing his white garb, with his grey hair tied in a black ribbon and his feet shod in old army boots. And this superstition seemed to take flight and travel round the settlements, so that now, when the Dyaks encountered the rajah, they tried to overcome their awe by gestures of ordinariness, offering him mangoes to eat or shaking his hand, pumping it up-and-down, up-and-down, in the way of a white man's greeting.

When they saw him now, staggering a little in the heat, his forehead running with sweat, three Dyak men came out of the shade of their huts and led him inside, where they sat him down on a floor of fresh palm leaves and brought him water in a wooden bowl. The rajah thanked them. He inhaled the cooler air of the hut and the piquant smell of the men's bodies and felt himself soothed a little. He closed his eyes and had a sudden longing to surrender to sleep in this place, which was far away from Leon and his anger. But he suspected that he might offend the Dyaks by falling asleep the moment he'd crossed their threshold, so to distract himself and stay awake, he reached into the pocket of his robe and brought out a pile of tangled string.

'Cat's Cradle?' he asked.

The men clapped their hands with delight. At the door now, two women stood looking in at the rajah prone on the palm floor and put their hands over their mouths, suppressing laughter. One of the Dyak men snatched the string away from Sir Ralph and, in seconds, had untangled it and fashioned it into the overlapping loops around his fingers needed to begin the game. He held these out to the rajah, who drank more water from the bowl, then began delicately picking at the string to make a first figuration.

The Dyaks laughed. The 'cradle' was then passed to another, who contrived something far more complex with it. Sir Ralph stared at this, wondering where he might go with it and the men watched him closely, enjoying his puzzlement. At last he decided to lift two of the loops down and outwards, thinking to undo the last construction and begin again, but it wouldn't come apart and once again he was struck by the Dyaks' ingenuity in this simple game. He made a new move, but saw that it could easily be unravelled. The third Dyak beat his own thigh with pleasure as the strings were passed to him. Winning against the 'Deity' always seemed to give him vivid pleasure.

When the game was over, Sir Ralph yielded to sleep. As soon as he woke up, he could see that the sun was beginning to set and that he would have to leave quickly if he were to find his way back to his house before dark. But he found that some rice had been put near him and a bowl of arak, and he knew that this hospitality couldn't be refused. So he yielded to the idea that he might spend the night with the Dyaks. This held only one terror for him – that the tribe would offer him one of their women.

The three men who had welcomed him and with whom he'd played Cat's Cradle now sat near him, watching him very intently. Then, an elderly woman came in, carrying a bulky parcel wrapped in banana leaves, which she set down before the rajah and the men gestured for him to open it.

The leaves slipped away easily and Sir Ralph gaped at what he saw before him: a pair of worn boots he had last glimpsed hanging over the edge of a hammock in his garden. He took the boots and held them tenderly against his chest. He saw the Dyaks shaking their heads sadly.

'Englung man,' said one of them. 'Lost, you see, rajah. Vultures eat face. We put this lost man in the ground. Branches above: his cradle.'

The rajah said nothing for a while, then in a hoarse whisper asked, 'Did you kill him?'

'No, Sir Raff,' said the oldest of the Dyaks, 'we told you, this was a lost man. In Borneo, lost men die.'

NO NEARER TO CERTAINTY

When Valentine Ross arrived at Henrietta Street, to be told by Sir William that Jane had taken the early train for London, a first feeling of disbelief turned swiftly to anger. He'd walked with passionate strides from Edgars Buildings, in joyous haste to see his fiancée and to present to her at last, in front of her father, a valuable emerald and diamond ring that had once belonged to his mother. He had spent part of the night polishing the ring in methylated spirits and he saw it afresh as a thing of great beauty. But now, without any word or warning, its intended recipient had abandoned him.

'*Why?*' he cried out. And then could not prevent himself from adding crossly, 'London? She did not have my permission to go to London!'

Sir William looked at him with a calm but accusing stare. 'She did not *need* your permission, my dear Ross,' he said. 'Her Aunt Emmeline has suffered a heart attack and is gravely ill. She sent for Jane. As you know, Emmeline and Jane are almost like mother and daughter. Jane could not hesitate.'

Ross turned away and stared out at the street. The sun was shining on the soft colours of the stone and putting a bright glaze on the black-painted railings. Though struck by the calm beauty of this scene, he felt that such beauty had no value, but was merely a meaningless arrangement of once-pleasing but now pointless things, if Jane had indeed left the city. The ring seemed to burn in his pocket. In the weeks when he'd walked about in the euphoria of at last possessing his mercurial Angel, he had felt himself to be the most fortunate man in England. Now, she had suddenly left him again, and he could not stop a black fury from descending on him.

'Did Jane leave me no note?' he asked. 'I would have thought this was a courtesy she might have considered.'

Sir William, if not surprised by Ross's anger, then slightly surprised that he wasn't able to conceal or control it, laid a consoling hand on Ross's arm.

'My sister's condition appears grave,' he said quietly. 'Worry on this score took all else from Jane's mind except how she might get to London as quickly as possible. You will have to forgive her the lack of a note. She will return as soon as Emmeline recovers.'

'I hope it will be soon. And if she does not recover?'

'Why then, both Jane and I will be in deep mourning. My sister is a remarkable woman.'

'I understand this, of course. But are you saying that this mourning would mean the postponement of my wedding to Jane?'

'And mine to Clorinda?' said Sir William. 'Not necessarily, for life must go on. But I advise you, if you are to keep and hold my daughter's affection, you should understand the role that her aunt has played in her life and make all allowances for the love she feels for her.'

Not liking Sir William's chiding tone, Ross merely repeated his hope that Emmeline Adeane would make a quick recovery and strode quickly away to his surgery.

Here, he sat down in his comfortable leather swivel-chair, took a handkerchief from his pocket and dabbed at his brow. He had twenty minutes before his first patient arrived. These twenty minutes appeared to him too slight a time in which to compose himself. His mind was so aflame with conflicted thoughts about Jane that he could only feel towards this hapless patient an animosity he knew to be entirely unreasonable. Throughout his career as a doctor, he had often had to master the skill of putting his own emotions aside in order to concentrate on the case in hand. But on this occasion, Jane's abrupt departure for London appeared to him so thoughtless – or even spiteful – a thing that he felt quite undone by it.

He cursed her. He let himself wonder whether Jane had even used her aunt's indisposition as an excuse to go to London for some other reason. Although she had seemed to suffer some pain when he'd first made love to her, there had been no blood on the sheets, thus indicating to him that she was not a virgin. Was it possible, then, that she had taken a lover during her long stay at Tite Street and, despite her promise to marry Ross, would brazenly continue to visit him?

Ross took the emerald ring from his pocket and threw it into a drawer of his desk. He wished, at this moment, to have Jane by his side, not to hold or to kiss her, but to hurt her. How, he asked himself, have I arrived at such a pass, where the only woman I can love – the one woman I cannot live without, who arouses me beyond all reason – treats me with such disdain? Am I just a toy to her, to be thrown down or cast aside whenever it suits her?

He knew that his desire to hurt her was unworthy yet asked himself whether many husbands did not, in fact, keep their wives obedient to their needs and commands by imprinting bruises on their white flesh, an excellent and eternal flowering, the mark of the male? And he let himself believe, then and there, that when Jane returned to his bed, he would treat her much more roughly than had been the case so far.

At this moment, there was a ring on the doorbell and Ross, assuming that this announced the arrival of his patient, tried as hard as he could to put his thoughts about Jane from him entirely – but did not entirely succeed. When a knock on his door came, he stood up and composed his features into the calm and benign alignment he'd perfected in all his years of doctoring. But it was not his patient who came in, it was Becky.

Dropping her grudging little obeisance, she held out a crumpled small package towards him and said: 'Letter, Sir. Your servant brought it down from Edgars Buildings. He said it looked important.'

Ross took up the letter and saw that it was stained and torn and criss-crossed with the faded stamps of authority from postal offices in Singapore, Aden and Southampton and sealed with a blob of what looked like animal faeces flecked with chaff. For a moment, his heart was lifted by the thought that here, at last, was a letter from Edmund, but he saw directly that it was not Edmund's writing on the paper.

He dismissed Becky. He sat down at his desk, his mind now gone from Jane and travelling towards the possibility that some catastrophe had befallen his brother. His hands shook as he broke the crusted seal. He peered at a few lines of almost illegible writing and read:

Dear Dr Valentine Ross of 31 Edgars Buildings,
Please hear our prayer. Your brother, Mister Edmun, has fallen captured. He is prisoned by a Dyak tribe. This people take human heads. They ask me for silver in ransom. But I do not have what they ask. Send please money for release of Mister Edmun. They ask five hundred shillings. I am Malay Chief in this region and only I can speak to Dyaks. Please send to me and I will bring this brother to be free. Send to me, Chief Leon at Savage House, Kuching, in Borneo.

Ross read the letter several times. Each time, two conflicting thoughts asserted themselves, almost simultaneously. The first was that what had been written here did indeed describe some terrible crime that threatened to be inflicted upon Edmund; the second was that a trick was being played upon him – upon 'Dr Valentine Ross of 31 Edgars Buildings' – and that any silver paid in ransom would go straight into the pocket of Leon, the letter writer. These two interpretations kept sliding up and down in Ross's mind, as if on some complex moral vector, where nothing remained fixed. Where was the truth?

And he saw that however long he stared at the paper, however long he examined the marks which crowded it and the dirty crumbs which had broken away from the seal, he would get no nearer to any certainty. Yet what he also knew was that the fate of his brother – in the recent delirious times strangely absent from his thoughts – must now be brought back into the forefront of his mind.

ANTE-ROOM

Emmeline Adeane lay very still and looked up at what was above her. She saw a distant vaulted ceiling, as though she might have been in a concert hall or a church, but she had been reminded that she was in a hospital and that she had only one task to perform and this was to rest.

She wasn't a person who set great store by rest. It had always seemed to her that life was a gift, briefly given, and that those who sat and stared out of windows or who lay on day-beds, asking nothing of their bodies or their brains but a passive surrender to inertia and vacancy were despicable nonentities. She knew that her own life had been hard and that there had been moments when she'd fallen into despair, but she also believed she'd kept a bargain with existence: she had embraced the world; she had kept striving for truth in her art.

Now, her heart had faltered.

In her dreams, she imagined this heart, once so faithful to all her endeavours, coming apart in small but fatal rents, letting blood ooze out to clot around it, so that it was destined to struggle harder and harder to keep beating and would soon give up the fight and stop. Sometimes, in these dreams, Jocelyn Hulton appeared and stood above her, looking down at the damage her heart was suffering, with his hand covering his mouth, as if he feared he might vomit. Then, he walked away. In every dream, this was what happened: Jocelyn never spoke a word, but only turned and walked out, closing the heavy door behind him. And Emmeline usually woke up at this point and found herself once more in the hospital, looking up at the high ceiling. She wondered if, in its dark magnificence, it was calling to her spirit.

She knew that this call had to be resisted. She wasn't ready for death, yet it seemed to her that the nurses who visited her bedside, who gave her no help and no instruction but to take doses of laudanum and to lie still, were resigned to letting her go. And it was this terrible resignation that had led Emmeline to call out for Jane. Jane, she knew, would fight on her behalf. She would find the right words to rally her.

But if she was indeed dying, then she could think of no companion she would rather have at her side than Jane. She saw the scene, as if from afar: she lies and gazes, not up into the void, but into Jane's eyes, which are steady and kind. Jane holds her hand. This hand is already getting cold, but Jane massages it gently and Emmeline can feel what a thousand other sufferers have felt, the healing touch of the Angel of the Baths.

When Jane arrived in the hospital ward, Emmeline was sleeping. She saw that the bed sheet had been pulled right up to her aunt's chin, as if in preparation for its further unfolding, to cover the dead face, and she did not like this at all. Gently, she pulled the sheet back a little, and put her palm against Emmeline's cheek. She noticed that Emmeline's hair was tangled on the pillow and that it had not been washed and she did not like this, either. She wanted to take her aunt in her arms and carry her back to Tite Street – to the smell of turpentine and to the sunshine coming through the skylight – and let everything be returned to life and brightness and the perfume of a creative life.

A hard chair had been set by the bedside and Jane sat down on this, allowing her hand to rest lightly upon Emmeline's head, so that when she woke up, she would at once know that she was not alone. Only now did Jane begin to look around the ward. She saw that shutters had been closed across all but one of the narrow windows, so that the inmates of the beds were consigned to a peculiar daytime twilight. The air in the room was stale, unmoving, as though this air was considered almost unnecessary and was a foul, rationed quota deemed just sufficient for the fragile lungs which breathed it.

Jane peered through the semi-darkness, searching for a nurse, to whom she would have begged for a window to be opened, but she could see no one moving around the ward. And the female patients, each in her iron bed, appeared to be in a state of utter quietness, taut white sheets pinning them down, their bodies subservient to some fearful command not to move, as if rehearsing for the tomb.

And it then occurred to Jane that this ward was the one where the dying were put. Now and again, a nurse would pass through, administering the laudanum that kept them quiet and relatively free from pain, but mainly they had been abandoned. She suspected that no doctor came there. The doctors had relinquished all obligations towards these women, believing that nothing more could be done for them. Jane knew that they wouldn't blame themselves for this impotence; they would blame the women for passing beyond their collective store of medical knowledge. To walk around this ward would only have put them into a state of irritation.

That Emmeline had been put here now filled Jane with a righteous anger. Her aunt didn't belong in this ante-room of death and she saw now that it was her task to get her out of here before she suffocated in the darkness and floated out of her life on a sea of opiates.

She stood up and bent over Emmeline, shaking her gently by her shoulders and saying her name. Though she said it quietly, the beautiful word 'Emmeline' seemed to echo up towards the vaulted ceiling and circle there like the cry of a lone seabird following a ship. And this cry brought a nurse scuttling from some nearby room, carrying the lower section of a wooden leg, complete with its cleverly jointed foot. She went straight to Emmeline's bed and pushed Jane aside, using the leg as a weapon. Jane cried out and this cry seemed to wake a few patients from their slumber and the room was suddenly filled with the noise of lamentation.

'Now hear what you have done!' said the nurse. 'Whoever you are, you must leave at once. This patient must be left to die in peace.'

'No!' said Jane. 'No! I am not going to let her die. Her heart can recover.'

'It will not,' said the nurse, now gesturing with the leg towards Emmeline's breast. 'She will be dead by tomorrow.'

At these words, Jane pushed aside the terrible leg from her aunt's body and threw herself upon her and began begging her to wake up. She feared, at any moment, that she would be felled by the nurse, the wooden leg falling upon her neck like an axe, and – in her constant awareness of how human behaviour descended from one moment to the next into the farcical – saw how ridiculous this scene was becoming. And yet it felt right to her, that she was fighting for Emmeline. Her brave aunt could no longer struggle. Jane would be her defender and take her away from this cathedral of death.

The nurse didn't hit her. She retreated, in her heavy shoes, to wherever she had come from, but Jane knew that this was only to summon reinforcements and that she would probably be manhandled out of the ward and into the street. So it was with great urgency now that Jane begged Emmeline to come out of her drug-induced sleep and speak her name. But Emmeline's eyes remained closed. Her breathing was shallow, so shallow that it almost could not be heard. At the corner of her mouth, a tiny bubble of spittle bloomed and then burst.

Jane now sat on the bed, pulling Emmeline into her arms and rocking her back and forth, just as she might have comforted a weeping child. But it was she who now wept. She wept for all the suffering Emmeline had endured, for her loneliness, for her lost beauty, for her golem, but most of all for the love her aunt had given to her – the love of a mother – which, if Emmeline was indeed surrendering to the death prescribed for her here, she was going to lose.

A trio of people came: the nurse and two black-coated doctors.

Jane laid Emmeline down very gently, smoothing her hair from her temples and placing a kiss on her forehead. The trio did not touch her, but only waited, so close to Jane that she could smell the fustian of the men's coats and the tobacco on their breath.

She turned to them, seeing in all of them stares of implacable hostility, and told them quietly that she was Miss Emmeline Adeane's niece and herself a nurse and would be able to care for her in her own house. She informed them that on the morrow she would come back in a Hansom Cab. She asked if her aunt could be woken early and made ready for the short journey from the hospital to Tite Street, 'and thereafter,' she added, 'you will be released from all responsibility for her and I will be the one who takes it on, for I do it gladly and I know that it is what Miss Adeane would have wished'.

The nurse who had relinquished the wooden leg said nothing, but looked towards the doctors, waiting for one of them to speak.

'As I understood it,' said the elder of the two men with a sniff of irritation, 'this woman is not expected to survive.'

THE TREASURE HOUSE

The Hansom Cab from Paddington Terminus had deposited Jane first in Tite Street, where Emmeline's maid, Nancy had aired and warmed the room Jane had occupied during her long stay in London. And it was here that Jane had intended to return after she was cast out of the hospital in the early evening, but now the thought of being alone in Emmeline's house as the night came on was inimical to her. She wanted to talk, even to be allowed to cry, if that was what she found herself doing. And she knew where she had to go.

Relieved as she now felt that she had not sent her letter of renunciation to Julietta, she nevertheless told herself that she was not seeking out her lover, to be embraced again by her; she was seeking out Julietta *and* Ashton – her friends and Emmeline's, and with them she would find the comfort she needed.

As she approached the tall house in Tedworth Square, she caught a brief glimpse of a well-dressed young woman, who ran quickly down the steps and climbed into a waiting carriage.

Jane paused in the street, watching the carriage being driven away. And she felt, in that instant, that she knew what had just happened: Julietta was alone in the house and had been visited by one of her 'beauties'.

If Jane believed for a moment or two that she should turn round and go straight back to Tite Street, she also knew that she was unable to do this. The thought of Julietta in her bed, damp and somnolent after the passionate attentions of the young woman, woke in her such mixed feelings of jealousy and longing that all else disappeared from her mind except the need to see the lover she had almost sworn never to meet again.

She went up the steps of the house and rang the bell. The maid who answered the door, bobbing a little curtsey to Jane as she went in, was no older than seventeen and extremely pretty and Jane glancingly wondered whether this innocent girl was now and then invited into her mistress's bed. She was led into a large drawing room, where a fire was burning. Told that Mr Sims was abroad and that Mrs Sims had retired early, she asked the girl to fetch pen and paper.

The maid went out to find this and Jane sat down on a Louis XVI chair upholstered in pale blue brocade. She looked about her at the treasures acquired by Ashton Sims and his wife: the Ormolu clock on the marble mantelpiece, the China blackamoor holding aloft a gas lamp, the exquisitely covered sofas and chairs, the Georgian tables, the Turkey carpet, the Dutch paintings, the palms in huge ceramic pots, the silver candelabra, the oak bookcases filled with leather-bound editions of Ashton's authors' works, the dog basket lined with sheepskin … And she thought, all this is right for Julietta. She belongs to this world of expensive, perfectly arranged things, for she is Beauty Itself. She could imagine the palms longing to caress her with their leaves, the Dutch pitcher-bearer in one of the paintings gazing mournfully down upon her, wishing she could escape from the picture to hold Julietta against her bosom. If these thoughts were childlike and foolish, Jane didn't care. She felt herself to be seated, now, in some inner sanctum of human pulchritude. She could almost hear music rising from the floor or whispering from the walls.

When the pretty maid returned with the paper and pen, Jane wrote:

Julietta, my dearest,
*   I am downstairs, seated among your treasures. Please may I come to you? Emmeline is gravely ill and we may be about to lose her. I think that only you can comfort me.*
*   Jane*

She handed the paper to the girl, knowing perhaps that – if the girl could read – she would look at the note, but not minding whether she did or not, even faintly aroused by the notion that this very young woman had knowledge of all that went on in Julietta's room when Ashton was away.

Now, she was being shown into that room.

Julietta lay in an enormous bed, her hair uncoiled on the pillow, her arms bare above the sumptuous satin and brocade coverings. Even before the maid had retreated from the room Julietta sat up, revealing naked breasts, and called out Jane's name. Jane rushed to her and took her in her arms, smelling at once the musk of the sexual banquet she had indulged in with her 'beauty' and made bold enough by this to find Julietta's mouth and kiss her so deeply as to make Julietta begin to moan with pleasure and Jane thought that this kiss was like no other that she had ever had in her life.

And whatever ecstasies Julietta had indulged in only half an hour before, Signóra Sims, never sated, now pressed Jane's hand down between her legs to show how ready she was to begin again on one of those wild hours where both women surrendered all restraint and lost themselves in an orgy of loving.

In moments, Jane was naked in the bed, her clothes thrown down carelessly on the floor. At the bedside, Julietta's pet spaniel gazed up in sweet perplexity as Jane once again felt the melting touch of *la langue de Juliette*, known far and wide as the greatest bringer of pleasure a woman could ever know. And this time, because Jane had been deprived of it for so long and was so deeply frustrated by her love-making with Ross, the moment of ecstasy was so long and deep, it made Jane cry out.

Later, Jane put on her clothes and Julietta put on a satin gown and brushed her hair and the two women went down to the drawing room, with the little spaniel dog following them. It was now that Jane explained what had happened to her aunt and Julietta comforted her with the very words Jane ardently wished to hear. 'You will save Emmeline,' she said. 'Now that you are in London, she will be saved. It is as simple as that.' Then, to console them both, Julietta rang for the maid to bank up the waning fire and asked her to bring a jug of claret.

When she had done this and left and the logs were catching brightly again, Jane whispered to Julietta, 'I believe she comes to your bed.

Does she?' and Julietta answered without embarrassment, 'I go to her little room, sometimes in the night when Ashton is asleep.'

'And you give her *la langue*?'

'No. Servants are too unwashed. We masturbate each other and I leave. It is very innocent. We barely speak – only the unspoken whisperings of women and their needs. But I believe she loves me. Her name is Ellen.'

'The *world* loves you, Julietta! You are the most irresistible being I have ever known.'

'And I ...' said Julietta, taking Jane's hand in hers, 'I do believe I love you more than all the others. If it were not for Marco, I can imagine that I could leave Ashton to live with you, as man and wife, and we could be wild and wicked every night.'

Jane turned away and stared into the fire. The phrase 'man and wife' captured in that instant for her a vision of how happy a life with Julietta would make her and reaffirmed that the future she had chosen with Valentine Ross was a mistaken one. She knew now that she loved women, Julietta above all, but perhaps other women, too, if she knew how to ask for that love.

She felt that never in her life had she been more certain of anything: Tall Jane, the Angel of the Baths, was a lover of women and she would always be that. To submit to marriage with Ross would be to plunge them both into a lifetime of misery.

At this moment, Ellen came in with the claret and placed the jug and glasses at Julietta's elbow. Julietta reached out and touched the maid's shoulder and said, 'Ellen, I have been telling Miss Adeane what you and I do sometimes in the night, and she thinks it very touching and sweet.'

A bright blush spread across the girl's features. She opened her mouth to speak, but could find no words.

This seemed to amuse Julietta and she went on: 'Miss Adeane understands that this is very normal and innocent behaviour among uninhibited women and nothing to be ashamed of. Men take advantage of their pretty servants all the time and may often hurt them or get them with child. But we do not hurt each other, do we, Ellen?'

'No, Ma'am,' said Ellen. 'Not at all.'

'And I have never forced you into anything you don't wish to do?'

'No, Mrs Sims. For I do wish to do it.'

'There you are, then. All is well. You may go now.'

Ellen bobbed another curtsey and went out. Jane saw that the blush had spread round to that little bit of her neck just visible beneath her white cap and she found this captivating. The honesty and daring openness with which Julietta lived her life made her gasp; wherever she went, she found and took whatever she needed and refused to feel abashed by any of it. And Jane's own life, she knew, was not lived like this. It had been a constrained and dedicated life, the life of a virgin spinster, and only too late had she discovered an erotic world, with all its possibilities and joys. She felt, at that moment, that she wanted to howl.

She came and knelt in front of the fire and took a sip of claret and said: 'I thought I could marry Doctor Ross, Julietta. I agreed to be his wife in good faith. And I have tried very hard to love him. But I think I cannot go through with it.'

She turned and saw Julietta staring at her with an expression of alarm and was disconcerted that this should be the case. She had expected Julietta to understand her predicament immediately and to sympathise with her decision to abandon her marriage to Ross. After a long moment, Julietta said, 'I hear what you are saying, Jane dearest. But what are you going to do about the other great matter, then?'

'You mean about you?'

'No. I will always be here for you. I mean about your state.'

'What "state"?'

'Oh. You didn't know, Jane? You didn't know that you are pregnant?'

Jane gaped at Julietta. Like the maid, moments before, she could find no words.

'I suppose you hadn't realised, my poor darling,' Julietta went on. 'But I know. When I give *la langue* to a pregnant woman, the perfume of her cunt is different. I am never wrong.'

WHAT TAMINAH KNEW

It was at about this time that the White Rajah fell into a depression.

He tried to fight it off, but didn't seem to have the right weapons. Drinking arak lifted his spirits for a while, but then the darkness closed in on him again. Walking in his garden, seeing the bright parakeets in their aviary and the scarlet lilies all aflame in the sunshine could make him glad that he had ownership of these beautiful things, that his eye alone had seen how they might bring him solace, but then he would remember the hammocks, side by side, where he had lain with Edmund Ross and listened to his New Testament readings and he would feel his mind sliding down once more into an abyss of sadness.

After he had been shown Edmund's body, already decomposing in the forest floor, he had made himself help the Dyaks with the terrible task of digging it up, and transporting it on a cart to the grounds of his house. Here, not far from where the hammocks had once been strung, it was reburied and Sir Ralph reluctantly summoned one of the Catholic missionaries from Kuching to intone a Mass over the dead man's grave. Some of the Malay servants had attended this Mass, crossing themselves from time to time and showing careful respect for the foolish 'Englung man' who had perished in the forest, but Leon had stayed away.

Later, he asked the rajah why he wept for the 'Jesus boy' and accused him of taking Edmund secretly as his lover. And when he said this, Sir Ralph did a thing he would never normally think of doing: he slapped Leon's face. For a moment, it looked to Sir Ralph as though Leon was about to begin one of those physical fights they sometimes indulged in, both of them growling with anger and mortification and conflicted desire, but Leon only nursed his cheek, looked at him with disdain, then turned and ran away. He ran out of the house and was not seen again for three days.

Work had begun on the new portion of the Savage Road that would lead to the river and the site of the cannery and the rajah was interested to see the jungle being cleared, foundations laid and stones broken to form the hardcore of the new highway. The Chinese labour brought in by Leon for these arduous tasks toiled in the great heat. With their small, slim bodies and their wide, conical straw hats, they appeared to Sir Ralph to resemble little mushrooms, bobbing about, scrabbling for a place in the earth. He knew that this was an amusing way to think about them, which, normally, would have made him smile, but he discovered that it saddened him. The life of a mushroom, so brief, he now compared to his own existence in Borneo; he had popped up here, as though overnight, in his white clothes, with his burning red-brown skin beneath, and people had gathered round to stare at him. He had gained a footing in Nature's realm. Now, he was decaying. His heart was pulp. He would soon be gone.

He dated his decline into depression from two events: the disappearance of Edmund, and Leon's obsession with the cannery. He blamed his own inattention in both cases. Why had he not noticed straight away when Edmund had gone missing from their trek to the river? Now, Edmund was dead and he would, in due time, be obliged to search for the address of his brother in England and write to him, relating the sad news. But he put off doing this. He dreaded to be held to account for his failure to take care of Edmund.

And as for the cannery, why had he not refused to sanction the wretched fish factory? It was his money that was going to pay for it, not Leon's. And already great damage had been done. In the shaking hands of Septimus Scaife, so much gunpowder had been packed into his paper tubes and lodged at the feet of the mangroves that the resulting mighty explosion he had boasted about had not only blasted the trees out of the water, it had killed all the fish in a mile-long stretch of the Sadong. Their bodies floated to the surface, nudged along the current by the broken tree trunks. Hundreds of turtles also died and their severed limbs littered the river banks, vitiating the air and bringing vultures down from Mount Ophir.

When Leon was shown this sight, he stuck out his tongue and screamed at Scaife, threatening to scatter *his limbs* along the Sadong and accusing him of sabotaging the project deliberately. The rajah witnessed the engineer turn white and in his attempts to move backwards, away from Leon, fall over his own feet and land ignominiously on his bottom in the mud. He began to protest that the fish would return, that eggs laid upriver by the turtles would hatch, but Leon could only see a white man's ignorance, stupidity and malign intent. Without consulting Sir Ralph, he dismissed Septimus Scaife on the spot, telling him to leave Borneo 'within one day' and never return. He told the terrified man that if he had had a dagger in his belt, he would have plunged it into his heart.

The rajah was tempted to help Scaife to his feet, he looked so forlorn and foolish sitting there among the river debris, but he didn't dare to side with him against Leon. Furthermore, he was inclined to believe that Scaife — humiliated by being sent away from the rajah's house into a lowly cottage — had intended him some harm. Indeed he had always suspected it.

After the three days of Leon's absence, Sir Ralph went in search of him. He couldn't wait passively any longer, because over his sadness was now laid an intolerable frustration: Leon's absence from his bed.

For all Leon's bluster, the rajah knew that he sometimes crept away from this side of himself, to spend time with his mother Taminah. In the presence of his mother, Leon became more docile and quiet. He would often show Taminah tender affection. Sometimes, he swept her house and cooked a meal for her in one of her blackened pots. Sometimes, he helped her to wash her hair in the river.

It was to Taminah's house, therefore, that Sir Ralph made his way. He found Taminah sitting on her hard chair on her veranda. She was cleaning sweet potatoes in a bucket. Beneath the black beech stilts of the house, her pet cockerels stepped daintily around, searching for seeds and grains of millet.

Taminah stood up and the rajah bowed politely to her. He had brought her the gift of some pomegranates and she took them in her thin hands and smiled at Sir Ralph, then disappeared into the darkness of her house.

He hoped that she had gone to fetch Leon, but she only re-emerged with another wooden chair, which she placed beside her own, in the shade, and a small cup of arak, which the rajah took from her gratefully. Though he wanted to ask her straight away if she knew where Leon was, he preferred her to think that he had called on her only out of courtesy. In his fractured Malay, he began asking her if she had been troubled by the explosion upriver. She had heard it, she told him, and she had found dead subaru in the pool below her house. She had netted these and cooked them, but thrown them away because they had not tasted right.

'My son,' she said, 'he believes he will get rich from a cannery, but we who live along the Sadong don't wish for machinery to disturb the morning. And we do not trust Englung engineers.'

'Perhaps you are right,' said Sir Ralph. 'The one who came here was inept. But Leon may have gone in search of other people to undertake this. Has he?'

'I have not seen him since the last rain.'

'Ah …'

'But when I see him, rajah, I shall tell him this: there is a plateau now, where the mangroves are gone. What he must do is to build there. But not houses for fish cans.'

'Houses for families?'

'No, rajah, Sir. Houses for the sick and dying. A hospital.'

Taminah was scratching now at the strangely pigmented skin of her face. It was a sorrowful habit of hers which Sir Ralph had often witnessed and her cheeks were scarred with welts, where her nails had brought out pinpricks of blood. Sir Ralph took a long sip of the arak. Then he asked, 'Do we need a hospital here in the forest?'

'We will need it, rajah. I was in Kuching. I went there in my neighbour Rashid's mule-cart to buy tallow candles and paraffin for my lamp, and as we drove along the streets, Rashid said to me, "Taminah, can you smell it? And do you see how a vapour hangs in the air?" And I looked and saw it and then I breathed in deeply and I could smell it: the Mal de peste.'

'Dengue Fever?'

'I think it is already in Kuching. They say that government soldiers are going to bring in cannon to fire, to try to purify the air. But if it is already there, then it will travel to us and people will begin dying. And some will look to you to help them, rajah. For why are you called rajah if you cannot help the people on your lands?'

Sir Ralph laid aside the arak and looked out at the vibrant yellows and greens of Taminah's banana grove and the bamboos clustering down towards the river pool, and he thought – as he often did – how much he wanted everything to grow and thrive like these things, but what, in the end, could one man do against the catastrophes decided upon by Nature?

When Sir Ralph got back to his house, he found Leon lying in his room.

Leon looked pale and tired. He said he had been in Kuching 'to go with boys' and he needed to sleep now.

The rajah sat down on Leon's bed. If he had not had the conversation with Taminah about the Mal de peste, he might have been more wounded by the idea of 'boys' than he was, but what worried him principally now was that his lover had been in Kuching and might already have caught the sickness that was beginning there.

He reached for Leon's hand, but Leon moved it away. 'Boys,' he said, 'very exhausting. Want fuck all the time.'

The rajah stared at Leon – his smooth brow, his flattish nose, his sensual lips, his long black eyelashes – and thought, whatever he says to me, however he taunts me, I will never not be awed by how beautiful I find him.

'I'll leave you to sleep, Leon,' he said gently. 'But I have been talking with your mother. She tells me we must start building a hospital.'

'I know,' said Leon. 'I know all about it. Bad fever. Those boys tell me while I am fucking them. I make a joke. I say "is that why we are fucking then, to keep death from the door?"'

Sir Ralph ignored this and said, 'Taminah suggests we build long-houses and make bamboo bunks – for the sick – where the cannery was going to be sited. On that new plateau.'

'I know,' said Leon again. 'No fish factory now. No money for Leon. No money for you, rajah. My beautiful idea kaput.'

OUT OF REACH

Jane left Julietta's bed at dawn and walked back to Tite Street.

She asked for hot water and washed herself. She felt dizzy from lack of sleep, but was now concerned only with getting back to the hospital to rescue Emmeline. She knew that the day in front of her would be long and difficult, but her hours with Julietta had been so extraordinary, they had given her both peace and strength.

As she washed herself, she looked at her body in the mirror. It appeared to her the same as it always appeared. If she was indeed pregnant, it would still be so early in the process that she told herself she wouldn't even think about it – not yet. Carrying Julietta in her heart and in her blood, she would now begin her fight to get Emmeline back. She had brought to London the gown she wore as the Angel of the Baths and she would now put this on. All the skill she possessed would be directed at making Emmeline well and placing her gently back in the life she loved.

She ordered Nancy to go out and buy fresh loaves, milk and oysters and to ask at the chemist for a strong fruit cordial and a balsam of camphor. She supervised the laying of clean starched sheets on Emmeline's bed and searched her studio for books she might read aloud to her, pressing to her breast the poems of Tennyson, Browning and Christina Rossetti. She prepared a warming pan. She mixed tooth powder in a small dish. Then she went out into the neglected garden and searched the tangled area for flowers. She found a few pansies clustering under brambles and picked these and arranged them in a little cut-glass vase, which she placed on Emmeline's dressing table.

She took one of Emmeline's turbans from a hat box and put it into a canvas holdall.

Then she set forth in a Hansom Cab for the hospital. On the short journey, she found herself summoning thoughts of her own mother, never known by Jane, her life ending only minutes after her daughter's began. Her name was Alice. By Sir William's account, Alice had been 'a person to whom human kindness came as easily as breathing' and it was often said of her that she had never 'done any wrong in the world'. And Jane thought now, 'I have done wrong – in the eyes of English society, which forbids love between women. I will do wrong again.' And she wondered, with sudden sadness, whether this kindly mother, this perfect Alice, would have cast her daughter out from her affection because of her sexual transgressions. Was it better, she wondered then, that Emmeline had had to play the motherly role – she who had given birth to nothing but half-formed creatures, ejected from her body in agony and memorialised in a clay golem, but who seemed to understand so well what was in Jane's nature and in her heart? Had Alice died, knowing that her daughter would come to need a different mother?

If these thoughts had something strangely hard-hearted about them, Jane also knew that she had never needed Emmeline more than she needed her now. It was only to her aunt that she could reveal the dilemma she was in, certain to receive Emmeline's calm wisdom on how her future might unfold.

Jane held herself very tall as she went in through the high doors of the hospital entrance. The long corridor which led to the room where Emmeline lay was deserted except for a thin woman kneeling on a slatted wooden board, scrubbing the stone floor with carbolic soap and a pail of grey water. As Jane walked by her she removed her coat, letting the woman see her white nurse's gown beneath and the kneeling woman stared up at her in perplexity, as if she'd seen someone or something unearthly. Jane strode on. Feeling choked by the strong smell of the carbolic, she realised that her heart was beating very fast.

She entered the vaulted space she'd termed 'the ante-room of death'. As before, it was empty of nursing staff and very dark, with all but one of the window shutters closed. She saw that a large wooden table had been placed between the two rows of beds and on this were laid out small bowls of junket, with, in each one, a stubby wooden spoon, such as one might give to a child to feed itself. Junket was a food Jane found repellent, but at least it was sustenance of a kind, indicating that the dying women were fed from time to time. She snatched up one of the bowls and made her way to Emmeline's bed.

She was about to sit down beside her aunt and try to persuade her to eat some junket before she prepared her for the journey back to Tite Street when she looked down and saw that the person in the bed was not Emmeline: she was a small woman with a shrivelled forehead and tiny hands, like the claws of a little jungle animal.

Jane looked all around her, then walked slowly down the ward, examining the occupants of the iron cots – pale, startled faces, many scalps shorn of hair, bony fingers clutching at sheets or holding onto the iron bed-heads, as if to anchor themselves to what remained on their time on earth. When they saw Jane, one or two of the women called out to her, reminding her of the way the sick called to her at the Baths. These people did not call her 'angel'. They did not know who this tall stranger could be, but only that she looked strong and that she was *there*, and not hiding from them, as the other nurses so often chose to do.

The crying out of the patients did at last bring forth a portly Matron, too fat for her uniform, cramming the last morsel of a jam tart into her cheeks. A few sticky crumbs came tumbling from her mouth as she shouted at Jane, 'What in the world are you doing here? Did you come to steal the patients' junket?'

Jane held herself very still. She allowed the Matron to come bustling very close to her before she replied calmly, 'I came looking for my aunt, Miss Adeane, to take her home.'

'Who is "Miss Adeane"?' said the Matron.

'Miss Emmeline Adeane, the artist. I came to see her yesterday evening. I informed two of the doctors that I would be returning this morning to convey her home.'

'Well,' said the Matron, 'I know of no such person. I have been here since six o'clock, doing the roster, and no one of that name is on this ward.'

Jane pointed to the cot where Emmeline had lain. She was about to say that this had been Emmeline's bed, when the Matron surprised her by snatching the bowl of junket out of her hand and slamming it down onto the table, after which she turned tail and began to walk away.

'Where is my aunt?' Jane cried out.

The Matron was almost at the door when she said, 'if a female patient who was here yesterday is not here today, then there is only one place she will be: in the morgue.'

She was gone then and Jane stood very still, trying to catch her breath. She put a hand to her throat, as if to ease the passage of air. She was aware of some of the dying women attempting to sit up, to see her more clearly, this stranger in a white gown who had been stricken by the words of the Matron. One of them reached out a beckoning hand to her, and Jane, wondering if this woman knew what had happened to Emmeline, moved towards her, but as she did so, the patient made a frenzied gesture towards the bowls of junket on the table, then pointed to her mouth. Jane turned to fetch the food for her and as she did so, other women began calling out for the junket and Jane wondered if they were often tortured like this – food being placed near them, but not within their reach.

She began distributing the bowls, placing them gently into trembling hands. All of this she did with her thoughts peculiarly absent from her actions. It was as if these things were being done in order, simply, to keep her breathing until she found the will to undergo the next moments of her life.

The hospital morgue was housed in a deep cellar.

Jane was led down to it by one of the doctors she had seen the evening before. He gave her a steadying arm. His former impatience with her appeared to have been mastered. Jane thought about the last time she had been in a morgue, in Paris. All that had been asked of her then was pity; now, she had been plunged into her own sorrow.

The doctor told her that Emmeline had died 'in her sleep' not long after she'd left. 'In cases like hers,' he said, 'where the damage to the heart is great, we always pray that death comes quickly.'

'Are you telling me,' said Jane, 'that my aunt did not suffer?'

'No. I'm not quite saying that. She would have suffered when the attack came. But once she had arrived here, we put her very soon into a state of sleep, and there her suffering ended. It was all we were able to do for her.'

They descended lower. The foetid smell of the morgue assailed them as they neared it. The doctor lit a gas lamp and as the white light blossomed up, hissing like a sudden wind, Jane could see that all the benches on which the dead were habitually laid out were empty – except one. And it troubled Jane that her aunt, who had lived such a scintillating, gregarious life, should be quite alone in the hospital morgue. She knew that this was a childish thought, but nevertheless she couldn't stop herself from weeping at Emmeline's terrible loneliness.

The doctor handed her a handkerchief, whipped from his coat pocket, and together they went to the bench where Emmeline's body was covered with a sheet. Unable to stop her crying, Jane asked the doctor to uncover Emmeline's face. With great gentleness, he drew the sheet back and there she was, revealed in death, the artist who had never known love's domestic consolations, but who had never ceased her courageous striving and made a life like no other that Jane knew.

Jane knelt down and put her arms round Emmeline's shoulders, quite as if she were still alive, and kissed her cold face. For a while, she laid her head on Emmeline's bony chest and just let her tears flow into the white sheet. The doctor withdrew a few paces, as if the tears were rain and he declined to allow himself to get wet. The hissing of the gas lamp was loud above her, the sound of life's obstinate persistence, even in this dark place. And perhaps it was this which inspired Jane to reach down into her bag and take out the turban she'd brought for Emmeline to wear on her journey back to Tite Street. Wiping her eyes with the doctor's handkerchief, she stood up and bent over the body, raising Emmeline's heavy head and carefully placing the turban upon it, tucking away the escaping strands of unwashed hair.

UNCTION UPON WATER

At about the same time that Jane was leaving the hospital and climbing wearily into the waiting cab, Ashton Sims arrived home from France and entered his house in Tedworth Square.

Told by Ellen that his wife was sleeping, Ashton went up to the nursery, where he found Marco and his nanny, Miss Paley. Miss Paley was sitting quietly knitting, in an armchair, while Marco rode on his rocking-horse, talking to it all the while, urging it to gallop faster and not shy at the sound of the wind in the trees. When Marco saw his father at the nursery door, he gave a shout of delight, tried to vault off the horse and fell over on the hard wooden floor.

Ashton and Miss Paley hurried to help him up, but Marco was a child who seldom cried; he just got to his feet and ran into his father's arms.

'Papa!' he said, 'do you know my horse's name?'

'Yes,' said Ashton, kissing his son, 'I believe I do. I think his name is Pippin.'

'No!' said Marco. 'His name *was* Pippin, but now it is something else.'

'Oh,' said Ashton. 'Did he not like the name Pippin?'

'No. He didn't like it.'

'And he told you this?'

'Yes, he did. Because he talks quite well, Papa. You don't think he can talk, do you, but he can.'

'On the contrary, I know that he talks very well. So what is his new name?'

'It's a secret, but I'm going to whisper it to you.'

'Are you sure you should – if it's really a secret?'

'Yes. Put your ear here, Papa. His name is Trebuchet.'

'Trebuchet?'

'Yes. It's my favourite new word. I learned it from a picture book. It's a weapon for attacking castles. And Nanny says you have to say it Tray-boo-shay, not Tree-bucket.'

'Oh,' said Ashton, laughing, 'but I rather like Tree-bucket! I think I even prefer it. Why not call your horse that: Tree-Bucket?'

Marco began giggling and Ashton thought that this was one of the sweetest sounds in the world, the happy laughter of his son. He hugged him close, then set him down to return to his rocking-horse.

'Does Mama know about Pippin's new name?' asked Ashton.

'Yes of course she does,' said Marco. 'Mama knows everything in the world.'

Made joyful by being with Marco, Ashton was about to suggest a game of spillikins, when Ellen appeared at the nursery door to tell Ashton that he had a visitor.

'It's Miss Adeane,' said Ellen, 'Miss Jane. She has some sad news to tell you.'

'What sad news, Ellen?'

'I don't know, Sir. She is in the drawing room.'

'I like Jane,' said Marco. 'She was here last night, wasn't she, Ellen? She and Mama were laughing. I heard them.'

Ashton noticed that Ellen blushed as she nodded. He knew what all of this suggested, but it was Ashton Sims's great and secret strength that knowing a potentially troubling thing only inclined him, not to apportion blame, but rather to alter his own perception of the matter, to steel himself to consign it to a part of his mind where it would no longer hurt him.

How many men could have done this? He wasn't sure that many could, given what rules and constrictions husbands felt justified in laying upon their wives and how angry and violent they could become if these were broken. But Ashton was not of this temperament. And he knew that his love for Julietta had a kind of magnificent *largesse* about it. It was a *world of love*, a wide, accommodating terrain of affection. Ashton truly didn't mind where his beauty of a wife sometimes took her pleasure, if that was her nature's inclination, provided she did not leave him. That alone would have left him bereft and angry. His greatest hope and expectation was that they could have more children and live in the domestic contentment they had both striven to perfect for many years to come.

This way of loving Julietta meant, therefore, that when he encountered one of her female lovers – and the witty and striking Jane Adeane was surely now included in that number – he felt no hostility towards them, but rather some kind of aesthetic bond, as though they and he had discovered themselves to be awed by the work of the same artist or moved by the same piece of music.

He found Jane kneeling by the fire, weeping.

When she told him of Emmeline's death, he got down beside her and put a tender arm round her shoulders. On his own account, he was saddened by the loss of a woman he had always liked and admired, but he knew by now what Emmeline Adeane had been to Jane and he was at some pains to find any words of comfort.

After a moment, he said: 'Jane, I am going to pour you a glass of brandy. Brandy may be much more help to you than platitudes from my mouth. Then I will get Ellen to wake Julietta and she will come and comfort you.'

He rose and rang the bell to summon Ellen, then poured the brandy and Jane took it gratefully. He led her to a comfortable chair and arranged a cushion behind her head. He saw that she was pale and trembling and that grief had somehow reduced her, so that she appeared smaller than she really was, as if pressed down and inwards by some intolerable weight. Between sobs, she murmured apologies for the state she was in and for troubling the household, saying she did not know where else to go …

'Hush, my dear Jane,' said Ashton. 'I'm very glad, and indeed touched that you came to us.'

'I would have given anything to have saved her, Ashton. In Bath, I know that I've contributed to the saving of lives, but I could not save hers …'

'Drink the brandy, dear girl. Take a gentlemanly swig! And then we will talk of Emmeline, if this is what you desire. Or we will remain quite silent, if it would help you more. But just know that you are safe with us.'

'My poor father!' said Jane suddenly, attempting to rise from her chair. 'I had quite forgotten. He will be so sad. We must send word ...'

'Don't fret. I will see to it. I expect he can be in London by tomorrow. And listen to me, Jane, all the legal paraphernalia of death, my lawyers, who also took care of your aunt's affairs, can take this on, if that is what you wish. You have only to say what you want.'

'Thank you, Ashton,' said Jane. And she added on impulse, 'You are a good man. I believe I know very few, but you are one of them.'

'No,' said Ashton, unable to prevent an edge of sadness from inflecting his voice, 'I am not good; I am only a pragmatist.'

Ellen came into the room at this moment and behind her, Julietta, still in her silken night robes, with her hair wild and exhaustion in her eyes. She went first to Ashton and kissed his cheek, to welcome him home, then flung herself down beside Jane. The scent of her body, after the glut of her night, perfumed the room with a scent so potent, it made Ashton's head swim.

'I heard, I heard!' cried out Julietta to Jane, 'oh my poor darling! Ashton, how in the world are we to comfort Jane? Let me take her in my arms. Come here, sweet angel.'

Julietta pulled Jane towards her and the two women clung together and sobbed, while Ashton stood very still, looking on, and Ellen stood by him blushing so hard one might have expected to see some vestige of a pink colour creep its way into the white lace of her maid's cap.

Given that he had been tasked with contacting Sir William Adeane, Ashton now excused himself from the room, quickly followed by Ellen. Sensing they had gone, Julietta began to kiss Jane's face and lick the salt tears from it and from her lips and then let her tongue probe the wet mouth, as if tears were the things with which it now delighted to quench a vast thirst. And it felt to the two lovers that their intimate world had taken on an oily, liquefied form in which sorrow and desire gleamed and trembled with rainbow colours, like unction falling upon water.

TABLEAU

Knowing nothing of what had happened in the last twenty-four hours, and no longer content to wait passively in Bath for Jane's return, Valentine Ross arrived at Tite Street on the afternoon of that same day.

In his pocket was the emerald and diamond ring, and all along his journey to London, he'd been instructing himself to set aside his anger with Jane for her sudden departure and to show her nothing but kindness. He had even decided that he might force himself down on his knees to offer her the ring. Yet he could feel inside him a residue of profound irritation with her which he could not shake. Since her father's return from Ireland, she had steadfastly refused to let Ross make love to her, and she would not even come to his rooms alone – another vexing assertion of her power over him.

He had begun ardently to wish that he did not desire her so incontinently and once again indulged in fantasies of subduing her in ways that would give him sexual release but which caused her physical pain. For how, he reasoned, could he bear to have a wife like this, who submitted to him in nothing and never would submit? Surely, this was a recipe for unhappiness as deep as black night? In terrible daydreams he bound her, face-down to his bed with rope, or even chains, whipped her buttocks till welts appeared on them, then entered there, a sodomite slipped from all bounds of tenderness or obligation – a man in *flagrante delicto* whose only intent was release through punishment.

Though he tried to lay such fantasies aside, they returned from time to time, causing him intense arousal, and this was so troubling to him that he had taken to revisiting the prostitutes at the Neck Tavern, but now paying additional sums to enact his cruelties with them.

Emmeline's maid, Nancy had let him in to number 2a Tite Street. He introduced himself to her as Miss Jane's fiancé and she bobbed a token curtsey to him. Ignorant as yet of Emmeline's death, she informed him that Jane had returned to the hospital, but was expected to bring Emmeline home 'as soon as she may be well enough'. He thanked her and asked her to make him a pot of tea.

Left alone in the hall, Ross wandered into the high space that was Emmeline's studio. The scent of turpentine was both pleasing to him and a cause of immediate unease. It was the perfume of the artist's work and in this large room he knew that what he was witnessing was the kind of dedicated endeavour of which he himself had never been capable. On an easel rested a half-completed still life of some china birds clustered around a wine bottle and he found himself admiring the way Emmeline had seen how the shapes of these objects made such a pleasing group.

Along the skirting were stacked canvases of differing sizes, some half-completed or rejected, some primed and pristine, waiting for new work. Although Ross expected to come across the portrait of Jane here and wondered what he would feel when he came face to face with it, there was no sign of it. He let his gaze shift above the stack of paintings, where, carelessly pinned to the wall, there were hundreds of charcoal sketches, essays upon ideas not yet fully formed: a human profile here, a naked foot there, a sprig of privet in flower, a bird in flight, a Chelsea costermonger with his cart, a wrought-iron gate, a rock rising from the sea ...

And Ross saw in all this a mind restless to capture what it beheld and try to transform the mundane and the quotidian, as well as the beautiful, into art. He felt that what he was looking at was the embodiment of the things Jane loved and valued. She'd gone running to London, without a backward glance in his direction, because in Emmeline she'd found somebody she deemed worthy of her adoration.

His next thought, as he looked at the quantity of brushes and palette knives on Emmeline's work table, was, could he, with the surgical instruments at his disposal, one day achieve some great medical triumph, some feat of salvation that would engender in Jane's heart the reverence and admiration of the kind she felt for Emmeline? He could see how different his world might appear to her, if only he could do this. His wife would no longer be haughty and teasing. She would live in awe of him. In bed, she would submit to whatever he chose to do. He would have vanquished her.

It was then that a new idea began to form in his mind: he would marry Jane and oblige her to come with him to Borneo, thus separating her from all that she knew and cared for, aside from him. Once on the Malay Archipelago, he would set about his task of rescuing Edmund, then establish himself – there in a primitive land, where superstition no doubt vanquished sensible medical practice – as the man who was bringing healing medicines and a surgeon's skills to an entire community, soon to be revered for hundreds of miles as a White God.

And Jane? What task could she find for herself except as his nurse, his inferior, his helpmate? And then in time, of course, she would be demoted even from that role. She would simply be Mrs Ross, the mother of his children. And there would be many children, for his lust would never be contained. Jane would become a lumbering figure, dragging her great height about in silent weariness. She would live for nothing except the love of her family. She would crave attention and tenderness from him, but he would ration it. He would make her go down on her knees and beg …

This reverie so preoccupied Ross's thoughts that he was startled when Nancy approached him to say that a tray of tea awaited him in the drawing room. He put down the palette knife he found himself to be holding. Though shocked by the violence underlying his scheme, he considered that in his Borneo plan might lie his salvation – the only salvation that he could envisage at that moment. He liked the mathematics of it. It would solve the complex equation he had been wrestling with for months: how to do his duty by his brother while at the same time committing himself to marriage with Jane.

Already, he saw the ship – one very like the *Rainsford* – waiting for him and Jane at Plymouth. He saw the cramped darkness of the cabin in which they would lie.

Nancy had served China tea, which Ross did not like. In the perfumed bitterness of it he understood how different Emmeline's tastes were from his own. Forced by his visit to the studio to admire her, he now felt that he might be obliged to dislike her on this account alone.

Setting the tea aside, he rang for Nancy. A great weariness was upon him and he urgently wished to rest before having to meet Jane. Indeed the idea of sleep was now so seductive to him that he closed his eyes and almost let himself fall across the padded Chesterfield on which he was sitting. But he also longed for a soft bed and, explaining that he had been travelling for a great quantity of time, asked Nancy to show him to a room upstairs.

The room she chose for him was small and dark, containing the kind of narrow cot which reminded him of his boarding school and he wondered if she had insulted him by offering him a servant's lodging. He had noticed that the way this girl looked at him was sly and it came into his mind that perhaps she had been privy to Jane's darkest secrets, and now felt nothing but pity for this 'fiancé', who knew nothing of them. For a moment, he considered taking the maid roughly by the arm and commanding her to tell him what visitors Jane Adeane had received at Tite Street, but, as if fearing that this was what he might be going to do, the girl had quickly fled away.

As soon as she'd gone, Ross left the allotted room and began opening other doors on the top landing. In the third room, he saw a peignoir belonging to Jane lying on a double bed and her hairbrush fallen onto a sheepskin rug. And these familiar possessions, glimpsed in the nights Jane had spent with him, suddenly touched his heart with anguish. Closing the door quietly behind him, he went towards the bed and gathered the peignoir into his arms and buried his face in its silken folds. Tenderly, he picked up the hairbrush and set it on a mahogany dressing table.

Though he knew that he should not let himself sleep here, he was unable to resist the temptation to do so. He removed his coat and his boots. He took the emerald ring out of his coat pocket, lest it fall out unnoticed, and set it on the dressing table. Then he lay down, cradling the peignoir as a child will cradle a garment belonging to its absent mother. In the scent of the peignoir he felt that he could recognise everything that resided in the soul of his beloved: her angelic power, her beauty and her passion.

It was dark when he woke. Through the window, Ross could see the flickering of a gas lamp at the further end of Tite Street.

He got up and put on his boots and splashed his face with water from a ewer on a washstand. He smoothed the bed and laid the peignoir across it, much as he had found it. Forgetting about the ring, he descended to the drawing room, sensing as he went down the stairs the quietness of the house and wondering whether Jane had not yet returned. He stood in the hall for a moment, noting that candles were burning in the drawing room. He felt hungry and hoped that supper might be being prepared in the kitchen, but there was no scent of cooking and such a heavy silence lingered about the place that he feared he was still alone, except for the sly maid, and was destined to wait out more useless hours before Jane appeared.

But when he pushed open the drawing room door, he saw her. She was lying, fast asleep on a chaise longue, with one foot dangling to the floor. By her side, resting her dark head on Jane's lap, knelt one of the most beautiful women Ross had ever seen.

For a long time, Ross did not move at all. His gaze remained fixed upon this tableau, as though upon a painting whose meaning he knew to be important but could not perfectly understand.

'BRITISH EMPIRE DOCTORS'

The arm of the Savage Road which led to the Sadong was now complete. Sir Ralph Savage walked back and forth on it, back and forth, back and forth until the sound of his own feet tired him. All the while, as he paced, he was admiring the road's straightness and the way the white stones sparkled in the sun. But what he was trying to see in it, above all, was a man-made entity which would *resist*. He instructed himself to have faith in the new structure, yet dreaded to witness the damage the heavy rains might nevertheless inflict.

At least the road existed. This made the rajah glad. Now, at its further end, Chinese labourers would begin building three large long-houses, on stilts, close to the river. The rajah had told them that these were to become a hospital and regretted saying this when he realised that many of them had taken fright at the idea of the sick from Kuching being brought here and simply run away.

To those who stayed loyal to his project he gave an impromptu address. Drawing himself up to his not inconsiderable height, tying a gold satin ribbon in his thick grey hair, and wearing his (by now rather ancient and rusted) regimental sword in his belt, he stood on one of the wooden crates that had contained Septimus Scaife's gunpowder and told his 'little mushrooms' that they were the heroes of his kingly domain. A hospital, he reminded them, is the greatest edifice a man can build. By doing this work, he interposes himself between life and death. It was for this reason that he had decided to pay those who remained till the end of the endeavour, not in base coinage, but in silver.

Staccato notes of astonishment came from the assembled labourers and then they began to applaud the rajah. He had not, of course, said *how much silver* he would give them. In the minds of some, perhaps it was a paltry sixpence and in the imagination of others a shining ingot or a three-tiered necklace. But the word 'silver' worked a kind of inevitable magic in Borneo at this time. Speculation about how great a quantity of silver ore Sir Ralph had hidden somewhere in his mighty house was widespread among the Malays under his rule and the rajah – despite fear of armed robbery – did not discourage this. He wished to be thought of as being as rich as Queen Victoria herself. He knew that such power as he had depended not so much upon his voracious will, as upon his fortune.

Returning from giving his address to the Chinese workers, Sir Ralph realised that for the first time in a long while, his spirits had lifted. He found himself retrospectively pleased with the image he had presented to the 'mushrooms': a strong, virile ruler whose compassionate heart and eccentric dress set him apart from other colonial masters. He found himself foolishly hoping that the forest itself had been listening and watching. For was the building of a hospital not a magnificent defiance against the depredations of Nature? He swore to himself that when the Mal de peste arrived on his lands, nobody would die of it.

Leon had been at his side during the speech. Indeed it had been Leon who had found and tugged into place one of Scaife's gunpowder crates for the rajah to stand on and then, in the middle of the address, had had a moment of intense worry that the box still contained dynamite unused by Scaife and might, by some means known only to science, ignite itself and blow the rajah into the sky.

But it had not happened and, as the rajah and Leon walked back down the new road towards the house, the Malay felt his love for Sir Ralph blossom up in him once more. The man, he told himself, was much too vain and much too 'English' in his soul to be admired entirely, but he was, in own peculiar fashion, a kind of hero, and Leon knew that his recent spate of anger with him was now past. He took the rajah's huge hand in his and caressed it.

Later, Leon sat down and began calculating how much black beech-wood, how much rattan and bamboo and how much palm leaf thatching would be needed for the three longhouses, how many cots and hammocks could be fitted into them and what space would be

needed for cooking areas and privies. He then began on sketches –
much like those he had done for the cannery – to be shown to the
workmen. These were deft, almost like the drawings done by a professional architect, and when Sir Ralph professed his admiration for
them Leon said: 'You like them? Then you make me overseer of this
hospital, my rajah. I will whip the coolie-boys and they will work very
well.'

'I hope there is no need of "whipping", Leon?'

'Whip with tongue. Keep everybody in line …'

'Whip with tongue? All right.'

'But there are two questions I do not know.'

'What are they, Leon?'

'First: silver. How much you give me, your overseer?'

Sir Ralph looked at Leon bent over his admirable drawings. The
complex question of how he was to reward his lover for being his
life's companion had never been satisfactorily answered in his mind.
He was in the habit of burdening him with gifts, some of which
found their way into Taminah's hut, but he seldom gave Leon more
money than he needed. He thus did not know how to answer this
question.

'I will give you what we both think is fair,' he said at last.

'That is no answer. For how much is fair?'

'It depends. Will the hospital be strongly built, or will it start
collapsing at the first rains?'

'You see my drawings …'

'The drawings are very good.'

'Then hospital will be good. No collapsing. And my job of overseer,
very hard work. So you must pay.'

'I will pay once the hospital is finished.'

Here, Leon set aside his sketches, took up a clean sheet of paper
and drew on it an irregular shape, shaded to look like a small boulder,
measuring five or six inches across. He passed this to Sir Ralph.

'You see my new drawing?' he said. 'This is a picture of the silver
you must give me.'

The rajah smiled. 'And what will you do with this much treasure?'

'I will get married. I will give a great banquet for my wedding feast.
But don't worry, my rajah, I will invite you!'

Sir Ralph laid his hand on Leon's head and ruffled his gleaming hair. The gesture was intended to say, I know you will always be able to taunt me with such threats, but for now, I choose to let them fly away – mosquitoes that whine in the air I breathe but do not bite me.

'It is thoughtful of you to say you will invite me,' he said. 'I will be delighted to accept. Now tell me, what was the second question you had for me?'

Leon was now laboriously writing the word 'silver' under his drawing. When he looked up from this, he said, 'Hospital no good, Sir Raff. This I see.'

'What? What do you mean, "no good"?'

'For hospital, we need doctors. Without that, hospital no good. You think there are doctors hiding under mangrove, or swinging up in branches with gibbons? We need British Empire doctors. Black coat. Tall hat …'

At the mention of 'British Empire doctors' the rajah's heart cramped with dread. Edmund had many times mentioned his brother Valentine, working as a doctor in the city of Bath, and it was to him that the rajah should have written, but from day to day, he put off this task. His excuse was that he had searched among Edmund's possessions for the brother's address and had not yet found it.

'We don't need such people,' he said. 'The Dyaks know many medicinal remedies. Doctors from England have no more knowledge of the Mal de peste or its causes than we do.'

'But why should they not help us? You say, rajah, you rule here to bring help to us – Sir Raff Savage helping Poor Ignorant Savage! You don't think this? Your Englung mind superior and us just nin-poops?'

'No. I don't think it. We know certain things; the people of Borneo know other things. We try to join our knowledge up.'

'Join knowledge up? That's what I say. Bring British Empire doctors to see our life. Look up at our sky and ask the Brahminy Kites "why is fever in the mist?"'

A BOUT OF SINGING

For a long time the bodies of fish and turtles killed in the explosion floated down the river past Taminah's pool. Then, one day, there were no more of them. The river flowed steadily on, but it appeared empty of all life except the clinging and curling fronds of water-weed. Taminah stood at its edge, wondering how long it would be before living fish returned.

At her back, were the juddering and breaking sounds of construction: beechwood piles driven into the earth to form the stilts of the longhouses, bamboo poles cut with great blows of the axe, accompanied by human cries, saws being worked with delicacy to create level planks for the flooring.

Knowing that her son had been put in charge of the building work, Taminah had agreed to help him by cutting and stitching palm leaves for thatching. An elderly Chinese worker, known only as Lin, a man whose body was so thin and deformed by the long labours of his life that he was unable to stand up straight, brought her great mountains of palm, carried on his bent back and let them fall on her veranda, sending the cockerels scurrying away on their long tethers. Taminah gave this man water and he thanked her and in his smile it was revealed to her that he had no teeth, and pity for him suddenly extended to wanting to cradle him in her arms and stroke his head. Each time he returned with more and more palm, this feeling of wanting to show Lin tenderness and affection grew stronger.

Leon came to the construction site every day. Taminah watched him and saw that he was putting on weight and that he strutted around in an arrogant way, arms folded across his chest, barking orders. The Chinese, whom he referred to as 'the rajah's little mushrooms', appeared afraid of him. And this new vision of her son as the overseer of the hospital made her aware that although she thought that she knew him, she had never before seen so clearly this side of his nature, which longed to wield power over others, even over his own mother, to whom he had always shown such careful respect. When he came up to the veranda, he now told her she was working too slowly. The frames of the longhouses were being assembled very fast, he announced, with some roof struts already in place. Yards and yards of the palm leaf thatching would soon be needed. She was falling behind in her important task.

Taminah told Leon that she was working as quickly as she could, but he commented that he had often observed her daydreaming instead of cutting, weaving and sewing.

'I am old,' she replied. 'You must allow the old their dreams.'

'Oh,' he said. 'What are you dreaming of?'

She didn't wish to admit to Leon that she sometimes dreamed about taking the old man, Lin, in her arms and stroking his head. She told him that she was thinking about the past, when he had been a tiny, beautiful child and his father had made him a little boat out of a turtle shell, in which he paddled about the pond and she had stood by, watching him with awe.

One evening at dusk – when the workers had gone to their huts and the three longhouses were almost complete, with a few cots already installed and privy trenches dug behind them in the bush – Taminah heard unfamiliar voices on the river.

She walked down to the new landing jetty put in below the longhouses and looked westwards and saw a procession of heavy canoes, four or five of them, coming towards her, against the run of the river. In the prow of the first canoe, stood a man with a flaming torch. He was waving it about, trying to cast light on the river bank, and now, when the longhouses came within his sight, he called out excitedly, gesturing to them and calling for the convoy to stop.

The current was strong and threatened to send the boats spinning backwards the way they had come. Taminah watched and listened and realised the voices were shouting in English. After the lighting of more torches, the canoes were manoeuvred in to the jetty and tied up.

Taminah stood very still, invisible in the descending darkness. She saw a group of men assemble on the jetty, perhaps twelve or fifteen of them. They wore wide-brimmed hats and underneath the hats, Taminah guessed that their faces were pale.

These faces were now staring, in the torchlight, at the newly built longhouses. And it was as if, for a moment, they didn't dare to move towards them, as though the longhouses might have been a forest mirage, or else a shrine to some god whose name and necessary rituals were unknown to them. But then two men set off towards them, holding high the torch, and carrying heavy rifles.

She saw them go into the first longhouse and for a moment the torchlight vanished. Then they came out again and began calling to their companions on the jetty, from whom a shout of joy went up and these men began unloading rolls of matting, bulging sacks, spades, guns and cooking pots from the boats. Bent a little by the weight of these things, the group now began to explore all three houses, and, finding them empty, as though providence had set them down before them as a miraculous gift, one group of them broke into a strange, tuneless bout of singing.

Leon had told her about this: that, under certain circumstances, white men had a habit of throwing all decorum aside and, upon some hidden signal, burdening the air with ribald song, the meaning of which was known only to them. It was this to which Taminah was subjected now. The unfamiliar sound echoed all around the forest at her back, driving everything else towards silence – even the river itself. And she knew that what she was witnessing was some complex turn of events, which no one had foreseen and which should not be happening.

The longhouses were being built as a refuge for the sick and dying when the Mal de peste made its terrible way from Kuching to the rajah's lands. But these men were not ill: they were loud and hearty and full of a kind of reckless cheer. She had no idea where they had come from or what they intended to do. She knew only that they had taken possession of the buildings her son had designed as a hospital and upon which so many people had worked for so long.

And she thought again of Lin, struggling up to her veranda with his back-breaking bundles of palm leaves, trudging to and fro like a donkey, never complaining and only accepting a cup of water if it was offered. She wished that he – and not these loud strangers – could have taken possession of a comfortable cot in a newly built house and laid himself down at last to rest.

The strangers made fires at the river's edge and cooked rice and drank and sang their songs far into the night.

In the early morning, when Taminah crept near to the jetty, where the canoes bumped against each other on the fast-running tide of the river, she could see strange objects, slightly resembling the bamboo cradles that white women made for their babies, set out on the mud. And Taminah decided that these things – which were and were not cradles – came forth from a white man's mind, just as the singing came forth from white men's souls, and that only the rajah would be able to determine what all of this might signify.

Taminah thus set off along the new arm of the Savage Road, heading for Sir Ralph's great mausoleum of a house. The sun was not yet up and, in the grey light, the road appeared to her as a ghostly, unpeopled highway which her own footsteps unfolded before her. The jungle all around her was almost silent, a tiny breeze just visiting the tops of the trees and sending its shiver through the air. And Taminah thought about the way sickness and fever were said to travel on the wind and in the damp mists of morning and how this terror might soon reach the very place where she was walking.

She was proud of the way she had turned Leon aside from his fish factory to build the hospital, but now, in the space of one night, it had been taken over by a gang of strangers. And so close to her own house they seemed! She fancied she could smell their sweat and the arak or the grog on their breath. It was as if, with their loud singing and their torches and their fires, they had moved the three new longhouses nearer to her pool than they were ever meant to be.

As she walked on, Taminah began to encounter one or two Chinese workers, emerging from the forest, going towards their day's labour on the hospital dwellings. She wanted to warn them what they would find there, but she kept silent. She was walking quite fast and she was some way from the river now. But at her back she suddenly heard the echoing sound of a rifle shot. She stopped on the road. Birds flew up from their roosts into the pale sky. A gibbon cried out.

DUTTON & CALDECOTT

Around a polished mahogany table, where a glass vase of feathery anemones had been placed to offer some colour and softness to a room which was otherwise drab and severe, the solicitors Mr James Dutton and Mr Bernard Caldecott now sat opposite their new client, Miss Jane Adeane. In front of Dutton and Caldecott lay a legal document written on thick cream paper, sealed with scarlet wax and tied with a red silk ribbon. This document was Emmeline Adeane's Last Will and Testament.

Jane, seated on the opposite side of the table, surreptitiously examined the faces of the solicitors. Her practised nurse's eye told her that they were both men in good health, enjoying a prosperous, rosy-cheeked middle age. They appeared *sane*, and she was glad of this. They had begun by telling her that they had 'acted' for her aunt for many years and she was relieved to believe that men like these had probably had no reason to practise upon her beloved Emmeline the small swindling tricks of which so many lawyers were capable. In short, she was disposed to trust them and to like them.

What she did not like was the presence of Valentine Ross at her side. It wasn't as if she had had to face the solicitors alone. With Sir William now arrived in London and Ashton Sims agreeing to attend, in order to introduce them both to Dutton and Caldecott, Jane felt that there was 'no need' for Ross to be there. But he had insisted that *as her fiancé* he had the right to be present at the reading of her aunt's Will. She had wanted to say to him that, as far as Emmeline was concerned, he had no rights at all. He'd never known her. He'd never shown the least interest in her remarkable life. It felt to her that Emmeline did not belong to him in any way. She belonged to her, Jane, and to her father and she belonged to Ashton because they had been friends for so many years; Ross was truly an interloper in the room. But she had said nothing.

If Ross knew something of Jane's feelings, on this score at least – and he almost certainly did – he was determined not to give way to being excluded. Indeed, he felt that now, more than ever, was a crucial time for him to exert his rights over the woman who had agreed to become his wife. But he saw clearly that in many ways, both small and large, Jane was continuing to defy him, using her grief over her aunt's death as an excuse to hold herself apart from him, showing him no tenderness at all and seeming unwilling to be touched by him. He wondered, in helpless desperation, if this behaviour was some terrible prelude to an announcement that their engagement was terminated. This fear made him unwilling to let her out of his sight.

The lawyers began a polite preamble to the reading of the Will, telling Jane and her father how sorry they were for the family's loss and concerned to let them know how dedicated they had been to the 'great artist'.

'We were at all times ready to offer advice to Miss Emmeline,' said Mr Dutton, 'and especially in matters of her association with galleries, whose fair and honest dealings with the artists they exhibit can never be guaranteed.'

'That said,' went on Mr Caldecott, 'we admired her independence of spirit and I venture to say, in respect of the Will we are about to read to you, that Miss Adeane never arrived at any important judgement without first considering all the facts with the utmost care. Mr Dutton and I have verified to our complete satisfaction that the Will has been correctly drawn up in all respects and that it represents Miss Adeane's last wishes, set down in good faith.'

Here, they paused. Jane heard Ross clear his throat, as if in preparation for making some comment, but he then seemed to change his mind and stayed silent. Mr Dutton untied the red ribbon binding the document and began to read.

The Will first set out some small bequests, mostly of paintings, to be given to friends, including Ashton and Julietta Sims, who were to receive 'two pictures of their choosing' and little Marco who was to have 'five guineas to be spent on toys that will gladden his heart'. A larger financial bequest left the sum of 'one hundred guineas to my beloved brother, Sir William George Adeane, which comes with my undying love to him'. At this point, Jane looked at her father and saw a tear course down his cheek. As he reached for a handkerchief, Jane touched his arm tenderly. Noting Sir William's sadness, Mr Dutton paused and signalled to his colleague. Mr Caldecott got quickly to his feet, went to a low cupboard and took out a decanter of ruby port and poured a small glass, which he handed to Sir William.

When he had drunk a swift draught, Mr Dutton resumed and said, 'we now approach the residue of Miss Adeane's Estate, which consists of a substantial sum of money, currently invested in stocks and bonds, and the ownership of her house, Number 2a Tite Street, which, as she is an unmarried lady, is hers entirely to give as she pleases, unencumbered by conflicting claims of kinship or by any mortgages, debts, pecuniary loans, entailments or legal impediments of whatsoever kind.'

Now, Caldecott stared intently at Jane, as Mr Dutton read: 'it is my final and incontrovertible wish that my house, designated as Number 2a Tite Street, together with the rest of my Estate, including all monetary investments, furniture and chattels, clothes and jewellery, be given absolutely to my beloved niece, Miss Jane Elizabeth Adeane and that my dear friend Mr Ashton Roderick Sims, together with the honourable firm of Dutton & Caldecott, Solicitors and Attorneys at Law, act as executors in this matter, to ensure that Miss Jane Elizabeth Adeane inherits her Portion precisely as stated in this, my Last Will.'

The room was silent. Jane stared at the solicitors, who were now smiling at her. She had heard what had just been stated, but could not, on the instant, take in the enormity of it. All that had preoccupied her since her aunt's death was grief for the loss of her. No speculation about what might be in her Will had entered her mind. If she had thought about the house, it was as some beautiful treasure which would always and ever be inhabited by Emmeline, even in her absence. Always, her pictures would hang on the walls and be stacked in the studio. Always, it would be filled with the sound of Emmeline's voice and with her laughter.

But now, all of this had passed to her! She saw it entire, forever containing the presence of Emmeline, and understood that there was logic in the extraordinary bequest, for perhaps it was only she – who had been a kind of daughter to her aunt – she alone in the world who could become the guardian of Emmeline's legacy, keeping her house just as it had always been and inhabiting it with love.

Jane lowered her eyes to the glass vase of anemones, liking the feathery raggedness of them. She knew that she would never forget this single detail in the offices of Dutton and Caldecott and that the moment would always be coloured by these flowers. And she realised with surprise that a small thread of happiness was being allowed to reside somewhere near her heart.

But something else was happening now. Valentine Ross was speaking. Nobody had asked him to speak, but he had leaned across the mahogany table, closer to the solicitors, intent upon bringing himself into the proceedings.

'Mr Dutton,' he said, 'I do not know if you and Mr Caldecott are aware that Miss Jane Adeane and I are engaged to be married. It is my hope that the wedding will take place as soon as the requisite period of mourning for her aunt is past, and thus before the year's end.'

'Ah,' said Mr Dutton, 'we did not know. Congratulations, Sir.'

'Thank you. However, in consequence of this, there is one important matter which must now be addressed.'

'Yes, Doctor Ross? What is that?'

Ross plunged on. 'I am not a student of the Law,' he said, 'but what I do know is that married women are not legally entitled to own property. Am I correct in that?'

'Yes,' said Mr Dutton. 'As things currently stand. There is a Private Members' Bill to come before the House in the autumn, entitled the Married Woman's Property Act, which would reverse that situation, if passed, but we doubt that it will pass. Is that not so, Mr Caldecott?'

'We fear it may not,' said Caldecott. 'But there will be further Bills …'

'Yes,' said Ross, 'but as things stand, as you say, if Miss Adeane … or rather *once* Miss Adeane becomes Mrs Ross … then such property as she may have been left would by law pass to me, as her husband? Am I correct in this?'

The solicitors looked helplessly at each other, as if neither of them wished to have the task of answering. But at length, both of them nodded. Then Ross turned to Jane.

'I only raise this, Jane, because it is an important matter and I wouldn't like you to be deluded into believing that this can proceed exactly as stated in your aunt's Will, when the reality will be different. But rest assured that I recognise that there is some injustice in the thing. Your aunt wished you to have the place and I will do nothing concerning the house without your consent. All decisions will be shared ...'

Miss Jane pushed her chair back and stood up. Mr Dutton and Mr Caldecott could only gape as the great height of her unfolded itself before them. Without looking at Ross – indeed feeling that she could not bear to look at him – she said: 'I would like to state, to all assembled here, that I think there is *much* injustice in the matter! And the greatest portion of this injustice is towards my beloved aunt. It was not her wish that her house be given to a person whom she did not know. She had a plan for the spaces she inhabited and which were precious to her and the plan concerned me and no one else. It concerned me because she knew I would keep everything safe for her, quite as if she might return among us one day. My aunt told me secrets about her life which nobody else knew. She shared her pain with me and it was me, I am told, she called for when she knew she was dying. So her bequest has a logic to it, which the law should respect. And I think it unkind of Doctor Ross ... I think it very unkind of Doctor Ross ... to try to undo that logic mere moments after it has been set out ... and I really think I cannot—'

Jane wished to go on and say that she couldn't forgive Ross. She knew that he'd done nothing more than point out a law of the land, but she cursed him for his intervention, and would have declared how wretched and thoughtless she found it to be if, at that moment, she had not been stabbed with a sudden acute cramp in her womb and remembered with terror her pregnant state. She sat down abruptly and, as she felt her father's arm come round her shoulders, she began to weep uncontrollably. Once again, Mr Caldecott sprang to his feet and hurried to fetch another glass of port from the low cupboard.

'SHE WAS COMPLETE'

If Ross understood that he'd blundered, which he did, he now only wished to make amends. In the carriage on the way back to Tite Street from the offices of Dutton & Caldecott, he longed to take Jane's hand. It came to him that this might be a good moment to offer her the emerald ring, which he believed he had returned to his coat pocket, but reaching for and not finding it, he then remembered that he had forgotten it! It still lay upon the dressing table near the bed in Jane's room. He cursed himself for this almost as much as for his tactlessness in the solicitors' office. How could such an important thing have slipped his mind? Once again, he was tempted to blame Jane's behaviour for his loss of control over his actions, but quickly decided that this was not quite fair. So he began to stammer that he was sorry to have spoken out about the property laws, but had only done so 'in order that everything should be clear from the outset'.

Jane did not like this word, 'outset'. For what did it indicate but a terrible 'setting out' on a life she now felt she would be unable to bear? She moved herself further away from Ross and said, 'I suggest we do not talk about it at present. It is too painful to me. And Father, may I ask that you and Doctor Ross return to Bath on the evening train? I am sure you should both be faithful to tomorrow's patients, and I would like to spend some time alone in what is, for the moment, my house – before it is taken from me.'

Silence fell in the carriage, as it lurched towards Chelsea. Jane was now feeling sick and only longed to arrive in what had always been designated 'her' room at Number 2a Tite Street and lie down on her bed and close her eyes. Sir William wished ardently that Clorinda had been by his side, imagining that she would have known – by some soothing Irish means – how to defuse the anguish which was visible on the three faces, rendering them strangely gaunt. But they could only go on like this, unspeaking, with Jane trying to master the nausea which was threatening to overcome her, Ross uttering silent curses upon his own impetuousness, and Sir William yearning to be in Mrs Morrissey's tea room, with her tender hand stroking his head and the sweet normality of a cream bun set before him on a china plate.

The men did as Jane had begged them to do and set out wearily on the return train to Bath at seven o'clock. Jane had left them long before, to go to her room, giving Valentine Ross no chance to hold her and beg her forgiveness and no moment in which he could have crept upstairs to retrieve his ring. On the journey westwards, he thought with desperation about the fate of this emerald, not knowing what Jane would deduce from finding the jewel suddenly there on her dressing table, but imagining that she might well assume that it belonged to Emmeline – and thus to her now – and could cast it thoughtlessly into a jewel box, among all the other items of value she now possessed.

Sir William tried to console his dejected future son-in-law by suggesting that Jane's crossness with him was born of her grief for the death of Emmeline. 'Sadness,' he said, 'often puts the human mind into furious angers, but it recovers, and in time Jane will recover. Delay your marriage a little and you will once again have a radiant and contented bride by your side.'

Ross replied that delay was the last thing he wanted. He did not mention the wretched question of the ring, nor say that he believed Jane was, little by little slipping away from him, that she no longer came to his bed and that only by marrying her quickly would he possess her once again. Neither did he mention the 'tableau' he'd seen in the drawing room of Jane and Julietta Sims lying in what appeared to him like passionate abandon on the day bed. He did not mention it because he didn't know how to think about it, knowing only that it was curiously troubling. He said, merely, that he was lonely.

He reminded Sir William that he had waited patiently for Jane for too long a time already and could not bear to wait any longer.

Sir William was sympathetic to these feelings. He wished his own marriage to take place as soon as his mourning for Emmeline was over. But this death had intervened. It had, perhaps, changed the future. For he had already seen in Jane a fiery response to her aunt's Will. He was sure, now, that she would not for long return to being the Angel of the Baths, but would become something else or even *someone else*, leading a bohemian life in London, using her legacy to become as much like Emmeline as she was able to be. How would Ross fit into this new life of hers? Perhaps he would run some expensive surgery from Tite Street, making far more money than was possible in Bath? Perhaps he would father children and be happy? Or perhaps, after all, what had happened today was fatal to any union between Jane and Ross and it would not now come to pass.

As darkness came down, when the train sped away from London and the silent fields of Berkshire offered their hedges and ditches and their sleeping cattle to the moonlight's painterly touch, the two men turned away from each other and stared out at the night. Both were tired and longed to be in a place where they might rest. For Sir William, that place was Clorinda Morrissey's bed, but Valentine Ross realised distractedly that his mind was so agitated that wherever he went now, he would find no real peace until or unless he was reconciled with Jane. As he fell asleep, he had a dream of being in a dark hutch aboard the *Rainsford*, with vast waves rearing up all round the ship, at each moment threatening to send it down into the deep.

Jane was also sleeping.

She woke to find Nancy at her bedside, carrying a bowl of broth for her supper, and as she drank this gratefully, feeling it calm her sickness, the two young women began to conjure memories of Emmeline: the way she regarded herself so critically in a looking glass, the way she would be 'lost' for hours in her studio, eating and drinking nothing, working on by lamplight and candlelight until she could hardly stand for weariness, the way she doted on ballotine of chicken and champagne, the way she arranged her provocative turbans so precisely on her head, the way she liked to dance, the way her moods could change with the changing of the hours …

'She was complete,' Jane found herself saying, not knowing exactly why she'd chosen this word, but knowing only that, for all her early sufferings, Emmeline had embraced her life. She had been the star of her own play. All the songs that had formed in her mind, she had sung.

'Of course,' Nancy said, 'she was often lonely.'

'I know,' said Jane.

'But after you came to stay and she painted your portrait, she said to me, I understand Jane perfectly now. Jane is with me and I won't be lonely any more.'

'I'm glad,' said Jane. 'This makes me glad.'

Nancy helped Jane to get up and she put on a grey silk robe given to her by Emmeline and she went down to her aunt's studio. Here, she lit a lamp and sat down on the ottoman, where Jocelyn Hulton had once lain and pleasured himself, watching Emmeline work. Conjuring this image brought the pottery golem back into Jane's mind and she suddenly felt an urge to see this object again and hold it – the only visible legacy of Emmeline's lost babies – in her hands.

She found it where it had always been kept, at the back of a cupboard, and she brought the box to the lamplight, opened it and look down at it. She hadn't remembered it as being so well formed as this, with a sad face which seemed to hold a human gaze. Had she not looked at it closely enough before? Or was it simply that the golem seemed to have greater life now that its maker was dead?

To respect this life, which was what she felt she wanted to do, Jane decided that she should try to mend the cracks in it. She took the lamp and began to search, among Emmeline's pots of paint, for some glue. When she found it, she selected a fine sable brush from Emmeline's great jar of brushes and palette knives, and working with infinite care to place just enough glue along the breaks in the body of the golem, imagined that she was a surgeon sewing up wounds, which, in time, would become almost invisible.

That night in her diary, she wrote: '*At the end of a momentous day, in which I inherited Emmeline's house and witnessed Valentine Ross attempt to snatch it from me, I rescued the golem. I was standing under the skylight in Emmeline's studio, where once the rain fell on her pottery wheel.*'

Her dreams that night were not of Emmeline but of her unborn child. The image she had of it – a mere shape as yet, a *thing* – alternated with visions of the golem, no longer brittle in its body but soft, like mud, and faintly warm to the touch. Unable to hold the foetus in her arms, she wrapped the golem in a shawl and cradled that and felt it move and try to reach out to her with one of its stubby hands.

Jane would have liked to have gone on dreaming, but she soon enough woke, sweating, and with a feeling of black terror at where her life had now brought her. She saw very clearly how Fate had teased her. It had brought her to the conclusion that she could not marry Valentine Ross. But even as she had arrived, irrevocably, at this decision, it had put his child in her womb.

CITIZENS OF THE WORLD

Sir Ralph, with Leon at his side, appeared before the strangers on the river bank. They had been busy making fires, boiling water and frying bacon, but at the sight of the rajah, they now abandoned these tasks to snatch up their guns.

'Who, in the flaming world, are you?' said one of them, pointing his gun with trembling hands.

Hearing the news of the sudden arrivals from Taminah, and guessing that these were ragamuffin European traders, Sir Ralph had taken the time to place a gold turban, adorned with jewels, on his grey hair and to dress himself in a voluminous white linen robe, tied with a golden sash, which billowed a little in the breeze coming off the water. He was a man who knew only too well how an outward show of magnificence could often subdue clamour and cause in the hearts of the onlookers an uncomfortable feeling of *smallness* and he'd decided this would be his weapon against them. While his wild blue eyes stared down the men, Leon stepped forward and announced, 'you are in the presence of His Excellent-Sea, Sir Raff Savage, Rajah of the South Sadong Territories and you are trespassing on his land. Please put away your guns.'

The men exchanged puzzled looks, while the Chinese labourers hung back, not knowing whether violence was about to break out. Slowly, some of the guns were lowered, but not all. Sir Ralph, meanwhile noticing the cradle-like objects which had baffled Taminah, strode forward and picked up one of these and held it in the air. In his most majestic and sonorous voice, he said, 'Sluice boxes! For the sifting of precious metal. You're styling yourself gold miners, we suppose?'

At this, the men, who were arrayed mostly in patched and tattered clothing, began to look sheepish and all but one of the guns were lowered. But then the oldest of the men, a scrawny carrot-bearded fellow, boldly approached the rajah and said, 'there's no *styling* about it. We're honest Australian miners. We almost made our fortunes in '59, but we went too late. A few tailings were left, but they didn't amount to much. We're the Disappointed of Otago.'

'The Disappointed of Otago?' said Sir Ralph. 'I see. So, in your disappointment, you've come to ransack Borneo? But let me tell you that you are deceived once again. There is no gold along the Sadong.'

'Excuse me, Sir Raff,' said carrot-beard, producing from a torn pocket a yellowed piece of paper, 'but I have a map here. I've worked on the tea clippers, going from Cape York to Guinea, see, and I paid an old-timer good money for this information. He worked a mine not far from here. He told me it was abandoned when a Fever broke out and everybody scarpered, but he vouchsafed to me – is that the word the likes of you would use: *vouchsafed* – that there's still gold in the ground. And the map will take me to it.'

'You don't argue with my rajah please!' said Leon.

'I'm not arguing, mister. I'm stating a fact. Look at the map for yourself.'

He waved the paper in front of Leon's face and Leon, disliking this very much, grabbed hold of the man's wrist and held it in a fierce grip.

'I told you, don't argue with my rajah!' he shouted. 'And now take your guns and your men and your canoes, before we set them on fire, and leave Sir Raff's precious lands!'

'Boys!' hollered carrot-beard, 'Armed and ready! Armed and ready!'

At this, the men raised their guns again and clustered round Sir Ralph and Leon. He lifted up his hands in the manner of a priest about to bestow a blessing and said, 'Listen to me, good souls. I'm a peace-loving man and there is harmony on Savage land. No blood is spilt here. Now, let me tell you that these houses you have occupied are being built as a hospital and you must leave them ...'

'We're not leaving,' said another man, in possession of some thick moleskin trousers too wide for his emaciated hips. 'Not unless you make us. In which case, we'll set them all on fire before we push off. You may be a "rajah", but who says that you "own" the ground we're standing on? And we think, from the sound of your voice, that under all that fancy dress you're just an Englishman, a loyal servant of the Queen. And you know what Australians do to loyal servants of the Queen? We truss them up in their flag and boil them alive!'

This was followed by laughter and cheering and before the rajah or Leon could speak, a third man stepped forward and said, 'we recognise no ownership of lands. We're citizens of the world. And we have as much right to dig for gold, wherever it's hiding itself, as you have to wear that golden topknot. So you go back to your palace, Rajah Excellent-Sea, and let us be.'

Now, there was more cheering and raising of fists and a shot was fired into the air, causing the Chinese workers to creep away into the shadows of the forest. When he heard the shot, Leon let drop carrot-beard's wrist and the yellow map drifted down onto the river strand. But before he could stoop to retrieve it, Leon's foot had ground it into the dark mud. This so enraged carrot-beard, who had carried the map next to his heart across fathoms of ocean and miles of river, that he lunged at Leon and knocked him to the ground.

In this instant, Sir Ralph understood that the woeful invasion could not, at this moment, be resisted, either by words or by the display of power residing in his 'fancy dress'. Staining his white robe in the mud, he reached down and helped Leon to his feet. His lover had been hit in the eye and seemed unable to speak. The rajah knew that he must be in excruciating pain, but that he would die rather than reveal his suffering.

Now, Taminah, who had been watching everything from a safe distance, came to her son's side. 'Ah-yeh, ah-yeh!' she began crying, trying to put her arms around Leon. 'Ah-yeh! Ah-yeh!'

And one of the miners called out, 'that's it, old lady. Take your baby home!'

The rajah retreated to his house and sat in the grandest of his parlours and looked about him at the objects of value he'd amassed and imagined the gold miners crowding in, stinking of sweat and mud, and helping themselves to his treasures and carrying them away. There would be raucous laughter as golden candelabra were broken like beech twigs and handed out like plugs of tobacco, rising currents of sniggering as a Ming vase was used as a pissoir. For the rajah had understood: these 'citizens of the world' had no more respect for man-made boundaries than did the forest. They felt that the succeeding seasons had ravaged them as harshly as they had tormented the trees. They were sticks of men. They tried to put down roots wherever the wind pushed them and their scarred hopes. Their own survival was all that counted.

It was this world of hungry, clamouring people which the rajah had fled when he'd decided to build his palace in the forest. If he knew that only his money and the authority bestowed upon him by a distant Sultan had made him master of his little kingdom, he had also sincerely believed that he would rule over a peaceable, thriving community, united in quietness and in love for their rajah. And Leon's tantrums aside, the years had passed without terror or catastrophe. He had truly believed that he was regarded as a benign ruler. As for his beloved garden, it had flourished to the point where the colours and scents of the flowers were of such intoxicating sweetness that Taminah had once fainted in a bed of lilies.

Now, all was under threat. If gold was found, word would travel by canoe along the river and then more and more boats would come crowding in, bringing more and more desperate men. It wasn't difficult to imagine them cutting down the forest, setting fires, spreading out from clearing to clearing until they arrived within sight of the rajah's lawns. And it was then, Sir Ralph supposed, that they would decide upon their mission to strip the spoiled rajah of his treasures. And, perhaps, they would not stop at the treasures – for why should one white man inhabit so many rooms, when they were living in shacks made of bamboo and palm leaf thatch? But again, why should they stop when they had taken possession of every room in the house? They would not stop. For the idea of torturing an Englishman who wore gold turbans on his head, whose squat little Queen pretended to rule over half the world, including their beloved Australia, would then begin to take root in their collective mind. Leon would not be able to save him, nor his servants. The gold seekers would truss the rajah up like an animal. They would take turns at relieving themselves in various ways upon or in his naked person. And then they would put a bullet through his heart.

LEON'S PLAN

The pain in Leon's eye, great though it was, didn't dismay him quite as much as the temporary loss of his beauty. When he looked at himself now, discovering the shiny purple swellings on his face, he decided that he looked like an insect, and he couldn't bear to let himself be seen, except by his mother.

Taminah stayed in his room with him, sleeping on a mat, bringing him food and water and arak, letting him rage by banging his fist against the wall. When the rajah came to his door he told Taminah not to let him in. Leon felt that his terrible resemblance to a fly would take from him all his sexual power over Sir Ralph and he was not prepared to let this happen.

So the two men stayed apart, both haunted by the arrival of the miners, both trying to work out how the usurpers might be sent away and neither of them finding a solution to something they had never predicted. If Leon let himself imagine different ways of killing them, these reveries soon enough fell apart. From their very appearance, Leon could tell that the gold diggers were anxious, watchful people, used to a life where danger always lurked, where vigilance was second nature to them. To kill one man, an element of surprise was needed; to kill a group of nervous, armed desperadoes much more than this was required. There would need to be a plan.

The plan soon enough formed in his mind, as he knew it would. By his nature and by his cunning, he was a man who found *solutions* to problems which eluded others.

When the swellings on his face had subsided a little, he tied a silk scarf round his head and around his wounded eye and rode to Kuching. He chose the best of the rajah's horses and the exertions of the ride put Leon into a strangely euphoric frame of mind. Though the sun burned down upon him and the dust cast up from the narrow highway threatened to choke him, he saw himself as he always longed to be seen: a man travelling through the world at capricious speed, ignoring danger, a brave and undaunted man who would overcome whatever adversity life placed in his path.

He refused to think about his failures. He'd believed in his fish cannery and he knew he had designed good housing for the factory he'd seen in his mind. It had not been his fault that the British engineer had been such a trembling fool. And now, though his plan for a hospital was also threatened, he believed he had seen how he could save it. Urging his stallion to an ever-faster gallop, he arrived soon enough at Kuching.

He dismounted and led the sweating horse through the bazaar which overlooked the Sarawak River. He had silver in a purse concealed round his waist. He passed a stall selling baby parrots in cages and noticed that the little birds were all huddled in one far corner of their prisons, with their backs turned to those who passed by. And he thought, this is how human life must be led if a man does not assert himself; he has to crouch in a dark place, with his face turned away from the world. But that man will never be me.

He went on past flower stalls and furniture menders and rice-sellers and stopped at last at a stall selling knives and daggers. Leon was not fond of guns, but he was seldom without his own kris and had, over the thirty-seven years of his life, let his worship of the shining blade develop into something almost mystical. He had never cut a man's flesh, but something in him was enthralled by the idea of doing so. The *cleanness* of the act, skin and flesh parting obediently in one magnificent downward thrust of his hand, letting flow a great fountain of blood, made him tremble with excitement. And here, at the modest stall, his practised eye fell upon one dagger which he longed to possess. He lifted it up, admiring its handle jewelled with lapis lazuli, and liking the weight of it – the kind of weight which had been perfectly judged for what a man's arm could be comfortable with, at the same time revealing to him the extreme damage the blade could inflict.

Though the dagger was expensive and might mean that he would not be able to pay more than one boy for the sexual release he now badly needed, Leon felt that he had to buy it. When he told the stall holder that he would take it for a price not much less than the one being asked, the man looked at him and said,

'You are wise in your purchase, Sir. This dagger has great power. But you must talk to it.'

'Talk to the dagger?'

'You must tell it the names of those you wish to harm and then it will do your work.'

Leon stared at the beautiful blue of the lapis. He knew only one man whose eyes were of this other-worldly colour.

To put his plan for getting rid of the Australian miners into action, Leon knew he would have to spend a night – or more than one – in Kuching.

After finding a stall selling dumplings and filling his belly with these, and drinking two cups of tuak, he made his way to one of the dilapidated houses where his 'boys' led a twilight life in rooms piled high with stained mats and where incense burned night and day to keep insects away and to mask the smell of stale semen, which was an aphrodisiac to some men and to others a terrible killer of desire.

Leon had a favourite boy here, a young Chinese by the name of Chang. Chang's skin was very soft, like the skin of a woman. He barely spoke, but just offered himself straight away, kneeling with thighs apart, in just the position Leon liked. Leon undressed quickly. The purchase of the dagger and the terrible thought of how he might one day use it had put him into a painful state of arousal and the rapid mounting of Chang was sweeter and more potent than it had ever been. When it was over he surprised himself by taking Chang into his arms and kissing him.

Afterwards, they sat side by side on a pile of mats and smoked and as Leon watched the blue smoke curl and billow about the small room, he knew that the time had come to put his plan into action.

He began asking Chang about the rumours of fever in the city and Chang told him that here, by the Sarawak River, you could hardly smell the Mal de peste, but that if you went into the centre of Kuching, you began to breathe it and taste it, the deadly miasma that brought sickness and death from Dengue Fever. Some people, he said, had already fallen ill and many were trying to get passage on a boat to Singapore.

'Where will I find those who are suffering?' asked Leon. 'I need to find two or three who are stricken down.'

'Why do you need two or three who are stricken down?' asked Chang.

'Because,' said Leon, 'I am going to save them. This is my mission, to take them away from Kuching. Perhaps I cannot save them. Perhaps they are too far gone into the fever, in which case they will die. But I am going to try to make them well, and what I must do for this is to take them to another place.'

'Where is this other place?' asked Chang.

Leon kept drawing smoke into his lungs and savouring its release as he described to Chang how he had built a hospital in the forest, but the hospital had been invaded by men from a faraway country, who were not stricken in any way except by a lust for gold and who were about to rape the land and destroy acres of forest with their foul and greedy diggings.

'At first,' said Leon, 'I could not see how I was going to persuade them to leave. I thought that I would have to try to kill them, but it is beyond me to kill so many.

'And then I saw how, if I brought in the sick and dying to my hospital, if I brought there the people for whom my hospital was designed, then these foreign men would be filled with terror. And what would they do? They are poor men whose hopes have been disappointed too many times to count and they may be reluctant to abandon what they think will be the source of their fortunes. But soon enough, they will go. They would rather live with their disappointment than die. For who would not? So eventually, they will get back into their boats, with all their cargo and they will sail away down the Sadong River and we will never see them again.'

Chang was silent. He looked into Leon's face, still half concealed by the silk bandage. Then he said: 'who will care for the stricken and the dying?'

'My mother will care for them,' replied Leon. 'I will pay her with silver and with objects that I have been given by the rajah. She will care for them for a little while and then they may die. Indeed, they will almost certainly die in due time. We will send their bodies down the river and imagine them arriving at the sea. And then we will be at peace once more.'

LILIES AND BRIARS

If Jane wondered at how often she succumbed to great tides of weeping in the wake of Emmeline's death, she also reminded herself that pregnant women were said to become emotionally fragile in the early months of carrying a child. She knew, too, that she wept for her future. To become the wife of Valentine Ross now seemed to her like entering the portals of hell. The engagement would have to be broken off before Ross learned of her pregnancy. And after that, she would never see him again.

But what would then become of her? She feared some violent anger in Ross which might destroy her. But not only that: she knew that society liked to turn its back on unmarried mothers, even perhaps the bohemian, emancipated portion of society which had clustered around her Aunt Emmeline. And so she would be quite alone and the child would grow up to be alone and friendless – and all because it had interested her, for a brief moment, to know what making love with a man was like.

Now, she cursed her own foolish curiosity and her physical greed. If only she had not done that, then a bright future might have awaited her. She would have been able to make whatever she chose of a life in London, close to Julietta, a life of wondrous freedom. Perhaps she could have started her own clinic in Tite Street, or perhaps again some new direction could have been found, some gradual discovery of The Thing which she had always believed attended her somewhere along the pathway of her life …

But nothing of the kind would be possible now. To her diary, she confided: 'Either I will become the unhappy wife of Valentine Ross, or I will be an Outcast Woman, trying my best to love and shelter a child. I see us now, the two of us, myself and a little girl, who already begins to grow tall, like her mother. Together, we wander Emmeline's high rooms, unvisited. We are waiting only for the years to pass.'

Ross bombarded Jane daily with letters, asking forgiveness for his 'ill-considered' outburst in the offices of Dutton & Caldecott and begging her to return to Bath. But she would not go. She replied that she was 'trying to assemble a beautiful service of farewell for Aunt Emmeline' and that until this was over, she would remain in London.

At Tite Street, on the days before the funeral, Jane received many callers, offering their affection and condolences. Among these were Emmeline's picture-framers, Mr Hartley and Mr Foulkes. They had brought with them the portrait of Jane, which had served as a stretcher to convey Emmeline to the doctor. It was now framed in ebony – Emmeline's emphatic choice – and, to Jane's eyes, it appeared fractionally altered, as though the subject in her white gown had aged a little during the intervening time when the frame was made.

Hartley and Foulkes propped up the portrait in the hall and they both looked from it to Miss Jane, now robed in black, and nodded their approval.

'If I may say,' said Mr Hartley, 'a very successful likeness.'

'And I notice another thing,' said Mr Foulkes, 'a likeness not just between portrait and subject, but a striking family resemblance between Miss Adeane and the late Miss Adeane.'

If Jane knew that this was flattery, that Emmeline had in her youth been a great beauty, while Jane, with her extraordinary height, was merely considered to be 'handsome', she was nevertheless gladdened by it. Anything which bound her retrospectively to Emmeline consoled her and she thanked Mr Foulkes and asked him if he and Mr Hartley would like to take a glass of sherry with her, while payment for the ebony frame could be handed over.

'Payment?' said Mr Hartley, 'Oh no, my dear Madam. Mr Foulkes and I are absolutely agreed, we would like to offer the frame to you as a gift to the late Miss Adeane, as a mark of our respect and appreciation. She trusted our humble firm with her work for many years and we wish you to know how much we valued this.'

Jane regarded the two men, who were both now advancing in years and both a little stooped from the hours they spent at the framing table, and she thought how, here and there in the world, often hidden away in some alley or winding street which few people ever trod, there were small yet wonderful oases of human dedication and kindness of spirit, and this gladdened her most particularly because she had *seen it* and not allowed it to pass her by.

Hartley and Foulkes courteously declined the offer of sherry and were in the very act of replacing their top hats on their balding heads and making for the front door when Jane turned again to look at the portrait, and came to a decision which surprised her. She asked the framers if they might be able to hang the picture there where it stood in the hall – the first thing visitors to the house would see as they came in.

'Ah,' said Mr Hartley, 'an excellent choice of location! The late Miss Adeane would have approved, I know. Do you have the necessary, Foulkes?'

'I have it,' said Foulkes and opened his frock coat to reveal a slim canvas bag attached to his waist, from which he produced a tape measure, a length of wire and numerous nails of varying sizes and conditions of rust.

So the portrait was hung in what Jane knew to be an ostentatious place, but she also knew why she had put it in the hall. The picture was the one thing shared completely between her and her aunt (each dependent on the other to bring it into the world, and both of them united in the secret of the golem) and so bound her to the idea that she had inherited the house *by right* and that only those who could bear to look at her portrait and walk by it without disdain would be allowed to enter there.

If Ross wanted to believe that he was punishing Jane by disdaining to attend Emmeline Adeane's funeral, he also knew that he was deluding himself. He was not there because Jane had not *deigned* to invite him. He sat in his rooms in Edgars Buildings, fighting dark feelings of intense hurt and anger. He said aloud to the peeling wall-paper of his sitting room, 'This cannot go on.'

Jane, meanwhile, was grateful that he was not beside her in the church. While the scented air was filled with passionate singing and Sir William gave a heartfelt oration on 'the great and generous spirit of my sister', Jane sat between Julietta and Clorinda Morrissey and both of them held onto her and let her cry. Ashton Sims, sitting just behind them, now and then reached out a comforting black-gloved hand and laid it tenderly on Jane's shoulder.

On the coffin, Jane had suggested, a large spray of lilies, expensively imported from Southern Europe, should be placed, but she had also gone out into Emmeline's untidy garden and cut branches of bramble and asked the florist to arrange these among the lilies, explaining to him that her aunt had been, on the one hand, as serene and beautiful as a lily but that she had only been able to persevere as an artist in a man's world by being 'brave enough to display her thorns from time to time'. If the florist was tempted to protest that he might scratch his delicate fingers with the wretched briars, he did not do so and when the arrangement was complete and laid on the casket, he prided himself that it was strangely pleasing 'and more original than any funeral spray he had ever seen'.

Respecting Emmeline's tastes, Jane ordered ballotine of chicken with pickled radishes and champagne to be served to the funeral guests at Tite Street. She walked slowly among them, her weeping now held in check by her sipping of her favourite drink, and was surprised and pleased to note that Ashton Sims had brought Guy Mollinet with him, the French author being in London for the launch of the English edition of his novel, *Morgue*.

'Forgive my uninvited presence,' Mollinet said to Jane, 'but as you know, all that pertains to death is of passionate interest to me. Ashton thought I might be moved by the English way of saying goodbye ...'

'You are welcome here, Monsieur Mollinet. Is the ballotine to your liking, or do they make it much better in Paris?'

'Oh, it is very good. For London.'

'Oh "for London"? Yes, I do see. And were you moved by the church service?'

'I thought the singing was quite fine, and I much liked the briars on the coffin. I suppose this is an English convention, is it, to remind us that life's road is difficult?'

'No,' said Jane. 'It was just something I felt was right for my aunt. The arrangements all fell to me, for it seems that Emmeline has left me almost everything she had.'

Mollinet's eyes widened at this. 'Everything she had?' he said. 'So you are now the owner of this house?'

'Yes I am,' said Jane. 'Except I feel that it will always belong to Emmeline and I will just be its guardian until she decides to return ...'

As she said this, Jane once more felt her eyes fill with tears and Mollinet reached out and laid his hand on her arm.

'My dear Mademoiselle Jane,' he said, 'may I say that I find you an exceptional woman. But listen to me, why do you and Julietta not come to Paris for a while? A change of city may help you recover from your loss. I can introduce you to many artistic friends – writers and poets ...'

At this moment, Julietta, seeing Jane overcome once more, appeared at her side and held her close, putting her dark head on Jane's shoulder. Mollinet laid upon this sight a surreptitious smile not entirely unmixed with yearning. If few Englishmen could have guessed that Jane and Julietta were lovers or let such an outrageous supposition even enter their minds, it seemed to the Frenchman entirely believable and probable that they were and he found this thought most marvellously arousing. A vision of the two women – the petite and beautiful Italian, the tall and handsome English girl – together in bed (with him as well, *bien sûr*) flitted across his mind in wildly gyrating colours.

'I was saying to Mademoiselle Jane,' he said, 'I do believe that you two should come to Paris again for a long *séjour*. What do you think, Signóra Sims?'

Julietta looked up at Jane. She was about to say to Mollinet that Jane was engaged to be married and would soon have to return to Bath, but Jane's challenging expression seemed to beg her to keep quiet on this subject, so she did not say this. Instead, she smiled at

Mollinet and said, 'I think we would both find that very tempting, wouldn't we Jane?'

Jane nodded. She was speechless because she had begun to wonder, on the instant, if, in some way that she couldn't yet define, an escape to France might not resolve her terrible predicament.

'There is only the question of Marco,' continued Julietta, glancing across the room at Ashton. 'I couldn't bear to be separated from Marco for very long.'

'Naturally not,' said Guy Mollinet. 'We can find you a large apartment, perhaps on one of Haussmann's new boulevards, and there will be room for Marco and his Nanny. We will teach him French. We will take him to the carrousel in the Tuileries ...'

'He is very fond of his rocking-horse, who has a French name: Trebuchet.'

'Trebuchet! How excellent. Is he a war horse?'

'I don't know. I believe Marco may think he is.'

'Then of course he must come, too. What could be easier than shipping an English war horse to France?'

'SOMETHING OF GREAT WEIGHT'

When the funeral guests had left, all except Sir William and Clorinda Morrissey, the subject of their marriage came gently to the surface and Sir William said, 'we hope you will not take it as any insult to Emmeline, Jane, if we now set a date in early September?'

'No,' said Jane, 'of course not. Emmeline would have wanted you to be married and I am so much looking forward to your wedding. And Father, I have been thinking, Emmeline has left me some very fine jewellery and I would love Clorinda to choose a beautiful piece as my wedding gift to her.'

'Oh jewellery, good heavens above!' said Clorinda. 'No indeed, that must all stay with you, Jane. I couldn't think of taking it.'

'But I will be so sad if you don't. There is far more than I will ever wear. Why do we not leave Father to fall asleep by the fire and go and look at it, at least?'

'I truly cannot take jewellery from you,' protested Clorinda, but Jane laid a gentle finger on Mrs Morrissey's mouth to silence her and Sir William said, 'I advise that you do as she suggests, Clorinda, for you know how vexed Jane can become if her commands are not followed.'

So the two women went up to Jane's room and she tugged from under her bed a large wooden jewel box. She set it on the floor and they knelt down beside it. Once the lid was opened, it was possible to pull out two little drawers, delicately hinged in brass and inlaid with black velvet. On the velvet rested a quantity of gems of every form and colour and Clorinda let out a gasp of wonder as the collection was revealed.

'You see?' said Jane. 'What a surfeit there is. How my aunt came by all this I am not entirely certain, but I know she had a weakness for sapphires, as you can see. Perhaps she could not pass a shop in Piccadilly without buying a sapphire as other people buy candied fruit? Perhaps she paid the jewellers with portraits of their wives and children? But now tell me what pleases you ...'

Jane picked up a sapphire necklace and held it against Clorinda's white neck. 'What about this?' she said. 'Or is blue the wrong colour for your wedding dress?'

'Well ...' stammered Clorinda, 'I had my eye on green and cream silk ...'

'Emeralds, then,' said Jane. 'There is no emerald necklace, but what about this brooch – emeralds and diamonds? Would that not be perfect for you? Or would rubies look very fine against green and cream silk?'

At the mention of rubies, Clorinda found herself blushing an embarrassing red and put a hand to her face to hide it. As soon as the box had been opened, her eye had alighted on a double-stranded ruby bracelet which had flooded her mind with temptation, but she knew that she should not even touch it. She fancied that if she laid her hand on it, there would occur some terrible painful burning. 'To tell you the truth,' said Clorinda, 'I am not very fond of rubies.'

'No? I believe I am not either,' said Jane. 'Perhaps it is their affinity with blood, is it? I think I will have to give them to Julietta, or perhaps just drop them down some convenient Chelsea drain! But do you like the emerald brooch?'

'It's beautiful. I like it very well, but ...'

'But what?'

'I just don't feel that this is right, to take your jewellery.'

'It's not mine, just as the house is not really mine. All of this was Emmeline's and she looked to find custodians of it after she was gone.'

'Nevertheless ...'

'Are you refusing to be one of Emmeline's custodians?'

'No, no. I wouldn't put it like that.'

Jane held out the emerald brooch in the palm of her hand. Even in the soft lamplight of her room, the stones radiated magnificence.

'Listen, Clorinda – you who are about to become my dear stepmother – would you do me the great favour of taking the brooch if I ask of you something in return?'

'Something in return?'

'Something of great weight. A weight that you might not be able to bear.'

Seeing sudden alarm on Clorinda's face, Jane reached out and pinned the emerald brooch to Clorinda's dress and said, 'the brooch is heavy, see how it pulls a little at the fabric of your bodice. Am I asking too much of you, to suffer the same kind of tug?'

'No,' said Clorinda. 'I'm sure you are not …'

'And can you promise to keep secret – from everybody in the world, including my father, for the time being – what I am about to tell you?'

'Yes,' said Clorinda, but the word came out strangely, seeming to cause the normally serene Mrs Morrissey a sudden moment of dyspepsia. Jane waited until this appeared to be past and then said, 'Well, I have made an important decision …'

'Yes?'

'I know that it's unfair of me to burden you with this. It is, I suppose, that I trust you absolutely.'

'You are right to trust me, Jane. I promise I will keep anything you tell me safely stowed away inside me.'

'Well, the death of my aunt has made me see the world in a new way. And I realise that I have made a great mistake in agreeing to marry Valentine Ross.'

'A mistake? Are you telling me—?'

'Yes. I know now that such a marriage would make me intolerably unhappy and I have decided that I cannot go through with it.'

Clorinda was silent. Her hand clutched at the brooch pinned to her dress and she stared at Jane in frank amazement.

'I see,' she said at last.

'Of course Valentine will be angry and my father will be upset, but I cannot help it, Clorinda. What I see in such a marriage is a desert of misery.'

'In that case, of course you are right to call it off. These things are absolutes and if we make the wrong choice …'

'It is in my mind to go to live in Paris for a while.'

'Paris?'

'Yes. They are laying out a new city some people are calling the City of Light. It will be very beautiful. And this is what I ask of my life, that it be new and beautiful.'

'Indeed. All lives should have some beauty about them. But love is the thing of greatest beauty, Jane. Do you really not love Doctor Ross?'

'No,' said Jane. 'I have tried to love him. For a while I thought I could. But now I feel that I do not even *like* him.'

Clorinda Morrissey was silent for a moment more and then she said, 'I cannot help but remember the day, soon after I opened my tea rooms, when you ... when you arrived a little late and Doctor Ross was all of an agitation waiting for you, and then you got up and went away with your cake uneaten. And I could see, even from my distance, that Doctor Ross was very unhappy ...'

'Yes. He proposed to me that day, and I turned him down. And it should all have been left like that, in a state where nothing more was possible between us. But while you and my father were in Dublin I went to his bed.'

'You went to his bed?'

'Yes. You're not shocked, are you, Clorinda?'

'No, no. Things of that kind have never shocked me.'

'He made love to me, but I didn't enjoy it – hardly at all. I know we are meant to enjoy this ritual, but I did not. Yet after that, there did not seem to be any way of distancing myself from the idea of marriage. I am to blame in this, Clorinda, I am to blame ...'

Seeing that Jane might be about to start weeping again, Clorinda reached out and held her tightly. If she struggled to think of words to comfort her, it was only because she felt afraid. Perhaps nobody knew better than she, whose eye was so accurately attuned to the joys and sorrows of her tea room clientele, how desperate was Ross's longing to make a life with Jane. What he would do now that he was to be sent back to a solitary existence without her, Clorinda could not predict, but the certainty that something ugly would occur clutched at her heart.

'What we must do,' said Clorinda at last, 'is to try to protect you from Doctor Ross's anger. What I suggest, dear Jane, is that you leave for Paris as soon as you can and that you write to him from there to tell him of your decision, but do not send your address. Would your friend Julietta be able to arrange matters in France?'

'Yes,' said Jane, 'but it will take a little time. Somewhere for us to live must be found and I have more business to attend to on behalf of Emmeline's legatees and papers to sign for the house ...'

'So when were you planning upon telling the poor man?'

'I don't know, Clorinda. All I knew until today was that I had to tell *someone* and I'm sorry for your sake that I chose you. But now that I've burdened you with news so heavy, please say you will accept the brooch?'

Clorinda again touched the beautiful jewel and the thought that it was an emerald and so contained within it the spirit of her Irish homeland moved her to say that she would accept it and treasure it for ever. This, in turn, emboldened Jane to say, 'there is just one more thing, Clorinda. I discovered this emerald and diamond ring on my dressing table. I'm not sure how it found its way there. Perhaps it was dropped and Nancy found it on the floor and put it there, thinking it was mine. But when I put it into the jewel box, I saw that it appeared to be all of a piece with the brooch. So here, please take the ring, as well. If we hold it against the brooch – look – we can see that the cut and colour of the emeralds are almost identical. They should not be separated.'

THE WOODEN HOOP

On the day that Clorinda Morrissey and Sir William returned to Bath, something happened to Valentine Ross which had never happened before: one of his patients drowned in the Hot Bath.

The nurse assisting him and Sir William in Jane's absence, who styled herself Nurse Marion, had accompanied the elderly woman, who was suffering from body tremors, the cause of which Ross was unable to diagnose, to the healing waters. Nurse Marion was the kind of sharp-nosed person who wished to give the impression of stern dedication to her calling, but who was addicted to the habit of making notes in minuscule neat writing upon everything that happened in the surgery and so was often distracted from actually observing the patients or listening carefully to what they had to say. This – together with the baleful fact that she over-starched her aprons and so walked about the premises crackling like a rasher of frying bacon – made Ross suspect that her time at Henrietta Street would have to be limited.

Now, when he heard about the death of his patient, who had 'slipped so silently under the green waters that nobody noticed' he was dismayed on two counts: that the patient had died for nothing but want of vigilance on behalf of Nurse Marion and that the whole sorry business had happened because Jane had deserted her duties, both as his fiancée and as his medical assistant. Indeed he felt that not only this, but *everything* that might go wrong in his professional life from now on was Jane's fault. She was selfish and proud. If she was an Angel, then she was surely also a witch? People could fall under her spell and be cursed. Death could occur. And nobody was at greater risk from her maledictions than he was.

These thoughts brought about in him the certainty that he would have to act. He couldn't remain patiently in Bath while Miss Jane drew out her mourning for her aunt for as long as it suited her. And, more importantly, he wished to *know*, once and for all, if Jane was deceiving him, either with some dilettante bohemian lover, or – and this thought caused him the greater amount of anger and repulsion – by going against nature and finding erotic satisfaction with her friend Julietta. As yet, he had no absolute proof of anything, but the tableau he'd seen in the Tite Street drawing room kept reappearing in his mind: Julietta's head on Jane's lap, an attitude of abandonment in both the women's bodies. The picture would not leave him. And he felt that he had endured these terrible suspicions long enough. He had to find out the truth, no matter what the consequences would prove to be.

When he announced to Sir William and Mrs Morrissey that he had decided to go to London with the intention of persuading Jane to come back to Bath and resume 'her rightful duties', he saw on Clorinda Morrissey's face a look of sudden and unmistakable panic.

'What is it?' he asked.

'Oh no …' said Mrs Morrissey, 'nothing at all, Doctor Ross. It is only that Jane mentioned to me that she had … she had much paperwork to be concluded with the solicitors, overseeing Miss Emmeline's legacies and so forth …'

'Well, in that case,' said Ross, 'I can be of assistance, perhaps. It's my opinion that women have a very poor and inadequate understanding of legal business. Their minds are unable to follow the logic of the subordinate clause.'

'Speaking as a businesswoman, I would not agree with you there,' said Clorinda and Sir William appeared to nod his concurrence. 'But in all events, I think, if I might venture to say … Jane will come back to Bath when she is ready to come back, and it would be wise of you—'

'You are about to say that I should leave her alone? But I don't think you understand my position. In a few months' time, Jane will become my wife. *My wife!* She is twenty-five and has had admirers, but no suitors of any seriousness. Therefore, I do her honour in marrying her. She must learn to get used to obeying me, at least from time to time.'

Sir William then drew Ross aside. In gentle tones, he said, 'I understand how you feel. The death of Emmeline has been difficult for us all. But let me remind you that Jane has always done things in her own way and in her own time ...'

'That may have something to do with the fact that you always spoiled and indulged her, Sir. But are you saying that this can be allowed to continue for the rest of our lives? I am to stand by while she behaves exactly as she pleases?'

'Well,' said Sir William, 'I would not phrase it like that, but you have known Jane for many years. You know what kind of woman you are marrying. Do you really imagine that she is going to change?'

'Yes,' said Ross. 'Because I wish it. Because unless she does ...'

'Well? What are you saying?'

'I do not know,' said Ross with a sigh. 'I do not know. But I think that, if she does not, then both she and I will suffer.'

When Valentine Ross arrived at Tite Street, he was told by the maid, Nancy, that Miss Jane was sleeping and could not be disturbed.

It was early afternoon. After ordering Nancy to bring him a bowl of coffee, Ross walked back into the hall and stared up at the portrait. He thought it conceited of Jane – vulgar, even – to have placed this large image of herself so near to the front door.

From the picture, she looked down at him with the ghost of a smile on her lips and he had to admit that Emmeline had indeed captured the essence of Jane: the power in her body, the challenge in her eyes and then this tremble on the edge of laughter about her mouth, this inability to resist teasing and mockery. But for all its accuracy – or perhaps because of it – he did not love the portrait. He especially did not like the object she held in her hands, a little ugly manikin, and couldn't imagine why Jane had agreed to be pictured with this. He decided that if he was going to live with Jane as his wife in Tite Street, the vexing portrait would have to be hidden somewhere out of sight.

He looked at his watch, then consulted the long-case clock in the hall. It was almost three o'clock. At this hour in Bath, Jane would always be with her patients and it surprised him that she should be sleeping. He reasoned that perhaps her grief for Emmeline had exhausted her, but then it invaded him like a wave of sickness, the sudden certainty that she was not sleeping at all: she was with Julietta.

He couldn't move.

If he thought of walking out of the house, to protect himself from seeing what he would not be able to bear, he dismissed this as only a prolongation of his agony. Instead, he turned at once and began running up the stairs. He knew his way, now, to Jane's room. He did not go in, but stood outside it, listening. At first he could hear nothing and for a second dared to hope that he had been wrong and that Jane was asleep after all. But then they came, the unmistakable sounds of sexual exertion, accompanied by breathless murmurations and followed by a little passionate cry. It was a woman's cry and the name she was repeating in her ecstasy was Jane's.

Ross's hand was on the door handle and he was a second away from turning it and opening the portal on the scene which had tortured him for what now seemed like some terrible eternity, but he knew that his agony was such that he would not be able to control himself. He would scream until his lungs burst. And then he would hurt Jane. He would have to hurt her. Violence was all that was left to him.

He ran back down the stairs, at headlong pitch, like a boy running for his life. In the hall, he collided with Nancy bringing the coffee. The bowl fell from the tray and smashed and the hot coffee spread, steaming, over the marble floor. Nancy's legs were scalded and she cried out in pain, but Ross paid this no heed.

He rushed into the drawing room. He stood still for a moment, wondering what would serve him best in his intent, then snatched up the poker from the hearth.

Now, he was standing in front of the portrait again, but this time he had a weapon in his hands. He later recalled wishing that the weapon was a knife, so that he could slash and slice at the canvas, but the poker was satisfactorily heavy and with it he began hitting the painting with as much force as he could summon.

He was not aiming at Jane's face, but at the lower part of her body, dressed in its lying virginal white gown, just below the place where her hands cradled the ridiculous manikin. And, little by little, Jane's gown was rent and torn and what Ross expected to see was her naked torso revealed in all its beauty and in all its shame. But the body did not appear. He kept smashing harder and harder with the poker at the canvas, but there was nothing behind the gown except a square of wall, and, when he saw this, Ross thought that this wall was a perfect representation of Jane Adeane's heart, so terrifying in its hardness, which had never yielded to him and never would. He began cursing Jane out loud, screaming that she was inhuman, that the abomination in her hands had been given more love than he would ever receive from her and that he hated her now, hated her with a loathing so strong that it would never leave him. He might live to be a hundred years old, but his detestation of Jane Adeane would last that hundred years and beyond …

Suddenly, she was at his side. She was crying out for him to stop his assault on the portrait. He saw her close up, now, her hair unkempt, her face oily, her eyes pools of venom. And the stink of her! As long as he lived he would never forget that fish smell of his once-beloved woman, caught in the act of her foul betrayal. He thrust her away from him, letting the poker fall. He pushed her against the wall. She was strong and she resisted him, but he told her she could not win against him, she could never win! For everything was at an end now. His loathing of her was complete. There would be no marriage. There would be no future. There would only be this last moment …

He tugged her towards him then pushed her violently back, so that her head hit the wall. In his delirium of pain and anger, he half expected the skull to break in two, but it did not break and Jane kept crying out and resisting and resisting, but he knew he could not allow this unbearable resistance, it had to be put down once and for all, so he pulled her towards him for a second time. Once more, he rammed her head against the wall. And now he felt her fall. All the resistance went from her and she lay unconscious at his feet, with blood seeping from the back of her head. And he thought, this is what I have wanted – ever since that day in a tea room when she rejected my proposal – I have wanted her lying before me, helpless and at my mercy and now, there she lies.

Perhaps he was about to kick out at her, kick her like the filthy animal she was, but then he felt himself being pulled away from her. The woman-stink was still there but he realised now that two other women had grabbed his arms, Julietta and the maid. He tried to wrench himself from their grip, but he was outnumbered, he was back to being the plaything of women, their toy, their fool, and all he could do was to keep cursing at the top of his voice.

Resisting all the while, he was dragged outside onto the steps. The steps were slippery in the rain that was now falling. And he knew that, in the next moment, he would fall, too. Julietta and the maid pushed him down the steps and into the street and he lay there, with his left leg twisted under him, staring up at the front door, which was now slammed shut.

In the next moment, a child came skipping by, bowling a wooden hoop. The hoop's steadiness and momentum was such that when its passage was blocked by the body of Valentine Ross, it lifted itself up and bounced over his anguished face and sped on.

Part Four

A BARGAIN

The Australian miners had tried everything they knew. Most of them were old hands, connoisseurs in the art of gold-seeking and proud of it. They had been told that the Borneo mine was exhausted, but they knew that if anyone could find the 'tailings' that remained, it would be them.

Slabs of black beech had been carefully laid in to prevent their diggings from collapse. They had broken their backs carting soil away to the river. They'd manufactured box flumes to bring water to their claims for sifting the dirt through their sluice boxes. When rats started to appear, feasting off decayed food and human excrement, they'd killed as many as they could and roasted them. They referred to them as 'ground squirrels' and declared that they remembered the delicate flavour of their flesh from the old Otago days.

They knew enough to dig deeply, to where the 'blue clay' lay. Sometimes alluvial gold was to be found at the river's edge, but these workings were some way from the river, and the true seams lay in depths that were hard to reach. Here, on Borneo, the 'blue' was stubborn. It just wouldn't show itself. Each evening at dusk, as Carrot-beard and his fellow diggers trudged back to where they had placed some of their group to guard their longhouses, they swore at another day lost, at another postponement of the dream which transfixed their minds.

As time passed, they faced a new threat to their hopes. In the largest of the longhouses, Malay women began to arrive, bringing with them sick and dying people and laying them down among the miners' possessions, leaving the diggers who had made their billet there no choice but to take up their sleeping mats and move.

Carrot-beard, whose name was Jim McKenzie, berated the guards. 'Women and invalids!' he shouted at them. 'Are you telling me they overpowered you?'

They had no answer to this, but one of them asked, 'Is that who we are? People who shoot women, who murder those who can't lift up their heads?'

And the miners' leader was checked by this response and didn't know what to say. He wondered if his desire for mastery of the situation, his longing to replace his own hard life with the easeful old age which gold would buy, had made him more heartless than he knew.

He made his way to the hospital, taking care to fill his pockets with bullets for his gun, but when he went into the longhouse, the stench of it made him reel back. He stood in the doorway, regarding the scene. The place wasn't yet crowded, but from the paillasses where the sick lay struggling with the ravages to their bodies came a low and terrible human cry, which froze McKenzie's blood.

Among the sufferers, who numbered eight or nine, two Malay women, with scarves wrapped around their faces, were working as nurses, offering medicine and swabbing the vomit-stained floor. When they saw the Australian gold-seeker at the door, they barely glanced at him, but lowered their eyes and continued with their work.

To find himself disregarded in this way troubled McKenzie almost as much as the sight and stench of the dying. He was a forceful and fearless man, used to being respected for his hardness, but what he saw here were people who had passed into a different realm of existence, where nothing signified except the struggle with death. He suspected that, were he to raise his gun and point it into the room, the nurses would take little notice of this, but merely see his actions as futile.

It was then that he began to feel afraid. He and his fellow miners had gambled much and travelled far on the wings of rumour. They had let themselves believe that there were fortunes to be made from the Sarawak mine, but as yet had found not an ounce of gold. And now, not only did they seem to be tiring themselves out for nothing, they were at risk from a contagion which could end their lives. Against most enemies, they had their courage, their weapons, their knowledge of hardship and their pride, but they had no arms against this. People said the Mal de peste came from the air. You just breathed it in and then it was carried on the exhalations of the dying, which was why the nurses wound cloths around their faces. McKenzie knew that it was only a matter of time before it reached him and the other men.

He returned to the goldfield. He knew how badly the diggings had besmirched the land, how the forest had retreated, with the trees felled for slabs and for firewood, leaving a desert of stones, earth and detritus. But it was that time in the early evening when the sun was going down beyond the rim of the forest and the earth's ugliness became almost invisible and the men were clustered around bright fires, drinking grog or arak, singing familiar songs. McKenzie found this camaraderie as consoling as anything he'd ever known. As he joined in the drinking and singing, he wondered if this – a harmony of men's voices defying the poverty in which they existed, asserting that despite so many disappointments they still lived in hope – whether this might, after all, be defence enough against death. But he didn't know.

The next day, one of the miners fell ill.

He wasn't much older than a boy, a young fella Jim McKenzie knew as Billy, whose father had found gold in Otago and squandered it all on a failed manufactory of leather goods in Yorktown. Seeing this enterprise go down and faced then with his father's suicide, Billy lived with the conviction that, in a heartless world, joining a gold rush was as likely a way to make money as any other. But he told McKenzie that when he found 'his' gold he wouldn't risk it on 'some futile endeavour' but rather exchange it at the Bank of Australia for enough silver dollars to last his lifetime.

But Billy had got no gold, and now the fever had laid him low. McKenzie heard some of his compatriots explain to the boy that he would have to be moved to the large longhouse, where the sick belonged, or else risk infecting them all. But only McKenzie had seen inside this place and he balked at the idea of putting Billy in there. He told all the men to move to the last and smallest of the longhouses, the furthest away from the hospital. He helped them carry away their possessions, aware as he did so of how few chattels a gold miner can call his own. Then he sent the diggers off for their day's labours, made Billy as comfortable as he could on his thin sleeping mat and told him he would leave his side only to beg some medicine from the nurses in the hospital and return straight away. As he left, Billy cried out to him, 'Don't let me die, Jim!'

McKenzie scratched his red beard. 'Do I look like a man who would?' he said.

As soon as he left Billy's side, McKenzie changed his mind. He began walking up the Savage Road to the rajah's house. He'd seen it at a distance before, but never trespassed inside its gates and now the whiteness and magnificence of it made him pause on the road. The day was fine and he saw the sun shining upon great banks of lilies in the garden and heard the cassowaries chattering in the aviary.

McKenzie stared in wonderment. This was how great wealth always showed itself: it killed the poor with its beauty. And no men, McKenzie reflected, are more susceptible to being wounded in this way than gold miners. Their day-to-day world is filthy and brutal, but their dreams are all of the luxurious life. They can imagine it without difficulty. They can envisage the fine clothes they would put on their backs, the polished silverware they would set out on their tables, the pictures they would hang on their walls. This other life is present inside them all the time.

McKenzie made his way to the rajah's door. A Malay servant, dressed in impeccable white, opened it a crack. From the crack, he observed the miner's dirty moleskin trousers, his frayed shirt, his face that was hollow with hunger under the red beard, and informed him coldly that the rajah would not deign to see him.

But McKenzie had been told, since arriving at the mine, that Sir Ralph Savage was a charitable man who tried to see the truth of things in the Sadong Territories and to make things better for everybody under his jurisdiction, not only for himself. The Australian was gambling on this now, on this unlikely strain of charity to be found in a rajah whose mind had been shaped by the self-serving hierarchies of the British Empire.

McKenzie stood his ground and told the servant that he had come to 'make a bargain' with the rajah and that he must be heard.

He was allowed into the hallway and told to wait there. He looked down at his dirty boots standing on the polished marble floor, then his eye was caught by a many-branched candelabra placed on an ebony table. It stood about two feet high and it appeared to be made of solid gold. It made McKenzie feel dizzy to see this. He could not help but imagine it lying deep underground, in the blue clay. He saw his pick breaking into the dark compacted earth, and then his eyes – which had searched for so long and found nothing – staring in helpless disbelief as the first glint of it was revealed …

This reverie was interrupted by the arrival of Sir Ralph. If he stood some way from McKenzie, it was not so much that he was afraid of him but because the stink of the miner's body made him wonder if this man was not already suffering from the fever. Wishing him to depart as soon as possible, the rajah asked him why he had come. He added that his servant had mentioned something about a bargain, but that as ruler of the South Sadong Territories, he was seldom forced into any kind of bargaining position.

Though disinclined to make any show of deference to the rajah, McKenzie forced himself to lower his head just a little as he said, 'you will appreciate, Sir Ralph, that I would not have come here, knowing how unwelcome I and my compatriots are on your land, unless it was with a proposition to put to you.'

'Yes?' said Sir Ralph. 'Speak up then, and be on your way.'

At this moment, Leon appeared. He stared disdainfully at McKenzie – the very same ignorant gold prospector who had given him his painful black eye. Leon wore a jewelled dagger at his waist and his hand now clutched the lapis lazuli handle. McKenzie took this in, but didn't back away and continued with his 'proposition' to the rajah.

'You see, Sir Ralph,' he said. 'One of my number has fallen ill. He is still almost a boy and cannot be allowed to die. But we have no medicine and no knowledge of the *peste* which had arrived on Borneo. If you will give me some antidote … something which will save Billy, then we will give up on the infernal mine and leave the island.'

Sir Ralph looked searchingly at McKenzie. Leon took the dagger out of its sheath and seemed to be measuring its sharpness against the palm of his left hand, as he said: 'There is no "antidote".'

The rajah now feared that Leon's anger against this starving, anguished man would lead to a fatal end and decided he must hasten his departure before this happened.

'I can give you some Jesuit's Bark,' he said, 'which seems to be effective against Malaria but the only cure for this fever rests in Fate's hand. I don't lie to you.'

'In the longhouse, there are nurses, giving medicine to the sick. I've seen them, rajah. Why is that medicine being given if it will not cure?'

'It is arak, not medicine. It is arak mixed with a little water. It can deaden pain. But most of those who suffer in that house will die. And your friend Billy will die. Indeed, I suspect that you will all die, now that the fever has entered the place where you sleep, unless you leave before tomorrow's sunset.'

The cruelty of this last utterance was so unexpected that it brought into McKenzie's heart a feeling of black despair. He stood there, all skin and bone inside his filthy clothes, watched by Leon's malevolent stare and felt himself begin to break.

'We have nothing!' he cried out. 'We endured storms and sickness and thirst to get here and all we find is barren earth. We live on the bodies of rats. I was told you were a compassionate man, rajah, but you show no pity.'

'Why should he show pity?' said Leon. 'You trespass on his land. You usurp buildings built by me as a hospital. You are despicable men.'

'No! We are not "despicable"! Rajah, Sir, I appeal to you. We are simply poor. You of all people should be able to see the difference!'

The rajah sighed. 'There are many on my lands who are poor, but they do not behave as you have done, despoiling the earth, stealing what is not rightly theirs. So you go back to your men and warn them that they are all going to die unless they leave.'

'I promised!' McKenzie burst out. 'I promised Billy I wouldn't let him die! Please give me something, rajah. Something to give me hope …'

'Hope of what?' said Sir Ralph.

'Give me that!' McKenzie shouted. He lunged forward with all the force his emaciated body could manage, grabbed the golden candelabra from the ebony table, and held it high in the air, out of Sir Ralph's reach. Leon raised his dagger, but McKenzie scuttled fast for the door while the rajah laid a restraining hand on Leon's arm.

That evening, the miners left the barren field for the last time and began to load their possessions into their boats. When these were in, they carried Billy to the door of the longhouse hospital and the elderly woman with the strangely pigmented face was about to take him in, when McKenzie realised that this was Leon's mother, and changed his mind. He told her they would take the boy with them and nurse him as they travelled and she gave them a vial of the medicine, which might have been only arak and water or something else, something which would save Billy, but McKenzie did not know which.

They laid Billy in the boat and cast off on the slow-running river. They gave him the golden candlestick to cradle in his arms, as a child would cradle a loved toy, to soothe him to sleep.

QUEEN OF THE ISLANDS

The ship left Plymouth at the beginning of August.

It shuddered and rolled through the early summer storms of Biscay and came into calmer waters off the coast of Portugal, where it took on more passengers and supplies before pressing upon the vast and empty seas that broke on the shores of Africa. After numberless weeks, or days counted at approximately eighty to ninety – in a world where everything was approximate and at the mercy of the wind – it would, or *might* reach its destination, which was Australia. One of its ports of call was Singapore.

It was an old three-masted brig, the *Queen of the Islands*, carrying English and Scottish emigrants who had decided to exchange the quotidian for the unknown and who carried with them all that they wished to salvage from their former lives, which was not much. Many were burdened with babies, both weaned and unweaned, some nurtured with precious care and some hauled around carelessly, like unnecessary luggage, as though they were not really wanted on the voyage and not expected to survive the journey. Already, before the coast of France was gone from sight, one baby had died, when its mother was too seasick to produce milk for it. The little body was wrapped in sacking and sent sliding down a plank into the ocean. The human parcel was so light, it floated obstinately on the waves for a good few seconds, before the water reared up in a sudden sweep of shimmering green and drew it under.

There were also convicts aboard. They were housed in darkness, in the space the seamen called ''tween decks', below the waterline of the ship, and they were almost never permitted, it seemed, to come up into the light, to breathe the fresh air. It was said that you could travel on this journey and never see them. For their crimes, they had been placed in a shadowy region where none but they would ever be found. But sometimes, as you climbed down towards the bowels of the *Queen*, you could hear the sound of hammering, as though these unhappy people had been put to keep building and repairing the ship, even as it sailed on.

Mostly, Valentine Ross kept to his cabin.

Remembering the 'hutch' he had been shown aboard the *Rainsford*, he was grateful that in this dark little space on the berthing deck of the *Queen of the Islands* he could at least stand upright. The bunk, where he was to spend so many uncountable nights, was hard and narrow, but there was at least a straw paillasse upon it and a pillow which might once have been plump with feathers, but which now resembled a slab of pastry dough.

Ross had stowed his few possessions, which included a pharmacopoeia containing tincture of Jesuit's Bark for fever and guaiacum for syphilis as well as opium, mercury and arsenic, in a sea chest, which also served as a table. In this materia medica resided Valentine Ross's one frail hope of a future. He spent much time on his knees, in a slumped attitude oddly resembling prayer, staring at the bottles and phials. With these, he thought, he might possess the power to rescue his brother from whatever maladies had befallen him. And if he could do this, then his life would not remain the futile thing that it now appeared to him – a life of empty yearning, failed endeavour and sudden, unanticipated cruelty. It would take wing again. He would have saved a beautiful soul.

He also carried with him the 'ransom' letter from Rajah Leon. He had read it so many times that the paper was cracked and faded. But no money had been sent. Valentine Ross had convinced himself that its writer was a blackmailer and a liar. Indeed, he was disposed to believe that almost everybody in the world was set upon a pathway of lies. People thought only of their own pleasures and satisfactions and were empty of compassion.

After the great ship had ploughed the furrows of Biscay and the wind had subsided, Ross was surprised to be woken on a dark dawn by a man bringing him fresh water in a tin jug, a sliver of soap and a frayed grey towel. The person was elderly and stooped – perhaps from a life spent ''tween decks', but with a face oddly etched with mirth and a voice of surprising gentleness. He announced himself as servant to the 'naval officer-type class of passenger', in other words to those lodged on the upper berthing deck. He apologised to Ross 'for having neglected my duties to you, Sir, on account of being stricken with the emetics'.

Ross regarded him from the safety of his bunk, unwilling to engage in any discourse and sternly disliking the idea that he was to be burdened with a servant, who might disturb his solitude at inappropriate moments, upon some irritating whim of the ship's timetable and its infernal ringing of bells. He therefore said nothing. The servant appeared untroubled by this. He poured the water into a canvas bowl, set on a gimbal, to try to keep the liquid from splashing out, side to side, with the roll of the ship, and announced, 'my name is Chesterfield and it is often remarked that I share a designation with a piece of furniture. You are quite free to comment in your fashion upon this, but I must tell you that I am unmoved by it. For a "Chesterfield" is a comfortable thing, bringing respite to the body, and what is a servant, Sir, but a useful object, upon which people may depend? I think my name is very fitting.'

Ross felt too tired and irritable to make any observation upon this. After a moment, he said: 'I do not need a servant. I can fetch my own fresh water. I wish to be left entirely alone.'

Chesterfield turned, wiping his eyes with the ragged towel, quite as if he was overcome by tears at being told that he was unnecessary. Then without saying another word, but with the shadow of a smile on his amused countenance, he placed the soap and towel beside the water bowl and went out. When he had gone, Ross sighed, closed his eyes and returned to sleep.

After just a few days at sea, Ross understood that the voyage had put him into a state of limbo. The ship made its difficult way through the Atlantic. But, for him, there was no feeling of being carried *onwards*, but only of being in some waiting room where the wind howled so loudly in the walls that he was becoming deaf. In this place, the present had no structure or purpose. His mind was drenched perpetually in memories of the past.

He told himself that if he were to engage his fellow passengers in conversation and learn something of their lives, he might be able to inhabit the days and nights with better grace, but he could not force himself to do this. Sunk so deeply into his own agonies, his head down, his arms folded and pressed against his chest, he knew he appeared almost as a madman might appear. On the rare occasions when he walked about the decks, or took a meal at a communal table, he saw what he created in people's hearts: a feeling of unease. It was as if they feared he might do them harm, and a part of him believed they were right to fear this, because he could no longer accurately judge what he was capable of doing or saying.

When asked what he did for a profession – not wishing to risk having his doctor's skills called upon during the voyage – he told his fellow passengers that he was an archaeologist. He invented a site on one of the hills surrounding Bath where a Saxon burial pit was supposedly being unearthed. And he found, as he anticipated, that nobody was truly interested in a past so distant from them. They had left England and its violent history behind them. They didn't want to think about slain bodies and axe-heads of stone. They were going to the New World, which perhaps they imagined as a place of untouched vacancy, where History had never made landfall, where they would hold untroubled sway for the rest of their lives.

For Ross, the past was his only real habitation, yet it felt as though it had unfixed itself from any irrefutable truth and become fluid, offering him different versions of events he had thought would remain stable forever. When he remembered, for instance, the day in boarding school when he saved Edmund from his bullying peers by grabbing the tallest of the persecuting boys and holding him out of the dormitory by his feet, he was now not certain whether he had not let go of the child and watched the body fall. It seemed to him that he remembered a falling. He could now believe that he had seen the boy on the ground, his neck broken. He could hear some loud commotion before he himself was grabbed by the arms and led away ...

Led away where?

It could not have unfolded like this because he, Ross, would have had to endure the fiercest punishment and there was no punishment, only this memory of the boy lying on the grass and the sound of people's fear. And it came to him then that what he was imagining was what he now knew himself to have been capable of, not what he actually did. If he was a person *who was capable* of letting a twelve-year-old boy fall to his death from a window, was he also capable of murdering the woman he loved?

He learned a little of the ship's lore. Ropes were 'sheets', sails were 'shrouds', wooden berths had the narrowness of coffins. All, he noted, was being made ready for death.

For death was everywhere. It kept climbing towards the *Queen of the Islands*, in the unceasing purpose of the waves in hurling themselves upon the vessel to break over the gunwales. The sea and the wind waged never-ending war with the old brig. And this struck Ross as a wretched state of affairs, that the elements on which the ship depended for its journey appeared perpetually intent on its destruction.

He asked himself if he would mind dying and recognised that in some obstinate part of himself he was made angry by the idea that his life could end at the age of thirty-two. Yet what, really, was left to him? What could he find to fill up all the years that might lie in store? If Edmund's life could be saved by him, then at least there was honour in that and a real manifestation of the brotherly love he had never ceased to feel. But afterwards, what would remain to him? Would he sink into the debauch and the inertia that tropical climates could bring about in white men who have lost their sense of purpose and resolve? Would it not be better to stuff his pockets with some leaden object lying about the cluttered decks of the *Queen of the Islands* and say to the heartless ocean, 'take me into your dread deep, for I have earned nothing better.'

Of Jane, he tried not to think. He wanted to sweep the past clean of her, as though she had never existed and that part of him which loved her with such violent force had never existed either. But she was so mighty a presence, still, in his imagination, that she couldn't be erased. Her tall shadow seemed to follow him wherever he went and whatever he did. He saw her at the Assembly Rooms, in her red dress, wearing a feather in her hair. He saw her at the Baths, ghostly in her white gown, as the sick and dying reached out to her. He saw her lying naked in his bed.

He asked himself what was to be done to banish her from his mind, knowing that, until this was achieved, he would live a half-life, the pathetic life of a solitary mourner. He tried re-enacting his punishment of her, pounding her skull against the wall, letting her fall on the stairs, left for dead. But these imaginings weren't sufficient to rid himself of her. For he was unable to believe that he had had the power to take her life. She lived, still, didn't she? Couldn't he feel her stubborn head nudging against his heart?

VIGIL

When Jane had fallen against the wall, the foetus inside her, a tiny sac of half-made flesh, which had clung to her womb for five weeks, began to break from its mooring. After contractions which felt as though they were splitting her body in two, it was ejected out of her and washed across the hallway by a blood tide which seemed to have no ebb.

Julietta and Nancy tried to staunch the terrifying deluge with soft towels pressed against and inside Jane's vagina, but by the time the doctor arrived, Jane's face had lost all its colour and her hands and feet were as cold as marble.

She drifted in and out of consciousness. The throbbing in her head, where it had been struck against the wall, seemed to her to make a strange echoing answer to the agony in her womb. She could feel blood sliding down her neck, but she understood that this wound was invisible, as yet, in her hair. When she tried to cry out to Julietta that her skull had been bruised, she found that she couldn't speak.

The doctor carried her to the bedroom that had once been Emmeline's and laid her down on the wide bed. He placed pillows under her knees, to raise her legs in a vain attempt to stop the blood that was still flowing out of her. He ordered Julietta and Nancy to fetch furs and blankets to try to warm her. Aware now of her head wound, he got Jane to swallow a little laudanum. He saw that her lips were blue and her whole body was trembling. He spoke to her softly. He informed her that his name was Dr Wood. Then he told her what she already knew, that she had lost her child. Her large eyes stared up at him, but barely flickered. The doctor waited for her to say something, but she did not seem able to make any answer.

Dr Wood examined Jane's head and found a flesh wound and livid bruising, but no crack in the skull that he could detect. He cut away some locks of Jane's hair, matted with blood, which he put into an enamel dish. He then gently cleaned the wound with carbolic acid, laid over it a piece of lint soaked in carbolic oil and wound bandages in a tight helmet round her head. He saw her eyes close. He pulled a chair close to the bed and waited.

After taking the laudanum, Jane could remember very little. She told herself that she had to try to keep breathing, but it seemed to her that she had been transported to a grey wilderness where the air was so cold that she did not dare to inhale it. She found that she was swaddled in fur and the perfume of the fur was strangely familiar to her and this gave her hope that she wasn't alone in the wasteland she now inhabited. She reasoned that she might be among people who would know how to build shelters out of blocks of snow and that soon she might find herself carried into one of these and made warm again.

But this didn't happen. In spite of the fur, her whole body was convulsing with cold. She fancied she could hear the noise her bones made as they shook in their sockets, like the wooden bones of a puppet. And then she could no longer hear anything. She entered a tunnel of silence. It was black night in the tunnel, but a long way away she could see a tiny circle of light. She stared at this, not sure how she should interpret it. She knew she was moving very slowly towards it, but there was nothing to tell her whether it was the light of heaven or the light shining on some human shore.

At the bedside, Julietta had reached for Jane's hand under the furs and kept rubbing it to try to warm it, then laid it against her cheek and kissed it and shed hot tears upon it. She saw the doctor staring at her when she did this, but she cared nothing for what he thought.

She had sent Nancy to run to Tedworth Square, to bring Ashton to her side. She herself was still shaking from the violence Valentine Ross had inflicted and was frightened that the wretched 'fiancé' might decide to return. The household needed Ashton's protection. But more than this, if Julietta was going to lose Jane, she wanted the dear comfort of her husband and she had no doubt that he would give it. Whatever he knew or did not know about the erotic bond between the two women, his love for Julietta brought everything into the shelter of his forgiveness and acceptance. Moreover, she knew that he admired Jane – for her dedication to her work and for her wit. If she was now dying, Ashton Sims would wish to bear witness to that death.

While waiting for him to arrive, Julietta, speaking in a low voice, fearing to wake Jane from a sleep that might be beneficial to her, asked Dr Wood if he had lost patients before who had miscarried. He replied that he had. And in this case, too, there had been a fall and a haemorrhage which could not be staunched.

'It is,' he said, 'a sad reflection on the state of medical knowledge that we know so much about bloodletting, but do not know how, under certain circumstances, to make the flow stop. We just have to trust to nature.'

'What more can we do?' asked Julietta.

'Administer more laudanum presently. It lessens the shock of the pain and the brandy is a stimulus, which perhaps encourages new blood to form. But the next few hours will be telling. She will either be gone by nightfall or the bleeding will stop and she will begin a slow recovery.'

Silence then filled the room again. Jane's breathing was so quiet, it reminded Julietta of the breathing of a child. And thoughts of her little Marco, alive and bounding about his nursery, filled her with sudden joy. And she thought how Jane would never know this happiness, now, of loving a child. The bits and pieces of her baby's half-formed body had been strewn across the hall. The husband-to-be would never be allowed to return.

These thoughts led in turn to a decision in Julietta Sims which she never thought she would be able to make: if God would spare Jane Adeane, she would renounce her 'beauties'. She cared nothing for them, only for the excitement of the showy orgasms she alone was able to give them. Henceforth, she would love only two people, Jane and Ashton. She would bring Ashton more frequently to her bed so that they might conceive another child, a child whom Jane could know from its babyhood and grow to love, along with its adoring parents. In this arrangement, provided she could still have Jane as her lover, she saw a beautiful triangular domestic felicity.

Ashton came in and said good-day to Dr Wood, then stood and looked down at Jane's head protruding from its mound of furs and bound like an Egyptian mummy with her white bandages. Nancy brought in a chair for him and he, too, reached out for Jane's cold hand and held it, so that he and Julietta seemed to play the role of her keepers, and they hoped that they were leading her, not towards death's prison, but towards a resumption of her life.

All night, they stayed like this, barely moving. In the early hours, Dr Wood departed, leaving the laudanum jar by the bedside and promising to return at midday. Nancy showed the doctor out and then came back to the hall, where she had had to sluice away Jane's blood with her mop and scoop up the broken foetus in her bare hands. Now, she wept for the tiny embryo she had tipped into the night-soil bucket. Then she washed herself and changed her clothes, and made coffee on the range and took this up to Ashton and Julietta, who were talking about the terrible events of the afternoon, in soft voices, while outside the chimes of old St. Peter's Church tolled the hours.

Towards morning, Julietta went down into the hall and stared up at the damaged portrait, torn at the very centre of the picture. Pieces of the canvas hung down, revealing the wall behind, and Julietta was disturbed to see that it was in fact the area of Jane's womb which had been destroyed. And it shocked her to realise that Valentine Ross, wherever he had fled, might live the rest of his life never knowing that he had murdered his own child.

A STATE OF MARVELLOUS DREAMING

Knowing nothing of all this, Clorinda Morrissey was in Dublin.

Word had reached her that her niece Maire had 'succumbed', despite the expensive interventions of the Dublin surgeons and had been laid to rest in the little cemetery at the end of Bishop Street, where, in autumn, the rowan trees shed a carpet of orange berries onto the graves.

Michael Morrissey wrote to Clorinda that '*the thyroid gland, once removed from poor Maire's body, may have caused her other organs to act wrongfully, being turned against their proper functions, so that she and we endured distress beyond your imagining.*'

Clorinda wished to reply that nothing was 'beyond her imagining'. She had lived through the famine. She had seen the Liffey freighted with dead bodies. She had seen the stomachs of babies burst from the gas of starvation. But she knew, also, that now her quarrel with Michael had to end. He had lost one of his beloved girls. She would have to show mercy towards him, no matter what it cost her.

She found him and his wife, Kathleen in a state of dumb sorrow. Michael was unable to go to work at the Anchor Brewery, he told her, 'because my legs just won't carry me there'. He sat all day by the smoky fire in the parlour, ladling on coal, watching the blue and yellow of the flames, choking on the smoke, spitting phlegm onto the dusty floor.

Kathleen sat near to him, playing with a pack of Tarot cards, whose predictions she did not fully understand, swearing at the figures as she turned them up. All around her, disorder accumulated. Unwashed crockery stood about in piles. Dirty clothes and bedding lay soaking in tin pails, never washed nor hung out to dry. Behind the chicken wire of the larder door, bread grew a patina of blue mould and potatoes put forth fibrous green shoots, quite as though the over-heated air was thickening itself into earth.

Worst of all, Clorinda saw, was the state of the other child, the younger child, Aisling. It was as though Michael and Kathleen had forgotten her existence, or, if they remembered it, treated it as though they had no obligation towards her. Aisling was eleven years old, but refused to go to school and the parents were too indif-ferent, it seemed, to care about this. They just sent her out into the cold street, to play on her own or with the toddlers who staggered about the road, chasing rats and squirrels, sitting down in puddles and laughing with woe. When she was allowed back into the apart-ment, she went to her mother and father each in turn, hoping to be hugged by them and they held her to them for a brief moment before they sent her to her room, the room she had once shared with the dead Maire, there to curl up on her bed with her toy pig, staring at nothing.

Clorinda could not bear the look of sadness on Aisling's face. She took the pails of washing into the communal laundry room in the basement beneath the tenement house. She set water on to boil on a blackened range. Then she came back and found carbolic soap and a washboard and took these into Aisling's room. She knelt down by the bed and took the toy pig out of the child's hand and gave her the soap. She said, 'would you like to help me perform a miracle?'

In the end, Clorinda had to bribe Aisling with money, but she told herself that this did not matter. Now, together, they soaped and scrubbed and pounded the washing: a penny for a shirt, two farthings for a pair of drawers, threepence for a petticoat, sixpence for a sheet. Very quickly, they grew hot and their hair became wild and rebellious in the steam, but they both felt strangely enthralled by the quantity of work they had to get through and they kept on for more than four hours, till most of it was clean and rinsed and hung up to dry.

Their hands were red and sore. They were hungry and parched. Clorinda returned to the room where Michael and Kathleen sat unmoving, snatched up her purse and two bonnets and went back to Aisling, whose pale face was now scarlet and smiling. Smoothing her own hair and that of the child, she crammed the bonnets onto their heads and led them out into the late afternoon, where a pale sun laid upon the empty street an unfamiliar glance of beauty.

Clorinda found a Luncheon Room which sold hot pork sausages and bread rolls. She ordered a jug of milk and four sausages and butter for the rolls and she and Aisling made a grand feast together, not caring if grease from sausages ran down their chins, and loving the milk, which was fresh from the herds of Kildare and full of cream.

When this was done, Clorinda ordered coffee, which her niece had never tasted, then sat back and looked at Aisling. She was no beauty. Her expression tended towards sourness as well as sadness, her complexion was blue-pale and her eyes were narrow. But enlivened by the work and the food and the coffee, she appeared to Clorinda like someone who had been absent from life and was now beginning to rejoin it. With strands of dark hair escaping from her bonnet and her cheeks an excited kind of red, she was almost pretty, and Clorinda now suddenly saw how she might save her, at least for a while, from her loveless life.

She began talking to Aisling about her own grandfather and the place where he had lived on the shore of County Clare opposite the Aran Islands. She said she had a longing to return there, to run on the strand, to gather pink cowrie shells, to hear the gannets calling. Then she asked her niece if she would like to make the journey with her to this place and watch the sun go down over the ocean and sleep in the silence of the wind. And the girl said yes, she longed to go away from Dublin, from the rain-soaked street and the crying babies and from the room where her mother came in at night to weep for the dead.

When Michael and Kathleen protested that Clorinda couldn't take Aisling away from them, (as she knew they would) she said nothing. She simply placed before Michael a Bank Draft, made payable to Mr Michael Morrissey of 12 Bishop Street, accompanied by a formal Note of Endorsement, stating that this was '*the sum of money still rightly*

owing to him and agreed by both parties, as his family's share of the ruby neck-
lace, designated an appanage of the Morrissey family' and saw his face lift
itself from contemplation of the coals and break into a wintry smile.
She did not tell him that her savings were now all spent.

'Take her, then,' said Michael, his eyes still fixed on the satisfactory
arithmetic before him on the table. 'See if she likes grubbing for
cockles in the sand.'

It was a long journey, by coach and by cart, but the weather was kind
and the feeling of travelling westwards, back towards the place where
she'd been happy as a girl, enthralled Clorinda. And she saw Aisling,
who had never been out of Dublin, enter a state of marvellous
dreaming at the sight of the green hills and the groves of ash and
the hedgerows in summer leaf.

They put up in wayside inns, where travelling salesmen seemed to
be the only other guests, going from farm to farm with smudged
brochures offering new steam-driven machinery that none but rich
landowners could afford. Against these men, adrift on their tides of
frustration and disappointment, they locked their door at night.
Clorinda was not surprised that Aisling wanted to reach out before
she slept to hold her aunt's hand. She clutched it tight. She told the
girl about her tea room, which had been born out of an old funeral
parlour, and how death and sorrow could be conquered by visions
of new things. She described the galas she had attended in Bath, with
their carousels and their fireworks, and told her about the handsome
Belgian acrobat who had fallen off his stilts and lain in the dust,
looking ridiculous. She heard Aisling laugh. And when the laughter
faded, the girl said, 'that was a strange feeling. I don't think I have
laughed very much in my life before, except once, at a mouse which
ran up the side of the bread bin and turned a somersault.'

When they came to the house, near Ennistymon, where the grandfather had lived his solitary life, they found it occupied by a pair of
sisters, the Misses McKinnon, creeping unobserved into middle age.
One of them, Miss Elizabeth, spent her days in the old barn, painting
pictures of birds and sailing ships, while the other, Miss Maeve,
milked their goats, fed their chickens and kept the house. And when

these woman saw Aisling, wearing her poor city clothes and with her bonnet all askew, they looked at her with longing. They had never had a child to love and now here was an eleven-year-old girl at their door, who was thin and lost-seeming, and they wanted to take her in and set before her the elder Miss McKinnon's oyster pie and make a bed for her with their best linen sheets and teach her the pet names of their goats.

Though Clorinda said that they would find an inn nearby in Ennistymon, the McKinnon sisters, learning that their house had once belonged to Clorinda's grandfather, would not hear of them leaving. They were shown to an attic room, now furnished with a wooden bed and a painted chest of drawers and hung with Miss Elizabeth's bright pictures, and when Clorinda went in there, she remembered what it had housed in her grandfather's time: a sewing machine with an old black handle and piles of cured animal skins, from which he fashioned the tawdry coats and mufflers which he sold to the people of Ennistymon and which kept him in silver sixpences and tobacco all through the winter.

Clorinda told Aisling that she had longed for one of Grandpappy's rabbit-skin coats and he kept promising that he would make her one 'to keep you warm in that sinful city of Dublin', but it had never come her way. But now, as she lay in the wooden bed, holding Aisling's hand, she fancied that the smell of rabbit and fox had lingered in the attic after all these years – the perfume of the past, caught in the wainscot and in the dusty space beneath the floor.

The weather held fine and the following day Clorinda and Aisling made their way over the dunes, where samphire used to grow, down to the wide strand, to see the Atlantic tides come roaring in. At the sight and sound of the sea, Aisling held out her arms, in the manner of a flying bird, and began to run in wild circles, then she cast away her boots, held up her skirts and pelted to where the ocean came sliding in over the sand. She let the water drench her feet, bringing her gifts of tiny stones and shells and drifts of bladderwrack. She let escape from her throat long-frozen cries of joy and Clorinda was able to see in that instant a different girl from the one she had known in the city. It was as if the person she had been, the facial expressions she had adopted all her life had been a mistake, a distortion of her true self, and now she had decided to become someone else.

Clorinda was just beginning to blame herself for what she had done, taking her niece away from the confined existence to which, in a mere few days, she would have to return her, when she saw Elizabeth and Maeve McKinnon coming towards them, carrying all the paraphernalia of a picnic. They stopped and laughed with delight at the figure of Aisling communing with the sea, then began to set out the picnic.

'There is elderberry cordial for the child,' said Elizabeth, 'and ginger beer for us. And cold mutton with relish and lettuce from our patch.'

'And apples from our ancient tree,' added Maeve, 'which we store all winter long in the outhouse, just as your grandfather used to do. When you and Aisling taste our apples, you may both feel that you have come home.'

A MAN WHO DISLIKED RIDDLES

Sir William hadn't accompanied Clorinda to Dublin, not only because he felt that he would not be welcome in Michael Morrissey's household, but also because he knew that he had neglected his patients of late and he was resolved to make amends to them now.

No sooner had he made this resolution, however, than a letter arrived from Ashton Sims, informing him of Jane's suffering, apparently from a bad fall. Sir William knew that he couldn't possibly remain in Bath when something terrible had happened to his daughter. According to Sims, Jane was 'so very much weakened by blood loss that my wife and I still fear she will not pull through, unless, perhaps, you come quickly to her side, to save her.'

Consulting his medical journals, he found scant new remedies for severe haemorrhage, only those he already knew: the exhortation to let the patient rest, the suggestion that a cocktail made from 'strong spirits, yolk of egg and mustard seed' could be beneficial to the body's ability to 'fashion blood'. Red meat, eaten raw, was also recommended, as was the 'slow chewing of spinach leaves' and these things he tried on his patients, with some small success.

Armed with this all-too-inadequate knowledge, Sir William posted a note of apology for his absence on his door, gave instructions to his nurse, to 'do what she could for those who pleaded with her' and set forth for London. Ashton Sims had not explained to him how or why Jane had become ill, but Sir William could not but think that her indisposition had something to do with Ross, who had never returned to Bath, but had instructed his servant to send on his things to a hotel in the West Country and only sent a scrawled message to say – without any explanation – that his engagement to Jane was at an end.

All of this news, together with Emmeline's recent death and Clorinda's absence in Ireland, made Sir William feel that he was suddenly bitterly alone. Running his hands through his thick grey hair, he wondered if his world was about to disintegrate into a state of sorrow he would not be able to bear.

He found Jane lying in Emmeline's bed, not sleeping, but in a state of prostration, too weak, almost to move her bandaged head. But, when she saw her father, her pale lips did widen into a smile and she held out a limp hand to him. He took her hand and kissed it, then sat by her, stroking a few strands of her hair back from her forehead, which was sweaty but cold, then transferring his own hand to her wrist to take her pulse.

He found it to be very weak and his practised physician's ear and eye would have suggested to him that his daughter was near death, except that she, above everybody that he knew, was possessed of an extraordinary strength of body and will. He only wondered, now, if she was heartbroken by Ross's unexpected departure and *wished* to let go her hold on life.

At present, however, he sensed that she was too weak for any intrusive interrogation. Sitting quietly in the room was a nurse engaged by Ashton Sims, so it was to her that Sir William addressed a few quiet questions. He learned that Jane had been persuaded to sip a little soup and that she suffered from an unslakeable thirst. He was also told that her consumption of laudanum for her pain was high and that her sleep appeared to be troubled by nightmares.

'Where is the pain?' asked Sir William. 'In her head?'

'Yes, sir. And in her womb which bleeds.'

Now, Sir William was silent. Jane, too weak to talk, gazed up at him, pleading with her eyes that he not condemn her. All this he saw and to answer her, he said, 'all that matters, Jane, is that you come back to us. To this end, I have heard some fanciful notion about the efficacy of yolks of egg and mustard seed. I wonder if our kind nurse could ask Nancy to go to one of the Chelsea markets for eggs and make a posset for you. Or is that too outrageous a demand?'

Again, he saw the curve of a smile on her mouth and took this for an affirmative answer. He nodded to the nurse and she went out, taking with her a water jug, which was empty, to refill it. Left alone with Jane, Sir William once again took her hand and stroked it gently. Jane closed her eyes. Sir William saw tears begin to run down her cheek and he knew that these tears were not only for the pain but for the recent catastrophe. He could guess at the reasons for it, but refused to name it, even to himself. He only sensed that there was a finality about it which, even if Jane survived, would bring about an alteration to their lives and that nothing in the future would be as he had once counted upon it being.

When the nurse returned, Sir William said to Jane, 'I am going to ask her to lift the bed clothes and examine you, to see whether you are still bleeding. Are you happy that she should do this?'

To Sir William's surprise, Jane turned her head to him and whispered the word 'portrait'. He did not know if he had heard her correctly and raised his head to silently interrogate the nurse.

For a moment, she looked away, unwilling to make any answer, but then she said quietly, 'the portrait of Miss Jane has been taken down and returned to the late Miss Emmeline's studio. Mr Sims told me to tell you, when you arrived, that you might wish to look at it.'

Sir William Adeane was a man who disliked riddles. In his own profession, when diagnosis was difficult, it put him into a mild state of anguish and this was what he felt now, anguish on top of anguish, that his daughter was holding to life by a frayed thread and that he was being sent upon some quest which might only increase his confusion.

He nevertheless stood up obediently and, reassuring Jane that he would be back directly, went out and down the stairs towards his sister's studio, a room which had always engendered strong feelings in him – feelings of both admiration and fear. He had never been told the story of the golem, never known that Emmeline had suffered quite so cruelly at the hands of Jocelyn Hulton, but he had often been afraid for his sister – for her vulnerability in a man's world and for her loneliness. He had sometimes seen her life as a kind of martyrdom to her art, and had never been able to decide if the sacrifice was worth the sorrow.

Now, as he walked towards the studio, he heard a ring at the door-bell and Nancy came out from her kitchen to answer it. Sir William waited at the foot of the stairs. The door opened to admit Ashton and Julietta Sims and when Julietta saw Jane's father, she rushed to him and asked, 'how is she, Sir William? Has she rallied? Is she out of danger?'

'I cannot say,' said Sir William, 'but I do not think the danger is past. And now she has asked me to go and look at her portrait.'

'Oh, the portrait, the portrait!' cried Julietta. 'Oh, Sir William, it will tell you the whole terrible story, but Ashton dearest, why do you and Sir William not go and sip a glass of claret in the drawing room and then everything can be made plain by that means, man to man.'

If there was a momentary look of terror on Ashton Sims's face, he quickly mastered himself, nodded to Sir William and said, 'probably that is best, that nothing is hidden from you. We believe it is what Jane wishes.'

'I must go to Jane,' said Julietta, 'I must go at once, poor darling, poor angel ...'

And she fled up the stairs, leaving the two men marvelling at the effortless speed with which she rushed towards her friend.

If it was difficult, at this time, for men who did not know each other well, to bring themselves to speak frankly about intimate matters, it was also the case that Ashton Sims, whose friends were the writers, publishers, artists and moral philosophers of the day, was used to discussing all the exquisite agonies afflicting the human condition. Thus, to relate to Jane's father the story of her pregnancy and cruel miscarriage – and its fearful cause – was not as painful for him as it would have been for almost anyone else.

He was able to tell the tale calmly and slowly and yet ... and yet ... even he could not tell it truthfully. About Ross's motive for hurting Jane he had had to 'speculate' only that Jane's fiancé had believed himself to be betrayed in some way. He could not bring himself to admit to Sir William Adeane that the cause of the man's violent outburst had been the knowledge that his own wife was Jane's lover.

Sir William, then, was left with the story as if told by an author who disdains to apportion to his characters reason and motive. And when he saw that this was how things would remain, he felt again his habitual impatience with the arrival of yet another riddle. But he also saw that Ashton Sims had gone as far with his dreadful tale as he was able to go at present. Sir William lit a cigar to calm himself and said, 'poor wretched Ross. I still cannot see how he arrived at such a crime.'

He puffed on his cigar for some moments, then he added, 'I believe he may finally have gone in search of his brother on the Malay Archipelago. I think we will never set eyes on him again.'

'Ah,' said Ashton. 'Well perhaps that is for the best.'

THE WHITE CLOUD

She could not rid herself of the feeling that she was drowning. It wasn't that the water choked her; it was the coldness of the sea in her veins. It coursed all through her, entering and leaving her heart, slowly insinuating itself into her brain, depositing ice crystals there, and the crystals flashed with wounding light.

Jane Adeane.

She could remember her name. She could breathe its syllables, still, but she did not know how long the name would last. It seemed to her that it had begun to flicker and dim and that when at last her name went dark, then her life would be lost.

In the frozen world she now inhabited, she remembered thinking of herself as 'her own lifeboat' in her great tallness. Perhaps she had even boasted about this, that in some way, her height set her apart from everybody else and would never let her drown. Yet now she knew that the freezing water would soon close over her head.

Images of her past rose up like faithful ghosts, to keep her company for a while, and then faded away. She saw the beautiful symmetries of the Baths and herself as their Angel, keeping watch, as the trusting people – the *smaller people* – floundered in the sulphurous water, all their movements impotent and slow, but their faces turned upwards towards her, begging for mercy, trusting her to save them. Yet it seemed that she could not save them, for when next she saw them they were in the Paris Morgue, set out for show on marble slabs, with water pouring into their closed eyes and out of their mouths and from between their legs, to rush past their feet and be sucked into the vortex of a metal drain.

She saw Marco. The little boy was swimming in the Baths, swimming without fear, not asking anything of her, but travelling round and round merrily splashing, and she hoped that this vision would last and keep her company for a while. She tried to remain still, to stop herself from shivering, so that Marco would stay as he was, buoyant in his life, destined to go on and grow into a man. But then the vapour rising from the Hot Bath began to grow dense. It formed itself into a white cloud around Marco and though Jane searched and searched, she could no longer see him.

So then it seemed to her that if Marco was gone, and the cloud obscuring him appeared to be growing larger and larger, it would soon engulf her, too, and then her end would be reached at last. She remembered that, for most of her life, she had had the notion of some momentous Thing towards which she was travelling. She had thought of it as something which would bring her happiness and renown, but now she understood that the Thing was death. It was within her reach. In moments, it would come …

But she allowed herself one last thought, about her own foolishness, walking through life so tall and blithe, convinced that some grand destiny awaited her, when all the time she had merely been striding towards oblivion. It almost made her laugh: the Angel of the Baths, wearing her white robes, so convinced of her singularity and her power, obliterated by a white cloud, impotent to save herself from joining the manufacturer of glue and all the other flawed and decadent people on their journey to nothingness.

Nearer and nearer came the cloud. Jane tried to retreat from it, but found herself up against a stone wall. So then she knew that what was asked of her was surrender. She closed her eyes. She waited for her own invisibility, but knew, still, that she was unreconciled to it. Something of her old pride and stubbornness kept surfacing in her. It understood that all was lost and yet it still fought on.

Then, with her very last ounce of rebellion – a rebellion worthy of Emmeline, going forth into the world wearing a jewelled turban, a rebellion worthy of an exhausted washerwoman who believes that moonlight will blanch her laundered sheets – she opened her eyes again. The cloud hung near. But something moved within it. It was a small shape, no larger than a child's bundle of washing, but then it seemed to take form and colour and begin to dance, waving its arms in the air. And Jane knew then that it was going to step out of the cloud and save her life. It was the clay golem and it came forth gleaming and soft, as if fresh from the pottery wheel.

Jane woke to find Julietta at her bedside.

She woke, too, to more words than she had had within her for a long time. She said Julietta's name and was able to reach out to her with both arms and Julietta held her and realised that Jane's body was no longer cold as it had been. She kissed her forehead and then laid her head on Jane's breast. She wanted to call out to Ashton and to Sir William that Jane was returning to them, but was so held by the moment that she could find no voice.

It was Jane who began to speak. She said, 'I have had visions. I saw death as a cloud and it was coming towards me ...'

'Hush, dearest,' said Julietta. 'Don't talk of any death cloud. Feel how warm is your face and your hand and your breast ...'

'Are they warm?'

'Feel.'

Jane reached up and put her hand on her cheek and she understood that she would now get well again and rejoin the world.

'Yes,' she said. 'Yes. They are warm.'

She could only lie still and gaze in wonder at the soft and comforting light in the room, at some roses arranged in a white vase on a little table, now beginning to shed their petals. Then she brought her eyes to the thing she longed to see above all others: Julietta's face.

THE GOOD SHEPHERD

As the *Queen of the Islands* heaved itself southwards through the Atlantic storms and its passengers tried to cajole the time with plans for their new lives in Australia, Valentine Ross kept obstinately to his cabin and only walked on deck in the deep of night, when, often, the sea seemed to be calmer and the stars, shining more brightly than they ever did in an English sky, attempted to seduce him with some intimation of wonder.

He resisted their attempt. He knew that wonder was gone from the world. He wished only to be left alone, not caring about the squalor created by his bodily existence in his cramped quarters. When his self-appointed servant, Chesterfield, began fussing round him, picking up dirty clothes, covering his chamber pot with a rag before taking it away, he asked the old man why he performed these tasks, 'when nothing signifies and it matters not at all to me that I should wear foul underwear or that my pot should overflow'.

Chesterfield stood his ground as best he could on the tilting ship and replied, 'it matters to *me*, Sir. I am a servant. While I am bound to this condition, I can only strive to do my duty as a servant in a way that will bring me no shame.'

'Shame?'

'Yes. You will say that it is a strong word to use, but it is the right word. For if we fail in the tasks appointed to us, what is there for us but that?'

Ross, who was lying on his bunk and suffering all the spinal discomfort of one who has lain there far too long, looked up at Chesterfield in surprise. He had had no stomach for any conversation with the old man, but now he had made an observation which Ross judged to be astute. He knew that he himself was mired in shame – for all that he had neglected, for his abject failure in love and for his wicked moment of physical cruelty – but he was not ready to speak about it, most particularly not to one so far beneath him in the terrible hierarchy of the world. Chesterfield, however, was not done with the subject. While busying himself examining the food stains on one of Ross's cast-off shirts, he went on to say, 'Now you, Sir, I deduce from the contents of your oak chest that you are a doctor. Is that the case?'

'Yes. It is the case. But you will swear, please, not to put this information about the ship.'

'I swear I will not put it about, Sir, but I only ask you, as a medical man, who has sworn an oath to do no harm, do you not, in your profession, wish to serve your patients as best you can?'

Ross looked down at his hands. He had wished it. He had sincerely wished it. He had striven to deepen his medical knowledge as the years passed. The notion that he had been able to relieve suffering had given him godlike satisfaction. And then …

After the fateful day in Mrs Morrissey's tea room when Jane Adeane had mocked him and refused him, that wish had gradually grown feeble and he had begun to let slip away from him his dedication to his profession. Hurt beyond endurance, he had no longer cared in the same way about trying to heal the sick and infirm. But it was not his fault; it was Jane's fault. She had rendered him indifferent towards those he should have helped. And in the end she had cancelled out his sworn promise to do no harm. She had tortured him to the point where he wished to kill her.

All this made a logical progression through Ross's mind as Chesterfield began gathering more clothes from the dirty floor, but he understood, deep in his heart's core, that he would never confess it to any living soul.

'I was a good doctor,' was all he said.

'But you use the past tense,' said Chesterfield. 'Why is that?'

'Because that is all there is,' he said. 'In the middle of an ocean, there is only stasis. All I know is the past.'

'Have you no plans for when you arrive in Singapore, Sir?'

'I will not notice Singapore. It has no meaning for me. I will only seek out some kind of native craft at the wharves there. Praus, I believe they are named. To convey me to Borneo.'

'To take up your doctoring again?'

'No. I go for only one reason: to save my brother.'

'From what, Sir, if I may ask?'

'I do not know. Now, when you have collected sufficient laundry, please be good enough to go away and leave me to myself.'

The old servant was slung about with a capacious canvas bag, into which he now began piling Ross's cast-off things. He did this hastily, almost in the manner of a burglar carrying off his swag, and this action of his brought to Ross's face an amused smile. He was tempted to say to Chesterfield that once he had washed and pressed the shirts and undergarments, he could keep them for himself, that his despair was so complete that he really did not care if he was forced to walk about the ship naked and submit to the ridicule of having his private parts exposed to strangers. But he held back from this. It was as if he believed that remaining covered up, indeed almost invisible in his wooden hutch, he might at last construct a new person, one who had eaten all his shame and let it pass through him into a stinking pot, taken away by a man whose only vanity was to believe in himself.

He asked himself how on earth this new Ross could be assembled.

It came to him that if he could recall more than a scant few genuine acts of kindness in his life, then these might act as a kind of guide-rail on which he could lean when the weather of self-loathing blew in.

He lay in his coffin-bed and tried to cover himself with a blanket of recollection. He took himself to the Wiltshire lanes and woods of his childhood. He carried a butterfly net. Ahead of him – always running on ahead and then suddenly stopping when he sighted an insect or a plant which interested him – was Edmund, blithe and happy in each passing moment, an innocent whose collecting zeal brought bright blood to his cheeks and laughter to his throat. Edmund would shout instructions to him: 'when we reach the field, tread softly, for plovers nest on the plough. Hark when the wind rattles the gorse, for we shall find bees clinging to the flowers. Watch the sky for us, so we are not lost in the dark.' And he always tried to obey his brother and then, at the end of an afternoon, guide them safely home. For it was in Edmund's nature to stray from the path, to lose his sense of direction, and more than once it was Valentine who had led his brother back, as the dusk came on, to where their mother waited in her parlour with a lit lamp and worry in her heart for her boys.

Here, surely, were acts of kindness, for which he had asked and received nothing. Neither Edmund nor their quiet Mama had ever shown gratitude towards him for guiding them safely through failing light, and yet all through his childhood, Ross had persisted in this role. And he thought now that here was something to set against shame and loathing. It also filled his heart, for a brief moment, with the belief that now, at last, he was once again embarked on the same mission – to be the one to bring Edmund home. This time, no fond parent waited for them. If there was a lamp burning in the house where they had once lived, it had been lit by strangers. Mother and father both lay in St. Mary's churchyard and the graves were over-grown. But Ross thought now that if ever he survived the sea journey, if at last Edmund was found, he would ask his brother if this was what he wanted, to be brought back to the valley where they had grown up and live chastely there, as though the intervening years had never been.

As he drifted to sleep on the tide of this dreamlike thought, he said again as he had said to Chesterfield, 'all I know is the past'.

Over the following few days, in worsening weather, as the Cape of Good Hope neared, Ross kept trying to steer his thoughts towards his childhood, looking there for acts of innocence and kindness. He'd loved his mother and had always tried to please her, but he had also known that Edmund was the son dearest to her heart. Often, Edmund would be praised or caressed in a kind of unceasing way which could cause Valentine terrible pain. But he almost never let his anguish become visible. He only strove harder to behave as his mother wished, and when she did put her arms round him or stroke his hair, he was able to bask in these moments of tenderness and congratulate himself on staying strong and hiding his jealousy of his brother.

And just summoning her presence, now, seeing her sewing by the parlour fire, was almost enough to bring him respite from his perpetual agitation. And yet it was not *quite* enough. The image of her kept slipping away from him, or else Edmund destroyed it by coming into the room and sitting at her feet. And when he did this, she laid aside her work to fondle his bright curls.

Perhaps it was this, the sight of her gentle hands entangled in Edmund's hair, that made Ross suddenly remember the emerald and diamond ring which had once belonged to his mother and which he had planned to give to Jane. And then he had left it in her room! He cursed and then cursed again. He had left it in her bedroom in Tite Street without meaning to do so, and had never had a moment to recover it.

The loss of this, the only thing of value he had had from his parent, now caused him intense agony. It suddenly felt to him that this had happened, not because of his own forgetfulness or inattention, but because of Jane's sorcery. She was a true witch! She had inherited a fortune from her aunt, but had somehow arranged to trick him into leaving his mother's ring behind, for her to add to all that she had taken from him. It was unbearable.

Ross went in search of Chesterfield, to ask him to furnish him with paper and ink. He would write a letter to Jane and post it back to England, when the *Queen of the Islands* stopped at Simon's Town to take on supplies. He would accuse her of bad faith, taking the ring into her own possession, when the conditions of that possession had been savagely betrayed. He would request that it be given to Sir William for safekeeping until his return with Edmund to Wiltshire.

He found Chesterfield shepherding a small group of convicts round and round the deck, as they enjoyed a brief respite from the dark hole in which they lived. The men wore leg irons and Ross could see that these had so chafed their ankles that many of them had to endure the agony of weeping sores. But Chesterfield was gentle with them, exhorting them to 'take good gulpings of fresh air' and to lift their white faces to the southern sun. And when Ross saw this, he retreated to his cabin without disturbing them. Confronted by people whose future was one of unremitting hard labour, who would never again be free, he pitied them. In these feelings of pity resided a guilty kind of joy.

THE MIDDLE CHILD

If Ireland had always been famed for the quantity of rain which fell upon it all year round, so that the bright greenness of the fields might be enough to dazzle the yellow eyes of the golden eagle, it was also true that one year in ten, a hot summer broke out and the green began to fade towards dry beige and above the hedgerows the air was a shimmering mirror.

It was such a summer which began after the arrival of Clorinda Morrissey and her niece Aisling in the house of the McKinnon sisters. Above the strand, the sky was the softest bird's egg blue and when the sun went down over the sea it flared such a brilliant crimson that the watchers on the shore, if they had witnessed sunsets over the Sahara Desert, might have compared it to these.

In this exalted kind of weather, a delightful lethargy fell upon the house. Miss Elizabeth spent less time at her painting and more time sitting in the shade of the apple trees, dreaming of all that she and her sister might offer to the young stranger who had suddenly appeared among them. Miss Maeve put her vibrant energy into contriving ever more mouth-watering picnics for them to take to the strand and teaching Aisling how to press wild flowers between the pages of the McKinnon family bible. As for Clorinda, she watched with tenderness all that was going on around her and kept asking herself the same question: was she compelled by moral right to return Aisling to her life in Dublin, or might she send word to Michael and Kathleen that their seemingly unwanted girl had found a new home and ask that she be allowed to stay there, at least until the summer was over?

She had no answer. She wished that Sir William was with her, that she might ask his advice on the matter, yet she also knew that this question was not his to decide; it had to be settled, in the end, by Michael and Kathleen and by Aisling herself. But why spoil the girl's continuing recovery from grief and rejection by asking it? She sensed that Aisling had no wish to address anything but the moment-to-moment wonders of this burning summer. She had 'adopted' a goat she named Iris. She sat in the long grass, stroking Iris's nose and pulling softly on her long ears. She fed her apples and dandelion leaves. She addressed her as 'my dearest little pet'. She asked Miss Maeve if they might take the donkey-cart into Ennistymon and purchase a bell to hang around Iris's neck, and they went and bought the bell and Aisling said 'now Iris will never again be lost'.

Then, one day, another girl appeared on the strand. She was about Aisling's age. She was dressed in a simple linen shift. Her hair was wild.

When she saw the Misses McKinnon and Aisling with them, she came skipping over to where they sat, under a frayed parasol. Maeve McKinnon got up and laid a kiss on the child's head.

'This is Charlotte O'Connor,' she said. 'Her father is the school-teacher. And here, Charlotte, are our new friends, Mrs Morrissey and her niece, Aisling.'

'New friends?' said Charlotte. 'I would like to have some new friends, so I would.'

'Well then,' said Maeve, why do you and Aisling not run off and see if you can find some cowrie shells?'

The two girls looked at each other and Aisling soon enough jumped up. Iris the goat, tethered to a post in the sand, also got to her feet, and the sound of the tinkling bell competed for a moment with the onrush of the sea. Aisling went to her and untied the tether.

'This is Iris,' she said to Charlotte O'Connor, 'and she is mine now, but you can play with her. She is very gentle.'

Charlotte straight away began to pet the goat. Then, without saying anything more, the girls went scampering off, with Iris bounding after them and what Clorinda saw in the way Aisling now moved, with ease and grace, was a manifestation of new and simple joy. Perhaps the McKinnon sisters saw it too, because Miss Elizabeth turned to Clorinda and said, 'Maeve and I, we have been thinking, with the summer being here and so fine a summer at that … we have been constantly saying that it might be a shame to return Aisling to the city. Haven't we, Maeve?'

'Oh indeed,' said Maeve. 'Of course, we know you have to get back to Bath, for your wedding, Clorinda. But why not let Aisling stay with us a little longer? Charlotte O'Connor is a sweet child and will surely be her friend. And then there is Iris, from whom Aisling does not wish to be parted. Why separate her from all this, to go back to a life of sadness?'

Clorinda was silent. She turned her face to where the girls were now playing at the edge of the water, with the goat bounding in circles all about them and the image came to her of Aisling escaping the room she had shared with poor suffering Maire, only to go into the street and try to sleep in an old baby carriage.

Taking Clorinda's silence for a hesitation, Maeve McKinnon went on, 'you know how correctly we will take care of Aisling, don't you? We will be as parents to her.'

'I know that,' said Clorinda. 'I do not doubt it at all. But I cannot be the one to decide. I will write to my brother. I will describe your beautiful world of consolations.'

'Let him see it as a kind of homecoming for Aisling,' said Elizabeth. 'For she now sleeps in what was once your grandfather's house. Surely, that is fitting?'

Knowing Michael as she did, Clorinda wrote only a short letter, taking care not to emphasise how the life Aisling was now tasting was so profoundly superior to that which he had offered her, nor saying anything about adopted goats or new friends, but merely suggesting that he and Kathleen be spared the burden of caring for her for a while and that the sea air would return to them a happy and healthy child when the autumn came.

Given Michael's antipathy towards the schemes and designs of other people as they touched upon his own life, Clorinda expected him to demand Aisling's immediate return to Dublin, but what he wrote in reply was strangely unexpected.

He first related how he had at last found the will to return to his work at the Anchor Brewery and then went on:

... the thing which has brought me a little back to myself and to life is the knowledge that I am to be a father again. Kathleen will give birth in the late winter and I have good hopes that the child will be a boy and that we will once again be a proper family.

As to she whom I will now call our 'middle child', let her stay at her pleasure with her new guardians and not burden us with her vexing cross-ness and habits of refusal. We are still grieving for Maire. The daily behaviour of the middle child had become impossible for us to endure and I do not wish to burden Kathleen with anyone or anything which could endanger the safe carrying of our son into the world. It is fortunate for all concerned that Aisling has been given hospitality elsewhere. If the Misses McKinnon have need of money for her sustenance, please give it to them and I will repay you, if you so wish, in due time.

It was now incumbent upon Clorinda to ask Aisling whether she truly wanted to remain in County Clare when she herself went back to England. She tried to imagine how the girl thought about her parents and their treatment of her, knowing that children who are not loved may often persist in the sad adoration of those by whom they are rejected. That Aisling never spoke about her mother and father did not necessarily mean that she did not mourn them.

Clorinda chose a time when the sun had gone and they could hear owls calling in the near-dark as they prepared for bed. As she brushed Aisling's hair she said, 'I have had a very kind request from the Misses McKinnon: that you stay here with them and with Iris until the summer ends. But you are under no obligation. I can return you to Dublin when I leave next week, and—'

'Oh no!' cried Aisling. 'Please let me stay! Aunt Clorinda, I shall die if I must go back to Bishop Street. Please do not make me leave. What would become of Iris if I deserted her? Her bell would sound and I would not hear it. She would pine and die!'

Aisling now broke into tears. Clorinda put aside the hairbrush and held the girl close against her.

'Never fear,' she said. 'The summer is long and you will be safe here while it lasts. And Iris will be safe.'

NEVER BEFORE SEEN IN BATH

The summer was indeed long and on an early September day hot sunlight was still falling upon Camden Street.

From the signs and awnings of all the shops along the whole length of the thoroughfare, bunting had been strung up and fluttered in the warm little breeze. Underneath the bunting, trestle tables had been laid out, covered with white cloths and piled with the choicest provisions, manufactured by the best cook shops in Bath. Champagne, punch and white wine had been chilled in silver buckets. Bottles of claret had been emptied into heavy decanters to inhale the warm air and let it amplify their dark perfume. The road had been closed to all horse-drawn traffic and in the very middle of it perched a string quartet, the musicians shaded by parasols attached to their chairs, playing some hastily learned bright airs from an Irish songbook.

And now the people began arriving. There were so many of them, it almost seemed as though everybody in the city had been invited – the whole of Bath crammed into one street on a hot September day! They pressed upon the pavement. The women fanned themselves against the heat. They stood by the trestles (trying to restrain themselves from snatching little tempting slices of game pie or galantine of veal) ready to applaud the arrival of a woman they had come to love and revere above many others in their crowded lives: Mrs Clorinda Morrissey. But she was no longer Mrs Clorinda Morrissey. This was her wedding day. When she emerged from the Laura Chapel and walked to Camden Street on the arm of her bridegroom, she had become Lady Adeane.

She wore a dress of cream and green silk, the over-skirt gathered up here and there by green satin bows, and a headdress that was a marvellous assemblage of feathers and ribbons, falling down to her shoulders. To her bodice was attached a beautiful emerald and diamond brooch and her eyes shone with unmistakable pride, for she had much to be proud of. She once toiled in a milliner's basement; now, she was loved by the cream of Bath society. And today she had become the wife of the revered surgeon, Sir William Adeane, a man who had lost his wife twenty-five years ago and never thought to marry again – until he met Clorinda and lost his heart to her cooking and to her courage and to the music of her voice. As he led her towards the great gathering on Camden Street, his top hat crammed onto his still-abundant white hair, his cheeks boyishly pink with blushing delight, his nose a little scarlet in the heat, he, too, became a darling of the crowd and all along the street there was such clapping and cheering, it was quite as if Queen Victoria herself had anointed the scene with her presence.

When the bridal couple were seated, waiters scampered round, wearing white gloves, ladling out punch, opening and pouring the wine, offering a first course of brawn with shallots and cucumber, upon which Sir William doted, and the guests fell upon the food. The sun was so bright, it glittered upon the aspic and made the glassware scintillate like diamonds. The chinking of cutlery was so noisily musical it almost drowned out the quartet, who were now attempting to aid the collective digestion by playing a little Mozart.

From the further ends of Camden Street, strangers began assembling to stare at the colossal sight of the street banquet, its like never before seen in Bath, and to wonder, if so many had been invited, why they had been excluded. They longed to join in. The waiters hurried them away, informing them that this was not a public gala, but a private wedding feast. Still, a few could not resist creeping back, not to try to steal food or even a tot of wine, but only to marvel at the miles of fluttering bunting, at the whiteness of the table linen, at the silver champagne-coolers and, most particularly, at the person (whoever he or she might be) whose mind had conjured such a piece of pure theatre, spreading out from the decorated shopfronts across the wide pavement and onto the newly polished cobbles of the road.

This mind was, of course, Clorinda's. She had dreamed of it first. She saw the sunlit day. She saw the street where her tea room quietly waited. And like an artist creating a beautiful picture, she set out the snowy tables under the blue sky and hung flags and garlands above them. Then, in her dream, two hundred golden chairs floated down from the chimney tops and arranged themselves, as obediently as infantrymen, along the tables. Music began playing: the old Irish songs she had heard in County Clare when the fiddle band came to her village when she was a child and all the men and women began twirling and hopping, trying to dance in their clogs and setting up such a pounding on the old earthen floors that the houses seemed to shiver and the babies and the cats began caterwauling like monkeys from some distant land.

When she woke from the dream, she said to Sir William that this was how and where she wanted their wedding feast: in the public street, with all her clientele invited and more food piled on the tables than was ever seen at the official galas that were the pride of the city. If Sir William demurred for a moment at the probable cost of realising this great vision, he also saw that it would be the last great wonder of his life and that it had about it something touchingly unique, something that only Clorinda could have imagined.

So here they were. Sir William turned to Clorinda and asked her, as he surveyed the guests intent upon a fine demolishment of a great side of beef, a mountain of veal cutlets, a gratin of potatoes in dishes the size of tea-trays, if she was content with her day, if it lived up to what she had seen in her mind. And she said to him, 'Can't you see it on my face, William? As long as I live, I will never forget such joy.'

At this, he stood up, wanting to make an impromptu speech before he and the assembled company were so stunned by the arrival of the fruit compotes, the apple charlottes and the rhubarb syllabubs that they lost all comprehension of where they were and on what glass of wine they were now embarked. He held up his hands, like a conductor readying his orchestra for the first note of a symphony. When the noise had diminished to a level at which Sir William could hear his own thoughts, he said, 'I will not keep you long from our great assortment of puddings, for I know that a pudding may be a much more marvellous thing than the sentimental words of an old man.'

To this there were cries of 'no, no!' and 'not true, Sir Will!' He heard Clorinda's laughter beside him and the thought that he would hear this in his house to his dying day put a choke into his heart and his next words were spoken with the kind of tremble in his voice which he always did his very best to subdue when talking to his patients.

'You all know,' he said, 'how long I have led a solitary life. Until last year, I believed that I would never love again. But then I heard a story. It was the story of a girl taken to stay with her grandfather, who lived in a lonely place, facing out to the ocean. She helped him gather sea-pinks for his table and samphire for his supper and she ran barefoot over the dunes and slept in a wooden cot with a doll made of rags.

'Can any of us say for certain what is going to move us, or what is going to leave us cold? I do not know why or how the story of the barefoot girl entered my heart, but it did. And then I looked at the face of the woman who told me the story and realised that it moved me too – moved me to feelings of love.

'And here is what this old man wants to say today: that he is overwhelmed with gratitude towards his bride, for revealing to him that love and happiness may be found towards the last turnings in the road of life and for agreeing to become the wife of someone who is so very out of practice at being a husband.

'All of you assembled here owe a debt to Clorinda Morrissey, for giving our city a beautiful little island of refuge and delight, and let me reassure you that I will not make so many demands on her time that the tea room cannot continue to exist. For it is the place where we come not only to savour a slice of Clorinda's fabled Victoria Sponge, but to pause in the onward rush of our lives, to sip the fragrant Assam and to ponder where we are going and what we have seen. The debt that I owe her is of profound significance and I want to thank her from the depths of my heart.'

Sir William had intended to end with a formal toast to his bride, but he had to sit down now, feeling as he did that any more words might choke him and that he would make a donkey of himself by starting to cry. He took Clorinda in his arms and kissed her and the guests began a lively clamour of appreciation, clapping their hands and stamping their feet. And as more strangers appeared at the end of Camden Street, lured by the knowledge that, given the 'sheer bloody racket' now disturbing the afternoon, something exceptional must be unfolding there, Jane stood up.

All eyes turned to her. The clapping faded away. Many of the wedding guests knew her, their beloved Angel of the Baths, but they had not seen her for a long time until this day. They had heard that she had been very ill, that her life had almost been lost, and these sufferings of hers were still visible in her features and in her tall frame, which seemed taller than it had ever been by having shed so much flesh from its bones. She was wearing a beautiful brown silk dress, but the bodice hung on her too loosely to do the dress justice, and her dark hair, fetchingly piled up with satin ribbons, was touched here and there with premature greyness.

When she began to speak, however, it was as if the 'former Jane', the one for whose healing touch so many people had longed, had re-emerged – in her calm demeanour and the way she held her hands so still and then in the strength of her voice, as she began: 'I know it is uncommon for a woman to speak on an occasion like this, but let me say that I believe the day is singular enough, uncommon enough, that it invites an uncommon response.

'My dear father has got married! He has spent, it seems, some twenty-five or more years practising – or more accurately *not practising* – for this day. Indeed I had come to believe that these long years of non-rehearsal would be so inevitably prolonged that instead of speaking at his marriage he would have to give the oration at his own funeral.'

Laughter crept over the edges of tables, bounced, here and there, off the round bellies of the wine-coolers. It was hesitant at first, then grew a little, as though the guests were waiting for the reassurance that Miss Jane was not as fragile as she looked. She waited for this little laughter to subside, then continued: 'I suppose I guessed, from Sir William's fondness for cakes and pastries, that he would become a faithful client of Mrs Morrissey's tea room. What I did not foresee was the dramatic alteration these sublime substances could cause in his brain, turning him from a sober physician into a veritable fool for love.'

The sounds of mirth rose up again. Sir William was laughing, too but his bride was clutching his arm, afraid, perhaps, that Jane was going to indulge in too much mockery, thus taking something away from the romantic words spoken by the groom a few moments before.

As if understanding this, Jane changed the mood of her speech and said: 'Love is the greatest blessing we can ever find. And if ever I wished great blessings upon anyone, it is upon my father, to whom I owe my life – not only the life that he begat, but the life that he recently helped to save. And I can think of no finer gift to offer him today than to say, Sir, you chose well. Your bride is a woman of exceptional gifts, of dedicated kindness, of touching loyalty and remarkably good taste in cream-and-green dresses; the butter-cream of her tea room confections, the green of samphire on the wild shores of her native Ireland. Ladies and gentlemen, noble Lords and Ladies, beloved friends and neighbours, let us drink a toast to Sir William and Lady Adeane!'

People rose – those who were not so constrained by their wide skirts or their intake of wine as to be unable to do so – glasses were refilled and the toast roared out over the dreamscape that was Camden Street, where the golden chairs had cascaded from the rooftop and cloths of white linen had settled on the tables, like snow.

A STORY OF GOOD AND EVIL

Jane stayed in Bath a few weeks more, to complete her recovery and when the autumn began snatching the leaves from the trees, she left for London.

She told herself that she wasn't leaving for ever, and yet she understood that after all that had happened, her gift for nursing, and indeed her will to perform all the tasks which it entailed, had been taken from her. The very thought of extracting rotten teeth now repelled her. The perpetual stink which accompanied illness made her gag. And she knew that the patience and fortitude she had once shown, especially in the matter of the male species and their ailments, had now deserted her. She felt that she never again wanted to lay her hands on any part of a man's anatomy.

Regarding herself solemnly in her looking glass, Jane saw that she looked older. The world, she thought, might take her for a woman of thirty or more. And this new appraisal of herself amplified the feeling that her youth was over and that she must now find some wiser, more independent Jane and some new direction for her life. She knew that many women in her predicament might be tied to financial dependence on their fathers, and she could imagine both the sorrow and the rage which they might feel. But, thanks to her beloved Emmeline, this was not Jane's case. Her house in Tite Street awaited her. She had enough money to refashion her life. And then there was Julietta ...

Once Jane was established in Chelsea, it became possible for Julietta to visit her as often as they wished. Having been near death, Jane's response to finding herself once more in the arms of her lover felt so overwhelming to her that when sated by sexual pleasure Jane found herself saying to Julietta, 'I love you too much.'

Julietta was silent for a moment, then said: 'I don't think one can ever love "too much". But perhaps you might find other women to bed, Jane, as well as me. Summon a few "beauties" to your house and see what happens. There is no shame in it. Then you and I will love more calmly.'

Jane looked into Julietta's liquid brown eyes. She asked her if, in all the long while she had been recovering from Ross's attack, Julietta had returned to her 'beauties' and Julietta replied straight away, 'I did not, Jane. I made a bargain with God. I promised that if he would spare you, I would renounce my beauties for ever. I would love you and Ashton, but no one else. We've both changed. Your love has changed me. The future can be calm.'

'And yet you're suggesting that I make love with other women?'

'Only if you wish it. I believe I will always be your "bride", but perhaps a few "bridesmaids" would amuse you and give you pleasure. Might that not be so?'

'I will think about it,' said Jane. 'I will think carefully about everything.'

One afternoon, Julietta, who was now pregnant with another child, brought Marco round to Tite Street for tea. Emulating Clorinda, Jane had instructed that jam tarts and sugar buns be made for him and when he had eaten his fill of these, he wandered into Emmeline's studio and came back to Jane and Julietta, carrying the golem.

He sat down beside Jane, cradling the little manikin as he might have cradled a tiny baby, kissing its ugly head from time to time. After a while, he turned to Jane and asked, 'What does it do?'

'Well,' said Jane, 'you ask me what it does and I think I know the answer to that: it comforts people.'

'How does it comfort people?'

'Well,' said Jane, 'remember how you swam in the magic water of the Baths? The water made you feel happy, didn't it? And I think there is something of the same kind of magic in the golem. Why do you not lay your face against it and see if a feeling of happiness doesn't come into you?'

Marco did as Jane instructed. She and Julietta watched as his soft pink cheeks pressed themselves against the rough clay and his dark curls brushed the top of the manikin's head.

'I'm not feeling happy yet,' said Marco.

'Ah,' said Jane, 'but you must be patient, Marco. Happiness is sometimes slow to arrive.'

'Why do you not close your eyes,' suggested Julietta. 'And perhaps imagine that the golem is talking to you ...'

They waited. Julietta took Jane's hand, as though they were expecting something important to arrive. Jane held Julietta close and the silence of the afternoon was suddenly broken by the sound of a drenching rain falling against the windows of the drawing room. Then Marco said, 'that's very peculiar, Jane. I had a pain in my arm from when I fell off Trebuchet, but now the pain has vanished away.'

That night, remembering her conversation with Marco, the beginnings of a story came into Jane's mind.

She told herself that she probably wouldn't be able to write such a thing, that 'real' writers – Guy Mollinet, Mary Shelley, Jane Austen, Charles Dickens and even Emmeline's detested Mr Wilkie Collins – had a vision of the world particular only to them and it was this which gave their work its power. She doubted that this was true for a woman who had spent almost ten years as a nurse. But she knew what pleasure and solace her reading had given her and remembered that she had found something of this same consolation in her diary jottings – in the *act* of writing. She dared herself to begin and see what happened.

She didn't yet know if her story might be only for children or whether its reach was deeper and wider than that, but her mind was held by it, whatever it was, and, as the night went on, it expanded and grew to the point where she renounced sleep and went down into Emmeline's studio. Shivering a little in the cool air of the autumn night, she picked up one of Emmeline's sketch pads and embarked on her strange tale.

She formed the golem into a creature of unbaked clay, soft and pliant. It had the ugly features Emmeline had described to her, before she had thrown it into the fire, but it grew a little larger in her mind. It took on a kind of human life: the living representation of all the children lost to Emmeline and even of her own lost child. And it was, as she had described to Marco, possessed of magic powers. The most important of these was the power of healing, an attribute once given to her while her life had been an innocent thing, and which, she felt, had been lost when that innocence was lost. By this reasoning, she knew that it was the very core of *herself* that she was seeking to capture in the story, but in another form, and it would be her imaginative understanding of this other form – the living golem – which would give the work verisimilitude and truth.

Jane set the golem down alone at midnight in the Baths and let it see the wonder of moonlight on the tiny ripples of the water. In its dawning consciousness, it knew that it belonged here. It bent down and scooped up a little water and rubbed itself with this, so that its clay flesh shone more brightly and became softer. And then it sat quietly on the edge of the Hot Bath, breathing the sulphurous steam and letting its head fall forwards in a contented sleep. It knew that on the morrow, when the people began arriving, hoping to be consoled by the waters, or even cured of their maladies, it would show itself to them and they would reach out to it, yearning to feel its mercy.

But when the morning arrived and the invalids came shuffling to the pool in their white shifts, they did not behave as the golem had predicted. So strange was its appearance to them that they shrank from the creature. They believed it to be evil. They would not let it near to them. It tried to speak, to reassure them that it only wanted to help them, but its clay lips kept sticking together, impeding sound.

The stewards of the Baths were summoned. They approached the golem and tried to pick it up and throw it into the street, but it let its muddy feet stick to the stones around the Bath, so that they couldn't move it. One of them shot it with a pistol but now it dragged its feet from the tiles and ran away. It smoothed its own wet clay over the pistol wound. It searched for a hiding place and crawled under a laurel bush. When the night came, the golem looked up through the laurel leaves and saw the beauty of the stars and wondered deep in its minuscule heart how it might predict the fabric of the world and the people in it – whether their souls were filled with starlight or with darkness.

What did it know of good or evil or sorrow? It only knew that it carried a burden. In its ugly body resided all the children who had never had a chance at life. And on their behalf, it had to fulfil its mission, which was to heal and comfort. But how was it to do this, if people feared it and wanted to wound or kill it? The golem looked up once more at the stars, but couldn't see them. They were now covered by cloud. Rain began to pelt upon the golem from the shiny laurel leaves and it began to understand that the rain could eventually turn its body into a shapeless form. It would soon be a mere lump of mud. And it looked around, in desperation, for protection from the sky ...

By the time Jane had got this far with her story, her body was no longer cold in the studio, but warmed to a beautiful heat by her immersion in creative fire. The dawn was breaking above the skylight and she set aside the sketchbook. She was tired and her head ached but she thought that she had seldom felt so happy. She asked herself if this was the Thing, the destiny towards which she had believed herself to be travelling throughout her life, and her feelings of joy in discovering her story at first suggested to her that it might be. But then she decided that her stubborn belief in a 'Thing' had probably been a deceiving and sentimental one – like the dreamy aspirations of innocent young girls, who could not yet understand that life seldom arranged itself around such self-congratulatory moments of arrival. Or if, sometimes, it did, then those moments quickly passed and all that remained to do was simply to struggle on down a long road upon which darkness would always threaten to encroach. But this didn't matter to Jane. She knew she had found a way forward and all that she asked of herself was to travel on with hope.

She got slowly to her feet and went down to the kitchen. The maid, Nancy, was not yet awake, so Jane banked up the range with coal and set water on to boil. She made a pot of strong coffee and took this back to the studio. She knew exactly what she was about to do.

She went to her portrait, now turned to the wall. She barely looked at her torn and damaged body, but only at her head and shoulders, and she found, as she hoped she would, that there was strength and purpose in her look.

She laid the picture down and using a thin chisel, pared away the frame put on by Hartley and Foulkes. Then she drew a chalk line across the picture, just below her shoulders, took up some strong scissors, cut the canvas there and eased the cut section off the frame.

She pinned it to the wall and sat down, drinking her coffee. From time to time, she glanced at it – no longer Emmeline's 'Woman in White' but simply Jane Adeane: a human face, an unrelenting gaze confronting the world.

'ONE AND THE SAME'

When the *Queen of the Islands* reached Singapore and its teeming commercial heart gave shelter to the travellers disembarking there, Valentine Ross immediately found his way to the nearest whorehouse. He remembered the apoplectic Harbourmaster of Plymouth saying that a 'satisfactory debauch' could be had in Singapore for the price of a tin tea kettle and he hoped that, by surrendering himself to all his wildest sexual imaginings, the darkness he felt in his soul would begin to lift and that a glimmer of daylight would return. But it did not return.

When he came out of the brothel, sated, tired and dishevelled, he found Chesterfield standing patiently in the dirty street, waiting for him. When he asked the old man why he lingered there, Chesterfield replied, 'just a feeling, Sir that somebody should be looking out for you.'

Ross regarded his servant's tired and weathered features, across which another of his obstinate grins now made its way. And he understood that, in Chesterfield's mind, he still had a role to play in the unknown future of a man who seemed to have no friends, who shunned society and all human discourse and was only clinging to life in the hope of rescuing his brother in Borneo. Setting aside a moment's irritation at being followed like this, as a dog follows its master, Ross then allowed himself to be moved by the man's loyalty. He knew that it was a long time since anybody had chosen to stay close to him. But now here was an ancient soul who had decided against helping to shepherd convicts to Australia and who wanted to be his companion on the next and final leg of his journey.

He thanked Chesterfield. He told him that he would pay him well and asked him to return to the harbour to seek out a ship travelling to Borneo. The only thing he longed for now was to sleep in a solid bed that did not tremble and pitch in the ocean's maw.

In the native prau which took the two men from Singapore to Kuching, Ross's spirits lifted for a while. The sky above him was a fierce and blameless blue. The delicate open boat, with its single vast sail, travelled so fast over the water that Ross yielded to the illusion that he was flying. He began to call to Edmund in his mind. He told him that he had been 'long delayed' but that he was here at last, speeding across the deep 'like a bird skimming the waves' and that he, Edmund, was the only person now inhabiting his heart.

He asked himself whether this was true and reasoned that it was almost so. Yet he knew that Jane was also there, a dark shadow which would always fall across whatever he attempted. And the knowledge that he would never quite escape from her, or from what he had done to her brought back to him his feelings of despair.

When the prau made its graceful landing at Kuching and Ross's trunk was lifted onto the quayside, he and Chesterfield stood looking about them in bewildered curiosity. Where Singapore had been crowded and noisy, this place was made strange and fearful by the silence which seemed to hang over it.

After a moment, they heard a cannon shot fired, then another and Chesterfield said, 'Lord, Sir, nobody mentioned we were sailing into an insurrection, did they?'

They waited. For the sound of running feet? For the appearance of militiamen? But nothing stirred. Ross looked out along the wooden quayside. He saw a line of what he took to be small shops or booths, but all of these had been boarded up. Ahead of them was a street of low houses, built so that the upper floors, resting on wooden stilts, overhung the lower ones, to keep them in the shade. The dirt road which ran between them appeared empty of people. On one side of the street, spreading trees which Ross could not name stood sentinel in the quiet. The only sound was the chatter of birds, high up in their branches.

'Perhaps,' said Ross, 'this is the place where people come to die?'

'Well,' said Chesterfield with one of his slow-burning smiles, 'it certainly doesn't look like Derby Day at Epsom.'

Chesterfield then hoisted the trunk onto his scrawny back, crossed the street and set it down in the shade of one of the houses. He instructed Ross to sit on his luggage and wait while he went in search of some conveyance to take them to the rajah's house. 'Give me money, Sir,' he said as he prepared to depart: 'it will be the only language anyone will understand.'

Ross put silver into his palm and watched him walk away with his awkward seaman's gait. As the old man rounded the corner of the street, Ross heard a church bell tolling.

It was late by the time a donkey, together with its Chinese owner and a small dray cart were found and they set off south-eastwards towards the rajah's lands and Ross worried that they might become lost in the declining light. But Chesterfield reassured him that the driver had told him, in his few snatches of English, that he knew the rajah's house – 'not "Rajah Leon" Sir, the rajah is Sir Ralph Savage, English person.' The house was so exceptional and so large that everybody in Sarawak knew it. It was 'a white mountain' nobody could miss. You could, he said, see it clearly in the darkness.

What he had also told Chesterfield, in answer to the old man's questions about the silence and emptiness of Kuching, was that Fever had visited the town. It had passed now, but not before almost half the population had been 'put into a pit for the dead' at its northern edge. But Chesterfield kept this information to himself. On the long voyage aboard the *Queen*, he'd understood only too well how fragile was Ross's state of mind. (On more than one morning, he had entered his cabin half expecting to find him dead from some poison taken from his doctor's bag.) He judged that his new master – if indeed this was what he was, if indeed he was master of anything or anyone – could not now be burdened with news of widespread death and suffering.

The cart went on and soon enough veered off the dust track to arrive on a white road, a little overgrown by the encroachment of the forest but clearly a well-made thing, whose pale stones laid before them a luminous carpet in the near darkness. And then they saw it rising out of the jungle, silhouetted against the purple sky, the vast

monument to wealth and power that was the Savage House, and Ross
knew that he had arrived at last at his destination.

Torches burned at the grand entrance to the mansion and Valentine
Ross stood and waited there, lit by the flames, with Chesterfield
hovering some way behind him, like a penitent at his back. Out in the
darkness, Ross could now hear the cries and screeches which he knew
was the music of the forest night. He wondered, fretfully, how Edmund
could have endured this never-ending lament, but now his heart was
beating wildly at the thought that at any moment his brother would
appear and he would take him in his arms. He told himself that their
roles were now reversed: he was the searcher, the seeker of new worlds
and Edmund would be the healer. Together, they would go on.

A Chinese servant guided Ross and Chesterfield into a hallway,
where bright logs burned in an immense marble fireplace. Chesterfield
set down the heavy trunk and his ragged features rearranged themselves into a condition of wonder as he took in his opulent
surroundings.

Ross gave his name to the servant and fancied he saw on the man's
face a momentary flicker of fear. Behind him, Chesterfield began on
one of the bouts of coughing which had afflicted him since the vast
sea voyage, so it was to the accompaniment of this human distress
that Valentine Ross and Sir Ralph Savage first set eyes on each other.

Sir Ralph, wearing one of his white robes and with his long grey
hair loose about his shoulders perhaps resembled a godlike figure,
albeit a little portly, a little too mountainous of girth to be anybody's
saviour, but Ross was nevertheless moved at the sight of him. He
bowed and held out his hand and the rajah took it and bestowed
upon Ross a long and thoughtful look.

Chesterfield had been unable to master his fit of coughing and
was now spitting into a red handkerchief, but across this unfortunate
commotion, the rajah managed a grave smile and said to Ross, 'I
would have recognised you at a hundred paces. You and your brother
are one and the same.'

They were brought into one of Sir Ralph's great receiving rooms.
While Ross was invited to sit, Chesterfield was left standing and it
was then that the old man felt his legs give way and he fell down in

a faint onto one of the rajah's most expensive embroidered carpets. Ross sprang to his feet and went to his side. He felt for a pulse and was relieved to find it, and began to apologise to the rajah, as though he feared that Chesterfield's inert form was now spoiling the symmetry of his room.

The rajah called for arak and the Chinese servant who had shown in the guests now hastened to pour a cup, which Ross tried to administer to Chesterfield. But he remained insensible to everything, gone temporarily into who knew what dream plucked out from his life of toil.

It was at this moment, with Ross kneeling by the old man and Sir Ralph commanding for himself a dose of arak, that Leon entered the room. He was wearing a jewelled robe and at his waist hung the dagger with its hilt of lapis lazuli. If Ross knew at once that this was the man who had sent him the lying ransom demand, he also knew, as he saw Leon's hand rest upon the dagger, that now – with Chesterfield laid out on the expensive carpet – was not the moment to risk any confrontation with him. He tried again to give his poor servant a sip of arak and was relieved to see him open his eyes and grin.

THE WHITE ROAD

Now, Valentine Ross was standing at the grave of his brother.

The rajah had laid turf over the earth mound and replaced the makeshift wooden cross with one made of marble. Written on the marble were the words *Edmund Ross, Englishman and Naturalist*. But no dates were inscribed on the small monument because Sir Ralph had not known precisely when Edmund's short life had begun, nor on which day it had ended.

Standing beside Ross were the rajah and Chesterfield. It had been Sir Ralph who suggested to Ross that he read some words from the bible. From the moment he'd heard Ross speak on the night of his arrival, he had been moved by how much like Edmund he sounded. Guessing, however, that the nature and temperament of the elder brother was quite different and that he would not be persuaded to take his ease in a hammock and recite verses from St. Luke's Gospel, purely for the rajah's consolation, he took the opportunity of putting the bible into his hands now and letting him choose what he would from it.

He and Chesterfield stood silently waiting. The old servant glanced uneasily at Ross, almost certain that strong emotion might prevent him from uttering a single word. Slowly, he turned the fragile pages of the great book. But at last he began, reading from St. Luke's account of the crucifixion:

'... And one of the malefactors which were hanged, railed on him, saying, if thou be Christ, save thyself and us,

'But the other answering rebuked him, saying, dost thou not fear God, seeing thou art in the same condemnation?

'And we indeed justly, for we receive the true reward for our deeds, but this man hath done nothing amiss.

'And he said unto Jesus, Lord, remember me when thou comest into thy kingdom.

'And Jesus said unto him, verily I say unto you, today shalt thou be with me in paradise.

'And it was about the sixth hour, and there was darkness over all the earth until the ninth hour ...'

Ross could not go on. He could not weep, either, but only felt in his heart a terrible suffocation, as though all through his body his faculties of speech and sound and movement had been brought to an end. He could do nothing except to stand there, staring down at the bible in his hands and beyond it to the grass mound. Yet through his mind came whirling memories of his brother. He saw him running – always running – in his never-ending quest to capture the marvels of the earth. His legs were strong and lithe, his golden hair was lifted by the wind, his arms waved his butterfly net towards the sky, and on his features was a look of rapture. That this joyful person had died, this favoured son, for whom their mother always tenderly worried and waited, and that he, Valentine Ross, less loved, had lived on in discontent and despair, having now no purpose to his life, made him want to howl with fury. But he knew that he could not even cry out. What life remained to him would be lived in silence.

It was Chesterfield who understood what he might be feeling and suggested to the rajah that Ross be taken inside to rest. Sir Ralph perhaps hoped that the mourner would resume his reading, or even say some words of his own over the buried body of Edmund, but he soon enough saw that the man appeared to be at the end of his forces. He took the bible gently from his hands and he and Chesterfield turned him round and together they began to walk towards the house.

When they led Ross into his room – the one which Edmund had once occupied – they found Leon there, going through the few possessions and medicines which remained in Ross's trunk. The rajah knew that the sight of Edmund's brother had woken all the old anger at the 'Jesus boy', and this, when they and all around them had recently suffered such depredations from sickness and invasion, dismayed him to the point where he found himself promising to Leon that if Ross did not 'sail away' of his own accord, he would refuse to give him shelter for more than a week or two. But now, he saw, to his weary dismay, that Leon had not been reassured sufficiently by this promise. He was suspicious and jealous of the doctor from England. And at all times, he wore the lapis dagger in his belt. He had said to Sir Ralph, 'one day soon, the dagger will talk to me and I will answer.'

'Whatever can you mean?' said the rajah.

'I mean,' said Leon, 'that the doctor has blue eyes, blue as lapis.'

Chesterfield tenderly removed Ross's coat and boots and laid him on the bed. The rajah led Leon to his own room and locked the door. He straight away took him into his huge embrace. He whispered to him that he loved him. He took the dagger from Leon's belt and held it to his own throat. 'If you do not believe me,' he said, 'then kill me. Don't hurt Valentine Ross, who has done you no wrong; put an end to me. But believe me, Leon, all I want is for us to be how we once were, for your anger to die. The miners have gone. The Mal de peste abated before it could take us. We've survived the catastrophe. We can rebuild all that has been destroyed, but only if you are at my side.'

Leon did not speak, but laid his head on Sir Ralph's shoulder. Part of him still obstinately wished to say that he was tired of being subservient to the rajah, that all he craved was to get money of his own, money enough so that he could go in search of lands to rule and a beautiful wife to own and a future of glittering power. Yet he knew that the great energy of which he had always been possessed, the energy which had helped to create the white palace, which had dreamed of the fish cannery and wealth to be made in China, was diminished. How could such a tired man hope to find the empire that he sought? These days, he barely strayed from the house and his favourite pastime had become the confecting of sweetmeats, made from nuts and molasses, which he consumed in bountiful quantities and did not mind that his stomach had grown as round as a barrel and that his strong arms were like those of the Buddha, fleshy and inert.

What remained, he knew, was the strong passion between him and Sir Ralph. Even now, as he leaned against him and inhaled the familiar perfume of his body, he felt it stir in him and he decided that this, a feeling he refused to name as love, but which nevertheless could bring him more pleasure than any other that he knew, might have to be enough to give his life meaning and contentment – at least until his former strength returned, until some other ambitious scheme took possession of his soul. He put his arms round the rajah and sighed. And he knew what the sigh signified: it was a moment of surrender.

Ross slept a little and when he woke, it was dark in his room. He lay there, listening to the wild cries of the tropical night. He had no idea of time. It was as if he was floating on sound and as the dawn cast a grey light through the window he longed to be floated out of the confines of the room and set down in the vastness of the forest.

With difficulty, because he was weak, he tugged on his coat and boots and went down through the silent house and out into the garden. The bright beds of Canna lilies mocked the pallid streaks of dawn, but Ross refused to give such showy flowers his attention. The time for such things was past.

He walked away from the house, not minding the cool air on his face. He soon enough strode in among the overarching trees and then found himself on the white road he had admired upon his arrival. He had no idea where the road led, but he found himself moved by it once more. He imagined all the hours and weeks of labour which had gone into its making. It seemed to him almost like a living thing, coiling and twisting on and on, defying encroachment by roots and blown seeds, a man-made entity of beauty and purpose.

The sky was growing lighter all the time. To his left, Ross could now see a strange open space, where all the trees had been felled, where the ground was pocked with deep trenches and where peculiar makeshift machinery stood abandoned. He knew that such a troubling sight would normally have made him pause here, to understand the significance of this place, but he found that it held no interest for him. It was as if the road was calling him on and on and would not let him pause or rest. And he realised now where it led: it led to the river.

The sound of the bush was loud all about him and the dawn sky was flecked with the dark shadows of birds he did not recognise. Aside from these, he felt himself to be quite alone until he saw a strange sight coming towards him. An old woman, whose face was pigmented with white blotches, was pushing a barrow in the direction of the rajah's house. Her load was clearly heavy and the barrow wobbled and swayed over the white stones and when they came nearer to him, Ross saw that reclining in the barrow, with his head on a yellow embroidered cushion was a Chinese man, so ancient and bent that he resembled the kind of skeleton to which flesh and sinew still obstinately clung, but whose eyes, in his emaciated face, were touchingly bright and lively.

Ross stopped for a moment, to nod a greeting to the elderly woman with her human load, and fancied he saw a thin smile crease her features. But she did not pause. And he had the sudden thought that this was a road upon which no one ever lingered, no matter in which direction, but only obeyed its onward call.

Ross knew that his walking should have made him warm by now. He remembered how his climbs up Beacon Hill towards Charlcombe had always brought bright blood to his cheeks and how his heart had seemed to beat more strongly the higher he went. But now, he did not feel it, that heat and euphoria that comes with exertion, and even though the sun was just beginning to rise above the trees, he was still cold.

He eventually came to a place where the road diverged and became two. He stopped for a moment, noticing that here, perhaps because of carts or barrows turning round, or travellers on foot changing their minds, piles of stones had been cast loose from the road's surface, and he saw these loose white stones as a kind of unexpected treasure, yielding itself to him in this dawn which seemed to have no date nor hour attached to it, but to be quite outside time.

He bent down and began to fill his pockets with the stones, holding each one lovingly in his hand before placing it inside his coat. Then he looked up and wondered which arm of the road he should take. His hands caressed the stones. He listened intently for some instruction inside him, bidding him go this way or that, but received none. So he closed his eyes and walked blindly on down the left-hand fork and after a while he realised that the sound of the Sadong River was now very loud. He could tell that this was a river far swifter, far more heartless in its intent than any he had known in England. He could imagine its wild passage, round boulders, down rapids, swirling in eddies, throwing spray towards the sky, carrying all in its embrace.

When he reached the river's edge, he touched the stones in his pockets once more, choosing to see an affiliation between them and himself: bodies made from the earth, tenacious in the way they clung to it, but susceptible to storms, to displacement and destruction and to man's incessant journeying this way and that.

Before lowering himself into the river Valentine Ross briefly considered whether he should remove his boots, but he knew this consideration to be futile and foolish. For there was only this now: a man and a surging river, and of the man he wished there to be no trace.

SNOWBERRIES

She had been named for the world of dreams, but also for the ash tree and when she walked past a little grove of these, on her way to school in Dublin, she saw that they appeared dead, with their few remaining leaves the colour of rotten plums and hanging like rags from the branches. When she got home, she said to her mother, Kathleen, 'the ash trees are all dead' and Kathleen replied, 'of course they are. Everything dies in winter.'

Aisling felt that she was dying. She was back in her old, sad room, with Maire's bed just two feet away from hers, a bed kept clean with fresh linen, quite as though Maire would walk in one evening and lay her head down on the white pillow.

At school, she found it difficult to work. All she could think about was the house on the western shore and the little pen where Iris was kept, knowing that by now it might all be blanketed with snow and that the goats, who had no fleeces on them like sheep, might die of cold.

She thought, too, of her friend Charlotte and the collection of cowrie shells they had amassed, and of the small wooden box Charlotte had found in her father's schoolhouse. The box had once contained chalks. The two girls had polished it up and made it a thing of touching beauty by gluing the shells to the lid. It had been this little object that Aisling had offered as a parting gift to Miss Maeve and Miss Elizabeth McKinnon when the time for her return to Dublin came round, and they, who had been holding back their tears, had let them fall onto the children's gift.

*

Aisling had tried to tell her parents about the great sea strand and the sight of sunlight on the thrilling waves, about the paintings hanging on the walls of the cottage, about the picnics Miss Maeve never tired of preparing and about Iris, with her soft ears and her pleading eyes. But Michael and Kathleen never seemed to want to listen to any of this. All they talked about was the imminent arrival of their son – whom they had already named Liam – in December. 'He will be born just in time for Christmas,' they told the girl they now referred to as their *middle child*, 'so you see, Aisling, we must give all our thought to how we can make him welcome. And we believe you should play an unselfish part in this. We have discussed what you might do and we have decided that Liam should have his own room for his little crib. He must not be disturbed in the night. Babies need a lot of rest. So we will move your bed into the parlour and you can sleep there. You will have your tea with us when your father gets home and go to bed when he decrees. You will grow used to the lateness of the hour.'

So this was to be it, then: her new brother would share the room with the ghost of Maire and she would share the parlour with the china cupboard and the mice and be forced to stay awake while her father drank stout after supper. Perhaps Maire's old toys, which she had never been allowed to touch, would be given to Liam? He would grow up in the soft embrace of his mother's arms. His father would work overtime at the Anchor Brewery to buy good food for his boy. In his quavering voice, ruined by the chewing of tobacco, Michael Morrissey would sing to his only son …

When the time for the birth approached and Aisling saw her bed shoved into the parlour, so near to the burning grate that she feared she might catch fire in the middle of the night, she wrote a letter to her aunt:

Dear Aunt Clorinda,

Please, I beg you, come and take me back to Miss Maeve and Miss Elizabeth. Please, please, please, please. Charlotte told me I could attend the school which her father has and learn my lessons there. Please, please, please come. My bed has gone into the parlour because my brother is coming.

I am burning by the coals and there will be nothing for me at Christmas
and I am missing Iris so much.
If you do not come, I will die.
From your niece, Aisling xx

The voyage across the Irish Sea was long and rough, but Clorinda
endured her sickness without fuss and went straight from the port-
side to Bishop Street, where she found Kathleen, huge in her ninth
month of pregnancy, packing Aisling's few clothes and possessions
into a sack.

Not bothering to enquire how her sister-in-law might be faring
after her journey, nor offering to brew tea, she said, 'oh it's you, then.
But what do we call you now. M'lady, is it?'

Clorinda ignored this. She looked around the cluttered room and
saw Aisling's bed, jammed in close to the fire. Kathleen delved into
her apron pocket, handed Clorinda an envelope and said, 'Michael
has left ten shillings, to be put towards Aisling's keep. But as I understand it, we're doing those spinster women a favour, so we are. No
child of their own, have they? And no husbands to give them one.
So they kidnap somebody else's girl! But they will be punished, by
my reckoning. They will soon come to see what a bad-tempered child
she is.'

Clorinda sat down on Aisling's bed. She asked Kathleen for a drink
of water. She was parched from her seasickness and made nauseous
afresh by the sight and smell of the unventilated parlour. She wanted
to describe to Kathleen how, at the house near Ennistymon, Aisling
had shown no bad temper at all, that she had, in fact, behaved like
a different child, but she kept silent. All that mattered was getting
Aisling away, starting early the next morning, retracing the journey
across Ireland they had made together in early summer, until at last
they arrived at the ancient house and Maeve and Elizabeth McKinnon
came running out to meet them.

Frost had rutted the roads and made the horses slip and stumble.
Clorinda and Aisling clung together under a tartan rug in the draughty
carriage, but Aisling said she wasn't afraid of anything now. If a wheel
fell off, it could be put on again; if the carriage tilted over, no one

would be harmed by more than a bruise. She was going to her 'new home' and God would find a way to bring her safely there.

As they neared the sea, warmer air seemed to waft in and at the next pause in the journey, Aisling found a bush of snowberries growing by the wayside and asked if she could pick a few branches to give to Miss Elizabeth 'for using in her painting'. Clorinda agreed, so they journeyed on clutching the snowberries, tied together with a thread from a sack which had once been filled with hops for the Anchor Brewery, but which now contained all that Aisling possessed in the world. As the dusk came on, the white berries lit up the dark interior of their carriage with an obstinate sprinkling of light.

But they were almost there, now. They had passed through Ennistymon. They could hear the rush of the waves. And then, in the darkness, they could see the flicker of the oil lamps burning in the kitchen window of the cottage and even before the horses had been pulled up, the front door was opened wide.

ACKNOWLEDGEMENTS

This novel owes a debt to the following works: *Letters from the Malay Archipelago* by Alfred Russel Wallace, ed. John Van Wyhe and Kees Rookmaaker (Oxford University Press), *Darwin's Moon, A biography of Alfred Russel Wallace* by Amabel Williams-Ellis (Blackie), *Into the Heart of Borneo* by Redmond O'Hanlon (The Salamander Press), *Almayer's Folly* by Joseph Conrad (Penguin Books), *Charles Darwin, Victorian Mythmaker* by A. N. Wilson (John Murray), *Science and the Practice of Medicine in the Nineteenth Century* by W. F. Bynum (Cambridge University Press), *The Butchering Art, Joseph Lister's quest to transform the grisly world of Victorian medicine* by Lindsey Fitzharris (Allen Lane), *How to be a Victorian* by Ruth Goodman (WW Norton), *Inside the Victorian Home* by Judith Flanders (WW Norton), *The Short Life and Long Times of Mrs Beeton* by Kathryn Hughes (4th Estate), *Rites of Passage* by William Golding (Faber & Faber), *Roads to Ruin: The Shocking History of Social Reform* by E. S. Turner (Penguin Books), *The Plimsoll Sensation: the Great Campaign to Save Lives at Sea* by Nicolette Jones (Abacus), *A Charming Place: Bath in the Life and Novels of Jane Austen* by Maggie Lane (Millstream Books), *Tales of the New Babylon: Paris in the mid-19th Century* by Rupert Christiansen (Minerva).

My old friend and colleague, Malcolm Bradbury said to me early in my writing life that 'serious novels are not just written, they are *rewritten*' and while I still agree with this, I know that the process of successful rewriting depends hugely on the editorial judgement of an author's 'first readers'. Mine were Bill Clegg, Alison Samuel and my beloved partner and dedicatee of this book, Richard Holmes. All three gave generously of their time and their intelligence and enabled me to make the journey from first draft to final MS without excessive psychic pain or too much mourning for my long-lost editor, Penelope Hoare.

A lively email exchange with Neel Mukherjee on the subjects explored in this book kept me amused and sustained. Clara Farmer was astute in putting to me a series of important additional questions and I want to thank her and the marvellously supportive team at Chatto/Vintage: Rosanna Boscawen, Richard Cable, Beth Coates, Rachel Cugnoni, Tom Drake-Lee, Charlotte Humphery, Victoria Murray-Browne, Fran Owen, Stephen Parker, and Mari Yamazaki. I also owe a huge debt of gratitude to my friend and agent, Caroline Michel. She is like a beacon of never-faltering light in her writers' lives, or perhaps an island of mercy.